Vale of Tears

Λ Novel

Peter T. King

Λ Roberts Rinehart Book

TAYLOR TRADE PUBLISHING

Lanham • New York • Toronto • Oxford

Taylor Trade Publishing
A Roberts Rinehart Book
An imprint of The Rowman & Littlefield Publishing Group, Inc.
4501 Forbes Boulevard, Suite 200
Lanham, MD 20706

Distributed by National Book Network

Library of Congress Cataloging-in-Publication Data

King, Peter T., 1944–
    Vale of tears : a novel / Peter T. King.
      p. cm.
    ISBN 1-58979-062-6 (hardcover : alk. paper)
    I. Title.
    PS3611.I584V35 2003
    813'.6—dc21   2003008788

♾™ The paper used in this publication meets the minimum requirements of American National Standard for Information Sciences—Permanence of Paper for Printed Library Materials, ANSI/NISO Z39.48-1992.

Manufactured in the United States of America.

Vale of Tears

To those who were murdered
on September 11, 2001
. . . and their families.

"to thee do we cry, poor banished children of Eve;

to thee do we send up our sighs, mourning and weeping in this vale of tears."

— from the "Hail Holy Queen,"
a Catholic prayer of intercession

Author's Note

V ale of Tears is a work of fiction set in the past and in the future. The events it describes, which center around the tragic attacks of September 11, 2001, and their horrible aftermath, are based on fact. Events occurring in the future are necessarily based upon speculation and surmise.

This book proceeds along alternating tracks. The odd-numbered chapters are fiction; the even-numbered chapters are based on fact. Characters—real and fictional—proceed along both tracks.

It is accepted wisdom that our world was changed forever by September 11th. It is now a world of extraordinary danger and diabolical adversaries. *Vale of Tears* describes the scope of that danger and the depravity of those adversaries. It describes how vulnerable we can become if we lower our guard—for even the slightest moment—and if we fail to recognize that our terrorist foes comprise a worldwide network with operatives active within our borders.

Vale of Tears also describes, however, the sacrifice and heroism—not just of those who were murdered on September 11th, but of their families and of the American people. The spirit and resolve that arose from the flames and rubble of September 11th resulted in an America that is stronger than ever before. And it is because of that spirit and resolve that we will prevail over the forces of international terrorism.

The late morning sun radiated brightly throughout the clear blue spring sky as the Delta shuttle flight from Washington, D.C. descended smoothly onto the westernmost runway of New York's LaGuardia Airport. It was only another few minutes before the pilot guided the 737 along the runway and inched it toward Gate 5 of the Marine Air Terminal, where it came to a firm but gentle halt.

Congressman Sean Cross was situated in an aisle seat in row 14. As the all-clear bell sounded its unobtrusive tone, Cross stood up and removed his suit carrier from the overhead compartment. Standing partially in the aisle while waiting for the fifty or so passengers who had been seated in the rows ahead of him to make their way toward the plane's exit door, Cross looked at the watch on his left wrist. It was barely half past eleven, the perfect time to beat the Friday rush-hour traffic crush. The trip to Cross's home in Seaford probably wouldn't take more than forty minutes.

Not that Cross would be doing the driving. For the past three weeks—ever since he had begun receiving vague phone and mail threats from self-proclaimed Islamic terrorists—the Nassau County Police had been providing Cross with around-the-clock protection whenever he was in New York. The Capitol Police were doing the same when he was in Washington. Cross was not particularly concerned by the threats. He'd gotten them before, usually after he'd said or done something controversial, and nothing had ever happened. Each time, the Nassau Police Special Investigation Bureau and the Capitol Police would assign Cross security details, which usually lasted four or five weeks.

These latest threats had come after Cross made a series of speeches and follow-up media appearances calling for increased government surveillance of Muslim charities in Nassau and Brooklyn that, he charged, were fronts for Islamic terrorists. As best the SIB could determine, the threats had come from individual malcontents and probably posed no real danger. Detective Brian Sullivan, who headed Cross's security team, had telephoned Cross yesterday to tell him he expected the detail would be pulled at the end of next week.

A Port Authority cop walked Cross from the plane and through the terminal.

Sullivan was waiting for Cross just outside the entranceway of the terminal. He was seated behind the wheel of an unmarked police vehicle. As Cross strolled out of the terminal, he thanked the cop. Sullivan popped the trunk of the four-door black Ford Crown Victoria. After placing his suit carrier in the trunk, Cross opened the right front door and sat down in the passenger seat.

"Flight okay?" asked Sullivan.

"Yeah, Sully. Everything went great. How's the traffic?"

"Very light. You'll be home in no time."

"Good."

"You still have the rest of the day open?"

"Yeah. I'm just gonna hang out."

"That's smart. A day off won't kill you. How about the rest of the weekend? Any changes?"

As Cross was telling Sullivan his schedule for Saturday and Sunday, the detective was driving the car from the airport and making a right turn onto the service road leading to the eastbound side of the Grand Central Parkway. Their casual conversation was interrupted by ringing from the cell phone mounted on the floor just below the car radio. Sullivan pressed the green *call* button, and Cross instantly recognized the distinctive, hard-edged voice of Sully's boss, Detective Lieutenant Ed McCabe. Cross also recognized that the voice betrayed concern—serious concern.

"Sully, is the congressman with you?"

"Yes, sir."

"Be prepared to take evasive measures."

"Yes, sir."

McCabe hesitated for the slightest moment before continuing in a particularly strong voice.

"We have a major incident unfolding. A possible terrorist attack on Old Country Road in Westbury."

"Any details in?" asked Sullivan, his eyes narrowing and scanning the parkway lanes from left to right as he turned the car into the center lane and accelerated to 70 mph.

"This happened only about three minutes ago, but we know enough to know that it's bad. Very bad. There were two massive explosions, one right after the other, at the Empire Plaza office complex," answered McCabe, referring to the two thirty-story buildings that had opened just six months before and were already leasing 90 percent of their office space.

Cross and Sullivan looked at one another as McCabe continued.

"I heard the blasts from here at headquarters, and right now from my window I can see the sky filled with balls of fire and mounds of black smoke," said McCabe, who was at the two-story police headquarters building on Franklin Avenue in Mineola, one block south of Old Country Road and less than three miles west of the Empire Plaza buildings.

"Any reports from the scene?" asked Sullivan, his voice firm and clinical.

"Yeah. A cop radioed in that he thinks he saw two fuel trucks—maybe three—heading toward the buildings just before the explosions."

"Eddie, this is Sean. Any other incidents being reported?"

"Not in Nassau that we know of, but we're getting something about a fire in Brooklyn. I don't know what the hell that's about, but I'll call you back as soon as I get anything definite. In the meantime, Sully, stay in constant touch with headquarters."

"Yes, sir."

"Sounds like bad shit, Sully," said Cross, as he reached forward, pressing the radio's *on* button.

Sullivan nodded grimly. Cross tuned the radio to 880 AM, the CBS all-news station. They listened intently to the purposeful tones of the veteran news anchor Jacqui Eaton.

"As our Long Island correspondent Patricia Gartland just reported, the Empire Plaza office complex has been rocked by a series of massive explosions, causing a raging fire that appears to be out of control and is spreading into the nearby shopping mall. Now we have on our newsline WCBS reporter Dawn Carbone, who is at the scene of what appears to be another large fire in downtown Brooklyn."

"Actually, Jacqui, I'm about a mile and a half from the fire," said Carbone, shouting to be heard over the din of what sounded to be an endless cacophony of blaring sirens. "I'm at the corner of Atlantic Avenue and Flatbush Avenue, west of where the fire broke out about ten minutes ago at the Twenty-third Regiment National Guard Armory along Atlantic Avenue between Pacific Street and Bedford Avenue."

"Dawn, from where you're located, how clearly can you see the fire, and what can you tell our listeners about it?"

"I can see it very clearly, and already I can tell you that it is as large a fire as I have ever seen. The flames have engulfed the entire armory and are shooting above the building. Also, large clouds of black smoke are billowing from the roof of the armory."

"Is there any word yet on casualties or fatalities?"

"Nothing yet. But the fire seems to have spread so fast that there has to be great concern for anyone who was in the armory."

Cross took his cell phone from his shirt pocket. Before he could press a button, it rang. It was his wife, Mary Rose.

"Are you listening to what's happening?" she asked.

"Yeah, it's on the radio. Westbury and Brooklyn. I was just going to call you."

"You okay?"

"Yeah, I landed about ten minutes ago. Sully's driving. We're on the Grand Central, just past Queens Boulevard. Are you at home?"

"Yes, I'm in the den watching it on television . . ."

"How does it look?"

"Terrible. Horrible. Both places. The flames and the smoke are incredible."

Sean then inquired anxiously as to the whereabouts and safety of the other family members. Fortunately, Mary Rose had reassuring news:

—Kara, their daughter, had been at a corporate board meeting in Melville. She'd called from her car to say she was heading to her home in Seaford, which she'd just moved into with her husband John. To play it safe, she was taking side roads and staying off the parkways.

—John was in lower Manhattan. This time, unlike the World Trade Center attack, he was not close to the danger zone, even though from his office window he could look across the East River and see the smoke-filled skies over downtown Brooklyn. He told Kara he'd stay in a friend's apartment uptown until things quieted down.

—Danny, their son, had left for Tokyo on a business trip just yesterday. It was the middle of the night in Japan, but Mary Rose had called him in his hotel room to tell him what was happening. He said he was fine and would monitor it on CNN International.

"Thank God everyone's accounted for," said Sean.

"'Thank God' is right," answered Mary Rose. "What about you? Are you coming home, or are you going to do something crazy?"

"Right now, I guess I'll go to Westbury to see what's happened. But don't worry, I'll stay back. I'm not going to get in anyone's way."

"Okay, but let me know as soon as you learn anything at all."

Cross pressed the *end* button on his cell phone and looked toward Sullivan.

"Sully, everything alright at home?" asked Cross.

"Yeah, everything's fine," answered Sullivan, who'd just phoned his wife.

"It looks like those bastards have hit us again."

"It's still early, of course, but I'd say it has to be terrorists."

"Islamic?"

"Who else is attacking Americans?"

Cross turned the radio back on and scanned the news stations. WCBS, WOR, WABC, WINS. They were all on headline, bulletin status—even WFAN, the all-sports station—virtually giving minute-by-minute accounts:

—Nassau Police confirmed that eyewitnesses had reported seeing three fuel trucks hurtling toward Empire Plaza and exploding either on impact or just before impact.

—NYPD was refusing to confirm or deny reports that minutes before the explosion two men were seen running from an oversized furniture truck parked on Bedford Avenue next to the armory.

—The president was about to meet in the White House with his national security advisor, homeland defense secretary, and FBI and CIA directors.

"Jesus, Sully, we've been here before."

"You're right, Sean. This is the same feeling I had when the World Trade Center was hit. And then the Pentagon. It was a spiral of disaster."

"Yeah. September 11th has to be the worst day ever."

September 11, 2001

The Morning

I t was just after 7:30 when Sean Cross got up from his bed to open the blinds on the window of his eighth-story apartment overlooking Washington, D.C. The State Department was off to the left. The Pentagon, slightly more distant, was straight ahead. The sky was exceptionally clear and filled with the brightness of the morning sun. *Great day for flying*, he thought. *Mary Rose's plane should be right on time.*

Tonight would be the annual congressional barbeque on the south lawn of the White House—the first of George W. Bush's presidency. Most members of Congress and their spouses would be there. Mary Rose had expected to fly down last evening, but torrential rains in New York and an almost violent thunderstorm had canceled all flights out of LaGuardia. She was rescheduled for this morning's 8:30 Delta flight, which was due to land at D.C.'s Reagan National Airport at about 9:40. Their son, Danny, who worked as a trade analyst at the Commerce Department and shared the Washington apartment with Sean, would also be at tonight's barbeque. Sean had called in a favor from the White House staff to get Danny an invitation.

As Danny prepared to leave the apartment for his ten-minute trip to work on the Metro subway, Sean looked at the living room clock and saw that it was barely eight o'clock.

"Leaving a little early aren't you?" asked Sean.

"Yeah. But since I'll be ducking out early for the barbeque tonight, I figured I'd get a head start this morning. Unlike congressmen, I take my job seriously," answered Danny with a sly smile.

"I'm sure the president will be delighted to have such a comedian at the White House tonight. Anyway give me a call during the day, and we'll work out the details for tonight."

"It should be a great time. Talk to you later."

Sean Cross walked out the front door of his apartment complex at about 8:45. His chief of staff, Tom O'Connell, was waiting in his black Jeep Cherokee.

"Anything happening?" Cross asked as he got into the front passenger seat.

"No. Everything's under control. Mary Rose's plane is on schedule. As soon as I drop you off at the Capitol, I'll go out to the airport to pick her up."

It was barely five minutes later. O'Connell was driving eastward along Virginia Avenue, stolidly navigating the three-mile, fifteen-minute trek to the Capitol through the morning rush-hour traffic. Scanning the front page stories in the *Washington Post*, Cross heard the cell phone ring and O'Connell say, "Yeah Kevin." It was Kevin Finnerty, Cross's press secretary. "Christ," said O'Connell, seemingly more annoyed than concerned and pausing to allow Finnerty to continue. "Okay Kevin. Stay in touch. We should be in the office in about ten minutes."

Putting down the paper, Cross looked over toward O'Connell.

"What was that about?" asked Cross in a casual, almost matter-of-fact tone.

"A plane crashed into the World Trade Center. One of those commuter planes."

"Where'd Kevin hear about it? On television?"

"Apparently they just broke into the *Today* show with the news. But Kara had called him just before that."

"Kara?"

"Yeah. She had been talking to John on the phone," said O'Connell, referring to Kara's husband, who worked several blocks north of the World Trade Center, "when he saw the explosion from his window. He thought it was a bomb or a plane. So Kara called Kevin right away to tell you."

Cross's immediate reaction was that something like this could screw up tonight's barbeque. Then he thought of Mary Rose and her 8:30 flight, which could have been in the area of the World Trade Center just about the time of the crash.

"Are they sure it was a commuter flight?"

"You thinking about Mary Rose's plane?"

"Yeah."

O'Connell's cell phone rang again. "Yeah, Kevin." Pause. "Call Delta right away and find out where the 8:30 flight is." O'Connell's face betrayed concern as he told Cross: "Now they're saying it was a passenger jet. Apparently the fire and the smoke are just incredible."

Cross said nothing. He stared out the car window onto Constitution Avenue. Coming up on his left was the far end of the White House south lawn. Obviously there was now more to worry about than whether or not tonight's barbeque would go ahead on schedule.

The silence was relieved by another call from Finnerty. He told O'Connell that Delta said the 8:30 flight had been held and had never taken off. It was still out on the runway. But Delta couldn't give any reason why the flight had been held in the first place and what the plans were now. O'Connell told Finnerty they'd be in the office in five minutes. As Constitution merged with Pennsylvania Avenue, the massive dome of the Capitol Building stood directly in front of them.

"What do you think?" O'Connell asked Cross.

"It's easy to get paranoid. But I hope they're not bullshitting us. I hope the fucking plane didn't really take off and they're just telling us this story about the runway."

Cross was interrupted by the ringing from his own cell phone. It was Kara.

"Anything on Mom's plane?" asked Kara, who was counsel to European Air and understood all too well the brutal reality of airline disasters.

"Kevin says Delta told him it's still on the runway."

"Any details?"

"No."

"You better stay on that," said Kara, striving mightily, with incomplete success, to conceal her apprehension.

"Have you heard any more from John?"

"I just hung up the phone. He said he's never seen anything like it. He knew right away that it couldn't be a commuter plane. It's just massive. Flames and black smoke just shooting out. All sorts of debris flying through the air."

"We're pulling up to Cannon now. I'll call you as soon as I get up to the office."

"Stay in touch."

"You too."

Cross's office was on the fourth floor of the Cannon House Office Building. Cannon was the oldest of the three House office structures. For several years now Cross had had enough seniority to move into more spacious and luxurious quarters in the Longworth or Rayburn Buildings but had opted for what he perceived to be Cannon's sense of history and character.

Ordinarily Cross would stay with O'Connell when Tom took the Jeep Cherokee into the parking garage in the bowels of the Cannon Building. Today, however, to save time, O'Connell dropped Cross at Cannon's northeast entrance on the corner of Independence Avenue and 1st Street. Getting out of the Cherokee at exactly 9:00 a.m., Cross said to himself as much as to O'Connell: "You never know what the day is going to bring."

This entranceway is on the second-floor level. Walking up the few stairs and through the revolving door, Cross was greeted by two Capitol Hill police officers, who appeared not at all concerned about—if even aware of—the World Trade Center accident. He nodded toward them, mumbled a "good morning," and forced a smile. Walking up the two flights of stairs, he crossed the fourth-floor landing and turned left into the hallway leading to his office, which was the second on the right.

Five young people—three male, two female, all in their early-to-mid twenties—were strolling toward Cross. He recognized them as staffers from neighboring offices. Sipping hot morning coffee from Starbucks cups encased in java jackets, they seemed far more interested in working out their lunch plans than concerned about the cauldron that, no doubt unbeknownst to them, was raging in lower Manhattan. They passed Cross and gave friendly "hellos" just as he turned and opened the door to the reception area of his office. It was 9:03.

The two desks on either side of the door were empty. Adam Paulson and Kerry Ann Watkins, who sat at those desks, were in the rear office, photocopying the key stories from the morning papers, which they'd gotten off the Internet.

Instinctively, but with no sense of anticipation, Cross looked up toward the television set on top of the bookcase directly to the right of the couch that faced the front door. "Jesus, they have tape of the crash," he mumbled to himself as he saw the huge jet fly directly into the tower and explode into soaring flames. Turning left into his private office, he placed his suit jacket on the coat rack, sat down behind his desk, picked up the remote, and turned on his television.

It took him several seconds to realize what it was that he was hearing and what he had seen. That was not videotape. It was a second plane hitting the other tower. The South Tower. "My God," he thought. His cell phone rang. It was Kara.

"Another plane has hit," she said.

"I just saw it on television."

"I was talking to John when it happened. He saw it all the way. The plane was coming straight in his direction. It was aimed right into the World Trade Center."

"What's John doing?"

"He left immediately. He's got to run down twenty-eight flights and then get out of the whole area. Any word from Mom?"

"No. I'm going to call her cell phone."

"I hope John will be okay."

"Don't worry. Once he gets out on the street, he'll be fine. The cops know just what to do when something like this happens," answered Cross, hoping against hope that Kara would not see through his obvious deception—since *nothing* like this had ever happened before.

"John doesn't have a cell phone."

"Kara, John will be fine," said Cross with a firmness based on nothing but vague hope.

Cross telephoned Danny at the Commerce Department.

"I guess you've heard," said Cross.

"Yeah, just before nine a guy down the hall turned on his television and told me about it. It looks bad," answered Danny, who hesitated for a moment before asking, "How's Mom's flight?"

"Delta says it's still on the runway, but we can't track it down. I'm going to try Mom now on her cell phone."

"Let me know right away."

Cross dialed Mary Rose's cell phone number. He was answered by a recording. Waiting for the recording to conclude, Cross took a deep breath so he would sound at least reasonably calm when he left his message on her voice mail.

"I'm sure everything is okay with you. You probably know by now that two planes have crashed into the World Trade Center. It looks as if they were terrorists. Call me as soon as you get a chance so we can work out where you'll be going and how you'll get there. Talk to you soon."

Cross put down the phone and walked to the reception area, where Adam and Kerry sat at their desks in silence, staring up at the television atop the bookcase. Seated on the couch was a confused college student who was scheduled to begin his internship that day. Cross stood in the doorway to Tom O'Connell's office. O'Connell was seated at his desk, pressing the remote and racing from channel to channel. Turning away from his television set, O'Connell asked,

"Any word yet?"

"No. I left a message on her voice mail. Have you tried Delta?"

"I've only been here about two minutes, but I've called them about five times and all the lines are busy. I'll keep trying."

"You should also call Anne in her car and ask her to turn around and go back to LaGuardia," said Cross, referring to Anne Kelly, who ran his district office in Massapequa Park and had driven Mary Rose to the airport that morning. She was also two months pregnant.

"Will do."

By now Kevin Finnerty and other staff members had come in from the rear office. They were all looking up at the television set and at one another. Cross decided to say something. But not about his own concern. "This has to be terrorists. This is going to be a long day. So we better dig in," stated Cross, who then handed Adam a five-dollar bill, saying, "Do me a favor and go over to the Korean place. Get me a large coffee and a toasted English. I need some Goddamned energy."

"Sean," Kerry Ann interrupted, "Danny's on line one." Cross went back into his office, closed the door and picked up the phone as he sat down behind the desk. It was 9:20. Danny asked for an update on Mary Rose. Sean said everything was the same. Danny said he'd been talking to Kara, who was very concerned about John. Sean's cell phone rang. He looked immediately at the incoming number. "Danny, that's Mom on the cell phone. Hold on, and you can listen in." Cradling the office phone between his shoulder and left ear, Sean pressed *send* on the cell phone and pressed it to his right ear. It was 9:21.

"How're you doing?" he said exuberantly.

"I don't know how I'm going to get to Washington," she answered with some annoyance. "The pilot said they're shutting down the airport."

"Where are you?"

"They're bringing the plane in from the runway. I'll be getting off in a few minutes."

"Did you get my phone message?"

"No."

"Don't you know what's happening?"

"No."

"New York is under attack," answered Cross, feeling his voice shake as he heard himself say words he never remotely envisioned ever having to say. "Terrorists have attacked the World Trade Center."

"Oh my God!" she shouted, then said, "Wait, the pilot's making an announcement."

Cross could hear the drone of the pilot's voice through the cell phone but couldn't make out any of the words. The moment the announcement ended, Mary Rose said very tensely:

"He said New York City has been attacked. Terrorists have bombed the World Trade Center and we should get out of the airport as quickly as possible."

"Anne is coming back to get you. Wait in front of the terminal. She should be there soon."

"I can't believe this is happening. Everyone on the plane looks like they're in shock."

"We've been worried about you. Danny's been on the other phone all the time, so he's heard everything I've said. Why don't you call Kara and tell her you're okay. And make sure you keep your cell phone on in case I have to call you or if Anne has any trouble getting back into the airport."

"Be safe."

"You too."

Turning off his cell phone, Cross spoke to Danny on the office phone he held in his left hand.

"You heard all that?" asked Sean.

"Yeah," said Danny, "that's a relief. Now we just have to track John down."

"Let's hope everything'll be fine. I'll let you know as soon as I hear anything."

Cross rang O'Connell on the intercom and told him Mary Rose was okay.

"Thank God for that," said O'Connell. "Anne just called and said she should be at LaGuardia in ten minutes. She also said the expressway is filled with ambulances and emergency vehicles heading toward the city."

"What a fucking day," replied Cross.

Relentlessly scanning the channels—every station, regular TV and cable, was covering the World Trade Center—Cross was drinking the coffee and eating the English muffin Adam had gotten him. He phoned his mother in Seaford and Mary Rose's mother in Atlanta to tell them that Mary Rose, Danny, and Kara were all safe and accounted for. *No need,* he thought, *to say anything about John.* Cross then watched President Bush go on the air from Sarasota, Florida, where he'd been visiting a grade school promoting his education program. The president said this had probably been a terrorist attack. He left immediately for Air Force One.

At 9:35 Kara called with the good news.

"John's fine," she said. "He got out of the building okay and was able to squeeze into a cab going uptown."

"Where's he now?"

"He called me from a pay phone on 59th Street. He was going to take another cab over the bridge and go right to the apartment in Forest Hills.

"That's great news—and I guess Mom called you?"

"Oh my God, yeah. I'm going to call her now and tell her about John. Then I'll go to your house in Seaford, and John will come out later on the train."

"That's smart. It's important to try to keep everyone in one place today. Things are hard enough without having to be searching for one another."

Cross turned off his cell phone. He noticed that whatever channel he was watching had switched from the World Trade

Center to its reporter at the Pentagon. *I wonder if they're talking about going to war already?* It was 9:43. He heard the reporter say that just minutes ago there'd been an explosion at the Pentagon, probably on a helicopter landing pad. This didn't register on Cross's Richter scale. Compared to what was happening in New York, a helicopter crash—as bad as it must be for the guys in the chopper and their families—wasn't really that significant. Cross pressed the remote to get back to a channel that was covering the World Trade Center. Instead that channel was also at the Pentagon, and its correspondent said he was hearing reports that a jet may have crashed into the Pentagon. *Jesus Christ!*

In the few seconds it took Cross to walk from his desk to Tom O'Connell's office, the network announcers were reporting that a jetliner had indeed crashed into the Pentagon and that a massive fire was raging out of control. "We're at fucking war," Cross told O'Connell. "I'm evacuating everyone from the office. You, Finnerty and I will go to your place," referring to O'Connell's house on 15th Street, about half a mile north of the White House. "It's centrally located, and it'll be our base of operations for the day. I'll also call Danny and tell him to meet us there."

Cross told everyone to leave the building immediately, except for Finnerty, who would drive him to O'Connell's house. As Cross went back into his office to telephone Danny to tell him they'd be going to O'Connell's, he heard the news announcer say that a fire-bomb explosion was being reported on the Washington Mall. Shaking his head, Cross dialed Danny's number at Commerce. The line was dead. He dialed it again. It was still dead. And then once again—with the same result. Cross knew how close Commerce was to the Mall area.

"Can't get through?" asked Finnerty from the office entrance-way.

"No. The line's dead," answered Cross, wondering to himself what else could possibly happen and realizing that it was barely an hour ago that it had all begun.

After trying Danny one more time and still getting a dead line, Cross called Mary Rose to tell her about the attack on the Pentagon and that he and Danny would be at O'Connell's house. He said nothing about Danny or the fire bomb on the Mall. Unlike the shock and dread she'd demonstrated just a half-hour ago, Mary Rose now displayed an eerie calm. A sense of acceptance. Almost stoicism. *War does harden us very quickly.* Mary Rose did tell him that Anne had called her and would be there in two or three minutes. As Cross hung up, Finnerty walked in, smiling for the first time that day. "Danny called when you were on with Mary Rose. He's fine. He's leaving the building now to meet us at Tom's. He'll stop at your apartment first." It was 9:55.

Cross put on his suit jacket and was walking toward the front door of the office when the phone rang. Kevin picked it up at Kerry Ann's desk, just inside the front door. Cross heard him say: "The congressman is just about to leave, but I'll see if he can talk to you for a few minutes." It was Channel 12 on Long Island. Doug Geed and Carol Silva were the anchors. They wanted to do a live phone interview—a "phoner." The screen would show live footage from Washington. Viewers would hear Cross's voice and see his name across the bottom of the screen. Cross said he would do the interview. He stood at the desk facing the front doorway, which was opened. Cross saw staff people from the other offices walking hurriedly down the hallway. Their faces showed concern but betrayed no panic. Over Cross's shoulder, atop the bookcase, was the television set. The sound muted, it was turned to CNN.

The Channel 12 interview began—Cross's left hand holding the phone, his right hand in his pocket.

Silva—"My God, Sean, what's going on?"

Cross—"We're still trying to figure it out. The idea is to keep calm and find out."

Geed—"What's happening at the Capitol?"

Cross—"All the buildings are being evacuated. The definite feeling is that Washington is a city under siege."

Silva—"Is there a precise place where members of Congress are supposed to go?"

Cross—"Actually there is no set plan or one place where we all go. I'm going to a location with two members of my staff."

Geed—"I'll assume the response to this will be like something we've never seen before."

Cross—"First we must stop it. Then we must find out who did it, and there has to be an organized, systematic, and overwhelming response against whoever did this."

Silva—"Is this the beginning of a war?"

Cross—"We have to assume that anything can and will happen. I can assure you the military is on full alert . . ."

It was 9:59:04.

Silva—"Oh, my God!"

Geed—"Oh Sean—the tower collapsed . . ."

Cross turned quickly and looked unbelievingly at the CNN picture.

Silva—"Half of one of the buildings!"

Geed—"My God! It's beyond belief."

Silva—"The entire tower has collapsed."

Geed—"The smoke from the buildings is going for blocks and blocks and all the way to the water. Pray for us all."

Staring at the Armageddon-like devastation engulfing the television screen, Cross realized there was nothing he could say. The absolute horror of this catastrophe defied words or description.

Cross—"Let me get out of here. They're telling us to evacuate the building."

Silva—"Thanks Sean. Please stay in touch."

Cross and Finnerty said nothing, merely nodding their heads as they left the office, went into the hallway and headed toward the southeast corner of the building. Avoiding the elevator, they walked down three flights of stairs to the first-floor exit opening onto the corner of 1st and C Streets. The Cannon Building appeared to be almost entirely evacuated. The Longworth and

Rayburn Buildings had also emptied out, and the sidewalks of C Street were filled with people, mostly young—probably all staffers—walking eastward. They looked serious, tense, but not at all frenzied. It was almost as if they already realized their world had changed forever, without notice, and they were somberly making the adjustment to this new world—as uncertain and perilous as that world might be. The Capitol Police were out in full force, but they had only to coordinate—not direct—the orderly departure of this virtually silent throng.

Settling himself in the passenger seat of Finnerty's silver Volkswagen Golf parked in the outdoor lot on C Street directly south of Cannon, Cross saw the pained expression that came over Kevin's face and heard the exasperated tone of "Oh, shit" as Kevin turned the key in the ignition. The engine went on but the fuel gauge read *empty*. There was just about enough fuel to get them to the nearest gas station, which was six blocks away on Pennsylvania Avenue. By the time they made it to the Exxon station, got the tank filled, and were on their way to O'Connell's house, it was 10:20. O'Connell had just made the trip to his house in less then fifteen minutes. Now, however, cars leaving Capitol Hill filled the streets bumper to bumper.

Cross and Finnerty were to sit in traffic on Massachusetts Avenue, directly parallel to Union Station, which was on their right, for more than an hour. At the most, they inched less than a block during that hour. The car windows open, the duo alternated between talking to stray reporters walking by on the street and listening to the cascade of bulletins being reported on the car radio. The reporters on the street were vainly attempting to keep pace with a story unfolding so quickly and so different in scope and impact from any they'd covered before. The radio reports ran the gamut of categories. The all too true—the collapse of the World Trade Center's North Tower at 10:29. The possibly true—a car-bomb explosion at the State Department, just blocks from Cross's apartment. The obviously untrue—the bombing of the Capitol Building. (The majestic structure was in clear view of Cross and Finnerty at all times, and there was not a hint of an explosion or fire.) The possibly relevant—the crash of a jet in a Pennsylvania farm field.

Several times Cross got out of the car and walked westerly for a block or so, as much to break the monotony as to find out if there were any hope of movement. There were cars, trucks, and buses as far as he could see. Except for emergency vehicles, nothing was moving. Still, no horns were blaring, and no drivers were shouting or gesturing. For at least this moment, equanimity and calm prevailed on Massachusetts Avenue as hundreds of people, stuck in their cars on a terrifying September day, accepted that so much was beyond their control.

Getting back into the car after his third sojourn, Cross was struck by how much this stalled procession of vehicles reminded him of the famed footage of the Iraqi army's highway of death in the closing hours of the 1991 Gulf War. Miles and miles of vehicles, defenseless then against an aerial attack; today on Massachusetts Avenue—an exploding jetliner. Yet Cross felt no fear. Nor, apparently, did Finnerty. Certainly it wasn't courage. It must be that same fatalism or stoicism he'd heard in Mary Rose's voice when he told her the Pentagon had been attacked. *All we can do for now*, Cross thought, *is try to locate our families and stay strong. Panic or fear won't help a bit and will only give those bastards another victory. And they've already gotten too many fucking victories today.*

It was virtually impossible to get a cell phone call through to New York, but Cross finally connected with Mary Rose at about 11:40. She was at their Seaford home with Kara. John would be arriving in about a half-hour on the LIRR. The Massachusetts Avenue traffic had finally broken, and Finnerty was pulling the car in front of O'Connell's house as Cross concluded his conversation with Mary Rose. His family was safe, and as he stepped from the car into the bright sunlight, Cross allowed himself to feel a certain warm glow of relief. Then he heard the rumble of trucks. He looked toward his left and was jerked back to harsh reality. It was a convoy of Army National Guard troops. Heading south. Toward the White House. We were under attack. And at war.

3

Maintaining a constant speed of about 65 mph, Detective Sullivan drove the black Ford easterly along the Grand Central Parkway, which became the Northern State Parkway as it crossed the border into Nassau County. Sullivan and Cross had been in regular contact with Ed McCabe at Nassau Police headquarters and were closely monitoring the radio news reports. There was nothing new on the Westbury and Brooklyn attacks except that both fires were raging infernos. There were no details on casualties, but there was the hopeful report from a WCBS reporter that "a good number" of employees had been seen escaping from the rear of the Empire Plaza buildings.

As they passed the New Hyde Park exit, Cross looked slightly rightward toward the southeast and said, "Jesus, Sully, look at that."

"The whole sky is filled with black smoke. That must be a helluva fire."

"I hope they're right about some of the workers being able to escape out the back."

"I hate to even think about being in there."

"What exit do you plan on taking?"

"Probably Post Avenue. That's the most direct."

"Sounds good," said Cross, his voice trailing off as he stared toward the ever-blackening sky.

Post Avenue led directly south to the fire scene on Old Country Road. The state police had closed off the parkway exit with flares and sawhorse barricades. Sullivan was okayed to go, however, as soon as he flashed his badge. The trooper, looking in the driver's side window, said to Cross, "Congressman, you'll see when you get there how bad this is. Just make sure you tell the president we're with him all the way. We can't let them get away with this." "Thanks. I'll be sure to tell him," answered Cross. "Believe me. That means a lot."

The parkway exit was more than a mile north of Old Country Road. But the air was thick with smoke, a smoke that became more pervasive each block along the way. Sullivan parked the car about two blocks north of Old Country Road, across from the western boundary of Holy Rood Cemetery and a block south of Nassau Republican Headquarters.

Post Avenue was filled with trucks and engines. Rescue vehicles and ambulances were there as well. When Post crossed Old Country Road it became Merrick Avenue, and that was also filled with fire vehicles and equipment, as was Old Country Road going east. Neighboring fire departments had responded—not just Westbury but the adjacent communities of Carle Place, Mineola, Levittown, and East Meadow, as well as those farther away such as Seaford, Baldwin, and Valley Stream.

Standing in the northside intersection of Old Country and Post and looking toward the southwest corner, Cross got his first clear look at the burning structures. The enormity was beyond anything he had contemplated. The flames and smoke extended, it appeared, almost to the heavens. Cross had no experience dealing with fires and didn't pretend to have any knowledge of firefighting, so he listened quietly and intently as the Westbury fire chief, Hughie Forde, briefed him.

"Congressman, this will have to be quick, because the situation might change at any moment."

"No problem. Tell me what you can."

"Very simply, this is a bad fire. Fuel trucks with explosives, it doesn't get much worse than that. But, thank God, we've actually had some good luck. The combination of the new construction methods—more concrete, less glass—plus the angle of the trucks when they made impact confined the fire to the front end of the buildings and to the first few floors for about six or seven minutes. And even when the fire did break loose toward the upper floors, it took about another ten minutes before the flames engulfed the back of the buildings. So a helluva lot of people did get out. We also caught a couple of other breaks. One of the big brokerage firms—Sandner & Manning—had a golf outing today. Plus, some people who come in at seven o'clock on flex time had gone out for lunch."

"Chief, any numbers yet?" asked Cross, realizing Forde had to get back to his command post.

"About thirty-five dead and another hundred injured," answered Forde, his jaw clenching. "I said we got some breaks, but this will still be the worst tragedy in the history of Long Island."

"Thanks, Chief. Keep up the good work."

Turning from the blazing buildings, Cross walked toward the car, saying, "Sully, I might as well get out of here. All I can do now is get in the way."

"Yeah. It's probably a good idea to get home and touch base with your family. The next few days could get pretty crazy. There's some reporters over there though who have some questions," said Sullivan, gesturing toward a group of reporters cordoned into a roped-off area next to the cemetery.

"Sure, it shouldn't take too long."

Cross was right. The reporters were subdued. Their questions brief and direct.

—Do you think Islamic terrorists were behind these attacks?

They would have to be the main suspects at this time.

—What action should the president take?

I can't speak for the president, of course, but I am absolutely certain he will take whatever military action he has to—and it will be overwhelming and lethal.

—Should anything else be done?

Clearly we have to be more aggressive and take much stronger action against terrorists operating right here in our own country, our own communities.

—Do you have any specific proposals?

I'll leave it at that for now.

As Cross was concluding his remarks to the final press questions, he could see Sullivan edging slowly away from him—maybe ten feet or so. His phone was pressed to his left ear, his right hand cupping the receiver as he spoke. It probably didn't take longer than fifteen seconds, but Cross took notice because Sully was otherwise always within arm's reach, ready to spring on a moment's notice.

Sullivan was silent until they got into the car. Then he turned toward Cross saying, "Sean, it's just gotten a lot worse. That was Eddie McCabe again. There's been an explosion in a Long Island Railroad Tunnel."

"Which one? What happened?"

"Apparently a bomb went off in a train that had left Penn Station, going to Babylon. It was on the city side. Just before the East River."

"Christ, it went off in the tunnel?"

"Yeah, the same tunnel you've done so much yelling about."

Cross did know the tunnel—too well. Actually there were four tunnels running alongside one another and extending from Penn Station across the East River to Long Island City, where the LIRR trains began their ascent from this subterranean netherworld. Not only were these tunnels themselves fire hazards, their emergency exits were almost nonexistent. The emergency stairwells, for instance, which descended ten stories, were extremely steep and barely more than two feet wide, making it virtually impossible for rescue workers to maneuver their way down when passengers were attempting to make their way up. And the ventilation systems were incapable of removing smoke or providing fresh air during a fire or explosion in any weather or at any time of the year.

Cross had been fighting this case for years, arguing that the federal government had to entirely reconstruct these tunnels as a matter of national security. That in their current dilapidated, antiquated state of disrepair they constituted an open invitation to terrorists. He was confronted at every turn, however, by southern and western interests who saw his proposal as just another giveaway to New York. So the most he was able to get were nominal amounts, barely sufficient to maintain the inadequacy of the status quo.

"Jesus," said Cross, "that could be a Goddamned disaster. Any details?"

"It happened less than ten minutes ago. Apparently it's chaos. Firemen trying to get down. Smoke everywhere. No word on casualties. But it's early. The reporters are just hearing about it."

Sullivan maneuvered a U-turn amidst the fire vehicles and drove north on Post Avenue toward the Northern State Parkway, where they'd go east and get off at the first exit to take the Wantagh Parkway south toward Cross's Seaford home. The trip should take about ten or fifteen minutes.

As Cross turned the radio back on to WCBS 880 AM, the newscaster was reporting that "terror has struck New York yet again today, and hundreds of commuters are struggling for their lives, trying desperately to escape from a tunnel filled with smoke and fire."

"Christ, those fuckers really nailed us," said Cross. "Any word from Brooklyn?"

"There's actually some good news on that. Part of it, you know, is used as a homeless shelter. But there were only a few people in the armory when the explosion went off, and they think everyone got out. Apparently, though, the fire is just incredible. There must have been some device inside, as well as the truck itself."

"It could be that the attack on the armory was merely symbolic. You know, an army installation, located so close to a Muslim community, being blown apart after all these years— that's a pretty good prize."

"That armory must have been there forever."

"Back in the 1800s anyway. Also my father worked there as a cop fifty years ago. They used to use it during the winter as a training location for the Police Academy," said Cross.

"A lot's changed in fifty years."

"A lot's changed in two hours!"

Turning the corner onto Madison Street in Seaford where Cross's house was located, Sullivan's trained eyes reflexively scanned up and down the road.

"Looks like the Seventh Precinct has you well covered," said Sullivan, subtly pointing to one unmarked blue Ford across the street from the house and a nondescript black van about fifty feet farther down the street.

"I guess that's encouraging," answered Cross with an ironic grin, realizing that while it is a good thing to *have* police protection, it wasn't such a good thing that the police thought you *needed* their protection.

"I assume this is pretty much standard for New York congressmen after these attacks," said Sullivan, "but it's especially true in your case since you've been so aggressive against these fundamentalists."

Cross took his suit carrier from the trunk, and Sullivan walked him to the front door.

"I'll head back to headquarters," said Sullivan. "But if you're going anywhere, just let me know. I can be here in twenty minutes."

"Thanks. Right now I'll just field calls for a while and try to find out what's going on, especially with the LIRR. That could be catastrophic. But I think I should go back into Westbury later on, probably about seven o'clock or so."

"No problem. Just give me some lead time."

Mary Rose opened the front door, Kara stood in the entranceway just behind her. Sean kissed Mary Rose and hugged Kara.

"Brutal day," he said, putting his suit carrier off to the side on the floor, placing his jacket over a chair and dropping himself down on the living room couch.

"At least we're all alive," answered Mary Rose.

"I'm just so happy that John decided to stay in the city. Otherwise he could have been on that train."

"Yeah," said Cross, in a tone so low that it was about inaudible. "Unfortunately a lot of other people weren't so lucky."

During the next several hours Cross, alternately and simultaneously, monitored the television and radio and received seemingly one phone call after the other. As the day went on, however, a certain order was emerging from the chaos and fog of war.

—The Empire Plaza fire in Westbury was under control. Chief Forde's estimate had been very accurate. There were thirty-eight dead and 116 injured. Of the injured, two were critical with third-degree burns; the others were expected to make full recoveries. The numbers were devastating but could have been so much worse.

—The Brooklyn fire had been more difficult to get under control, primarily because of three secondary explosions that had gone off in the armory during the first hour after the initial blast. Fortunately, the casualty count was low. One National Guard employee and three homeless people were hospitalized with smoke inhalation, and two firemen had minor burns from one of the secondary blasts. All were expected to recover fully. The armory itself was severely damaged, affirming Cross's initial thought that this target had been primarily symbolic.

—The LIRR tunnel conflagration was as tragic as Cross could have dreaded. A hundred ninety-eight passengers and four firefighters dead; 110 passengers and six firefighters suffering from smoke inhalation, with eight of those passengers in critical condition—the others were expected to live.

—The president had put all armed forces on full worldwide alert and had ordered the FBI and CIA to launch full-scale, all-out investigations.

Mary Rose and Kara had stayed in the house all afternoon with Sean, their eyes riveted on the television. Danny phoned in from Tokyo to make sure everyone was safe and to say that Japanese television was showing nonstop footage of the three attack scenes. And John got to the house about 5:30. A guy from work had given him a lift.

No one was particularly hungry, but Mary Rose put together some hamburgers and they sat at the kitchen table taking minimal bites of meat as they tried to make some sense of the day.

"Are you surprised by how bad this is?" Mary Rose asked Sean. "I thought we had them on the run."

"We do have them on the run," Sean answered. "Their training camps have been destroyed. We've seized incredible amounts of their money. And we're locking up Al Qaeda leaders and breaking up their cells all over the world."

"And we haven't had any real attacks since the World Trade Center and the Pentagon," interjected Kara.

"The bottom line is," said Sean, "that you can never be completely safe when you're dealing with hard-core fanatics. Yeah, we've done a great job of disrupting them but you just can't protect yourselves everywhere, all the time."

"Any idea how they put this together?" asked John.

"If I had to guess, I'd say this was done entirely internally," answered Cross. "There's just too much surveillance and international monitoring for this to have been coordinated overseas like the World Trade Center was. It's also harder for them to be sneaking guys into the country."

"So it was people living here?" asked Mary Rose.

"I think it had to be," answered Sean. "And it was dirtbags living here a few years. That means they used money that was over here, got all their supplies and gear over here, and made their plans over here. Right here among all of us."

"We've got to be talking about more than just a few people, then," said John.

"Absolutely," said Sean. "Besides the people directly involved planning it and carrying it out, there'd have to be others they'd come in contact with when they were putting it all together."

"So basically you're saying that they pretty much have their own army and support network right here in New York," said Mary Rose.

"What I'm saying is that Al Qaeda has trained killers living among us and that there must be a lot of others out there who know what Al Qaeda is doing and either let them do it or actually help them," answered Sean.

"Which means," said Kara in her characteristically direct tone, "that these low-lifes are all murderers, no matter how much or how little they actually did. Whether they crashed the trucks into the buildings or just kept their mouths shut, they're responsible for about 240 Americans being murdered today."

"Kara, you're 100 percent on target," said Cross.

"What happens next?" asked John.

"As far as we know, these attacks are all that's out there for now," said Sean. "But we don't know for sure, so the feds are already in. Checking, for instance, for any chemical or biological agents. The FBI, the NYPD, and the Nassau cops are squeezing all their sources as hard as they can—not just to find out who did it, which will be tough enough, but to try to head off anything else."

"What do you think?" asked Mary Rose.

"I think this is it for now. That's their M.O. But you've got to cover everything."

"Dad, you still going to Westbury tonight?" asked Kara.

"Yeah, I'll go in for awhile. Sully's coming by in about ten minutes. I just want to see what's going on and at least show a presence. The firefighters deserve that. They've done a great job."

"When are you due back in Washington?" inquired John.

"Right now the schedule says Tuesday afternoon, and unless something else happens, they'll probably keep it that way. But I have Tom and Kevin flying up tonight. We have a lot to do this weekend. In fact, Anne has already started in the district office. We've got to get the names of any victims who were from the district and start reaching out to their families to see if they need any help. One thing we learned from the World Trade Center is that we've got to start early. There's just so many complications that develop with funerals, identifications, insurance and a million other things you can't anticipate."

"It's a great day," said John ironically, "when you realize that you've had enough experience to consider yourself an expert in dealing with disasters."

September 11, 2001

The Afternoon and Evening

Entering Tom O'Connell's house in Northwest Washington, Cross first sought out the television. He found it in the living room and went directly to it. The last he had seen was almost two hours ago, when the South Tower was collapsing and being subsumed in a mushroomlike cloud of billowing gray smoke that plunged downward and then rampaged mercilessly through the streets of lower Manhattan.

Now much of that cloud had abated, as well as the cloud from the North Tower. The view on the television screen was a grotesque overlay of smoke, dust, and debris. Through that overlay Cross could make out the twisted steel, the mountains of wreckage, and the still-raging flames. It was Dresden. It was Hamburg. It was hell. It was a nuclear winter in September.

It took another forty-five minutes or so before Danny arrived at O'Connell's, carrying with him a bag of sandwiches and buns. Not having a cell phone, Danny could not be contacted, and his delay had caused some concern—particularly since there had been the reports of a car-bomb explosion at the State Department, just blocks from the apartment Sean and Danny shared.

"What'd you do, take a tour of Washington?" Sean asked with a gruff smile.

"I got myself lost finding you these delicacies," answered Danny, opening up the bag to proudly display six saran-wrapped, ready-made bologna sandwiches.

"We greatly appreciate your thoughtfulness," said O'Connell, as he attempted to extricate a sandwich from its saran enclosure. "But, seriously, how was it out there?"

"Besides getting lost," Danny answered, "it did take me longer than I thought it would. I didn't want to get on the Metro, so I walked from Commerce to the apartment."

"What about the report of a car bomb at the State Department?" asked Finnerty.

"That was bullshit," answered Danny. "Nothing happened at all. I did go up on the roof of the apartment, though, to look out at the Pentagon, and that's really bad. I could see all the flames and smoke. I'm glad I wasn't in that."

"How was the walk over here from the apartment?" asked Sean.

"Except for making one or two wrong turns, it wasn't that bad at all. A lot of people had left work and were on the streets. It was very interesting. People didn't seem scared, but nobody was talking either. Just looking straight ahead. Sort of like they were each in their own world. Me too, I guess."

"Any troops?" asked O'Connell.

"Yeah, that caught me off guard. I guess I should have thought about it, but it was jarring to see army troops on American streets."

The devastation of the World Trade Center had caused the destruction of telephonic transmission facilities affecting hundreds of thousands of cell phone users. That destruction, plus the massive flow of frantic phone calls in and out of the New York area during that day, made it laborious and frustrating to get through on a cell phone. But Sean used Tom's land line in the house to call Mary Rose, and they reassured one another that all the family members were safe and accounted for. He also did several telephone interviews with Channel 12, mainly to let Long Island viewers know that Washington was not panicking. Additionally, Cross received several phone calls from Felix Grucci, the Republican congressman from eastern Long Island, who'd stayed in New York that day to be with his mother, who was to have had heart surgery in St. Francis Hospital in Nassau County that morning. Once the towers were hit, of course, all nonemergency surgery was postponed, and all transportation out of New York was closed down. Cross told Felix what was happening in Washington, and Grucci relayed to Sean what he was seeing and hearing on Long Island. Neither congressman particularly edified the other, but it was reassuring just to make the contact.

That morning, after the World Trade Center and the Pentagon had been attacked, Cross—along with the other 434 members of Congress and the hundred U.S. senators—realized that Congress did not have an emergency evacuation plan. So, for those first few hours, Cross and all the others—except for the very top leaders of the House and Senate—were entirely on their own, with no formal means of communicating with each other or getting direction from their leadership. In midafternoon Tom O'Connell did get a call from a member of Congresswoman Carolyn McCarthy's staff saying he'd heard that the Capitol Police were giving a briefing at their headquarters on Capitol Hill for senators and congressmen. After checking with the police switchboard and confirming the report was true, O'Connell drove Sean and Danny to the meeting.

The streets of downtown Washington, normally radiating with energy and teeming with lobbyists, lawyers, and political operatives, each rushing urgently to their next meeting so they could make their next deal, were empty. Barren. Desolate. Except, of course, for the National Guard troops in trucks and police standing watch on street corners or driving their patrol cars. Leaving downtown D.C., O'Connell drove east on Massachusetts Avenue toward Capitol Hill. Approaching North Capitol Street,

Cross looked right and saw the Dubliner—the down-to-earth Irish pub he regularly frequented for relaxing meals and a few pints. Through its front window Cross could see people standing around. They didn't appear to be saying much or drinking at all. *Probably patrons from the adjacent Phoenix Park Hotel,* he thought. Past the Dubliner, he looked directly up North Capitol Street on his right toward the north side of the Capitol dome. The street was closed to all traffic, with burning flares placed across its entrance and police officers standing menacingly behind those flares.

The Capitol Police headquarters was located only several blocks away at 119 D Street, N.E., just north of the Senate office buildings and next to the Monocle restaurant. O'Connell displayed his House credentials and was allowed to park the Jeep in the lot down the street from the headquarters. Walking toward headquarters, Cross saw that a yellow tape reading "Police Line Do Not Cross" was connecting the lamp posts up and down the street. Police—uniformed, plainclothes, and SWAT teams—were positioned throughout the street. Behind the tape on the north side of the street, directly across from the headquarters, was the media stakeout. There must have been fifty or so photographers and reporters—print, radio, and television—and about twenty television cameras. Some reporters were talking to Congressmen standing just inches away from them but in the street and on the other side of the yellow tape. Other reporters were trying to make calls on their cell phones; others were getting ready to give live television reports; and others were sitting on the grass, staring out and saying nothing.

Cross immediately realized that whatever meeting there had been had broken up. Congressmen were milling about the center of the street, standing in small groups and speaking quietly. "Did they tell you anything?" Cross asked Tony Ripo, a congressman from Chicago. "Not much," replied Ripo, "just that the House and Senate leaders have been evacuated to a secret location. There's supposed to be a more detailed meeting in a few hours, about six o'clock I think."

As Cross thanked Ripo and started to walk toward the headquarters entrance, Republican congressman Rory Andrews walked up to him and said animatedly, "How many times did I say that this was exactly what was going to happen if Clinton didn't change his policies? I knew this was going to happen. I just knew it. This is all Clinton's fault. *You* heard me say it."

"Yeah. I did," answered Cross, nodding his head but not having a clue what Andrews was talking about.

Cross then spoke to several of the police officers he knew, asking how they were, if they had spoken to their families and thanking them for all they were doing. He then walked toward the media stakeout, where he saw Elaine Povich of *Newsday* standing behind the yellow tape.

"Tough day, Elaine."

"This is the worst."

"You hearing anything we're not?"

"I was going to ask you that same question," she said, forcing a weak smile.

"I guess we're not much help to each other. But I'll let you know if I learn anything at the next meeting."

"Thanks. Earlier, some of your fellow Republicans were really attacking Clinton and blaming the CIA and FBI. What do you think?"

"This isn't the day for that shit. We've just suffered the worst attack ever on our country. This is a time to draw together, not point fingers, and we have to get back to work."

"Thanks, Sean, see you later."

Cross then asked O'Connell to drive Danny and him over to his office in the Cannon Building before they headed back to O'Connell's house. Again, the congressional credentials got them through the police checkpoints at each corner and intersection between police headquarters and Cannon. Traveling south on 1st Street, Cross saw no vehicles except the emergency rescue trucks at the east entrance to the Capitol grounds—their function today being more to thwart car bombs than provide medical assistance.

Entering the same Independence Avenue doorway as he had this morning, Cross asked the two police officers at the door if it was okay to go in. "Sure, Congressman, you can go to your office, but you'll have to move quick. We're closing the building in twenty minutes, at exactly three o'clock." "No problem," said Cross. "You're the boss."

Sean and Danny walked the two flights of stairs to the fourth floor. All he wanted from his office was his Rolodex of phone numbers, since he didn't know how long Cannon would be closed or whom he might have to call in the next few days. Danny wanted to use the phone to let some of his friends overseas know that he was safe. Sean picked up the Rolodex and then found the camera and film he'd brought with him to the office that morning for this evening's barbeque. Waiting for Danny to complete his calls, Cross walked slowly throughout the office. It had been less than five hours since he'd left, but it seemed like a lifetime. Pens and unopened correspondence lying on desks. Unread newspapers left behind on chairs and on the tops of file cabinets. The phones hushed silent. The office door was wide open, but there was not a sound from the morgue-like hallway.

Cross turned on the television in the reception area and realized that the reporters in lower Manhattan had already made the psychological transformation to being war correspondents. And the news from the World Trade Center was still all bad. Paula Zahn was reporting on CNN that there could be as many as 265 fire department fatalities—*265!* Cross knew that the worst tragedy in the history of the fire department had been twelve, back in the late '60s, and it had taken the FDNY years to get over that trauma. Just this past June the city had virtually come to a halt when three firemen were killed in Queens on Father's Day. And if there are 265 firemen, how many cops? How many people working in the buildings? And how many on the planes that went down? And when does the count go so high that you become numb? When does the tragic become the routine?

Cross's questions were partially answered just a few hours later. Watching the television in O'Connell's house, he saw World Trade Center Building Seven collapse and crumble to the ground in another explosion of dust, steel, and debris. To the television reporters, and indeed to Cross as well, it was just one more incident. And this time no one was killed. The fact that it had been a forty-six-story structure that prior to today would have constituted the largest building collapse in the history of New York City went very much unreported.

Yet as the horrific events unfolded across the television screen, Cross also realized that America would not allow the death and the suffering of the day to overwhelm its spirit or vanquish its soul. Just watching the firefighters and the cops and the rescue workers and the ordinary New Yorkers fighting back and demonstrating defiance, Cross knew that an unquestionable national will and resolve were rising from this funeral pyre of twisted steel and crushed body parts. New York had taken the enemy's best shot, and it was still standing. More than ever Cross was proud to be an American, and so proud to be a New Yorker.

That's what made the congressional gathering at police headquarters that evening so disturbing. The pompous posturing of self-important politicians stood in such stark contrast to the quiet selflessness of those struggling through the flames and amidst the ruins. The meeting, which began just after six o'clock, was intended to be an update of what was known, what was being done, and what might be anticipated. It was held in a large, auditorium-like room. There appeared to be about 250 members of Congress in the room, plus staff and, in some cases, family members. Cross was accompanied by Finnerty, who did the driving, and Danny, who after taking a look around the room whispered to Cross that "some of these guys are going to act stupid."

At the front of the room were Bill Livingood, the sergeant-at-arms, who was responsible for House security, and Fr. Daniel Coughlin, the House chaplain. The House leaders—Speaker Denny Hastert and Democratic leader Dick Gephardt—had been moved to a secret location immediately after the Pentagon had been attacked. They conducted the meeting by speakerphone from wherever they were. Hastert's message—concurred in by Gephardt—was that unless anything further occurred, Congress would go back into session the following morning. In the meantime the military, the FBI, and the police would determine the possibility of additional attacks and the extent to which security would be increased and new procedures implemented. This all sounded reasonable to Sean—but Danny turned out to be right. Hastert and Gephardt had barely finished speaking when shouts of disapproval rang out from the crowd. Several congressmen actually stormed to the front of the room to shout into the speakerphone positioned on the desk.

"This is an exercise in cowardice!" bellowed one.

"Unless you can tell us that you have specific knowledge of a specific plot to attack the Capitol, then we must go back into session tonight," explained the other. "The American people want to see us."

Hastert's patient attempts to explain that going into session tonight would put an unfair burden on law-enforcement and spread public resources too thin at a time of national crisis were met with hoots of derision.

"I told you these guys were assholes," whispered Danny.

Cross shrugged and looked around the room. It was maybe only 20 percent who were acting like morons, but they marred the moment—the moment when they should have been emulating the quiet courage of the people fighting their way though lower Manhattan, instead of acting like juveniles. *Of course the cops don't have any specific intelligence of an attack tonight,* thought Cross. *But that means nothing. They didn't have any idea about the attacks this morning either. Christ, the Pentagon is in flames just a few miles from here, and we're asking the cops to change their security plans because some self-important congressmen want to be on television tonight, and they want to be part of a story that is larger than us all.*

Finally, they compromised and agreed to assemble on the Capitol steps in about an hour. They wouldn't go into the chamber, but they would be seen on television.

"Are you going to the Capitol?" asked Finnerty.

"No, the cops have enough to do without putting up with us showboating," replied Cross. "Let's just get a beer and something to eat at the Dubliner. Maybe it'll help us get our heads together."

As they left the headquarters building, Cross saw Danny smiling to himself and asked what was so funny.

"I know this isn't a day to be laughing about much," answered Danny. "But I couldn't help it. I was just imagining Denny Hastert sitting in a cave somewhere with Gephardt and the two of them listening to all that bullshit."

"If he's smart, he just might stay in the cave," said Finnerty.

After a quick dinner at the Dubliner of a corned beef sandwich and a pint of Harp beer, Cross returned to O'Connell's house to watch President Bush address the nation. It had been a long, tiring, and tortuous day for the president. He'd been meeting with schoolchildren in Sarasota, Florida, when the Twin Towers were hit. After giving a brief statement at 9:27 that this had probably been a terrorist attack, Bush left immediately for Air Force One, beginning a circuitous route that would not return him to Washington, D.C., until 6:57 that evening. First he'd gone from Sarasota to Barksdale Air Force Base in Louisiana, and then to Offutt Air Force Base in Nebraska, the home of the Strategic Air Command, where he conducted a National Security Council meeting by video teleconference. At both bases, air force personnel in full combat gear—with drawn M-16s—surrounded the perimeter of Air Force One and the buildings to which the president was brought. When Air Force One finally touched down at Andrews Air Force Base that evening, it was accompanied by a squadron of F-16 fighters.

Sitting somberly in O'Connell's living room, just a few feet from the television screen, Cross found the president's Oval Office address effective and moving.

—"Terrorist attacks can shake the foundation of our biggest buildings but they cannot touch the foundations of America. These acts shatter steel, but they cannot dent the steel of American resolve.

—"Today our nation saw evil, the very worst of human nature, and we responded with the best of America.

—"I've directed the full resources of our intelligence and law enforcement communities to find those responsible and bring them to justice. We will make no distinction between terrorists who committed these acts and those who harbor them.

—"Good night and God Bless America."

Finnerty drove Sean and Danny back to their apartment. Except for the occasional solitary pedestrian, the police squad cars, and the army trucks, the streets were barren and silent. Arriving at the apartment house, Sean and Danny walked through the empty lobby and took the elevator to the roof. Standing against the perimeter wall, they looked across the Potomac toward the Pentagon, where raging flames of red and orange were illuminating the blue-black September sky. It struck Cross that throughout that entire day virtually his entire focus had been on the World Trade Center and the New York victims and rescuers. But here, barely a few miles away from his apartment, hundreds of Americans who served this country lay dead or injured. What an abomination! "We've got to kill the bastards who did this," said Sean, as Danny slowly nodded his firm approval.

Sitting in their living room apartment, Sean and Danny watched the ongoing news reports of the day's tragedies. They sat quietly, each sipping a beer. The room was barely lit by one small lamp on a corner table. With all the confusion, chaos, and horror of the day, this was the first real opportunity Cross had to focus in any depth on what was being reported. And as he watched, Cross realized how much of the day's essence he had missed. Yes, he knew that the planes had crashed into the towers. That the towers had become boiling cauldrons of flames, smoke, and death. And that the towers had collapsed and thousands of good people had died. But, until now, Cross had seen this only from the perspective of a horrible, grotesque tragedy. He had not thought of real individuals—real people—actually dying, or of just how they died. But tonight, with no family members to worry about or briefings to run to, he was focused, and he realized he was not ready for what he was seeing. It was one thing to see the top floors of the North Tower engulfed in flames; it was another to see the people who worked on those floors standing in the windows desperately waving for help, knowing all the while that within minutes they would be burned to death or forced to jump. Nothing in these people's lives had caused them to expect this moment. They weren't soldiers going into combat, cops chasing perps across rooftops, or firemen going into a burning building. No, they were ordinary people who just a few moments before had been sitting at their desks so they could make enough money to pay their bills and take care of their kids. Now they were confronted with having to decide whether to burn to death or jump a hundred stories to the concrete below.

And the firefighters and the cops. Sure, it was their job to put their lives on the line. That goes with the territory. But not confronting the fuel and flames of a 767 jetliner. Not being trapped in the crushed rubble of what had been two of the most enormous structures in the world.

But it was the faces of people trapped at their office windows that so completely haunted him. Faces racked with desperation and fatalism. Facing the unimaginable and knowing that it was inevitable.

The phone rang, and Cross picked it up on the second ring. Tom Barfield was on the line. Tom and his wife Janet were old friends of Cross from New York. He'd been a successful bond broker with the firm of Cohen & Fitzpatrick. He'd left the firm just about a year ago after a heated dispute with Harold Rubin, the principal owner in the firm. Cross knew that Cohen & Fitzpatrick's offices were in the North Tower of the World Trade

Center and was friendly with a number of guys in the firm. They were Irish-Americans who supported Cross for his efforts on the Irish peace process and had contributed to his campaigns. They were good guys. But he hadn't thought of them this day. Until he heard Barfield's voice.

"Jesus, Tom, it's great of you to call. This has been some day."

"Yeah. I was just talking with Mary Rose. Janet and I heard you on Channel 12 a few times today, and I thought I'd touch base with you to see how you're doing."

"I'm doing as well as anyone. I have nothing to complain about at all. Everyone's safe and accounted for. How are your guys doing?"

"You mean our friends from Cohen & Fitzpatrick?"

"Yeah."

"Not good," answered Barfield, who hesitated for a moment before continuing. "It's bad. Very bad."

"Do you have any numbers, any estimates?"

"Sean, are you sitting down?"

"Yeah."

"More than six hundred."

For a long moment, Cross said nothing. Then he continued.

"How about our friends?" asked Cross.

"A lot of them were hit," answered Barfield, offering no names.

"Farrell?" asked Cross hesitatingly, referring to their mutual friend Farrell Lynch.

"Yeah, Farrell's dead, and so is his brother."

"And Eamon?"

"Eamon's dead too. Sean, they're all dead. Every one of them."

Cross said nothing.

"How about the firemen and the cops?" asked Barfield, seemingly anxious to shift the focus. "Any word on them?"

"Fr. Mychal Judge, the fire chaplain who was killed. I knew him through Steven McDonald," replied Cross, referring to the New York City police officer who'd been paralyzed years before.

"He was a good guy. And Pete Ganci, the chief of the department, I didn't know him, but he lived in my district, in Farmingdale."

"I suppose more of the names will be coming out from the Fire Department tomorrow."

"Yeah. Now they're saying that count is over 340 and the cops—NYPD and the Port Authority—are about sixty."

"I never thought we'd ever see a day like this in our country," said Barfield angrily.

"We've got to make sure they pay."

"I thought Bush was terrific tonight. Right on the mark. But he's got a helluva job ahead of him."

"He sure does. But I really think he can do it," answered Cross.

"So do I. But the country's got to stick together."

"That's the truth."

"Listen, if you and Mary Rose can find the time this weekend, maybe we can get together for a drink. I know Janet would love that."

"Great idea. We could all use some friendship."

Hanging up the phone, Cross stared at the television for a few more minutes—seeing again the faces of the people in the windows. Danny had already gone to sleep. Turning off the television and the living room light, Sean walked toward the bedroom. The images of the doomed people in the windows seared his mind; he looked through the top dresser drawer until he found two Ambien sleeping pills left over from a recent congressional trip overseas. He took the pills, got into bed, and fell into a sleep that was deep but hardly restful.

The morning sun shone brightly through the window of Sean Cross's local congressional office in Massapequa Park. Sitting at his desk, drinking a cup of coffee, and eating a buttered roll he'd bought at the deli across the street, Cross was reading through the Saturday papers, which detailed the devastation from yesterday's attacks. The fires were under control and largely extinguished, but the death tolls were rising—Westbury was up to forty-two, and the LIRR 208. Brooklyn still had just a handful of minor injuries, though the Armory was in ruins.

It was just after eight o'clock when Brian Sullivan, who'd been alone in the outer office, walked in to tell Cross that Tom Barfield had arrived.

"Jesus, Tom, you're right on time," said Cross, shaking hands with Barfield.

"It's only because I was afraid that if I were late, you'd finish off all the buns and doughnuts," answered Barfield, grabbing himself a cheese Danish from a table in the center of the room and sitting down in the chair directly in front of Cross's desk.

"At least you brought your own coffee," said Cross.

"It was in self-defense. I didn't want any of that swill that you usually give me."

"Excuse me. I forgot you were once such a big restaurateur!"

"Yeah. Now I'm just big."

"Seriously, Tom, thanks for coming by. I really appreciate it."

"Are you kidding? I'll do anything I possibly can to get those pricks."

Sean Cross and Tom Barfield had first crossed paths about twenty-five years ago when Cross was starting out as a town councilman and Barfield was the proprietor of one of Long Island's most elaborate restaurants—Barfield's of Rockville Centre. It was the type of place you'd much more expect to find in Manhattan than Long Island—especially at that time. It was elaborate, the food was top dollar, and it was frequented by assorted athletes, celebrities, politicians, and people who wanted to be seen with people who wanted to be seen. Not content with being a young Long Island version of Toots Shor, Barfield sold the restaurant and immersed himself in the financial services maelstrom of lower Manhattan. It was tough, and it was a fast track, but Barfield did well. Very well. Maneuvering and moving—always upward— Barfield moved from company to company, culminating in his eight years at Cohen & Fitzpatrick, which was located on the top floors of the World Trade Center's North Tower.

For whatever reason, there was a disproportionate number of Irish-Americans at Cohen & Fitzpatrick. Mostly blue-collar, neighborhood-type guys who had worked their way up on their own and, with the help of the boom years of the '90s, made big bucks. Cross had known a number of these guys or their families through his involvement in Irish-American organizations over the years and his role in the Irish peace process. Barfield had organized several fund-raisers for Cross at Manhattan gin mills with the Cohen & Fitzpatrick guys, and they'd always raised good money. Barfield ended up leaving Cohen & Fitzpatrick in 2000, however, after a sustained fallout with Harold Rubin, the firm's principal owner. Since Cross could never understand what the bond business was all about anyway, he couldn't fully comprehend the nuances and complexities of Barfield's dispute with

Rubin, but he knew that Tom felt strongly about it, and he assumed that Barfield was right.

Barfield was blessed with the indefinable capacity to land invariably on his feet. So when he left Cohen & Fitzgerald, Barfield lined up some heavy-duty partners and formed a security firm—the Barfield Group—which specialized in protecting corporate executives. Since it was always Barfield's style to go top shelf, the new company spent large amounts of up-front money recruiting high-quality, high-priced retired FBI agents and NYPD officers with intelligence backgrounds. He also made large capital investments in state-of-the-art technology. Almost from the start the company did well, and now it was doing very well.

As the company got going, Barfield began to view it as more than just a financial investment. His executive style was direct and hands-on, which meant that he spent a lot time with his professional investigators, learning how they assessed risks and planned strategies. Inevitably this made him aware of the threat posed to Americans by Islamic fundamentalist groups and the extent to which these groups pervaded many levels of the Muslim community in New York.

"How was the scene in Westbury last night?" asked Barfield.

"The firemen did a great job. It's amazing how so many different departments could be so well coordinated," said Cross.

"The death toll is up?"

"Four more. But they think that will be it."

"And it looks like the hospitals are able to handle all the injured."

"Yeah, so far no problems."

"Sean, are the cops telling you about anyone they're zeroing in on?"

"No. I get the impression they have a lot of general suspects but nothing specific on anyone."

"I agree with that—there are certainly a lot of suspects. Maybe this will wake people up about how dangerous the situation is."

"I thought the World Trade Center would have done that."

"It did—but not enough. That alerted Americans to Al Qaeda as an international threat. But those hijackers hadn't been in this country long, so most people didn't realize how much of a domestic threat we have, that there really is an enemy within."

"So you think the guys who pulled off yesterday's attacks have been here for a while?"

"I'm almost certain of that. The government really has tightened the borders since the World Trade Center. Sure, some can still get in. But so many had to be involved yesterday, they couldn't have been guys who recently snuck in. Also, this took so much coordination the government would have intercepted some communications if it were being run from overseas. No, I'm convinced this was planned, coordinated, and carried out by guys who were here at least four or five years."

"You think they're based in New York?"

"Yeah. Primarily Brooklyn, Long Island, and also Jersey."

"Actual Al Qaeda cells?"

"Remember, what I'm giving you is mostly second hand. I can't swear to it but it but I think it's good information, and I think there are actual cells."

"Are a lot of your clients targeted or threatened by Islamic terrorists?" Cross asked.

"Some are. But we can never be sure who is and who isn't, so I try to keep as close an eye as possible on these characters. And the ex-cops and feds working for me are pretty tight with their old jobs, so they get a lot of inside shit that helps me out."

"Sounds pretty good to me."

"So getting back to your question about these cells, it's not just actual Al Qaeda members we're talking about. They have a strong support network in the Muslim community, besides the people that are members."

"Tom, I agree with you completely. I was talking with Mary Rose, Kara, and John about that last night. I don't have the details you have about actual operatives, but I know they couldn't do it on their own."

"We're on the same page."

"I keep interrupting you. What can you tell me about the actual terrorists—the Islamists?"

"The Muslim community is the most radical and terrorist of any immigrant group that's ever come to this country. And this has been going on for the past ten to fifteen years."

"Here I am interrupting you again. But didn't they say the same about the Irish? Let's be honest. You and I know quite a few IRA types in Queens and the Bronx."

"To me there's no comparison between Al Qaeda and the IRA. But that's another debate. The bottom line is that the IRA never worked against the United States. And most of the micks over here who supported the IRA considered themselves 100 percent pro-American, and believe me these Muslims don't."

"September 11th proved that."

"Anyway, beginning somewhere is the late '80s or early '90s, Islamic fundamentalists started organizing—first in Brooklyn and then out here. They would meet in mosques and conduct training in everything from car theft to bomb making."

"Did the people running the mosques know this was going on?"

"Yes. In fact I'd say most of them actually encouraged it. You have to remember that even though most Muslims over here probably don't support bin Laden and Al Qaeda, the militants have taken over the mosques. Our intelligence is that 80 percent of the mosques are controlled by radical Islamists. And these people are absolutely committed to destroying America."

"Where else did they train besides the mosques?"

"A lot of it was right here on Long Island. There's quite a few ranges out here, and these dirtbags were trying out all sorts of weapons. They also had actual training camps upstate and in Pennsylvania."

"Nobody bothered them? The cops or the FBI?"

"No, because they weren't bothering anyone. Let's face it, Islamic terrorism wasn't our main concern in the early '90s."

"Even after the first World Trade Center attack in '93?"

"No. Unfortunately, too many at the top in Washington thought that was just the work of a few wackos or terrorists. Remember, Clinton never even came to the World Trade Center in '93."

"What about later on? We had Khobar Towers, the African embassies, and the *Cole*."

"Yeah, but they were overseas. The government just wasn't as concerned about a domestic attack as it should have been—except for the millennium, and once Y2K was over and that turned out okay, we let our guard down again," said Barfield.

"That all changed after September 11th. Hasn't the cops and the FBI working together disrupted a lot of their training?"

"Certainly they're not going to the outdoor ranges or the training camps any more, but these fucks operate very well in the shadows. They can still meet in the mosques or in private homes or apartments. Plus Muslims don't stand out any more. There's more than two hundred thousand Middle Eastern immigrants in the New York area."

"Which makes it a lot easier for the Islamists to blend in . . ."

"Especially when so many in that community look the other way."

"So, what's the story? Are we looking for a fucking needle in a haystack?" asked Cross.

"Not necessarily. I'm certain there's at least three guys the FBI has in its sights right now—even if it's not saying anything to anyone."

"You've got my attention."

"Each of them is in a different category, but I'm convinced they're all connected, and I'd be damned surprised if—with an operation as sophisticated as this was—they weren't involved."

"Fire away."

"The first is Ali Abdullah. He's a top religious leader. An imam. For almost ten years he's headed a very radical mosque in Brooklyn, on Atlantic Avenue. But for the past two or three years, he's been spending a lot of time at that new mosque they've opened out here on the north shore. Abdullah's a real bad actor. Hates America. He's probably the closest thing to that blind sheik in Jersey City who was behind the World Trade Center bombing in '93."

"Wasn't Abdullah part of bin Laden's inner circle?"

"Yeah, he was right in with him—especially when bin Laden was in Saudi Arabia. He's got a lot to say."

"Who's the second guy?"

"A guy called Khalid Mustafa. He fought in Afghanistan against the Russians and came to the United States in 1991 or '92. He's considered to be their best explosives expert. He lives out here in New Hyde Park, but he spends most of his time in Brooklyn. He also does some traveling to Detroit and to Canada, where he meets with other questionable characters."

"What does he do for a living?"

"Officially he works for one of those furniture stores on Atlantic Avenue—going back and forth from the store to the factory and making deliveries—but the FBI always thought that was a cover to give him the opportunity to move around freely inside the terror network."

"So far you're drawing a pretty grim picture. Who's next on your list?"

"Mohammed Hawasi."

"Hawasi. I've heard of him. Isn't he supposed to be mainstream?"

"He'd certainly like you to think he is. He's a very successful antiques dealer, but you probably know him through the charity he heads—the Islamic Medical Relief Service Foundation."

"Yeah, that's the one."

"Well, I hate to disillusion you, but that foundation is a total fraud. A front. The only medical service they provide is to Al

Qaeda fighters who are wounded. Everything else goes to guns and explosives—mostly explosives."

"Why doesn't the Justice Department shut it down?"

"They want to, and they've been trying like hell. But Hawasi is clever. There's some very elaborate money laundering going on. Still I've heard that just last week Justice thought they had enough and were ready to drop the hammer."

"It looks like they were too late."

"Too late to stop these attacks, maybe. But I don't think shutting down the foundation or even locking up Hawasi would've stopped the attacks. The plans were too far along for that. The important thing, whether or not they ever close down Hawasi or his foundation, is that the FBI must have picked up a lot of leads—who Hawasi meets with, who gives him money for the foundation, what mosques he goes to, who deals with him, buying and selling all those fucking antiques . . ."

"You think the antiques place is a front?"

"Absolutely. Just another way for those guys to launder their money."

"Where do you expect the FBI to go from here?"

"The first thing they're doing—and this is a big change from pre-9/11—is reaching out to the NYPD. There's a helluva lot more cooperation than there ever was before. The president will kill them if he hears that there's any turf battles going on."

"I'm glad you've got some fucking good news to give me."

"Don't expect too much more of it for a while," said Barfield with a wry smile.

"That's reassuring," rejoined Cross. "You're at your best when you're acting like a fucking undertaker!"

"Anyway, the feds and the NYPD have already been working on some of this, but they have separate operations going as well. So they'll compare notes and see if they can make any new connections. The best thing, of course, would be if Abdullah,

Mustafa, or Hawasi have been dealing with any of these guys the NYPD has been tracking."

"As the experts say, that would certainly help connect the dots."

"Sean, from your end in Washington, do you expect the president to take any extra military action because of these attacks?"

"I suppose it's possible, but I honestly can't think of too much else he can be doing. We pretty much have them on the run everywhere. There're no training camps that we know of. They have no base of operations. And we're getting great cooperation from just about all of the intelligence agencies—the Brits, the Russians, the Japanese, the Filipinos, and even most of the Arabs, especially Jordan and Egypt."

"So you're pretty certain this was a home-grown operation?"

"You know better than anyone that nothing's certain in this business. And there could have been some collaboration from overseas. And a few people could have slipped into the country. But I really think that would all have been only incidental to the operation. This was nothing like 9/11, where they were recruiting in Germany and flying back and forth from here to Europe. As big as this one was, I still think it was a local job."

"Have you been contacted by any of the victims' families? I assume that'll keep you busy for a while."

"Yeah. Anne Kelly said she and the rest of the staff were here last night, almost until midnight, taking calls from relatives. In fact, the staff will be coming in again in about ten or fifteen minutes to handle any calls that we get today."

"Is this about people who are missing?"

"No, this time it looks as if there won't be any missing. It might be a small blessing but—unlike 9/11—every family will probably have a body to bury."

"What are the calls about?"

"To be honest with you, a lot of the calls end up being referred to the police or the medical examiner. But in some cases the victims were veterans, and their families want to have them buried in a veteran's cemetery. Some families want us to expedite visas for relatives overseas so they can come to the funerals. And then some people—who didn't lose any relatives or friends—just want some reassurance that we're all not going to be blown up."

"What do you tell them?"

"That it doesn't look as if any more attacks are imminent but to be careful—whatever that means."

"Does that help?"

"Yeah, believe it or not, in most cases it does."

"This sounds morbid, but when will the funerals start?"

"Jews, of course, are buried right away. So they'll start tomorrow. But the others—I'd say some on Monday, most of them Tuesday or Wednesday—and the rest Thursday and Friday."

"Are you going to try to make the funerals in your district?"

"Yeah, whatever ones I can—and if I can't make the funeral, I'll try to stop by the wake. But another thing I've learned after September 11th is that you miss a lot more of them than you can make. There's a lot of overlap, and besides I've got to be back in Washington by early morning on Tuesday. So I'll do the best I can."

"Any personal friends this time?"

"No, so far it doesn't look like it."

"I suppose that makes it a little less stressful anyway."

"Yeah, I guess."

Wednesday, September 12, 2001

Sean Cross awoke at 6:30 on Wednesday morning. About an hour earlier than usual. For a fleeting moment he allowed himself sanctuary in the delusion that the previous day's events had been a dream. That lower Manhattan and the Pentagon were not in ruins. That thousands were not dead or missing. That America was not at war.

Rubbing his eyes and shaking his head loose from the final remnants of the sleeping pills, he soon realized all too well that yesterday's horror was all too real. He lay back for a few moments and stared at the ceiling, summoning the energy to get out of bed and face the day.

Walking over to the television and turning it on, he saw that the rescue crews at the World Trade Center were still working from the night before. The flames continued to burn but—on the television screen at least—the air seemed less filled with smoke, dust, and debris, while the rescue workers, mostly firemen, seemed more intense and driven.

Opening the bedroom blinds, Cross saw that smoke was still spewing from the Pentagon. The sun was bright. The sky was a brilliant blue. But there was nothing beautiful about this day. There was just too much death for that.

Life, of course, and the nation had to go forward. And, at the most superficial level, it did appear that it was going forward with a sameness in the routine it had followed before. And yet it was all so different. Like most days, Tom O'Connell came by to pick Cross up at about 8:30. Usually there'd be political small talk or discussions about legislation coming up that week. During today's ride, however, they alternated between silence and discussing body counts and the possibilities of more attacks. At Cross's office in the Cannon Building, staff members—usually effusive—greeted Cross and one another with somber nods. The front-page headlines of the newspapers on their desks said it all:

New York Times—U.S. ATTACKED

New York Daily News—IT'S WAR

Newsday—ACTS OF MASS MURDER

Albany Times Union—FREEDOM UNDER SIEGE

USA Today—ACT OF WAR—TERRORISTS STRIKE; DEATH TOLL "HORRENDOUS"

Boston Globe—REIGN OF TERROR.

And there was the headline on the page-one lead story in the *Wall Street Journal:*

Streets of Manhattan

Resemble a War Zone

Amid Clouds of Ash

Shortly after 9:30 Cross did a telephone interview from his office with Channel 12. Viewers on Long Island saw a live shot of the smoldering ruins of Ground Zero as they heard Cross's voice. His message was identical to yesterday's: *The American government is fully operational, and it is essential that we stand as one.* It was pretty much the same message he would soon give in a speech on the House floor.

Assured that it would not interfere with police operations, Speaker Denny Hastert had decided to call the House into session that morning. He requested a large turnout in the chamber to send the clear message that terrorists could not successfully interfere with the workings of American democracy. The Speaker's office had announced that the first hour would be reserved for one-minute speeches. Because Cross wanted to speak about the attacks, he arrived about ten minutes early and took a seat in the front row on the right side of the chamber.

When Hastert ascended the Speaker's podium at 10:03, the House chamber was almost full. The House chaplain, Father Coughlin, delivered the opening prayer:

"O God, come to our assistance.

"O Lord, make haste to help us.

"Yesterday we were stunned, angry and violated. Today, Lord, we stand strong and together. Yesterday changed our world. Today we are changed.

"Now we turn to you for your guidance and sense of eternal truths which built this Nation as we begin a new day of building security and peace through justice."

Hastert then led the House in the Pledge of Allegiance, which was virtually shouted by the House members, venting their rage and demonstrating their solidarity. This was the type of unity Cross had been praying for. Seated in the visitor's gallery was the prime minister of Australia, John Howard, who'd been scheduled to address a joint session of the House and Senate this day. In his characteristic, understated manner Hastert stated, "Due to the events of yesterday, the chair wishes to announce that the joint meeting to receive the Honorable John Howard, prime minister of Australia, scheduled for today, will not take place.

"The chair wishes to acknowledge, however, the presence of the prime minister today, and extends, on behalf of the House, his appreciation for the solidarity of the Australian people in this very difficult time."

The House members stood as one, extending a sustained ovation to this stalwart ally, as the prime minister stood and waved from the gallery. The Speaker then recognized the majority leader, Dick Armey from Texas, who announced that after the one hour of speeches was concluded, the House would go into recess so that the chamber could be swept for an intelligence briefing that would be given to the members that afternoon. Armey, a gruff Texan who'd never evinced much positive feeling for New York, condemned "yesterday's terrorist acts" and concluded emotionally, "Let me assure you, by the time the 435 members of this body have spoken, the world will have no doubt about who we are, what we will stand for and what we will not stand for."

Armey was followed by the minority leader, Dick Gephardt, who echoed the same theme: "This Congress, in a nonpartisan way, will work as hard as humanly possible to make sure that our people have the safety they demand and deserve, and that terror is defeated completely and finally.

"Make no mistake, this was an act of war against the United States and all our people and we will not be divided. All of us, the president, the Congress, and the American people, are today, and will be tomorrow and in all of the tomorrows, totally and completely united in our determination to begin the process of healing and to take swift action to see that the people who committed this horrible crime are properly punished."

Cross was gratified by this demonstration of unity and national purpose, and when he walked to the lectern in the well of the House, though he had no text or notes, he knew exactly what he wanted to say: "Mr. Speaker, yesterday was an act of war upon the United States. Our country as a nation will never be the same again. But from that tragedy, from this moment of death and destruction, we must rededicate ourselves to our principles. We must stand behind our president as commander in chief; stand together, not as Democrats or Republicans, but as Americans, vowing to find out exactly who it was that is responsible for this heinous act and to do all we can to eliminate them from the face of the Earth, and also those who would harbor these terrorists.

"Also my heart goes out to the victims, many of whom live in my district and the adjoining districts outside of and within New

York City. Already the names of friends and relatives are coming in, so we personally know how tragic this truly is. I just want these families to know that our hearts and prayers are with them. And we give a special debt of thanks to the police officers and the firefighters who gave their lives."

Concluding his remarks, Cross walked to the rear of the chamber to listen to several of the speakers before returning to his office. He soon realized that the necessity to have national unity was not appreciated by all Democrats. Leaning against the gold railing, Cross saw Mike Cleary, a Democratic congressman, approaching him. Cross said in a low tone, "Tough days ahead of us . . ." Before Cross could get any further, Cleary interrupted: "Well, this proves that all that missile defense shit is a fucking waste of time. It wouldn't have helped at all yesterday." Instinctively Cross rejoined: "All it means is that we need different defenses for different enemies," before catching himself. *Is this all this guy can do today is try to make some cheap partisan point that doesn't mean anything anyway?* thought Cross. *Fuck him. Why even bother?* Cross turned away and walked from the House chamber back toward his office.

As Cross stood at Independence Avenue waiting for the red light to change, another Democratic congressman, Dave Dunne, came up alongside him. This time Cross could almost see it coming. "Bush showed nothing last night," said Dunne. "Nothing at all." Shaking his head, Cross answered dismissively: "I guess it depends on how you look at it. I thought he was terrific." The moment the light changed Cross stepped quickly from the curb and crossed the street. *Some of these guys just don't get it. They just don't fucking get it.*

Cross arrived for the intelligence briefing just before one o'clock that afternoon. All the House members were required to enter the chamber through the glass door in the Speaker's lobby. The main doors were sealed shut. Once inside everyone was instructed to turn off all cell phones and beepers. Finding a seat in the third row on the right side, Cross looked around the chamber and estimated there must be at least four hundred members seated or milling about.

The administration had sent an assemblage of heavy hitters to conduct the briefing. Standing in the well of the House, waiting to begin the briefing, they looked pained but determined.

First to speak was John McLaughlin, the number two guy at the CIA.

—The case wasn't airtight, but all evidence pointed to Osama bin Laden and his network.

—These attacks were part of a very complex operation and must have had a year or more of planning.

—Intelligence reports begun in March of this year showed that bin Laden was planning something "spectacular."

—Bin Laden's M.O. is to have many targets.

—It's too soon to relax our guard.

—We are reaching out to foreign intelligence agencies.

Attorney General John Ashcroft then made his presentation.

—The country is not in paralysis or disability.

—The president considers these attacks acts of war and will use every resource available.

—The Justice Department is conducting its most serious investigation ever and is following leads all over the country.

—We will not tell details of sources and methods of investigation.

Ashcroft concluded by giving telephone numbers for tips and assistance.

William Mueller, the FBI director, who'd been in the job for only a week, followed Ashcroft.

—It's essential that we prevent another attack.

—We're looking for co-conspirators here and overseas.

—Three of the four planes were taken over with knives.

—At least one hijacker had training as a pilot.

—There will be FBI-CIA coordination.

Transportation Secretary Norm Mineta, a former Democratic congressman, discussed airline security.

—He'd been in the bunker with Vice President Cheney yesterday when he gave the order to bring down about 2,100 planes in two hours.

—New security procedures must be implemented.

—We would err on the side of caution, such as by prohibiting curbside check-ins.

Tommy Thompson, the Health and Human Services secretary, said that five disaster medical teams had been deployed, five morgues had been set up and that there was a shortage of O-positive and O-negative blood. Joe Albaugh, the federal emergency czar, after announcing the president had signed a disaster declaration, finished up by saying how moved he was by what he'd seen at the World Trade Center site. "Please go home tonight and kiss your kids," he concluded, his voice breaking.

Considering that it was barely twenty-four hours since the most horrific attack ever made against our country, this was a pretty informative briefing, thought Cross. *We know who's responsible. We're going all out, here and overseas, to track down those responsible and to prevent another attack. Full disaster resources are being provided for the dead and injured.*

The first questions—from Democrats—indicated support and sophistication. Maxine Waters, the firebrand congresswoman from Los Angeles, asked for more details on bin Laden, and Nancy Pelosi, the leading Democrat on the Intelligence Committee, inquired whether the recent assassination of a Northern Alliance anti-Taliban leader in Afghanistan could have been a prelude to yesterday's attacks. Both appeared satisfied by the answers they received:

—The CIA has been after bin Laden for several years, acquiring enormous data on him and achieving some successes against him.

—The assassination most likely was tied to the attacks.

This cooperative spirit and sense of harmony were soon shattered when Democratic congressman Jonah Goodman used his question time to berate the briefers. He said he was insulted and angry. The briefing had been a farce. He'd been told nothing he didn't already know. The administration was withholding information. He was particularly indignant that McLaughlin and Mineta had left before he got to the microphone. The fact that they'd gone to the other side of the Capitol to brief the Senate was no excuse. This was an insult to everyone in the House. Yelling and shouting erupted on the Democratic side.

This was what the partisan die-hards had been waiting for. Their political juices are flowing. There's only about thirty or forty of them carrying on, but they sound like a pack of fucking morons! thought Cross. *They're a fucking disgrace.*

Disgusted that an intelligence briefing dealing with the deaths of thousands of Americans had descended to the depths of the *Gong Show,* Cross left the chamber and walked out into the Speaker's Lobby. Turning on his cell phone, he saw he had a voice mail message. To get a clear connection, Cross stepped out onto the Capitol balcony to listen to the message. It was Kevin Finnerty. His voice was somber, the message direct. "Jimmy Boyle called. His son, Michael, is missing. They think he's dead." Cross pressed the *end* button and stared blankly toward the Cannon and Longworth Office Buildings, standing stolidly and directly across from him on the south side of Independence Avenue. It was a bright, clear day, but to Cross the midafternoon air reeked with the sad stench of death. *Michael Boyle. Jesus, this is getting close to home. This is horrible.*

Sean Cross and Jimmy Boyle had been friends for more than twenty years. They had a lot in common. Though they hadn't known each other as kids, each grew up in Sunnyside, an Irish-American, working-class enclave just across from Manhattan on the Queens side of the 59th Street Bridge. Sean and Jimmy lived in different parishes. Sean in Queen of Angels; Jimmy in St.

Raphael's. Since neither parish had its own school, Cross and Boyle went to St. Teresa's in neighboring Woodside, where Dominican nuns took perverse pleasure in smashing kids' heads until they rattled like trash cans filled with broken toys.

Jimmy had been a veteran New York City firefighter and union leader, twice being elected president of the Uniformed Firefighters Association (UFA)—once in the early 1980s and again in the early '90s. Retired from the FDNY, Jimmy was now working as an investigator for the Brooklyn district attorney, Joe Hynes. Jimmy's son Michael, just turned thirty-seven, was following in his father's footsteps—tough fireman and outspoken union activist. All the firehouse insiders knew it was only a matter of time before Michael would be a candidate for UFA president. Mike also shared his father's zeal for politics, enjoying the skirmishing, the elbowing, and the give-and-take. Just last year he'd run a very successful fund-raiser for Cross in the Belle Harbor section of Rockaway in Queens—a fund-raiser that Cross enjoyed pointing out was more successful than any event Jimmy had run for him the previous twenty years. This year Michael's cousin was running in the Democratic primary for a City Council seat in Queens, and Michael had been active in his campaign. Primary day was September 11. Cross knew that Mike had intended to be on the ground, in the district, getting out the vote that day.

Cross had to call Jimmy right away. But he would do it from the solitude of his office, with the door shut tight, not from the open-air balcony of the Capitol Building. Walking though the Speaker's Lobby, Cross glanced fleetingly into the House chamber, long enough for him to see the congressmen who were still gesticulating and orating about their injured pride and damaged egos. Shaking his head in disgust, Cross telephoned Finnerty, who told him that Jimmy was at home and appeared to be composed. Cross called Mary Rose, Kara, and Danny. Mary Rose, of course, knew Jimmy, while Kara and Danny were friendly with Jimmy's younger daughter Jeanne.

Back in his office, Sean's conversation with Jimmy went about as well as a phone call about a tragedy could go. Finnerty had been right. Jimmy was composed. Sad and devastated, but composed. And, of course, not at all self-pitying. Jimmy said that Michael had called him at about 8:30 yesterday morning from the Engine 33 firehouse in lower Manhattan to tell him he'd finished his tour and was heading to Queens to work in his cousin's primary. About fifteen minutes later the first plane had hit the Trade Center, and Jimmy had had a clear view of the Twin Towers from his corner office just across the East River in downtown Brooklyn. When Jimmy saw the second plane hit, he had known immediately that it was a terrorist attack, and his fireman's instinct took over. He raced downstairs and took off by foot across the Brooklyn Bridge. Jimmy remembered that the first time the Trade Center was attacked in 1993, the bombers had gone to the J&R Music store, just east of Broadway, to admire their handiwork. That's where Jimmy would head. When he got over the bridge, however, the streets were filled with people escaping the scene. Working his way through the crowd, Jimmy had just gotten to Broadway when the South Tower crumbled in a devastating explosion of dirt, ash, smoke, and body parts. Jimmy dove into the doorway of 250 Broadway, where he waited until the air cleared enough for him to brave his way down to the flame-engulfed North Tower. It was when he got to the corner of Barclay and West that the North Tower collapsed, the force of the explosion throwing him to the ground and the dark, swirling smoke temporarily blinding him. Fortunately, his union experience kicked in, and he remembered that District Council 37, the public employees union, had an office down the street. Jimmy felt his way along the side of the buildings, patiently making his way through the pitch darkness to the side entrance on Murray Street. As Jimmy waited in D.C. 37's lobby for this blinding sandstorm of death to begin to lift and realized that he would live, it struck him that maybe Michael hadn't gone to Queens. Maybe he had jumped on the rig. And sure enough, after talking to firemen on the scene a short while later and then going back to the fire-house, Jimmy realized that Michael had done what he was afraid he'd done. Gone back on duty. Jumped on Engine 33. And run into the North Tower, where he was killed. Sure, he was still officially listed as missing. And some family members and friends held out hope. But Jimmy'd been around too long to rely on any string of false hope. Jimmy knew his son was dead and that he had been just across the street from him when he died. Mike's lifelong friend David Arce was also dead. Arce had worked with Mike on Cross's campaigns. Cross had told Jimmy he would come by his house over the weekend. In true Jimmy Boyle style, Jimmy had asked Sean if there was anything *Jimmy could do for him!* "Jimmy, you'll never change," answered Cross, feigning exasperation and smiling grimly to himself, before saying good-bye.

Just as Cross hung up, Finnerty came through the door, saying that Channel 12 wanted to go live in one minute with a phone interview.

"What do they want?" asked Cross.

"An update on what you were told at the briefing," answered Finnerty.

"That was classified. So I can't tell them much."

"Well, then, tell them that."

"Okay."

The interviewer was Danielle Campbell, always pleasant and knowledgeable.

"Congressman Cross, what can you tell us about the intelligence briefing you and the other members of the House just received?"

"As you know, Danielle, it was classified, but I believe it's okay to tell you that Osama bin Laden appears to be the main suspect right now. I think what's more important, however, is that all our intelligence agencies and administration officials are doing all that they possibly can and . . ."

"Congressman, I hate to interrupt you but we have just had several Democratic congressmen on with us, and they're saying that the briefing was inadequate and that the administration is holding back information."

"Danielle," Cross replied, his voice rising, "I wish these Democratic congressmen would realize that just one day ago our country suffered the worst attack in our history. That thousands of people were burned and crushed to death. That a massive rescue effort is still going on. It's time for all of us to act as Americans and not cheap-shot partisans."

"Thank you, Congressman. And as our viewers can tell, feelings are high on Capitol Hill today."

"Fuck those Democrats," said Cross to himself, putting down the phone and looking over at Finnerty. "They're showing their true colors."

"Well, I got one more for you today. Catherine Crier wants you on her show on Court TV. You'll be on with David Dinkins."

"Live?"

"Yeah, over at the studio on East Capitol Street."

"When?"

"In ten minutes."

"Thanks for the warning. Let's go."

Sitting alone in the Washington studio, illuminated by klieg lights and waiting for the interview to start, Cross glanced at the monitor and saw David Dinkins having his mike adjusted as he sat calmly in the Manhattan studio on Third Avenue. As always, the former mayor of New York City was impeccably attired, his dark blue, double-breasted jacket contrasting with his white shirt, off-white tie, and white breast-pocket handkerchief. Cross didn't know Dinkins that well, but they'd met a number of times over the years and had always gotten along with each other. After his election as New York City's first African-American mayor in 1989, Dinkins's tenure had been marked by racial unrest and turbulence, such as the Crown Heights riots in 1991, and he had been defeated by Rudy Giuliani in 1993. Through it all Dinkins had always been the perfect gentlemen, exuding class and dignity. Still, Cross didn't know what to expect today. Dinkins was a liberal, and too many of the liberals Cross had encountered today had been rabid in their attacks on Bush. Another political reality was that, going back to the Vietnam War, the African-American community had been consistently critical of American foreign policy. Cross suspected this might be especially true if there was talk of attacking Afghanistan, since many African-Americans identified with Muslims. Cross's concerns were allayed early in the show when, after several perfunctory questions had been asked and answered, Dinkins stated, "The one thing we must remember is that President Bush is our commander in chief and we must support him as our leader. It is essential that all Americans stand behind our president."

Gratified and moved, Cross replied, "I want to commend Mayor Dinkins for his leadership in saying that we should all support the president as our commander in chief. This is one more patriotic act in his long and distinguished career."

"Sean, did Dinkins surprise you? Did you expect him to be so supportive of Bush?" asked Finnerty, as they left the studio.

"To be honest, after all the Democratic bullshit I heard today, I was surprised," answered Cross. "But maybe I shouldn't have been because, however much you might disagree with him, Dinkins is a real person. He's been through a lot, and he realizes this is life and death—not like some of the morons down here."

"How about the African-American angle?"

"That could be increasingly important. If blacks are willing to give that type of strong, visceral support to Bush when we're fighting Muslims, that is a helluva sense of unity."

"I guess we owe David Dinkins a big one after today."

"We certainly do, because this country is going to need all the help it can get before this is over."

7

"Good morning, Congressman Cross," said Dr. Abdul Ahmed, as he stepped from behind his large oak desk to shake hands. "It's a pleasure to see you. Thank you so much for coming."

"It's my pleasure," answered Cross. "I hope the meeting can be productive for both of us."

"Congressman, please sit down. It was very generous of you to agree to come to my office."

"It was no problem at all. There's too much going on to stand on ceremony. Though I must say that if this were a more peaceful time, I might have attempted some humorous remark about the mountain coming to Mohammed."

"I hope the day never comes when you and I cannot share a bit of humor."

"I hope that as well, Dr. Ahmed."

Born and raised in Islamabad, Pakistan, Dr. Abdul Ahmed had immigrated to the United States about twenty-five years ago and now, as head of surgery at the Long Island Regional Heart Center, was acknowledged to be one of New York's premier cardiac surgeons. Cross and Ahmed had first met in 1993, shortly after Cross had been elected to Congress. Ahmed headed a group of Pakistani and Kashmiri Americans, most of whom were doctors, who wanted to increase the Muslim community's involvement in American politics. Cross found Ahmed and his group friendly and responsible. They wanted advice on how to become a political force the way the Irish, Italians, and Jews had done before them—and the way the Indians were doing now. One difficulty facing Muslims was that most of the Muslims in this country came from countries that had no history of democracy—except for Pakistan, on a very intermittent basis. India, Pakistan's historical enemy, was, by contrast, the world's largest democracy.

Cross, nevertheless, had formed a solid working relationship with Ahmed and his fellow Muslims, primarily because they agreed on a number of significant foreign policy issues.

—Though it was more often a military dictatorship than a democracy, Pakistan was a far more consistent U.S. ally than India, and Cross supported increased American military cooperation with Pakistan.

—Cross urged American military intervention in the Balkans to stop what he called Serbian "genocide" against Muslims in Bosnia and Kosovo.

Even on issues where there was obvious disagreement—such as Cross's strong support of Israel—Ahmed was unfailingly polite and cordial. Those same good feelings prevailed when Cross spoke at Ahmed's mosque—the North Shore Islamic Center. Never during any of these meetings and gatherings did Cross encounter or discern even a hint of anti-American bias or hatred. That's why in the first days after September 11 he had defended Muslim Americans and insisted their civil rights be protected. This support, however, soon turned to disappointment and anger as the Muslim American leadership failed to demonstrate the absolute support for the war against terrorism that Cross believed was particularly warranted in their case. *Yes, bin Laden was wrong, and we condemn the attacks of September 11*, the Muslims would say, *but it is also wrong for Americans to be bombing innocent Afghan children.* Cross had no patience with that attempt at moral equivalency. So Cross's relationship with Dr. Ahmed and the Muslim community generally had grown increasingly distant and frayed in the months after September 11. Still, when Dr. Ahmed telephoned him at home last evening asking for a meeting to "discuss these horrific tragedies," Cross had said yes and suggested Ahmed's private office on Northern Boulevard as a suitable venue.

"My good friend, it has been too long since we have had a chance to speak frankly and at length," said Dr. Ahmed, with an accent marked by distinct Pakistani intonations but easily understandable. "The events of last Friday threaten not just America, which is my country, but the Muslim community, which is my people."

"You're right. We have been friends and friends should be able to talk honestly and directly and not have to worry about hurting each other's feelings."

"I can't disagree with that."

"Fine. I know that you're the one who asked for the meeting, but if it's okay with you, I'd like to go first," said Cross, indicating in a polite but firm tone that he didn't want the agenda to be set by a discourse from Ahmed about the repression of Muslims everywhere in the world, including New York.

"As you wish," answered Ahmed, after the slightest hesitation.

"What happened last Friday was an absolute disgrace. It was a crime against humanity. It was mass murder. And the injuries are horrific. I just came from the burn unit at the Medical Center. They've never seen anything like it. I . . ."

"You know we have condemned the attack."

"To be honest with you, I don't know that you have condemned it *enough*. It's the same as after the World Trade Center attack. There's not enough outrage. It's too cute and nuanced."

"How can you say that?"

"Very easily. You're Americans. All you should be saying is that the ones who did this were murderers. We don't need any criticism of American policy in Afghanistan or the West Bank or Iraq. Save that for another day."

"Our people are very concerned about the way our Muslim brothers and sisters are being treated in the Middle East and about possible retaliation against us in this country."

"As I said, you can talk about the Middle East some other time. Today your brothers and sisters are the innocent Americans who were killed and injured . . ."

"With all respect, Congressman, I distinctly recall all the speeches you gave about the way the British were persecuting the Irish in Northern Ireland."

"With all respect to you, Doctor, if the IRA had ever attacked Americans, I would have disowned them in a second—and I would have waited a long time before I started talking again about what was going on in Northern Ireland."

"Injustice is injustice. Why not talk about it?"

"Because talking about it soon after an attack on America can be interpreted as a justification or rationale for the attack. And that's exactly what you did after the World Trade Center when we had the ecumenical brotherhood service at the mosque."

"I don't see how you can say that."

"Very easily. Just a month after Muslims carried out the worst atrocity in American history, Catholics, Protestants and Jews went to your mosque to show solidarity with the Muslim people. They all called for brotherhood and unity. And what did the imam do? And Dr. Masri? They accused the Americans of bombing innocent Afghanis and killing Palestinians. In fact, it wasn't until two months later that the imam finally admitted that bin Laden was even involved."

"You have a very selective interpretation of events."

"It's an American interpretation."

"All killing of civilians is wrong—no matter who does it."

"I didn't hear you saying anything about civilian casualties when we were defending the Muslims in Bosnia and Kosovo and bombing the hell out of the Christian Serbs."

"You have to understand the strong feelings in our community about American policy. We can be good Americans and still criticize government policy."

"You can't criticize it in the wake of a terrorist attack and expect people to take you seriously."

"Are you saying we have no right to be concerned about innocent Muslims being attacked—even in this country?"

"You know I'm not saying that. My God, the president went out of his way to denounce any retaliation against Muslims, and the fact is there were very few attacks. And every one of them was universally denounced."

"Let me get back to the point I started to make before. We think American policy in the Middle East is much too supportive of Israel. Many of us think that Jewish interests in this country have too much influence in determining our policy toward the Palestinians and the Arab states. Under your theory, how can we possibly raise these issues without having our loyalty questioned?"

"It's not that difficult at all, once you accept that your main priority must be security of our country, the United States. Everything else must be secondary. As you know, I happen to disagree with your view of Israel and the Middle East. But you raise valid points that should be part of our national debate. But you can't be tying them to Al Qaeda or bin Laden if you want other Americans to take you seriously."

"We try as hard as anyone to be good Americans, to become a part of American life. You yourself always said that we were ideal neighbors—we worked hard, there was no crime or welfare, and we never asked for anything. Now we're being ostracized for something we had nothing at all to do with."

"You're right. In so many ways the Muslim community makes tremendous contributions to this country. And I'd be the first to tell you that I personally have always been treated very well, in all my dealings with you—whether it's at the mosque, in your homes or at formal events."

"So, my friend, what is the problem?"

"The problem is that there is a disconnect about where the ultimate loyalty of *some* of your people lies."

"Congressman, we have been talking frankly—yet not directly to the point. Please tell me exactly what you think we should be doing that we're not."

"Besides condemning the terrorist attacks, your people must step forward and cooperate with the police and FBI. Tell them everything you know. In other words turn in your own people."

"And you're suggesting that we're not?"

"Except for the occasional incident like the arrest of the cell in Lackawanna, I know that you're not."

"How can you be so sure?"

"First, the police and FBI people that I talk with—and some of them are pretty high-ranking—tell me that they get no support."

"I can't accept that."

"As I was starting to say—whether or not you want to accept it—all the evidence bears out what these guys have been telling me."

"What do you mean, evidence?"

"The evidence that the terrorists who carried out last Friday's attacks were sleepers who'd been living in your community for years."

"How are you so certain of that?"

"The FBI, the NYPD and the Nassau Police are convinced these operations were carried out by guys who were here at least five or six years."

"Why?"

"For one thing immigration has been tightened since the World Trade Center attacks, and it's much harder for the Al Qaeda crowd to get into the country. Also, the method that was used in Brooklyn and Westbury—truck bombs filled with tons of TNT, aluminum nitrate, and aluminum powder—is almost identical to what Al Qaeda used at the American embassies in Africa back in 1998. So these were guys who were trained a while ago."

"You think that's conclusive?"

"It's conclusive enough, and besides the FBI has other evidence."

"That you can't tell me about?"

"No."

"Very well, I won't pursue it."

"There is no need to pursue anything. This isn't a debate. We shouldn't be trying to score points. It has to be clear to you that this attack came from within the Muslim community. All I'm saying is that the time has come for good people like you to spread the word in your community that the time has come to step forward. And believe me, I'm saying this as a friend."

"I appreciate that. It's just so difficult for me to accept that you and I can interpret the same situations so differently. My heart was broken when the World Trade Center and the Pentagon were attacked. Everyone I spoke to in the Muslim community felt the same as I did. We felt a special debt and obligation, because it was Muslims who carried out these atrocities. Yet you tell me, and I accept you at your word, that this sorrow and anguish did not come across to the American people."

"No, Doctor, not to the extent it should have—because there was always the sense that you were holding back. And I can't emphasize enough how much the lack of cooperation with law enforcement has hurt as well."

"But you do accept *my* good faith?"

"Absolutely. If I didn't, I wouldn't be here today."

"And I will accept what you have told me as advice from an old friend. Let me talk to several of my colleagues, and I will be back in touch with you."

"I appreciate that and look forward to hearing from you."

"Are you going back to Washington today?"

"No, not until tomorrow. After I leave here I'll be going to two funerals—one in Seaford, the other in Lindenhurst—then I'll be stopping by the Medical Center this afternoon to talk with some of the victims and their families."

"You have a difficult and trying day ahead of you, my friend."

"Well, it's not something I look forward to, but I can't complain. I'm not dead, and I'm not injured, and no one in my family is either. So I'm ahead of the game."

"That's a healthy way to look at it. In the meantime, I will do what I said about talking to some of my friends."

"Thanks, Doctor. I look forward to hearing from you."

Driving down Wantagh Parkway toward St. William the Abbott Church in Seaford to attend what would be the first of many funerals, Cross told Brian Sullivan that he thought the meeting with Dr. Ahmed had gone well.

"Do you really think that he got the message?" asked Sullivan.

"Yeah. It took a while. But more got through to him than I expected," answered Cross.

"When do you think he'll get back to you?"

"That I don't know. He said he had to talk to some of his friends."

"Are they doctors as well?"

"As far as I know they are. But there could be some other guys that we know nothing about."

"Any chance that Ahmed is connected to a terrorist group?"

"I'd really be surprised if he was, because he is a good guy. I think his problem—and a problem with a lot of their leaders—is that they don't realize they have an obligation to turn in their own kind."

"Do you think he himself would know anyone who's actually involved?"

"No. I think the most we could hope for is that by speaking out forcefully, he would make it acceptable for good people in the community who might know something to come forward."

"Did you mention any of the news that Barfield gave you?"

"You mean the guys the feds are focusing on—Abdullah, Mustafa, and Hawasi?"

"Yeah."

"No. Even though I think Ahmed is a good guy, I don't trust him that much. He might feel he should tip them off."

"If you had to bet, when do you think you'll hear back from him, one way or the other?"

"I'd say about ten days—but, even then, I don't know how helpful he'll be."

"I guess we'll have to wait. Right now you have a funeral to go to."

September 13–14, 2001

As Sean Cross drove toward Capitol Hill with Tom O'Connell on Thursday morning, he knew that indeed a new day had dawned. The shock and confusion of the previous two days were gone. A part of the past. Now it was time to go forward. Time to even the score. And time to start doing whatever had to be done to keep this from happening again.

The day's business began in the Rayburn Building, where a group of Republicans was meeting with Jim Woolsey, who had been Bill Clinton's first CIA director. Woolsey had resigned during Clinton's first term in protest of the president's virtual refusal to spend any time being briefed by Woolsey or to show any real interest in CIA matters. Feelings became so raw that Woolsey had endorsed Bob Dole against Clinton in 1996. This morning Woolsey was focused, almost somber. He had no definite answers but very strong views. Bin Laden was not alone. There was a "loose network of terrorism," of terror groups and governments that supported them. He felt certain there was some level of Iraqi involvement in Tuesday's attacks. Woolsey was angered that CIA human-intelligence sources on the ground had been so degraded. It had been bad under Carter; good under Reagan; and, except for Y2K, bad again under Clinton. Woolsey also castigated those in the Congress and the Clinton administration who had imposed restrictions on the CIA, making it almost impossible to penetrate groups like Al Qaeda. Since 1995, for instance, the CIA had been unable to recruit anyone who'd been at all involved with human rights violations. Very simply, Woolsey said, you're not going to find anyone who can get close to bin Laden if he has to have totally clean hands. But more than what Woolsey said, it was how he said it that struck Cross. Here's a guy who'd seen it all. But the seriousness of his tone and the gravity of his demeanor this morning made it clear he'd never seen or envisioned anything like what had happened two days before.

Cross and Woolsey shook hands and exchanged solemn smiles as the congressman thanked the former director for his thoughtful input. Cross then left the Rayburn Building and walked across South Capitol Street to the Longworth Building, where the House Republicans were gathering in the first-floor conference room. Cross was gratified that unlike the self-righteous fulminating that had gone on at police headquarters on Tuesday night, today's mood was appropriately subdued. Denny Hastert spoke first, saying that several votes would be taken on the House floor that day and that he wanted to get back to a normal schedule as quickly as possible. The principal speaker was Nick Calio, the White House's point man on Capitol Hill. His main message was that the president was in command of the situation. In answer to entreaties that the president travel to the World Trade Center site, Calio said the White House staff wanted him to go but that the president wouldn't sign off on it until he was absolutely assured that a presidential visit would not in any way interfere with the rescue operation.

As the meeting ended, Cross walked over to the Capitol Building and went to the House floor. The main bill on the calendar was special legislation, introduced in response to the September 11th attacks, to award $250,000 to the survivors of police officers and firefighters killed in the line of duty. Cross spoke briefly but emotionally, citing the heroism of New York's cops and firemen, and giving specific mention to Father Judge and Michael Boyle. It was almost twenty hours since he'd gotten the news about Mike Boyle, but Cross still felt a tremor go through him as he heard Mike's name leave his lips.

Back in his office in the Cannon Building, Cross got a phone call from Anne Kelly. She'd been talking to Jimmy Boyle, who had watched the speech on C-Span; he was very thankful that Cross had spoken about Michael. *Jesus, I'm glad I gave Jimmy something to be thankful for,* thought Cross. Just then, Tom O'Connell came through the door.

"While you were on the phone with Anne, the White House called," said O'Connell. "There's a meeting with the president this afternoon at the White House, and you're invited."

"Who else is going?" asked Cross.

"It looks like the downstate New York delegation, plus the guys from Connecticut and New Jersey whose districts are close to Manhattan, and maybe Virginia, because of the Pentagon."

"I guess the senators are going?"

"I'd think so—certainly Hillary and Chuck will be there."

"Anything else?"

"Yeah. The president told Giuliani and Governor Pataki that he's going to Ground Zero tomorrow."

"That's great. It'll show solidarity with the city and be a real shot in the arm for the guys working down there. They must be getting exhausted. See what you can do to get me on the trip."

"I'll do my best."

Cross and O'Connell left for the White House meeting at about 2:30 that afternoon. As O'Connell was driving his Jeep from the Cannon garage, Cross's cell phone rang. It was Gerry Adams, calling from Belfast in Northern Ireland. Cross had been involved in the Irish peace process for about a quarter-century. During that time he had formed a strong friendship with Adams, who headed Sinn Fein, the political wing of the Irish Republican Army. Years before, Cross had been one of the first Americans to endorse Adams as a legitimate political leader. That move had damaged Cross with the establishment media and had cost him significant support among Republican leaders. Cross's faith was vindicated, however, in April 1998, when Adams signed the Good Friday Agreement with the Irish and British governments, bringing an end to decades of heated fighting and atrocities on all sides. Despite complications, delays and crises in subsequent years, the Good Friday Agreement continued to work, as Adams demonstrated his ability to move from revolutionary outsider to skilled political inside player.

"Sean, how are things? All of us over here have been thinking of you and praying for you ever since we first heard of the attacks."

"Thank you Gerry. It's very thoughtful of you to call. I really appreciate it."

"My God, Sean, it's no bother at all. I would have rung sooner, but we were told straight away that you and Mary Rose were well, and I know how busy you must be with it all. I understand you lost many in your constituency."

"Yeah. We have no idea what the final count will be, but it will be well over a hundred."

"It's difficult to even begin to comprehend something that large. The suffering must be horrific. Father Judge's death is particularly devastating."

"It is. But we're on our way back."

"I'm sure you are. I just want you to know how much the people of Ireland are saddened by this. Our hearts are with you."

The phone call concluded, Cross stared vacantly out the passenger window onto Pennsylvania Avenue. After a long moment he turned to O'Connell and said, "That's just another example of how much our world has changed. Think of all the years and all the conversations I've had with Gerry and the other guys in Ireland about bombings and shootings and who was killed and who was wounded. And here, on September 11th, in less than two hours, we had more people killed than were killed in thirty years of fighting in Ireland."

"And Gerry Adams is calling to console us! What a turn-around," said O'Connell.

The scene in the reception area of the White House West Wing was one of somber confusion. More than twenty representatives from the House, plus the senators from New York, New Jersey, Connecticut, and Virginia, were milling about, speaking in hushed tones and trying to find out if there were any new developments. There were also the all too many discussions of mutual friends who had been killed or were still missing. Chuck Schumer asked each of the New York representatives if they'd stand together in asking the president for a special twenty-billion-dollar aid package to rebuild New York. Each said yes. Schumer said it might be a tough sell.

Just a minute or two after three o'clock an attractive young woman came down the hallway leading from the Oval Office and said the president would like to meet with the senators first. In ordinary times that would have prompted at least one congressman to make a halfway humorous remark about rank and privilege, and second-class citizenship. But not today. Today nothing seemed very funny.

After about ten minutes went by, the same attractive aide reappeared and invited the House members into the cabinet room for the main meeting. Filing into the room, each looked for their place card that indicated seat location. Some were seated with the senators at the large, dark wood, rectangular-shaped conference table that dominated the room. Cross's seat was in the row behind the table. He would be facing toward the president, who had not yet entered the room. Apparently, Bush was still in the Oval Office with Chuck Schumer and Hillary Clinton. Behind the president's chair was a window, which spanned the length of the room and looked out onto the Rose Garden. The moment he looked toward the window, Cross felt a tremor. It was still another reminder of what our world had become. Patrolling the grounds—just outside the window—were Secret Service

SWAT teams in military camouflage fatigues and full battle gear, with heavy machine guns in their hands.

Just then the door to Cross's right opened, and President Bush entered the room from the Oval Office. Upon seeing the president, Cross and the others stood and broke into spontaneous applause. Schumer and Clinton followed the president into the room, as did Condoleezza Rice, the president's national security advisor. Schumer was smiling. The president took his seat at the center of the table and looked about the room for a moment.

Cross was not particularly close to Bush or his White House staff. Not that it was personal, but Cross had supported John McCain against Bush in the 2000 presidential campaign, and in politics the guy who wins takes care of the guys who were with him. Especially in presidential politics. Cross hadn't been with Bush, and he understood the rules of the game. Still, Cross thought that during the previous seven months he'd established a decent working relationship with the White House and a cordial relationship with President Bush himself.

Even during the most bitter days of the presidential primary season, Cross had never been one of those who thought Bush wouldn't be up to the job. What Cross did think during the primaries, and what he continued to think during the first half year of the Bush presidency, was that George W. Bush was an able guy, an easygoing guy very much at peace with himself who could get it done. Not charismatic like Kennedy or Reagan perhaps, but neither was he consumed by neuroses or anxieties like Johnson or Nixon, or hampered by glaring personal weaknesses like Clinton. Bush was solid, and he had enormous respect for the office. In many ways, Cross thought, George W. Bush was a Harry Truman–type guy—and Truman was considered to have been a pretty good president.

This day, though, in these first moments, Cross thought he was seeing a George W. Bush different from the one he'd seen before. As the president began speaking, Cross saw a figure who knew he had been thrust into a defining historical moment and would be forever judged by how effectively he responded to that challenge. There was a resolute strength to his demeanor and a confident authority in his delivery. Cross had read volumes about wartime leaders—especially the World War II leaders—and, yeah, it was still early in the game, and maybe he was seeing what he wanted to see, but right now Cross was more than confident that George W. Bush would measure up.

The room was still. The president spoke somberly and calmly. Right at the start he announced, almost in passing, that he would approve the special twenty-billion-dollar aid package for New York. *No wonder Schumer was smiling.* Then he turned to the main purpose of the meeting, discussing the horror and depth of the terrorist attacks. He was effective. Perhaps too effective. Sensing that the emotional level in the room might be too high, the president said self-deprecatingly, "I have been moved, but I am not going to let senators and congressmen see me weep in the cabinet room!" After the briefest hesitation, laughter spread through the room—as much as an emotional release as an affirmation of Bush's deadpan humor.

The president continued, "I don't want you to go out and scare our citizens, but the threats are not over. We are at war." Cross found himself taking a deep breath. Everyone had known, of course, what the attacks meant, but hearing the president of the United State actually use the word "war" for the first time was jarring—jarring but reassuring. This president would not be attempting to dodge or finesse reality. Pausing for effect, the president then added, "The vice president has been evacuated to Camp David." Cross felt himself taking another deep breath. He hadn't expected this. The evacuation of a vice president. It had never happened before in the history of the country. Looking quickly about the room, Cross saw that the others were also startled. Bush must have sensed this reaction as well, quickly adding "that's why we invited you here today." Again there was loud—this time mostly nervous—laughter.

The president went on:

—America must go forward. This is a war against terrorism. I will hold some cards very close to my vest. I'm *very* serious about hunting down those who are responsible. So far the overseas response has been positive. Putin stood down the Russian troops when we went to DEFCON 3. We must find out where others stand. Musharraf in Pakistan is the first guy—he gets a chance. I haven't spoken to him personally but someone very close to me has. Here at home, the military will not be used as police. AWACs and F-16s were protecting Washington, D.C., New York, and seven other cities. They are still protecting Washington and New York. The perimeter around the White House has been extended. Airport security has never been higher, but there could be hijack pilots at large. People ask me if I'd urge a member of my family to fly—it depends on which one! [prompting more laughter]. There is a problem with our borders—we're checking trucks coming from Canada into Michigan—and it's causing problems with the autoworkers.—

The president paused again, and looked solemnly around the table and around the room, before concluding, "Blood lust is high, but there must be a purpose to our response. I will not use a two-million-dollar weapon to attack a four-dollar tent. Through tears I see opportunity."

Sitting back, the president invited comment.

—Senator Warner of Virginia said we must support our commander in chief just as he'd supported President Bush's father in the Gulf War in 1991.

—Senator Specter of Pennsylvania said we already have the legal basis to go after bin Laden, because he is guilty of the 1998 African embassy attacks.

—Congressman Charlie Rangel, the raspy-voiced veteran from Harlem, said—very much as David Dinkins had the day before—"Mr. President, we are fortunate to have you as our commander in chief."

When Senator Joe Lieberman of Connecticut said that the "challenge will be to maintain the interest of the public," the president agreed, adding, "I was just telling Hillary that in a month the people might be more interested in why the Yankees lost the pennant, and I'll have to let them know why I'm taking military action."

Then it was Chuck Schumer's turn. From the look on his face, Cross could tell that Chuck had a lot to say. He only made it part of the way.

"Mr. President," said Schumer, "When I asked you to give twenty billion to New York and you immediately said 'yes,' well, Mr. President, I was just at a loss for words. I . . ."

"Chuck," the president quickly interjected, "that was the reason I approved the money."

The room broke into the first truly uproarious laughter of the afternoon, and, at least for this one moment in time, the usually voluble Schumer was indeed at a loss for words.

—Hillary Clinton, back in the White House for the first time since she was First Lady, said that she knew the tremendous pressure that faces a president and that we must politically and personally stand united.

The president concluded the meeting by thanking everyone for their support and reminding them that this was "the first war of the 21st century." As Bush left the cabinet room, Cross shook his hand and wished him well.

A horde of reporters was outside the West Wing. The senators and congressmen stood in front of the array of microphones and expressed their support for the president and the importance of the country remaining united. As the questions droned on, Cross edged away and walked toward Tom O'Connell's Jeep Cherokee.

"How did it go?"

"Pretty heavy stuff. But the president was good. Serious when he had to be—which was most of the time. But he used some humor to break the tension."

"Anything new?"

"Yeah, Cheney is being evacuated to Camp David."

"Holy shit! Did you have any idea that was coming?"

"No. It took everyone by surprise."

"Has this been announced?"

"No."

"You don't intend to leak it to anyone do you?"

"Christ, no. This is too serious for the usual fun and games."

As Cross walked into his Cannon office, Kevin Finnerty told him that Lynne Duncan of ABC News had just called. She wanted to know if Cross could tell her anything about the meeting.

"No. Tell her I can't. She's an old friend. But I'm not going to fool around with this stuff."

"You can't tell her anything at all?"

"Zero."

"Okay, but this is a first."

"Don't be a wise guy."

About three minutes later, Cross finished trying to explain to Danny why he couldn't tell him over the phone what had gone on at the White House meeting. That he'd have to wait until tonight. Just then Tom O'Connell came in and told him to turn on CNN. Cross pressed the remote and watched and listened: "CNN has just learned that Vice President Cheney has been evacuated to Camp David for security reasons. This marks the first time in our nation's history that the government has been forced to take action like this. President Bush announced the Vice President's evacuation at a meeting of senators and congressmen held at the White House this afternoon. That meeting concluded less than a half-hour ago."

"So much for national security," said O'Connell.

"I'm sure it would have come out soon enough anyway. I just didn't want to be the one who did it."

"Maybe we are coming back to normal faster than we thought!"

It was shortly past noon on Friday when Cross climbed onto the Capitol Police's passenger bus that was parked at the foot of the steps on the House side of the Capitol. The sky was gray and overcast; the ground wet from the rain that had fallen earlier. The White House had decided the evening before to invite pretty much the same House members who'd been at Tuesday's meeting to join the president at Ground Zero. Cross, of course, had immediately accepted and from looking around the bus, it appeared most of the others had as well. He was wearing a dark green, nylon, zippered jacket he'd borrowed from O'Connell. The others were also dressed casually.

Virtually surrounded by a heavy police escort, the bus made its way from the Capitol, arriving at Andrews Air Force Base in Maryland just in time for the delegation members to go directly to the distinguished visitors lounge and watch the television as Bush spoke from the National Cathedral in Washington. It was a national day of "prayer and remembrance," and a capacity crowd within the cathedral, led by former presidents Ford, Carter, Bush, and Clinton, looked up from their pews. Countless millions across the nation and the world—including the congressmen gathered at Andrews Air Force Base—watched on their television screens as the president walked to the pulpit. They looked to him for leadership in this darkest hour, and he did not disappoint.

—"On Tuesday, our country was attacked with deliberate and massive cruelty. We have seen the images of fire and ashes and bent steel."

—"Just three days removed from these events, Americans do not yet have the distance of history. But our responsibility to history is already clear: to answer these attacks and rid the world of evil. This conflict was begun on the timing and terms of others. It will end in a way, and at an hour, of our choosing."

—"God bless America."

Around the television set in the lounge there were nods and smiles of quiet approval as the president concluded his remarks and stepped down from the pulpit. The House members and the accompanying White House staff then turned and filed almost solemnly out the glass doors of the lounge toward the blue and white Air Force jet that would fly them to LaGuardia Airport. President Bush was to leave a short time later on Air Force One.

The flight to LaGuardia took about forty-five minutes and was uneventful. Talk was muted, and each member appeared apprehensive about the scene of devastation that awaited at Ground Zero. The only activity occurred when the plane passed over lower Manhattan. Then Cross and the others craned their necks to see through the left-side windows. He got a brief view. Peering through a break in the clouds, he saw smoke and empty space where the Twin Towers had been. Minutes later the jet was setting down on the runway of LaGuardia's Marine Air Terminal. This was the terminal used by Delta for its shuttle flights to Washington and Boston. But there were no flights at LaGuardia today. Nor had there been any since Tuesday morning.

It was just after 2:30 p.m. The members walked directly from the plane to the bus awaiting them on the tarmac. The weather was better than expected. As in Washington, it was gray and overcast, and there was the slightest mist in the air. But the rain had stopped falling, and it appeared it would stay away for the rest of the day. An NYPD escort led the bus from the airport along a route familiar to these New York passengers—Grand Central Parkway to the Brooklyn-Queens Expressway to the Long Island Expressway and through the Midtown Tunnel into Manhattan. It sounded complicated, but this afternoon, especially with so little traffic on the road, it would take less than twenty minutes. Cross had made this sojourn countless times, but today as the bus went along the LIE and approached the tunnel, he took one extra look at St. Raphael's Church on his right, the church that Jimmy Boyle had attended as a kid.

Coming out of the tunnel onto Manhattan's streets, the bus encountered more traffic than there'd been in Queens but nothing like the usual Friday afternoon madness. No gridlock or incessant horn-blowing. No cab drivers or jaywalking pedestrians shouting curses and epithets. Cross was delighted to see, however, that the streets were far from empty. This was no ghost town. Just three days ago and only a few miles south of here, Manhattan had suffered the most unspeakable attack in American history. And if the streets were not as crowded or as vibrant as before September 11th, in most other cities today's turnout would be considered a pretty busy day.

As the bus went west on 34th Street, there were no sirens or lights from the NYPD escort, and the bus stopped for red lights. *No need to create any more tension for these people,* thought Cross; *besides, we're right on schedule.* The conversation in the bus was still solemn, very similar, it seemed, to the expressions of the New Yorkers walking the streets—somber but undaunted. But there was nothing at all somber about the scene along West Street as the bus—now going south—approached the vicinity of Ground Zero. Hundreds of people lined the streets cheering, waving American flags and holding up signs, thanking and encouraging the rescue workers who'd come from all over the region and country to do what they could. The windows of the bus were shut tight, but its passengers could clearly hear the crowd's defiant cheers of *USA! USA!*

The bus parked just north of Chambers Street. Stepping from the vehicle, Cross and the others were met by an air filled with a harsh, sulphurlike odor. The streets, still wet from the morning rain, were covered with what looked like a muddy white ash or a thin concrete mix. Within seconds Cross's shoes were caked in white. Walking the several blocks to the site, Cross saw that the left side of West Street was lined with dump trucks waiting their turn to haul away debris. Down the side streets on the left, however, were crushed fire vehicles and other badly damaged emergency vehicles. Along the right side of West Street were countless television satellite trucks and hordes of reporters and their camera crews. The sky was still gray, but there appeared to be an occasional ray of sun. Every half-block or so, down the center of the street, there were checkpoints—NYPD, the National Guard, and Secret Service. At each stop the Capitol Police officer and Secret Service agent escorting the congressional delegation would flash appropriate ID and be waved on. Cross recognized the National Guard insignia—it was from his old unit, the "Fighting 69th." He thought ironically of the times they would sit around the armory on 26th Street and Lexington Avenue joking about what a good job they must be doing, because the whole time they'd been in the Guard no one had ever attacked New York! *I guess no one will ever joke anymore about New York being attacked,* thought Cross.

Though planned less than twenty-four hours ago, the trip was pretty well orchestrated. The House members walked until they got to the corner of West and Vesey Streets—the northern boundary of the site. They were assigned to a roped-off area on the northeast corner. Directly across, on the southeast corner, were such notables as former mayors Koch and Dinkins, and Cardinal Egan. It was approximately 3:15.

Thirty years before, Cross had worked for a law firm on Vesey Street just blocks east of this corner. That was when the Twin Towers were being constructed. He knew the area well, but today, as he looked into this abyss of destruction, he could not get his bearings and felt strangely disoriented. Hundreds of majestic floors of steel, concrete, and glass had been reduced to five stories of rubble. Surrounding buildings had been blown apart. Others had countless windows shattered. There was smoke, and there were flames, under control but still burning. Firefighters were searching feverishly for survivors. Cops, some uniformed and others in blue nylon NYPD jackets and baseball hats, patrolled the site. Cranes and heavy-duty construction equipment were spread throughout and amidst the ruins as hard hats— mostly ironworkers—labored continually. The mission was to locate and rescue survivors. But, as Cross soon learned, there would be no survivors. A cop he had known for years, Tom Curtin, spotted him and walked over.

"Did you ever think you'd see something like this?" asked Curtin.

"Not in my worst dreams. But I'm amazed this operation is so well coordinated already. Especially the rescue work," answered Cross.

"Forget the rescues. That's all newspaper talk. We have to do it for morale. But there's no way with all that crushed debris and those flames burning that anyone could be alive. It's impossible."

"You sure?" asked Cross, not knowing what else to say.

"Sean, I wish to God I were wrong, but that's the truth."

"Thanks for being straight with me, Tom."

Moments later Cross said hello to Tom Fitzsimmons, a cop he recognized from the bomb squad. Cross couldn't imagine anything bothering this guy, but his voice was shaking as he told Cross what he'd seen on Tuesday morning.

"It was just a few minutes after nine. Both towers had been hit. I came running down Liberty Street, figuring 'how bad could it be?' But I couldn't believe what I was seeing. Jumpers. One body after the other. Flying through the air. Crashing and splattering on the sidewalk. It was the worst. The fucking worst."

The bomb squad cop said nothing else. He just stood there, slowly shaking his head. Cross put his right hand on the cop's left shoulder and said, "Take care of yourself."

Minutes later two cops from Cross's congressional district—Paul Grupp and John Kissane—walked over to say hello and to thank Cross for all that Congress was doing. His answer was quick and direct: "Are you kidding? Thank *you* for what *you're* doing."

Cross also recognized a guy in full fireman's gear standing off to the side, catching his breath and drinking bottled water. It was John McCreedy. Cross had gone to high school with McCreedy more than forty years before. He'd still see him every few months when McCreedy would stop by the district office to reminisce and offer his views on myriad world affairs. McCreedy had the time to visit and converse because he was retired. Retired from the FDNY for more than a decade, McCreedy had served many years there and was pretty banged up when he got out. His hip was in particularly bad shape.

"Hey John, what are you up to?" yelled Cross toward the middle of West Street.

"Sean, I figured I might find you down here," answered McCreedy, walking with a pronounced limp toward the cordoned-off area on the corner.

"How long you been here?"

"I came down on Wednesday. I had to do something to help out, but I think this is it. The hip is killing me."

"How's it been?"

"To be honest with you, I don't know how much good I've done, and I may end up giving myself a heart attack—but it's been worth it for me."

"I'm sure it has."

"I can't even describe it. The first day here, they were stopping all traffic at 14th Street. So I had to walk down from there. I had my hat and my gear and I'm limping down the middle of West Street and all those people along the side were cheering and applauding. And it didn't stop, all the way down."

"Did it make you forget about your hip?"

"I felt no pain. All I could think back to was all those years when I was working in Brooklyn—in East New York and Brownsville—where we'd answer a call and people would be cursing and throwing bottles and all sorts of shit at us."

"It's too bad it took this—for you guys to finally get the credit you deserve."

"I'm alive. I have nothing to bitch about," said McCreedy, looking toward the burning rubble.

Cross looked at his watch. It was just after four. The schedule said the president was due at 4:10. But there was none of the flurry and movement that preceded a president's arrival, so Cross assumed there was a delay. He asked K. C. Crowley, a female Secret Service agent, if she had any information.

"Yeah. I just got an update. The president landed at McGuire Air Force Base in New Jersey—instead of JFK. That must have been for security reasons. Then they helicoptered him to the Manhattan heliport. He should be here in about twenty minutes or a half-hour."

"Thanks, K.C."

As he waited, Cross made cell phone calls to Mary Rose, Danny, and Kara describing for them what he was seeing and how much devastation there was. He also spoke with and listened to the hard hats assembled behind him. They were waiting anxiously, hoping to catch a glimpse of the president. This was when it first struck Cross how much Bush had resonated with blue-collar Americans. These guys had watched him carefully over the past three days. They knew that because of the rush of events, what they were seeing was unguarded and unscripted. And they liked what they saw. "The guy's got guts," was the most common refrain.

When the president arrived, it was amidst a convoy of black limousines, SUVs, and camera crews. As Bush stepped from his car, Cross saw he was wearing a gray work jacket and jeans. An American flag was in his lapel. It would be twenty minutes or so before Cross would see Bush again. The president was walking to various spots and meeting rescue workers throughout the massive site and would be working his way back around toward West and Vesey. The president was out of view, but the air was filled with electricity. The *USA* chants were constant. American flags were everywhere. "We love you, George," and "Kick their ass!" shouted the hard hats, even when Bush was entirely out of their sight. At one point Cross heard a loud roar, followed by sustained chants of *USA! USA!* It was only that evening, when he was watching television, that Cross would see the footage of George W. Bush standing on a pile of rubble and forever defining his presidency by embracing a retired firefighter and shouting into a bullhorn to the roaring crowd: "I hear you. I hear you, the rest of the world hears you, and the people who knocked these buildings down will hear all of us soon."

It was about ten minutes later that Bush approached the corner where Cross and the other congressmen were standing. Cross shook his hand and said, "Great job, Mr. President." Cross then stepped to the side, and pointed to the hard hats behind him, saying "These guys love you. They're your people." The president reached forward, shaking one blue-collar hand after the other.

There was a major vote scheduled in Congress for late that night or early Saturday morning. It was the resolution authorizing the president to attack Afghanistan. The Air Force jet would fly the congressmen from LaGuardia to Washington so they could make the vote. Cross, however, had decided not to return to Washington. He hated to miss such an important vote, but the funeral for Pete Ganci, the New York City fire chief, was being held in Farmingdale on Saturday morning. Cross believed that was where he belonged. Ganci had been his constituent. The FDNY had come to symbolize what the struggle was all about. Besides, as important as it was, the resolution was going to pass overwhelmingly without Cross's vote. If some future opponent wanted to attack Cross for missing the vote, so be it.

Cross got off the bus with the others at the Marine Air Terminal, said his good-byes, and got into a car with Tony Lacorazza, a Secret Service Agent who would drive Cross over to parking lot 4 at the US Airways terminal, where he'd left his car on Monday morning. The lot had been packed tight that morning, and Cross had been forced to park a good distance from the terminal. This evening though, as Lacorazza dropped him off outside the lot, Cross saw that his car was one of the few remaining. The lot was virtually barren. The terminal itself was shut down. The only signs of life were the Port Authority police officers standing guard at the terminal doors. Looking at the nearly empty lot and the shuttered terminal, Cross again thought how different it had all been just four days before. Just as history's line of demarcation was B.C. and A.D., so too the lives of all those who'd been alive that day would be *pre*–September 11th and *post*–September 11th.

Cross exited the parking lot and the airport. It was almost 6:30, and it was Friday evening. Most other Fridays would have seen bumper-to-bumper rush-hour traffic on the Grand Central Parkway. Tonight, though, the road was clear. And as dusk approached, all that could be heard was the roar of the F-16 swooping low in the darkening sky.

9

It was shortly after seven o'clock that evening when Sean Cross got out of the cab in front of Bobby Van's Steakhouse on 15th Street about three blocks from the White House. That afternoon he'd gotten a phone call from Tom Barfield.

"Tom, I didn't know you were going to be in town," said Cross, sitting behind the desk in his Cannon office.

"I didn't either. It was a last-minute deal, a security agreement with a new corporate client near Dupont Circle," answered Barfield. "It just came together last night."

"Once again money goes to money, and I'm still breaking my ass trying to get by on a government salary."

"You're breaking my heart."

"I assume you called for a reason."

"It's been almost three weeks since we met in your office, and I've been trying to piece together what I can for you."

"Any luck?"

"Nothing dramatic. So far all I've gotten are bits and pieces, but I'm still certain the three guys I mentioned to you—Abdullah, Mustafa, and Hawasi—were involved somehow—so I'll stay on it from that angle."

"Is there another angle?"

"There might be. We may have caught a break."

"What kind of break?"

"It's a break you and I might not be too happy about—but there might be an Irish connection."

"Are you kidding?"

"No. I'm not kidding at all. I'm deadly serious."

"When can we get together?"

"I'm not flying back to New York until tomorrow morning. So how about tonight?"

"Dinner?"

"Yeah."

"Seven o'clock okay?"

"That's fine."

"The usual place?"

"Yeah. And I'll be bringing someone with me."

"Great. See you at seven at Bobby Van's."

Bobby Van's was a New York City-style steakhouse located in the very heart of Washington, D.C. Frequented by D.C.'s inner circle, it had been a hit almost from the day it opened about five years ago. Whether at lunchtime or dinner it was filled with power brokers—including cabinet secretaries, senators, congressmen, reporters, and lobbyists—exchanging rumors or cutting their latest deals. The owners—Joe Smith and Joe Hickey—also operated a place with the same name in Manhattan, on Park Avenue just north of Grand Central Station. The two Joes alternated as to who would operate which Bobby Van's on which night. Tonight it was Joe Smith's turn to be running the show in Washington.

Born and raised in Belfast, Smith had moved to the United States about twenty-five years ago—but not before he'd been involved in the fighting that beset Northern Ireland at that time, and for so many years before and after. Cross got to know Smith pretty well after the Belfast native moved to New York. Cross never asked the extent or nature of Smith's involvement in Ireland, but he knew it had been significant. Smith had grown up with Gerry Adams. Others he'd grown up with had gone to prison or been killed by the British army. Smith still maintained a close relationship with the Sinn Fein leadership in Ireland, including Adams. But Smith was also in tight with America's power structure—whether it be the mayor or governor in New York, or cabinet members and congressional barons in Washington.

"Congressman Cross," the neatly attired Smith proclaimed in an almost stentorian tone as Cross entered the restaurant, "it is indeed a pleasure to have you grace us with your presence this evening."

"No, Mr. Smith, the pleasure is all mine."

"Seriously, Sean, it's good to see you, indeed it is. I just got a call from your man Barfield. He said he's running about a half-hour late. Can I buy you a drink while you're waiting?"

"I'll never say 'no' to that."

"Grand. Do you want to drink at the bar or go right to the back room I reserved for your dinner?"

"Let's go right to the table in the back room. You've got half of official Washington sitting at the bar."

"Do you have national security secrets to be telling me?" asked Smith with a broad smile, walking toward the reserved room.

"Actually, I don't have much to say at all. But why let them hear anything?"

"A man after my own heart," said Smith, sitting at the table and gesturing toward the waiter. "What are you drinking, Sean?"

"I'll have a Manhattan on the rocks."

"Get the good congressman here a Manhattan, and I'll have a red wine," said Smith to the waiter.

"Business looks better than ever," said Cross.

"Jesus, Sean, it certainly is going well. I tell you, this is a great country!"

"It must be if guys from Belfast can make it!" said Cross with a wry smile.

The waiter brought the drinks. Cross and Smith clicked their glasses together and wished each other luck.

"Speaking of doing well, Tom Barfield's not doing too badly for himself either," observed Smith.

"No. Tom has always made money."

"Is he helping you out on these latest attacks?"

"Nothing official. But he's got a lot of contacts and he's able to fill in some of the blanks for me."

Raised in a culture guided by the credo "whatever you say, say nothing," Smith asked nothing more about Barfield or the purpose of tonight's meeting.

"The last few weeks since the attacks have been brutal," said Smith. "I'm up in New York three or four days every week, and I can see it in the people. It was a body blow, so it was. Far fewer killed than the World Trade Center and nowhere near the property damage or devastation, of course, but it was such a shock. There was just too much a false sense of security. I suppose we thought September 11 was behind us."

"You're right. It's human nature to hope for the best, but the bottom line is that this is going to be with us for a long time. And we have to find a way to condition ourselves to it."

"You really think it's going to go on that long?" asked Smith.

"Yeah, I do. Listen, I wish it could be over tomorrow, but there's a lot of them."

"You mean overseas?"

"I mean overseas and here. I have no doubt there are sleeper cells throughout the country."

"Christ, Sean, the FBI and the cops are everywhere. That must be having some impact."

"Sure it is. We're making it a lot harder for them. But we can't stop everything. We can't bat a thousand."

"I tell you, the more this Al Qaeda shit goes on, the more I realize how lucky we were that it didn't happen when we were trying to bring Gerry and the boys in from the cold."

"Not to name-drop, but I had this exact conversation with Bill Clinton a few months ago."

"Great minds think alike."

"Obviously. Anyway, I asked him whether he thought he'd have been able to give Adams a visa or keep the Irish peace process going if September 11th had occurred first."

"What did he say?"

"He said 'no.' The American people wouldn't have been in the mood to be distinguishing between groups of terrorists or between terrorists and freedom fighters. And, to be honest with you, I couldn't blame them."

"So we got lucky that Ireland was on the radar screen during the mid-nineties, before anybody knew very much about Al Qaeda or bin Laden."

"Yeah, for once there actually was 'the luck of the Irish,'" laughed Cross, all the while trying to anticipate what Barfield might be telling him later that evening about an "Irish connection."

"I suppose all the funerals are over with back in your district?"

"It looks like it. There was one on Monday morning for some poor guy from the LIRR who'd been on the critical list with terrible burns. It was really a blessing that he died. But all the others are expected to recover."

"I see the LIRR trains are running pretty well again."

"Yeah, there are still some delays. But it's not that bad."

The waiter opened the door. Tom Barfield walked in accompanied by a middle-aged guy. The guy was well dressed and appeared to be in pretty good shape. He looked as if he might have been a cop of some sort. Cross and Smith greeted Barfield, who introduced the guy as "Frank Hennessy, an old friend." The waiter took the drink order—red wine for Barfield, Scotch and water for Hennessy. Smith wished everyone a good evening and left, closing the door behind him.

"Sean, sorry for the cloak-and-dagger routine," said Barfield, "but I didn't want to be talking over the phone."

"No problem. Plus it gives us a chance to get a decent meal."

"No offense, Sean, but it doesn't look as if you've been missing too many meals lately."

"Always the comedian."

"Seriously, Sean, I asked Frank to come along tonight because he's come up with some interesting information. He's retired FBI and has been with my company for a few months."

"To be honest with you, Tom, when you dropped the 'Irish connection' on me this afternoon, it confused the hell out of me—so Frank, what do you have for us?"

"Let me start with a name you might remember—Fiona Larkin," said Hennessy.

"Of course I remember Fiona," answered Cross. "How could anyone forget her?"

Cross had first met Fiona Larkin about fifteen years before, during one of his visits to Belfast. These were the very early days of the peace process, when Gerry Adams was transforming the Irish republican movement from paramilitary to primarily political. Fiona was in her early twenties then. She was also strikingly beautiful—shoulder-length red hair, sculpted cheekbones, and a great body. She was smart, with a lively personality to match her hair. Fiona was from the young generation of Catholics who'd taken the fullest advantage of Northern Ireland's educational system, graduating from Queen's College in Belfast with high honors. She was also from the generation of Catholics who refused to accept second or third-class citizenship. Her main job at that time was researching position papers for Sinn Fein candidates. As far as Cross could tell, Fiona was highly respected by the Sinn Fein leadership, and she in turn supported Adams's efforts to move from bullets to ballots. She appeared to be on the political fast track.

After Bill Clinton gave Adams his first American visa in early 1994 and during the next several years when the peace process was accelerating, Fiona was always at the Belfast meetings that Cross and other congressmen attended, and Cross considered her to be a part of the Sinn Fein inner circle. So Cross was surprised to learn—just prior to when the Good Friday Agreement was signed in April 1998—that Fiona had left Sinn Fein and was supporting a dissident breakaway group styling itself the "Real IRA." Cross also learned that Fiona was living with Rory McAllister, the Real IRA commander in South Tyrone. The Real IRA went on to carry out a string of botched attacks, causing large numbers of civilian casualties and losing the group what little support it might have had. Then in 2000 McAllister was shot dead by one of his own men in an internal feud. The Real IRA went defunct, and Cross heard nothing more about Fiona Larkin—until Frank Hennessy just now mentioned her name . . .

"I thought you'd remember Fiona," laughed Hennessy. "She was active during the days we were still surveilling guys like you."

"How the hell is she involved with the New York attacks?"

"I don't know for sure if she is actually involved or not, but like Tom told you, there is a 'connection.'"

"What kind of connection?"

"A friend of mine in the Irish police tells me that about two years ago Fiona got involved with Abdul Bajal, who was the leading Al Qaeda man in Dublin. And just last week she was spotted leaving a small restaurant in lower Manhattan with Ramzi Haddad, one of Mohamed Hawasi's henchmen."

"Tom, Hawasi's one of the guys you mentioned to me," said Cross.

"Yeah, Hawasi's got that Islamic medical foundation and the antiques business," answered Barfield.

"This is going too fast for me," said Cross. "We've just gone from the Real IRA in Belfast to Al Qaeda on Atlantic Avenue, and—not for nothing—but why the hell did Fiona Larkin hook up with a Muslim terrorist?"

"That's why I brought Frank along," answered Barfield. "It does get complicated."

"Let me just lay out everything I know about it," said Hennessy.

"Fire away," said Cross.

"To start off, there are about twenty thousand Muslims in Ireland. And they came from a bunch of countries. Egypt, Libya, Algeria, Yemen. They started arriving in the late '80s and early '90s, and for the most part they're good people."

"Which is more than you can say about a lot of the Irish!" interrupted Barfield with a wide grin.

"For the most part they settled around Dublin, and they have several good-sized mosques," continued Hennessy. "There's two in the center of the city and one in Ballsbridge."

"How do those rich snobs in Ballsbridge feel about having a bunch of Arabs living among them?" asked Cross.

"From what I understand," said Barfield, "they think they're 'quaint.'"

"Anyway, a few years ago the Gardai's Special Branch," said Hennessy, referring to the undercover unit of the Irish police, "started getting reports of Al Qaeda activity in Dublin. From what they could piece together and what they got from the Brits and the FBI, they centered on this guy Abdul Bajal."

"Where's he from?" asked Cross.

"He's a Saudi, by way of Egypt," answered Hennessy. "He also did some fighting in Afghanistan."

"He was running an actual cell?" asked Cross.

"The Irish think that, in total, there were about ten active members in the cell and maybe another twenty or so who gave them support," answered Hennessy.

"What were they up to?" asked Cross.

"There were no actual operations carried out in Ireland," answered Hennessy. "What they did was meet regularly in a mosque in the center of town. Their main jobs would be things like providing stolen and false visas and passports to Al Qaeda operatives passing through. They'd also launder cash and hold it until it was needed for operations on the mainland."

"How would they launder it?"

"Through a front called the Islamic Holyland Children's Foundation," answered Hennessy.

"We think that's part of the link to Hawasi," interrupted Barfield, "the foundation in Brooklyn, the Islamic Medical Relief Service."

"Was Bajal definitely the top guy?" asked Cross.

"The top guy in Ireland," replied Hennessy, "but he got his orders from an imam in England."

"England?"

"Yeah, in north London there's a mosque in Finsbury Park. Moussaoui, the twentieth hijacker, used to go there sometimes. So did the other guy, Richard Reid, the shoe bomber."

"When did the Irish find this out?"

"Most of it by 2000 or early 2001," answered Hennessy.

"What did they do about it?"

"They didn't think they had enough to arrest them. A lot of the evidence might not have held up in court. Besides Bajal wasn't causing any problems in Ireland, and we have to remember that Al Qaeda wasn't as big on the radar screen then as it was after September 11th. But the Special Branch did keep a surveillance on the mosque in Ballsbridge, the foundation's offices, and Bajal's apartment in south Dublin—until just before September 11th, when Bajal gave them the slip."

"Where'd he go?"

"They found out later on that he apparently went to England by boat and then made his way through Europe and finally got to Indonesia—but when Bajal actually left Dublin, the cops didn't make that much out of it; in fact, they weren't even sure he'd left."

"What did they do after the 11th?"

"The Special Branch raided Bajal's apartment, the foundation, and even the mosque. That's when they realized all that this guy was up to."

"Like what?"

"As expected, they found visas and passports and all sorts of fake ID. They also found plane tickets and records showing that Bajal had spent a week in an apartment in Montreal in the fall of 1999 with Ali Rakin just before Rakin left for Jordan."

"Wasn't Rakin one of the guys nabbed in a millennium plot in Jordan?" asked Cross.

"That's the man."

"Bajal does move in some bad company."

"There's more. The cops went through the computer at the foundation offices and found plans for explosives and maps for the London Underground and the New York subway system."

"Any idea where Bajal is now?"

"They're certain he's in Indonesia."

"No more sightings in Ireland?"

"Nothing, and they're watching very closely."

"How about Canada—since he did stay there, you said, with Rakin?"

"As far as we know—the Irish, the Brits, and the FBI—he's not in Canada. But you can never know for sure, because the Canadians are so damn uncooperative."

"Even the spooks—the CSIS?" asked Cross, referring to the Canadian Security Intelligence Service.

"The CSIS is actually O.K. But it's the government and the immigration officials that are totally useless—and arrogant about it."

"Is there any word on any activity by Bajal at all since September 11th? That's a few years ago now."

"There was nothing at all until Fiona Larkin suddenly reappeared. Ironically enough, one of our FBI guys from the old Irish squad . . ."

"You mean the guys who spent twenty-five years running around New York trying to find the IRA," said Cross.

"Yeah, he was tipped off by one of his old sources—some New York City mick—that Fiona'd been seen lately in a few pubs in Manhattan and the Bronx. The source thought the IRA must be back in business. He had no idea that Fiona had joined up with the Muslims."

"I didn't have the slightest idea myself," said Cross. "I just assumed she'd disappeared into the woodwork."

"That's what we all thought," said Hennessy. "After McAllister was killed, Fiona was gone. Nobody heard a word from her. Apparently though, from what we've been able to piece together, she met Bajal about six months or so after McAllister was shot and got caught up in his fundamentalist, anti-Western frenzy."

"Was she living with Bajal in Ireland?"

"We now know that they were an item, but actually living together, we don't know."

"Wasn't Bajal under surveillance during this time?"

"Yeah, and the Irish cops have no record of anyone seeing the two of them together. We think she put her revolutionary training to good use—meeting Bajal in places where they wouldn't be spotted. In any event, we now know that she has been living with him ever since he got to Indonesia."

"What the hell was Bajal's attraction?"

"Who knows what any broad sees in any guy? But in this case I'd say it was Fiona's attraction to danger, that revolutionary zeal she had . . ."

"As misguided as that zeal was," said Cross.

"That's the truth. She broke with Sinn Fein and the IRA because she decided Adams was selling out the republican movement for politics."

"But Gerry had been saying for the previous ten years at least that they had to go into politics and make it work for them. And I thought—during all that time—that Fiona was one of Gerry's strongest supporters. So I was really surprised when she split from Sinn Fein."

"So was the Sinn Fein leadership."

"Did they ever figure out why she left?"

"This is strictly amateur psychobabble—especially since it's coming from a bunch of micks—but they think Fiona joined Sinn Fein in the first place because it was the most radical and revolutionary movement in Ireland at the time and that she stayed with it for so long because she convinced herself that Adams was just suckering the Brits in—that he never really believed in the political route. But in late '97 and early '98, when she saw that Adams and McGuiness did want a political solution, she left and joined up with that Real IRA crowd."

"I guess that makes as much sense as any theory."

"And that would explain why she got involved with McAllister and even with Bajal."

"Yeah, McAllister was a true believer—no peace in Ireland until every Brit was gone. And the only way to get the Brits out was to send them home dead. Political compromise was treason."

"He certainly killed enough of them."

"He also killed a lot of civilians—including kids and women."

"Which is why he was called 'Mad Dog' McAllister."

"Is Bajal supposed to be charismatic like McAllister?"

"From the intelligence reports I've seen—the personality profiles—I'd say he's much more charismatic. He's supposed to have a magnetic personality—almost a cult following. Some of the speeches he'd give in the mosque would just about hypnotize the audience. Very much like a Hitler or a Castro. And the fact that he supported force and no compromise must have appealed to Fiona."

"How about the religious angle? Does Fiona actually believe in Islam?"

"No. Certainly not from a theological or spiritual angle. Apparently it was the message of using absolute force to destroy the West—especially the U.S. and Britain—that got her on the fundamentalist bandwagon."

"Did she actually convert to Islam?"

"The Special Branch thinks so. They also think that Bajal and Fiona got married. But neither the Irish nor the Brits have any idea how serious the conversion was. All they know for sure is that she believes in a jihad against America."

"I guess that's all we have to know. The rest is just philosophical and theological bullshit. What do you think she's meeting with Hawasi's goons for?"

"That we don't know. But the guy she met with last week—Ramzi Haddad—is a bad actor. He's one of Hawasi's top men."

"Why would Al Qaeda risk sending Fiona over here?"

"They thought it was safe, since they have no idea we know about her. They assume we're just looking for Middle Eastern types, so some Irish-looking woman could move around easily enough without anyone taking notice of her."

"This guy Haddad that she met with—didn't Al Qaeda think that you'd probably be tailing him?"

"I'm sure they did, and that's another reason why they'd send Fiona. They figured that we'd only be paying attention to Muslim-looking people and we'd consider Fiona to be at just another business meeting."

"What is his business anyway?"

"He's some kind of furniture salesman."

"That sounds a little vague."

"That's because I never thought it was for real. I'm sure it's just a cover for his real job."

"Which is?"

"A strong-arm man for Hawasi."

"So the meeting with Fiona wouldn't have stood out?"

"No, not at all. In an average day Haddad will have four or five meetings—about half of them with non-Arabs."

"How did Fiona get into the country?"

"We think through Canada—since there's no record of her or anyone matching her description coming in through Kennedy or Newark. But, to be honest with you, she probably could have flown in, if she'd wanted to, and gotten through Customs okay."

"Even with all the increased security?"

"Yeah. Fiona could have slipped through the cracks. Remember, she's never been convicted or even charged with anything, and no one's heard from her in so long. And even Bajal has never been charged with anything."

"Anything more on Haddad's background?"

"The main thing is that he's not motivated by religion or ideology. He's always been a shady, borderline-type crooked businessman and shakedown artist. The feds are pretty sure that the relationship between him and Hawasi is one of mutual convenience."

"Any idea what went on at the meeting?"

"No. It lasted only about twenty minutes or so. And the place where they met—the Church Street Restaurant—is really more of a large coffee shop than a restaurant. The agent who was monitoring them said the conversation appeared to be very low key and businesslike."

"How did Fiona look?"

"She's still very good-looking of course, but she had no makeup on and was dressed very plain. She certainly didn't stand out."

"Any idea what she was doing in the Irish bars she went to?"

"One thing she didn't do was drink."

"That's a change. She used to love wine."

"It is a change—and it shows that Bajal really has had an impact on her, even if she's not into the theology. He's a very strict Muslim when it comes to booze. As to what she was doing, it seems like she was just talking with a few of those characters who used to support the Real IRA."

"Where did she stay when she was over here?"

"In Manhattan. At the Bliss Hotel on the Upper West Side."

"What did the FBI do?"

"They didn't pick her up or give her any idea they were onto her. They put a tap on her hotel room phone and a bug in her room. We also tried to intercept her cell phone calls."

"Any luck?"

"No. She's pretty clever."

"Do you think she knew she was spotted?"

"No. There's no indication of that at all. She's just been trained to be careful."

"How did she leave?"

"She went back through Canada. We put a tail on her until she got on a plane."

"And then?"

"Our guys picked up the tail at the other end."

"Indonesia?"

"Yeah."

"We have that kind of freedom of movement over there?"

"Ever since the Bali bombing, Indonesia lets the FBI and CIA do whatever they want, with no questions asked."

"This is all very interesting, but I have two main questions. What's the FBI analysis of why Fiona was over here, and, since I assume the FBI knows you're telling me this, what are they looking for from me?"

"They think she came here to work out the details with Haddad of an upcoming operation involving Hawasi. The FBI doesn't know what the operation will be, but they think the actual work will be carried out by some of Fiona's old Irish friends. Al Qaeda assumes that we're watching Muslims and that they can pull an end run on us by using Irish guys. I'm sure, though, that when Fiona met with her Irish friends she never said anything about Al Qaeda. Whatever they're asked to do, I'm sure they think it's for Mother Ireland, not Muslim terrorists. Our job is to find out what they're up to before it's too late."

"And my role?"

"They'd appreciate anything you can pick up from your Irish sources. You still seem to know your way around with that crowd."

"I'll see what I can find out. I think you're right, though. She would have to convince them that this was some sort of Real IRA mission. I can't imagine Al Qaeda having any support among even the most rabid Real IRA hard-liners."

"That's the FBI's analysis as well."

"What kind of timetable do you see?"

"Al Qaeda is usually very methodical about their operations— so the best estimate is that it will be at least six or seven weeks before anything would be expected to happen. In the meantime we'll be watching Haddad, Fiona, and the two micks she met as closely as we possibly can. What we have going for us is that we really don't think any of them has a clue that we spotted Fiona and that we're making any kind of connection."

"That's encouraging. Frank, I have one last question. When you're talking about the FBI tonight, sometimes it's been 'they,' other times it's been 'we.' What's the story? Are you in or out?"

"Officially I'm out, and I'm working for Tom. Unofficially, I'm helping the bureau out as a private contractor, or consultant. I realize that's a little blurred, and it's not the way the FBI usually does things but, as we all know, we live in a very different world."

"We certainly do," said Barfield, ordering another round of drinks.

Saturday, September 15, 2001

The morning sky was clear blue, and the sun shone brightly in the heavens. In just a few hours, at twelve noon, Sean Cross would be attending the funeral mass for Pete Ganci at St. Kilian's Catholic Church in Farmingdale. Ganci, the FDNY chief, had been the highest-ranking New York City fire officer ever to die in the line of duty. Cross did not know Ganci personally but knew of his reputation as a legendary firefighter. As Pete Ganci's congressman, Cross also knew that he had to be at the funeral.

Cross looked at the clock and saw there was no need to hurry. The first thing he wanted to find out was what the vote had been on the war resolution. He checked the morning papers, but the vote had come too late to make any of the deadlines. He walked to the den, turned on the television, and flipped from one channel to the next until he found the story he was looking for: the resolution had passed in the early morning hours by a vote of 420 to one. This almost unanimous tally affirmed Cross's judgment that his presence wouldn't be needed, but he still regretted having to miss such a significant vote.

"How could anyone have voted against that resolution?" asked Mary Rose.

"I don't know," answered Sean. "I suppose it takes all types."

"This is our survival we're talking about."

"I know."

"I mean that literally. It really hit me yesterday when I was at Roosevelt Field."

"How so?"

"I had to stop at the jeweler to get my watch fixed. When I was walking through the mall, all the department stores had signs and displays in the windows talking about Christmas sales. I thought 'How can they do that? We don't even know if we're going to be alive at Christmas.' And if we are, how can we ever celebrate anything again?"

"I don't know," answered Cross in a low voice. "I don't know."

It was shortly after eleven o'clock. Cross was driving east on Conklin Street, the main thoroughfare in Farmingdale. Anne Kelly, Kevin Finnerty, and John Sweeney were in the car as well. They were at least five blocks from St. Kilian's, but they had to stop. The Nassau police had put wooden barricades across the road. Large crowds of people were already lining the sidewalks on both sides of Conklin Street. A mammoth American flag was flying across the center of the street. The sergeant recognized the congressional plates on Cross's car and walked toward him. Cross lowered the window on the driver's side.

"Looks like you got some crowd already, Sarge," said Cross.

"Yeah, even bigger than we expected. But there's no problem at all. Everyone's quiet, very orderly."

"Everything on schedule?"

"Pretty much. The only delay might be if the mayor's a few minutes late. Right now he's still at the Feehan funeral in Queens," said the sergeant, referring to FDNY Deputy Commissioner Bill Feehan.

"It seems like Rudy's everywhere. He's really doing a helluva job."

"He sure is. I don't know where we'd be without him. He's holding the whole thing together."

The sergeant moved the barricade and told Cross he could leave his car in a reserved area about a block past the church. Cross thanked the sergeant and drove slowly along Conklin Street, angling the car into the designated spot east of the church.

"It's great that Rudy's going to be here today," said John, as they were getting out of the car. "I always thought Rudy was a terrific mayor, but for the past four days he's been absolutely heroic."

"Rudy certainly was the right man at the right time," answered Cross.

Cross had first met Rudy Giuliani more than thirty four years before in the summer of 1967, when they were law students interning at Richard Nixon's law firm on Wall Street. Each had just finished his second year of law school—Giuliani at New York University, Cross at Notre Dame. Giuliani was a serious student, an editor of the NYU law review; Cross was not as serious. Both were fixated on sports and politics—Giuliani a Yankee fan and Kennedy Democrat; Cross a Mets fan and Goldwater Republican.

There were twelve interns that summer. For no reason other than luck of the draw, Giuliani and Cross were assigned to work as a team. Also, since Giuliani lived in Bellmore and Cross had just moved to Seaford, which is only two LIRR stops past Bellmore, they ended up traveling back and forth to work together each day. Between the working and the traveling, they got to know each other fairly well—and for the most part they got along. Both were opinionated and too inclined to use cutting sarcasm as a weapon of first resort. But Cross felt that each had a respect for the other—certainly he admired Rudy's intellect and ability to think logically and argue articulately, though he did not admire the hair-trigger temper. They didn't see each other often in the subsequent years, but when they did were always cordial to one another.

Cross was not surprised when during the 1980s Giuliani attained national renown as a hard-driving federal prosecutor—

breaking the back of the mob in New York and carrying out high-profile investigations of big-name Wall Street financiers like Michael Milken and Ivan Boesky. Nor was he surprised by Rudy's prosecutorial excesses. That was part of the package.

It was the same when Rudy ran against David Dinkins for mayor of New York in 1993. The city had seemed to fall apart during the four years that Dinkins was in office. There were more than two thousand murders a year, race riots and harassment of Korean grocers in Brooklyn, and a general breakdown in the city's quality of life. Cross thought that if anyone had a chance of turning New York around, it was Rudy. At the same time, Cross didn't know if Giuliani had the temperament and patience to endure the inevitable delays, frustrations, and obstacles that are endemic to any municipal government but which permeate every nook and cranny of New York's political and governmental maze.

As it turned out, Rudy was a great mayor. He literally turned the city around and brought it back. Murders went down to less than seven hundred a year. Neighborhoods came alive. Times Square changed from a moral cesspool to a cultural and entertainment citadel. Revenues were up. Welfare was down. The budget ran surpluses. And the population increased by one million. Most importantly, perhaps, New York's quality of life had improved beyond all expectations. Graffiti, which had been everywhere—on the subway cars, garbage trucks, and building walls—was gone. The squeegee men, who would walk menacingly up to cars stopped at red lights, run a dirty wet rag or "squeegee" across the windshield, and then demand payment for their services, were gone as well. The streets were cleaner, and the subways safer.

Rudy, of course, was Rudy, and he did it his way—bruising egos and making enemies. But as far as Cross was concerned, Rudy had done what had to be done, as only he could do it. If political correctness was a casualty of the Giuliani crusade, so much the better. Still, when Giuliani was being mentioned in 1999 and 2000 as the Republican Senate candidate against Hillary Clinton, Cross let it be known he would consider taking

Rudy on. He did the radio talk-show and cable-television circuit, pointing to Giuliani's liberal stands on issues like abortion and reminding Republicans of Rudy's days as a Kennedy Democrat. All the while, however, Cross knew that if Giuliani wanted the nomination, it was his. Sean simply wanted to be available in the event lightning struck. At the end of the day, neither of them ran. Rudy was diagnosed with prostate cancer in April 2000, and Cross was passed over by New York's party leaders because of, among other things, his support of John McCain in the presidential primary and his staunch pro-life stand.

Cross and Giuliani had several chance encounters over the next twelve months—at Cardinal O'Connor's funeral in St. Patrick's Cathedral, at the Republican National Convention in Philadelphia, and at a Republican fund-raising lunch in Staten Island a month after the presidential election. Each time, Cross asked Giuliani how his health was and urged him to take care of himself. And each time, Giuliani said he was doing fine. Then in early May 2001, President Bush had a White House reception for the Yankees, who'd beaten the Mets in the 2000 World Series—the first "Subway Series" since 1956. Cross was a diehard Mets supporter, but he was attending as a lifelong New Yorker and baseball fan. Standing on the White House lawn, talking with Yankee manager Joe Torre and waiting for the president to come out from the Oval Office and begin the ceremony, Cross was suddenly tackled from behind. "Who the hell let you into a Yankee party?" the tackler demanded. Cross wondered who this madman was. He turned around and saw it was Giuliani.

"They needed a Mets fan here to give you guys some class," said Cross. "You look great. How're you feeling?"

"Actually, I couldn't be better. All the treatments are finished, and the doctors have given me a clean bill of health."

"That's terrific. I'm really happy for you."

"Make sure you get yourself tested."

"I told you before that I always do. I know how bad it can be. My father died from it."

"So did mine."

"I know."

"There's no reason why anyone should die from it any more. It's easy to detect and easy enough to get rid of."

"That's the truth."

"Listen, are you going to visit me in City Hall or Gracie Mansion? I've only get a few months left in my term."

"I'd love to."

"When you get a chance, give me a call, and we can work out the details."

"Thanks, Rudy."

It was the last week of July, and Cross was going over his schedule for August. Congress would be in recess the entire month of August and wouldn't be coming back into session until September 4th—just after Labor Day. Except for a four-day trip to Taiwan the last week in August, Cross would be in New York for the entire recess. Looking up from the schedule, he asked Tom O'Connell to call Giuliani's office and try to set something up. "When we were at the White House, Rudy was talking about getting together," said Cross. "Maybe it was just a weak moment, but give it a shot." Within the hour O'Connell told Cross, "There was no problem at all. Rudy's scheduler seemed to know all about it. You'll be having breakfast with him at Gracie Mansion on August 16th."

August 16th was a bright, beautiful summer day. Driving down York Avenue on Manhattan's Upper East Side, Cross turned left on 90th Street, which merged into East End Avenue, leading to the front gate of Gracie Mansion. Cross identified himself to the police officer manning the security booth at the gate. The cop obligingly told Cross he could put the car in the driveway, which was about thirty feet inside the gate and immediately adjacent to the mansion's main entrance.

Gracie Mansion overlooks the waters of Hell Gate, which is where the East River, the Harlem River, and Long Island Sound intersect. It was constructed at the very end of the eighteenth century by Archibald Gracie, a Scottish immigrant who'd amassed a fortune from a trading company he founded in New York. The mansion had gone through several owners until the city purchased it in 1896. During ensuing decades the mansion was utilized for such disparate public purposes as an ice cream parlor and as the home for the Museum of the City of New York. The mansion also went through alternating stages of neglect, repair, and renovation. Finally, in 1942, the city designated Gracie Mansion as the mayor's official residence. Fiorello LaGuardia moved into the mansion with his family, and each subsequent mayor followed suit. Increasingly, mayors also used the mansion for official functions and receptions. During the administrations of Mayor Wagner and Mayor Lindsay, a new wing was constructed that included three reception rooms decorated with antiques and reproduction furnishings. Mayor Koch established a conservancy to maintain and improve the mansion. This resulted in heating and electrical systems being replaced, whole sections of the structure being rebuilt, and works of art being displayed throughout the mansion. Gracie Mansion did indeed reflect New York's rich and unique heritage.

As Cross walked through the mansion's entranceway with Anne Kelly, he looked at the clock on the wall and saw that it was several minutes before nine o'clock. A female aide to the mayor welcomed Cross and said Giuliani would be arriving in about ten minutes. Like all mayors since La Guardia, Rudy had moved into Gracie Mansion with his wife, Donna Hanover, and their two children. But Rudy and Donna were going through a very public and tumultuous divorce, and for some time now he had been living with friends who had an upscale East Side apartment. He still used the mansion, however, for receptions and breakfast meetings, such as the one this morning.

Cross and Anne were standing in the room just inside the front door, sipping cups of coffee, when Rudy, accompanied by Joe Lhota, the deputy mayor, made his entrance.

"Sean, it's great to see you," exclaimed Rudy with a broad grin. "I'm glad you made it, but I'm sorry I'm late."

"You're not late at all," answered Cross. "It's not even ten after nine."

"So what do you think? Isn't this some place?"

"It really is."

"Come on, let me give you a quick tour in the back before we have breakfast."

Evincing an almost boyish pride and enthusiasm, Giuliani led the way through the mansion and out the back door. Outside, they walked the grounds—looking northeast toward the Triborough Bridge, eastward across the East River toward Queens, and then southerly toward the 59th Street Bridge, still packed tight with commuters braving the rush-hour crush to drive their cars from Queens to Manhattan. Squinting his eyes from the beaming rays of the morning sun, Giuliani said musingly: "This is an amazing city. There's nothing like it anywhere. The excitement, the challenges. There hasn't been a day since I became mayor that I didn't look forward to going to work." Cross nodded.

Walking back inside, they sat at the dining room table while the kitchen staff asked them how they wanted their eggs and whether they wanted ham, sausage, or bacon. Cross noticed how relaxed the staff—one woman and two men—was around Rudy. No sense of apprehension or air of tension. That meant a lot to Cross. Over the years he'd seen too many politicians in positions of power act like petty potentates, cruelly abusing those under them, almost reveling in their employees' discomfort and torment. The smiles and the bantering between Rudy and the staff indicated to Cross that no matter how demanding Rudy could be of his commissioners or how abusive he was to the media and political opponents, there was no reign of terror at Gracie Mansion.

Sipping from a glass of fresh orange juice, Cross asked Giuliani when he had first realized that he was actually succeeding in turning the city around. It had taken a couple of years,

Giuliani said, before he knew for sure. The numbers on crime and revenues and job growth had all been going in the right direction, almost from the start. But it wasn't until he sensed that the so-called permanent government—the civil service bureaucrats, the lobbyists, the contractors, the influence peddlers—truly understood that the game had changed that Rudy felt confident he was going to prevail. "If you didn't watch these guys all the time, they'd steal everything out from under you. They'd walk out of here with *this* and *this* and *this*," said Giuliani, pointing first to the silverware, then the salt shaker, and finally the sugar bowl. "These characters would have been terrific bank robbers."

Rudy was simultaneously wistful and defiant. He was already nostalgic about what he had attained and how far the city had come. He was also determined to keep a liberal from taking over City Hall and, in Rudy's eyes, taking New York back to its bad old days. Rudy didn't tip his hand as to how he intended to keep a liberal from office, but Cross felt certain he had a plan in mind.

Before Cross left, Rudy took him to a hallway alongside the kitchen and pointed out two photos taken at the identical location at Times Square—the big difference between the two being that one had been taken before Rudy took office, the other in this, the final year of his second term. The first was filled with sleaze and porno parlors, the second with family entertainment theaters and thriving restaurants. No contrast could have been more stark or vivid. Times Square was a metaphor for the rebirth of New York City. And as he shook hands with Rudy in the Gracie Mansion driveway that morning and thanked him for his friendship and hospitality, Cross knew that New York's rebirth would be Rudy's crowning legacy. What more could any New York City mayor hope to be remembered for? That had to be the ultimate. This was twenty-six days before September 11th ...

Today was September 15th. The fourth day of a very new world. Walking toward the front of St. Kilian's, Cross saw a large number of uniformed guys congregating near the church steps. They were greeting and talking with one another in somber tones. Cross recognized enough of them to realize they were retired firefighters. Grizzled veterans in their sixties and seventies who'd gotten back into their dress uniforms to pay respect to a fallen leader. Some of the uniforms might be a bit tight, but for the most part these guys were still in good shape.

"Hey, Jack, how're you doing?" asked Cross, as he shook hands with John O'Rourke, a Seaford neighbor and long-retired firefighter who'd been chief of the FDNY in the 1980s.

"I guess I'm doing as well as anyone could on a day like this," answered O'Rourke, who was wearing his chief's uniform. "Pete Ganci was really one of the best. A tough guy. A smart guy. He always knew what he was doing."

"He certainly showed guts on Tuesday."

"That was more than guts. He almost got killed when the South Tower came down. Then after he sent everyone else north, he went back down and got killed in the North Tower."

"It's like something you'd see in a movie."

"Except no one would believe it."

"Before Tuesday they wouldn't have. Since then you'd believe anything."

"Did you have a chance to get to the wake? He was laid out here on Main Street in the Farmingdale Fire House. He was a volunteer in that department."

"I was in Washington on Thursday and last night, to be honest with you, after I got back from Ground Zero, I probably could have made it but I just wanted to be with my family. Jack Kilbride, a city cop who's a friend of mine, went though and spoke to Pete's widow Kathy."

"She's a very strong woman."

"That's what Jack said."

"It's good that you're here today."

"Where else should I be?"

"You're right."

"There's a lot of retired guys here today."

"It's the same story. They felt they have to be here. Besides, I don't know how many active guys will be able to make it here. There's so many working at Ground Zero—not to mention the 343 who are dead. We wanted to make sure there was a good uniformed showing."

"One of the cops was telling me they couldn't even get a FDNY fire truck for today. They're all in use or were destroyed on Tuesday."

"They'll be using a Farmingdale truck."

"This is some turnout from the people," said Cross, looking back toward the blocks of ordinary citizens quietly assembled behind the police barricade.

"Pete deserves a good send-off."

"By the way, Jack, you're still able to fit into that uniform pretty well."

When Cross looked at his watch, it was ten minutes before noon. For blocks Conklin Street was bursting with people. A woman from the mayor's office approached Cross and said, "Congressman, we're asking the dignitaries and elected officials to line up across the street, directly across from the entrance. The cortege will be coming east along Conklin. We expect the mayor to be arriving in a few minutes."

Cross walked over to where the line was being formed. A number of local politicians, including Town Supervisor John Venditto and county legislator Sal Pontillo, were already in place. Also there were Peter Vallone, the Speaker of the New York City Council, and NYPD Deputy Commissioner Joe Dunne. They greeted one another in almost hushed tones and then stared ahead. A few minutes past noon the mayoral aide walked toward Cross and said almost in a whisper, "Congressman, the mayor will be arriving in about two or three minutes. If you come with me, we'd like you to greet him and then escort him back here."

The aide and Cross walked east on Conklin Street for about a block and a half and then waited for barely a minute. A motorcade of three Nassau County police cars and an unmarked black vehicle approached from the east. There were no lights or sirens. The cars came to a stop along the curb, and Giuliani stepped out from the back seat of the unmarked vehicle. Yesterday afternoon at Ground Zero Cross had spoken briefly with Giuliani. Maybe thirty seconds. Thirty seconds of controlled but intense rage. "Sean, they killed thousands of our people. Thousands of Americans. Right there. They're still burning," Giuliani had said, pointing toward the steaming rubble of what had been the Twin Towers. "We've got to get them. We've got to."

Today, as he walked toward Cross, Rudy seemed more subdued. Determined and strong but subdued.

"Must be some day for you," said Cross as he and Giuliani exchanged a firm handshake.

"Bill Feehan's funeral was very emotional. Very intense. So many people just loved the guy. And we'll be doing this for months."

"There's a tremendous crowd here."

"We'd better get going."

Giuliani and Cross stepped into the center of Conklin Street and started their walk toward the church. They'd taken just a few steps before people in the crowd began to notice Giuliani. Until that moment the assemblage had been still. Now people began to applaud. At first the applause was tentative. But almost immediately it began to swell and spread throughout the crowd for blocks westward along Conklin Street. Voices yelled *Rudy, Rudy,* and *USA.* Within seconds this clamor was almost deafening. Shouting to be heard, Cross exclaimed into Giuliani's ear: "They love you Rudy. You're keeping the country together." Giuliani said nothing but nodded appreciatively toward Cross and looked toward the crowd with a slight, self-conscious smile.

Arriving at the front of St. Kilian's, they took their places in the line of honor on the north side of the street. The crowd again fell silent. The midday sun was beating down brightly. Moments later the beat of muffled drums could be heard from the distance. This beat of drums grew louder and more intense. Cross turned his head slowly toward the right. It was the FDNY bagpipe band leading the funeral cortege. Several minutes later the band slowly made its way past the front of the church. It was followed by the engine from the Farmingdale Fire Department. Fastened tightly to the truck was Pete Ganci's coffin. Two firefighters stood on the rear of the truck as added assurance that the coffin would remain in place. The engine stopped in front of the church, just several feet from where Giuliani, Cross, and the other dignitaries were standing. Pulling up behind the fire truck were the black limousines carrying family members, including Ganci's widow, Kathy, and their three adult children. All of the family members, relatives, and friends who were in the procession got out of their cars and stood in silent formation as an FDNY honor guard unfastened the coffin, slowly lowered it from the back of the truck, and positioned it on their shoulders. The eight-man honor guard turned to face toward the church. Six priests were standing on the church steps. Fr. John Delendick, an FDNY chaplain, walked forward and blessed the coffin with holy water. The clergy then led the honor guard bearing the coffin, followed by the family and close friends, into the filled church. A firefighter escorted Giuliani, Cross, Vallone and the other officials through a door on the east side of the church and led them to reserved seats facing the side of the altar. Kathy Ganci and the Ganci family sat in the first row in the center of the church. Despite the personnel strain, the pews on the side of the altar opposite to where Cross was seated were packed tight with firefighters—active and retired. Loudspeakers transmitted the service to the thousands gathered outside on Conklin Street.

The funeral was moving. The eulogies by Giuliani and Tom Von Essen, the FDNY commissioner, were particularly eloquent and poignant. They focused on Pete Ganci the man—the firefighter who died with his men—and on the FDNY as the personification of America's strength and will. Rudy was eloquent, firmly in command, but speaking from the heart. Von Essen's eloquence was of a different sort—the eloquence of a former union leader so obviously devastated by the deaths of those he truly loved. Cross had known Von Essen from the days when Von Essen was first elected president of the UFA and Cross was starting in Congress. They both also attended St. Francis College in Brooklyn, though Von Essen graduated a few years after Cross. When Giuliani appointed Von Essen commissioner and he gave up his union presidency, it caused hard feelings among some of the rank and file, who felt Von Essen was selling out his members to be the boss. During his tenure, any controversial reform that Von Essen implemented was viewed by many firefighters as proof of his betrayal. Cross always thought the rap was unfair, but he knew how rough UFA politics could be. Von Essen always kept a stiff upper lip and insisted none of the attacks bothered him. But Cross was convinced they did. Today, as he spoke of Pete Ganci and the FDNY, Von Essen appeared wracked by pain and his voice almost broke several times. But he made it through to the end, fully earning the standing ovation he received.

As the mass was ending, the same FDNY escort officer who had led the dignitaries into the church came to take them out through the same door and line them up on the street. Exiting into the bright sunlight, Cross saw that the crowd was still there in full force. Walking alongside Giuliani, Cross said, "Rudy, I meant what I said before. Whether you know it or not, you've been keeping the country together. You've got to keep it up. The people need that." "Yeah, sure. Thanks," responded Giuliani, a blank expression on his face. *This guy is so caught up in what's going on he really doesn't know the impact he's having*, thought Cross. "Listen Rudy," said Cross, feigning exasperation, "even if you don't know what the hell you're doing, just keep doing it!" "Yeah, sure. Thanks, Sean."

The coffin was carried from the church to the strains of "God Bless America" and placed back on the engine, with the straps refastened to hold it secure. The pipe band played "America the Beautiful," an armed forces medley, and "God Bless America" again before leading the cortege westward from the church, again to the somber cadence of muffled drums.

As the crowd dispersed slowly, Cross spoke with a number of the firefighters, expressing his condolences for Pete Ganci and thanking them for all they were doing. Turning to greet a middle-aged Farmingdale couple he'd met at various veterans' functions over the years, Cross saw the mayor's aide walking toward him. "Congressman, the mayor's having a news conference on the side lawn, next to the church. He'd like you to join him." Cross excused himself and walked to the side lawn, which was just opposite the door they'd used to enter and exit the funeral.

Giuliani was standing in front of microphones for what appeared to be all of New York's television and radio stations, plus CNN and Fox. He was flanked by Peter Vallone, Tom Von Essen, and Richie Scheirer, the director of the city's emergency management office. Standing in front of them were about fifteen reporters—television, radio, and print. Usually they would be loud and jockeying for position. Today they were either silent or speaking in hushed tones. Cross walked onto the lawn and stood to Giuliani's left. Giuliani began the news conference by saying it had been his policy as mayor never to meet with the press at a funeral. He was making an exception today because he sensed that the reporters understood the solemnity of the occasion and would conduct themselves appropriately. *Ordinarily the reporters would take that remark as a patronizing insult and respond with sarcasm, invective, and abuse, which Rudy in turn would fire back at them,* thought Cross. *But today they're just nodding quietly.* Aside from paying tribute to Pete Ganci, Rudy had nothing to say that was particularly noteworthy. His main objective, as it had been for the past four days, was to assure New Yorkers that the city was working. That the mayor was in control. And that everyone should remain calm and confident. When he concluded, reporters asked a few perfunctory questions. Rudy answered the questions, again thanked the reporters for being so dignified, and began walking across the lawn to the waiting car. He and Cross shook hands. Cross said, "Rudy, remember, keep doing what you're doing." Giuliani smiled toward Cross and gave a slight wave as he got into the car.

11

It was early Monday morning. Sean Cross had just arrived at his district office in Massapequa Park and was looking through some mail on his desk when Peggy Moran, the recently hired receptionist, who was in her mid-twenties, told him, "There's a Lou Bianchi on the phone. He says you'll know who he is."

"Sure, put him through."

"Lou, how're you doing?" asked Cross. "I hope you're not calling to tell me I'm being arrested."

"Arrest you! I can hardly find you. I tried calling you in Washington, and they told me you'd be in New York for the week."

"There's a one-week recess."

"Another recess! Do you guys ever work?"

"Only when we have to. Anyway, what's up? I assume you've got some important things to do other than check on my work schedule."

"You're right. I'd like to get together with you in the next few days."

"It involves your job?"

"Yeah, I just got back from Hamburg, and I think you might be able to help on some people I heard about over there."

Lou Bianchi's "job" was deputy inspector in the NYPD's Counterterrorism Bureau, the elite unit that Commissioner Ray

Kelly had formed in response to the September 11th attacks. This anti-terror bureau comprised more than a thousand specially trained officers. It was global in reach—and, in many respects, superior to the FBI and CIA. Its primary task was to scrutinize reports of threats against the city. It wasn't unusual for the bureau to receive as many as fifty hotline terror tips a day. This unit also, of course, had to ensure the safety of the endless string of world leaders and dignitaries who visited New York. Most unique for a local police force, however, was the NYPD's decision to post anti-terror cops at overseas locations. The first postings were London, Lyon, Tel Aviv, and Hamburg. These were expanded to include Prague, Madrid, and Jakarta. So far the Counterterrorism Bureau was considered a success. But as the recent attacks in Brooklyn, the LIRR tunnel, and Westbury showed, a lot remained to be done.

Born and raised in Bensonhurst, Brooklyn, Lou Bianchi had been in the NYPD for thirty years, going on the job right after graduating from Notre Dame Law School, which he'd attended on a scholarship. He'd also served twenty-five years in the Army Reserves as an intelligence specialist, retiring as a lieutenant colonel. Bianchi moved up rapidly as a cop, making the dangerous arrests and breaking the tough cases. He was particularly successful going after big-time drug dealers and mafia bosses. Bianchi also had no problem with promotional exams—passing the sergeant, lieutenant and captain's tests on his first shot. No one was surprised when he was assigned to the new counterterrorism unit. Nor was anyone surprised that he was so hands-on—going on patrols, supervising the training, going head to head with the FBI and CIA, demanding more intelligence sharing, and visiting overseas posts. Last week he'd been in Hamburg meeting with his counterparts at Bundeskriminalamt, the German police agency.

Cross knew Germany was a hotbed of Islamic terrorism—particularly Al Qaeda. Mohammed Atta, the main September 11th hijacker, had lived in Hamburg for years, and the plot had been orchestrated from there. It was almost common knowledge that

Al Qaeda cells were still operating in Hamburg's Muslim immigrant community.

"I assume Hamburg was interesting," said Cross.

"That place is filled with terrorist activity," answered Bianchi.

"You think I might be able to help you?"

"Yeah. I'm aware of your contacts with Barfield and the Muslim doctor, and you might be able to fill in some blanks for me."

"Lou, anything I can do to help, I will. As far as I'm concerned, the NYPD has a better grasp of what's going on than anyone, including the feds. What day is good for you?"

"Any time in the next few days. Are you going to be in the city at all?"

"I'll be in Brooklyn tomorrow night. Danny and I are going to the Cyclones game in Coney Island. They're playing the Staten Island Yankees."

"That should work out fine. I'm still living in Bay Ridge—so I can get to Coney Island in no time. Plus no one should take any notice of us."

"Great. I'll call you tomorrow to work out the details."

The Belt Parkway traffic was surprisingly light the next day, and it was a few minutes before 6:30 as Cross approached the Ocean Parkway exit. He and Danny would be in their seats at KeySpan Park well before the game began at seven o'clock.

"I'm glad they moved the season up," said Danny. "It was crazy having to wait until the second half of June for opening day."

"That's the way it always was with Class A ball," answered Cross. "But it made more sense to start in April."

"You seem to get more out watching of these Class A players than you do from the major leaguers."

"Go easy on me. This brings me back to my youth. When I'm watching a ball game in Brooklyn, I feel like I'm back in Ebbets Field watching the Dodgers."

"It must be some long trip to go all the way back to *your* youth."

Bringing minor league baseball to Brooklyn and constructing a ballpark in Coney Island had been Rudy Giuliani's brainchild. Giuliani had arranged for the city to finance the building of KeySpan Park, and the Mets had provided a Class A, New York-Penn League team. This was the first time professional baseball had been back in Brooklyn since the Dodgers betrayed their roots and moved to Los Angeles in 1957. As a kid, Cross had lived and died with the Brooklyn Dodgers. He was part of that generation of New Yorkers who'd memorized every statistic about Brooklyn's fabled "Boys of Summer." He first realized how lousy life could be when he looked out his high school window at Brooklyn Prep and saw Ebbets Field being torn down. After Ebbets Field, Coney Island had been Brooklyn's most noted landmark. At one time—in the 1940s and mid-fifties—it was probably the most famous amusement park locale and beachfront in the world. Its prime symbols were the Cyclone roller coaster—hence the team name—and the giant parachute jump. Coney Island then endured decades of steady and unyielding decline. The crackdown on crime during the Giuliani years and the return of professional baseball reversed that decline.

KeySpan Park invoked Coney Island's nostalgic past. The Cyclone roller coaster was beyond the left-field wall. Out behind center field was the Wonder Wheel Amusement Park. Behind the right-field wall is the parachute jump—long in disuse but still majestic—and beyond that the boardwalk, the beach, and the ocean waves. Within the park the outfield walls were festooned with old-time billboardlike signs. Most importantly, the Cyclones had been a hit from day one, and their 7,500-seat ballpark filled to capacity game after game, season after season.

Ironically enough, the Cyclones had their own small bit of September 11th legacy. They had made their debut in the 2001 season and finished the regular season play with an outstanding 52-24 overall record and a .684 wining percentage. They had gone on to win the division title by beating the Staten Island Yankees and then had won the first game of the best-of-three league championship series. The next game, possibly the clincher, was scheduled for KeySpan Park the following night—September 11. The games, the series and the season were canceled—along with so much else of New York life . . .

"What time are you supposed to meet Lou Bianchi?" asked Danny, as they drove along Surf Avenue toward the parking area next to the park between 17th and 19th Streets.

"About nine o'clock, next to the ticket booth in the Wonder Wheel Amusement Park."

"I assume you're not going for a ride on the Ferris wheel."

"Don't be a wise ass. You know why I'm meeting him. He wants to talk about something he heard overseas."

"Aren't you worried that seeing the two of you together might tip some people off?"

"I suppose there's always a chance of things getting screwed up. But this is as good a venue as any. And it really is not unusual for us to get together. First of all, we both went to Notre Dame, and we've gone to ball games and fights over the years. He lives in Brooklyn, and I'm a Cyclones fan. Besides with all the noise and confusion from the rides and the people on the boardwalk, no one will be able to make out anything we're saying."

"I agree with you there. I can never understand what you're talking about."

Cross and Danny entered the park and found their seats on the first-base side of the field, six rows behind the Cyclones' dugout. They were in time to see the last few minutes of batting practice. The sky was darkening, but the field was brilliantly illuminated by the circular lights atop posts surrounding the perimeter of the park. And, no surprise, by the time the first pitch was thrown, there wasn't an empty seat anywhere. The Cyclones scored two runs in the bottom of the first and kept hitting as the game went along. In the bottom of the sixth inning, as Cross and Danny were each finishing a Nathan's hot dog and a beer, the Cyclones pushed across two more runs, extending their lead to 9-1. The clock on the giant scoreboard behind the left-field wall read 8:52. "We'll head out at the end of the inning," said Cross in a low but casual tone.

Exiting the ballpark, Cross and Danny turned left, walking parallel to the first-base line and toward the boardwalk beyond the right-field bleachers. Stepping onto the boardwalk, Cross was greeted with a burst of ocean breeze, causing him to zip the front of the blue and tan cloth jacket, which had been given to him by Local 338 of the grocery handlers' union. Walking east along the boardwalk—the ballpark on their left, the beach and the ocean on their right—Cross and Danny breathed in the cool sea air.

"It really is a beautiful night," said Cross.

"And you're here to talk about people who are trying to burn us all to death or blow us to pieces," responded Danny. "What a fucking world!"

In deepest right center field the outfield wall angled toward center field and away from the boardwalk, leaving open an area spacious enough to accommodate the Wonder Wheel Amusement Park, with its array of rides and games—including a 150-foot-high Ferris wheel and a roller coaster. An opening from the boardwalk led directly into the amusement park, with its garish bright lights and amplified carnival music. Off to the right was the ticket booth, which, in keeping with the motif, was thoroughly encircled with flashing orange lights. Just to the side of the booth was Lou Bianchi, wearing a Bay Ridge Bombers sweatshirt and puffing on a cigar. Protruding from his right rear pants pocket was what appeared to be a racing form.

"Hey Lou, how've you been? Waiting long?" asked Cross.

"No. I got here about five minutes ago. I enjoy watching the kids, seeing all the excitement, and hearing all the screaming and laughing on the rides, especially the roller coaster."

"Those things always scared the living shit out of me when I was a kid."

"Me too—but we've got more than that to worry about these days."

"You'll never fucking change. You don't take long to get to the point."

"There's a lot to talk about. Why don't you and I just stroll along the boardwalk? Danny can stay back and screw around with the video games until we're done."

"Don't worry about me. I'll be here when you're finished," said Danny. "I'm used to looking busy when I'm doing nothing. I had the perfect role model."

"This guy's onto you," said Bianchi with a grin, before turning serious again. "I don't expect any problems, but I've got backup just in case," nodding almost imperceptibly toward a homeless-looking guy sitting on a boardwalk bench just outside the amusement park and then in the direction of a very attractive blond in tight jeans and sweater leaning against the boardwalk railing and looking as if she was anxious for some guy to pick her up. "They're ready if any shit develops."

Danny gave a smile and ambled toward the video games, while Cross and Bianchi strolled very casually back onto the boardwalk, walking eastward.

"I hear that you're in regular contact with Tommy Barfield," said Bianchi.

"He really seems to have good contacts," answered Cross.

"You picked the right guy."

"I'm not trying to play amateur cop or fuck things up for the pros."

"Keep doing what you're doing. All I'd be worried about is some congressman or senator who thinks he's Dick Tracy or James Bond or tries to get cheap headlines by holding Sunday news conferences announcing some big 'disclosure.'"

"The old Sunday for Monday routine."

"What you're doing is fine. There's people you can reach that we could never get to."

"Like?"

"That Muslim doctor—Doctor Ahmed—and any of your Irish friends who might be connected with Fiona Larkin. Anything you get from them could be very helpful to us."

"Are you focusing on Ahmed?"

"Not him directly. But we think he might know something about Khalid Mustafa and what he's been up to."

"He's the explosives guy who works at the furniture store in Brooklyn."

"Right. But he lives out in New Hyde Park and he hangs out with people in Ahmed's mosque . . ."

"The North Shore Islamic Center."

"Yeah."

"But you don't think Ahmed's involved?"

"Nothing that we've come across leads to that. But we think he knows things that can help us—things that he probably doesn't realize the importance of."

"And the micks?"

"You're one of the only people I know of who's actually dealt with those people and not been indicted."

"Thanks for the vote of confidence. There's enough fucking mafia goons from your people who are no bargains either," said Cross, with a knowing smile.

"There's no such thing as the mafia," answered Bianchi with a loud laugh.

"So long as we understand each other!" replied Cross, faking a right cross at Bianchi's left shoulder.

"Ahmed and Larkin tie into what you learned in Hamburg?"

"Yeah. There's a lot of 'noise' out there. Even more than before September 11th. We're scared shitless that they're planning another spectacular—something much more than last month's attacks."

"And they were pretty bad."

"They certainly were."

"But the next attack—or attacks—could be worse. A lot fucking worse."

"What can you tell me about what you're picking up?"

"The problem is, we're picking up too much. First we have to decipher it, and then we have to try to figure out what's real and what's not. They're masters of disinformation."

"I assume you've narrowed it down somewhat."

"We have—which is why I wanted to talk to you. We're almost certain there's an Irish link, which would have to be Fiona Larkin. The Real IRA."

"How are you so definite about that?"

"We're picking up constant noise from Indonesia which is where Bajal is . . ."

"Fiona's boyfriend."

"Right. Also, the word 'clover' is appearing, and that was never used before."

"Clover?"

"As in four-leaf clover. Like a shamrock."

"A shamrock has three leaves. Like the Blessed Trinity. Didn't you Italian guys learn that? Or don't you believe in St. Patrick?"

"I believe you're a thick mick. Do you really think some Muslim terrorist transmitting signals from some cave really cares whether there's three leaves or four leaves on a shamrock?"

"I just thought you might be reaching."

"If we are, all the Brits—including MI5, MI6, and Scotland Yard—agree with us. So does the Irish Special Branch."

"Okay. You've got me outnumbered. What are you expecting the Real IRA guys to do?"

"Our best guess is that they'll be a smaller part of a larger operation. Smaller but still very deadly."

"Like what?"

"Car bombs. Some of those guys in the Bronx have been retired for years, but they could still put together some pretty lethal bombs."

"And Al Qaeda assumes we aren't paying any attention to the Irish."

"Exactly."

"But you think this would be the 'smaller' part of the attack?"

"Everything is relative. And conventional car bombs—even if they are detonated in a tunnel or on a bridge or in the heart of the financial district—will only kill or injure people in the immediate area."

"That could be a lot of people."

"Yeah—but a nuclear attack could kill tens of thousands."

"Nuclear?"

"That's right—or a 'dirty bomb,' a combination of standard explosives and radioactive materials. The German cops—the Bundeskriminalamt—are convinced Al Qaeda's coming after us with a conventional nuke or a dirty bomb."

"In that case the car bombs would be just a deadly sideshow."

"Very deadly—but not the main attraction."

"And the Irish know nothing about nukes."

"Zero. But remember we're still talking about the potential loss of hundreds—maybe thousands—of lives just from the conventional weapons."

"When I met with Barfield and Frank Hennessy, I told them I didn't think Irish guys would go ahead with this if they knew it was going to kill Americans."

"I basically agree with you. The micks could put the car bomb together and, without the Irish even knowing about it, the Muslims could take it from there. But that's still no fucking excuse. Even if they think it's going to be used against some British facility in the United States, they can't be involved in bomb making or any type of terrorism over here."

"Ever since the Good Friday Agreement there's no excuse for any paramilitary or terrorist attacks against the Brits anywhere."

"This could be sensitive, and we don't want to tip our hand at all—and I know Hennessy has also spoken to you about this—but I can't tell you how helpful it would be if we can get a pipeline into what they're planning. Get some idea of what Larkin told them."

"I understand completely what you mean about not tipping them off. But I do think there's one guy I can go to. He's well connected, and I've always found him to be totally straight with me."

"I'll leave that to you. I only ask that you stay in touch with me at every step so we'll be ready in case this does go the wrong way."

"Good enough. What about Ahmed?"

"That's the nuclear part. Without going into all the details, the Germans are certain that Al Qaeda has the capacity and is actively planning some sort of nuclear attack—probably a dirty bomb."

"And they think Mustafa's involved?"

"He's a top suspect. The guy who's masterminding it is supposed to be Ali Shibh, who has been in and out of Hamburg over the past five years. His nickname is 'the scientist.' The connection to Mustafa is that the two of them fought side by side against the Russians in Afghanistan. Apparently Shibh saved Mustafa's life, and they formed a lifetime bond. But apart from the personal tie, what they really share is an absolute fucking hatred of the United States. And there's strong evidence that they've stayed in close contact over the years."

"Any idea where the attack would be?"

"We think it would be by ship at one of our ports."

"And New York is the main target?"

"We don't know for sure. Christ, we've got ports everywhere. Philadelphia, Baltimore, Florida, the West Coast—everywhere. But my concern is New York—and let's face it, we always seem to be the one they come after."

"I'm no expert on this, but isn't stopping one of these attacks like finding a needle in a haystack?"

"It's probably tougher even than that. More than six million containers come into this country by ship every year—and nearly two million of them come into the Port of New York. The bottom line is we can't examine every container, and, even if we could, we haven't entirely perfected the technology to detect radioactive devices buried in these containers."

"And the damage could be extensive."

"A dirty bomb would be bad enough. But an actual nuclear bomb—which these guys could be capable of assembling—would be much more. Remember, ports are particularly vulnerable. They're flat, because they're right at the water's edge, so there's almost no shield against the materials spreading. Or for added psychological effect, they could detonate it when they're passing under something like the Verrazano Bridge and kill thousands of people in cars and trucks."

"What are you doing about it?"

"The only guaranteed protection is to intercept it before it ever leaves the overseas port. And we're really getting good cooperation—especially from the Germans."

"The Germans! I thought they spent all their time bad-mouthing the war-mongering Americans."

"That's all for public consumption. Believe me, their security people are absolutely petrified of Al Qaeda, and they know we're the only ones who can really stop them. They know they need us."

"They certainly have a funny way of showing it."

"What can I tell you? At least they're not as bad as the French."

"Thank God for small blessings."

"But no matter how much they help us, there's nothing as good as a tip or a lead."

"And that's what you're looking for from Ahmed?"

"That's what we're hoping for. We know that Ahmed has some personal contact with Mustafa. They're not close friends or anything, but they see each other at different events and functions, especially religious services. So it's very possible that Ahmed could tell you something he's heard from Mustafa that means nothing to him and wouldn't mean anything to you either—but could be a piece in our puzzle."

"Suppose Ahmed tells Mustafa that I'm asking about him?"

"Obviously, it would be better if Ahmed tells Mustafa nothing. But even if he did, it probably wouldn't be that damaging, because Mustafa knows that's he's on our radar screen. He knows that we know he's out there. He's just confident we'll never be able to pin anything on him."

"I'm actually supposed to meet with Ahmed next week."

"I knew that you reached out to him."

"Right after last month's attacks I told him that his community had to be more supportive—more cooperative. That they couldn't cover up for their own."

"How did he take it?"

"He actually seemed to be taken aback. But he told me he'd talk to some of the local Muslim leaders and let me know what they said. Anyway he called yesterday and said he'd like to 'talk over some things' with me. So we're on for next week."

"If you can give me anything at all, it would be a great help."

"What do you think? Do you expect him to be at all cooperative?"

"If I had to bet, I'd say he wants to help but is really torn."

"What do you mean?"

"I mean that if he actually knew for certain who planned or carried out the attacks, he'd give you their names. It would hurt him to give up one of his own, but he'd do it, because it would be so black and white. What he's afraid of is the information that's in the gray area—information on guys who might turn out to be strong fundamentalists, very anti-India or anti-Israeli, but not supporting bin Laden or Al Qaeda. He gives you the information; you turn it over to the FBI; the FBI checks the guy out; he comes up clean on Al Qaeda but gets deported because of some visa violation or gets harassed by the feds and he loses his business."

"How does that hit you?"

"I don't buy it. In ordinary times I'm as suspicious of government as anyone. Be we don't have the luxury any more of being 100 percent civil libertarians. I'm more worried about bin Laden than I am about the FBI. If it's a choice between some guy who's an illegal alien being deported or New York City being blown to pieces, I say fuck the alien."

"Sean, I agree with you completely. I don't accept their reasoning at all. We have to weigh the equities, and since 9/11 security trumps just about everything else. But you've got to remember that most Muslims coming to this country have had no experience with real democracy. They're not used to cooperating with the government."

"Even before September 11th that was a major problem with American Muslims—trying to convince them to get involved in politics, to become part of the system the way Indians have."

"With all its faults, India is the world's largest democracy."

"And the Indian community over here is very involved in our politics, which is one of the main reasons they've had far more influence in Congress with issues like Kashmir than the Pakistanis."

"Also, a lot of American Muslims automatically identify the government with a police state. We think government abuses are the exception; they think they're the rule."

"Don't we have the same problem with the Russians?"

"You have no idea what a fucking pain in the ass they are. There's a load of Russian immigrants right here in Coney Island. They get robbed, shot at—it doesn't matter. They just refuse to cooperate with the cops. The Sixtieth Precinct here has tried everything—handing out brochures that are printed in Russian; sending a command-post bus, a precinct on wheels, right into the streets of the neighborhood; meeting with local business and community leaders. Nothing works. The bottom line is that—based on their experience in Russia—they're convinced that once you walk into a station house, you never walk out."

"I've always been big for immigration, but we've got to find a way to convince these new immigrants that if they want to live here, they have to live like Americans, they have to assimilate at least part of the way."

"That's going to be a real challenge, especially with all the political correctness bullshit we have to put up with."

"Overall, how do you think your anti-terror unit is doing?"

"*Overall,* it's going great. We have a lot of resources; we're really moving well; and then we get hit like we did last month, and it's a real bitch, a real fucking downer."

"I suppose so long as any of those fuckers are alive, we have to expect shit like that to happen."

"You're right. We can set up the best defense in the world, and even then we have to hope for the best. The only way we can guarantee security is to kill them all before they get here."

"But you're satisfied the unit is doing as well as it can?"

"You can never be satisfied, but, yeah, I think we're doing a good job. The commissioner has brought in some top guys from the CIA and military intelligence, and we've assembled the best cops we can find. It's a terrific combination of guys with intel experience and tough street smarts. To be honest, when things are going along smoothly, this assignment is a cop's dream. It's everything a cop could ever hope to do. But when it goes bad, like last month, it's a fucking nightmare. You can drive yourself crazy thinking about the signals we might have missed or something we should have done to head it off."

"You can't be Superman. This is a tough fucking war, and we're not going to win every battle."

"But we will win the fucking war."

By now they had turned around and were coming back westerly along the boardwalk, toward the amusement park. Ahead of them, in the distance, beyond Brooklyn, was a clear view of the majestically lit New York skyline, shining brightly in the dark spring night.

"You know, for years I looked at that skyline," said Bianchi, "and never paid any attention to the Twin Towers."

"I was the same. To me the skyline was always the Empire State Building and the Chrysler Building. The Twin Towers were just there."

"Now they're not there. And when I look at the skyline all I see is where they should be. There's just that fucking void."

Cross nodded in silent agreement. After a long somber moment, he decided to change the tone.

"Isn't there something screwed up about an anti-terrorism cop wearing a shirt that says 'Bay Ridge Bombers'"? asked Cross.

"There probably is, and I'm probably screwed up," answered Bianchi smilingly. "Actually, it's a weekend softball team I've been playing on for twenty years. But yeah, I do appreciate the irony."

"I guess we have to try to keep some sense of humor, or we'll go nuts."

"If we haven't already," replied Bianchi with a loud laugh.

They were at the entrance to the amusement park. Cross noticed that the "homeless" cop was still there but had switched benches. Glancing over his shoulder, he saw the good-looking blonde strolling seductively about forty feet behind them and realized she must have been covering them the whole time.

"You guys are laughing so much, I assume you've solved everything," said Danny, walking casually toward them.

"It's either laugh or cry," answered Bianchi.

Sunday, September 16–
Wednesday, September 19, 2001

It was 11:30 on Sunday morning when Sean Cross walked into the Seaford Bagel Shop on the corner of Merrick Road and Washington Avenue. The line of customers extended through the store and almost onto the street. The few who were talking did so in hushed tones. Most seemed alone with their thoughts. Several, however, nodded toward Cross as he worked his way toward the back of the line. He had just dropped Mary Rose, Kara, and John at the house after attending a very unsatisfying 10:15 mass where the priest exhorted the congregants to examine their own consciences rather then hate the September 11th murderers. It had taken all the family members' powers of persuasion to convince Kara not to storm the rectory and confront the priest after Mass. Cross was at the shop this morning to buy a few dozen bagels to bring with him to Jimmy Boyle's house.

Cross had stopped by Jimmy's yesterday afternoon, after Pete Ganci's funeral. He had gone alone and felt apprehensive as he approached the front door of Jimmy's Westbury home. But there was no need for concern. Before Cross could even knock, a white-haired, middle-aged guy Sean recognized as a retired firefighter from Jimmy's union days opened the door, shook his hand, and shouted into the house, "Hey Jimmy, your friend the congressman is here." Stepping into the living room, Cross saw that besides Jimmy's immediate family—his wife, two daughters, and two sons—the home was overflowing with friends, neighbors, and retired firemen. From the kitchen came the unmistakable voice of Jimmy Boyle shouting back, "Congressman Cross himself! What an honor! Either that or he thinks there's a television camera around!" Seconds later Jimmy emerged though the crowd of bodies and faces wearing a broad smile and extending his right hand.

"Hey, Sean, it's great of you to come. How was Ganci's funeral?"

"There was a tremendous turnout. The streets were filled. And Rudy was good."

"Yeah, he's doing a terrific job. I wanted to go to Ganci's funeral, but I went to Father Judge's in the city at St. Francis."

"Father Judge was a good guy. How was it?"

"Very moving. Also a big turnout. I was talking to David Dinkins and then after the mass I was introduced to Hillary Clinton."

"I was on a television show with Dinkins the other day. He's really supporting the president."

"He was very friendly to me, asking about Michael. Hillary was good also."

Cross hesitated for a moment before asking, "Any word on Michael?"

"No," said Jimmy, walking Cross toward the corner of the room before continuing in a low voice. "There's no chance. I know that. Anyone they didn't find the first day is gone. But some people in the family still have hope, so I'm not saying anything."

"Jimmy, I'm really sorry about this."

"I know you are," said Jimmy quietly before reversing emotional direction and announcing in a loud, almost boisterous tone, "Here's our good congressman who was barely able to make it through his speech in the House the other day talking about Michael. I have the video if anyone wants to look at it. Can you imagine this guy?—all those years as a congressman and he still can't give a speech without stumbling. He's been out of Sunnyside for too long."

Looking on in quiet bemusement as Jimmy went through his routine, Cross thought *this guy just won't let you feel sorry for him . . .*

There were about ten workers—mostly high school kids—laboring feverishly behind the bagel shop counter, taking orders and moving customers along. Cross was waiting for only a few minutes before a cute, brown-haired girl—probably sixteen or seventeen years old—asked, "What can I get you?" "Three dozen bagels. Mix them up any way you want," answered Cross, walking toward the cash register and taking out his wallet. Almost two minutes later the girl approached him, carrying an enormous shopping bag, filled to the top with bagels.

"You're the congressman, aren't you?" the girl asked.

"Yeah," Cross replied. "I am."

"The manager says there's no charge for you, and thanks for what you are doing."

"There's no need for . . ."

"The manager says there's *no charge*," the girl interrupted, her young voice registering an adult tone of finality. "He says if you want this many bagels, you must be giving them to someone who needs them."

"Then let me give you a tip," replied Cross, attempting to hand her a five-dollar bill.

"Give it to a charity," she said with even more finality. "They need it more than I do."

"Thank you very much," said Cross with a smile.

As Cross walked from the store, a customer he'd never seen before said, "Keep up the good job. We need you."

Cross drove to his house and picked up Mary Rose, Kara, and John for the ride to Jimmy's house. On the way he told them about the bagel shop—the almost solemn silence of the customers, the generosity of the owner, and the thoughtful expression of support.

"What do you make of all that?" asked Kara.

"It certainly can't be because they like you," said John, wearing a broad grin.

"Thanks for being a comedian," answered Cross, also with a smile. "Actually I think it shows that the country is trying to get its bearings. There were more people there this morning than usual—which most likely means that more people are staying at home with their families, sitting down and eating with them instead of running off to the golf course or the mall. As for being quiet, that could be for a number of reasons. They could be sad or in a state of shock—or they could be worried that the guy next to them in line lost someone at the Trade Center."

"How about how they reacted to you?"

"For once I have to agree with John. I don't think it had very much to do with me at all. The people want the security of a strong government defending them against more attacks. They like the way Bush has responded. And since I'm the guy from Seaford who's in Washington, they identify me with what the president is trying to do."

"I also think the television shows you've been on have been a help," said Mary Rose. "People want to see that you're doing something—not just waiting for bin Laden to hit us again."

"You're probably right," answered Cross. "Several people in the parking lot after Mass said they saw me on the news with Rudy at Ganci's funeral."

"I was still so mad at the priest, I didn't hear what anyone said in the parking lot," said Kara.

The mood at Jimmy's house was pretty much the same as yesterday. Rooms filled to the brim with family, firemen and friends. Tables of cold cuts and coolers of beer and soda. And Jimmy holding court, doing all he could to keep everyone in good spirits at the same time that rescue workers were poring through tons of burning debris looking to find his dead son's remains.

Seeing them come in the front door, Jimmy walked hurriedly to embrace Mary Rose and Kara and give John a hearty handshake. Gesturing toward Sean, who was holding the large bag of bagels in his arms, Jimmy exclaimed, "Don't tell me this cheap bastard actually sprung for a few bucks! He must have robbed a bakery truck." Jimmy then proceeded to berate Sean once again for the speech he had given mentioning Michael.

"Kara, your father could barely talk. He was lucky he finished the speech. I've got a video right here anytime you want to look at it."

"Jimmy, I've seen and heard enough of my father's speeches to know how bad he can be," answered Kara, joining in with the joke. "I don't have to see him on a video!"

"Even your own daughter's onto you," laughed Jimmy, slapping Sean on the back. "Let me get you a beer. You look like you need one."

As they walked toward the kitchen, Jimmy turned toward Sean saying, "Thanks for that speech about Michael. It really meant a lot to us."

That afternoon Kara and John decided things had calmed down enough for them to return to their apartment in Forest Hills. Sean and Mary Rose drove to Jones Beach to take a walk on the boardwalk. The conditions were perfect—a mild breeze and a clear sky. Like at the bagel shop, the people on the boardwalk seemed more quiet and remote than usual. Also like at the bagel shop, some of the walkers slowed down long enough to wish Cross well. Then there was the young couple—both probably in their early thirties—who had something else to think about. They stopped and shook hands with Sean and Mary Rose.

"We're from north Seaford," he said.

"Thanks for saying hello," answered Cross.

"I'm a good friend of Charlie Milone," he said, referring to the Seaford Republican leader.

"Charlie's a good friend of mine also."

"How are things in Washington?"

"We're doing okay. The president's determined to get the job done. How are you doing?" asked Cross, more to be polite than anything else.

"I'm in the Naval Reserves. I just got notified this morning that I'm being activated."

"When do you have to report?" asked Cross, who'd not expected the conversation to take this turn.

"Wednesday. They gave us seventy-two hours."

"That's rough. Can you get everything organized by then?"

"I hope so," he said with a laugh.

"What choice do we have?" said his wife. "That's the deal he signed up for. You have to do what you have to do."

"You have a good attitude," said Cross. "We need people like you. Don't be afraid to call my office if you need any help."

"You just keep doing the great job you do in Washington," he said.

"Believe me, your job is a lot harder than mine," replied Cross as he shook hands with them and wished them well.

"Good luck," said Mary Rose.

Cross went to his district office in Massapequa Park on Monday morning. No decision had been made yet when Congress would come back into session. This was his first day in the district office since last Tuesday's attacks. Phone calls were coming in at a steady pace. Relatives of World Trade Center victims who were dead or missing and presumed dead needed information. Information most of them had thought they wouldn't be needing for another twenty, thirty or forty years. Information about death certificates, death benefits, funeral allotments, numbers to call to identify remains. Some of the callers were emotional and distraught. Others were numb, sounding almost zombielike. And some were petrified of this strange and lonely world into which they had been thrown without forewarning or preparation. Each staff member was taking the facts and details and either giving immediate advice or promising to get back to the caller with it. Anne Kelly, who was running the operation, made sure each caller was treated with patience and concern. Extra copies of all telephone messages were prepared for Cross's personal attention.

Besides the families of victims, there were the calls from ordinary constituents—good, decent Americans who wanted revenge against bin Laden, Afghanistan, and anyone else who stood in our way. Cross told the staff people to assure these callers that President Bush would absolutely take whatever military action had to be taken. Reading through the reports of these phone messages, Cross saw that, so far at least, no anger was being addressed toward Bush. No one was blaming him for what happened or implying that he wouldn't retaliate appropriately. And while there were some anti-immigrant calls, very few were anti-Muslim. If the people Cross had seen and met over the weekend and these phone calls were any barometer, the country was holding together pretty well.

Besides wading through the hundreds of phone messages, Cross seemed to be on the phone with Tom O'Connell and Kevin Finnerty in Washington almost continuously throughout the day, checking out rumors and trying to determine what Congress's schedule would be and how Cross would coordinate that with what he had to do in New York. As to the rumors, there was growing speculation that the president would be addressing a joint session of Congress—but that speculation was still unconfirmed, and no date was being proposed if he did decide to give the speech. It was definite, though, that Congress would be back in session the next Thursday morning, September 20th. Denny Hastert felt strongly that the country must see the government functioning as normally as possible, as quickly as possible. Cross agreed completely, but there was already a scheduling conflict. There would be a memorial service in Huntington that morning for Farrell Lynch, who'd worked with Tom Barfield. Farrell's brother Sean—who worked with him—had also been killed, and Cross felt he must attend the memorial service. This meant the earliest he could get to

Washington would be very late Thursday afternoon, since planes still weren't flying to Washington, and he would have to make train connections—the LIRR from Huntington to Penn Station and then Amtrak to Union Station—that would take at least four or five hours.

"You really feel you have to go to the service?" asked O'Connell. "The Speaker wants as many members back for the first vote that morning as possible."

"I understand where Denny's coming from, and I agree with him, but I really do think I should be at the service. I met Farrell through Tom Barfield, but I've known his mother and father for years. And for them to lose Sean and Farrell together—nothing could be worse than losing two sons."

"Weren't the mother and father active on the Irish issue?"

"They really were—back in the days when it wasn't very popular. And they always supported me—even before I went to Congress."

"No remains have been found?"

"No. Not for Farrell or Sean. That's why it's a memorial service and not a funeral."

"You just do what you have to do. I'm sure Denny will understand."

"Let's not beat this fucking thing to death. The United States Congress can survive without me for a few hours."

It was about 7:30 on Monday morning evening when Cross and Mary Rose got out of his car, which he had parked behind the bank directly across from Schmitt's Funeral Home in Seaford. The line of mourners was already out the door of the funeral home onto Merrick Road and back up Seamans Neck Road. The wake was for Tim Haskell, a New York City firefighter from Squad 19, who had been killed when the first tower collapsed. His remains had been found, but his coffin would be closed. By all accounts Timmy Haskell had been an outstanding firefighter and had had a great career and a full life ahead of him—until he was murdered on September 11th at the age of thirty-four. In ordinary times it would be difficult to imagine a family enduring a worse tragedy. But for the country—and for the Haskell family in particular—these were no ordinary times. Timmy's brother, Tom, an FDNY captain, had also been murdered at the World Trade Center on September 11th. He was thirty-seven years old. His remains had not yet been found.

Cross did not know the Haskell family personally. But he knew of them. There had been four sons and a daughter, they had all attended Seaford High School, and several had overlapped with Danny and Kara. They were outstanding athletes and were well known in the Seaford community. As they crossed Seamans Neck Road to take their place on the line, Mary Rose said, "Sean, I don't know how any mother could bear to lose two sons. I just can't imagine it." Just then a firefighter who'd been assigned to monitor the line walked up to Cross and said, "Congressman, thank you very much for coming. Let me take you and your wife inside."

Inside the funeral parlor the firefighter handed Cross and Mary Rose off to the funeral director, who led them to the front row of chairs directly in front of the closed coffin and introduced them to Timmy's mother, Maureen, and sister, Dawn. Sean and Mary Rose expressed their regrets, and the mother and sister thanked them for coming. Cross and Mary Rose then knelt in front of the coffin and said some silent prayers. As they got up, the director took them over to meet other family members standing off to the side of the very crowded room. There were two surviving brothers—Kenny, who was also a firefighter, and Kevin. There were cousins, including Frank, who was a firefighter as well. After Sean expressed his condolences and the brothers and cousins expressed their appreciation for his being there, Frank said, "Congressman, would you mind talking to a few of us in the back?" Cross looked in the direction where Frank had nodded and saw a group of firemen huddled in grief. "Sure," answered Cross and walked toward the rear of the room while Mary Rose remained up front to talk with the mother and sister. Cross shook hands with each of the firemen. They were cordial, but he could tell they had something to say.

"Congressman, are we going to do something this time, or is it going to be the same old story?" asked one fireman.

"Too many people died last week for us to sit around and do nothing like we usually do," said another.

Cross saw the other firemen nodding their heads in approval. He waited for a moment and then tried to reassure them that the president would follow through.

"Believe me, I understand what you're saying and why you're saying it. You lost a lot of guys. A lot of great guys. And I agree with you that we've put up with too much for the last few years. But I can't stress to you how strongly the president feels about this. I guarantee he's going to . . ."

"Excuse me, Congressman," interrupted another firemen, "it's not the president we're worried about. We love Bush. We know he wants to do the right thing and bomb the living shit out of those bastards. It's Congress we're worried about. And the media and the UN."

Before Cross could respond, at least four or five firemen joined in. "Bush is the best." "That guy is great." "Bush was down at Ground Zero. He knows the story." "Tell the president we're with him." "And tell the other congressmen the people support the president."

"Don't worry," said Cross, "I'll be sure to let the president know how you feel. I know it will mean a lot to him."

"Thanks for listening to us," said Ken Haskell, the firefighter's brother. "We can be a tough crew."

"No problem. As far as I'm concerned, I got off easy."

After they had shaken hands again and Cross began to walk toward the front to find Mary Rose, another Haskell cousin came over to Cross, handed him a letter, and said "Congressman, it really means a lot to our family that you were here tonight. When you get a moment, please take a look at this letter and, if you can, pass it on to President Bush. We think he's a great man." Cross thanked him and assured him he'd read the letter and give it to the president.

About twenty minutes later Cross and Mary Rose were at home, sitting at the dining room table, reading the letter addressed to the president. "On September 11th of 2001 when the tragedy of the day began to unfold, four members of my family—all New York City Firefighters—raced to the aid of victims of the World Trade Center disaster. Two have not returned. . . . Just like my country and my state, the face of my family has changed forever. . . .

"I would like to take this time to wish you God's blessing in this most difficult time. We trust your strength, your leadership and your wisdom in this crisis. We know that you will take the correct actions at the appropriate times. Our prayers are with you. God Bless you and God Bless America."

As Cross folded the letter and placed it back in the envelope, he said, "This letter and what those firemen told me tonight really says it all. The people in this country who've suffered the most support Bush. And they trust him. These are the people he has to have with him if we're going to win this war."

It was Tuesday morning. Exactly one week since the September 11th attacks. These attacks and America's response were still the only news stories being covered. Cross had barely gotten to his district office when Kevin Finnerty was on the phone from Washington with a list of press calls from television shows that wanted Cross that day. The first would be at Channel 12 in nearby Woodbury at twelve noon. The last would be at Channel 11 in the old Daily News Building down the street from Grand Central Station in Manhattan at 10:20 that evening—with four others in between. Cross said yes. Not only for any good it might do but because it gave him the opportunity to do something—to work the nervous energy out of his system.

Cross would be leaving for Channel 12 at about 11:30. Until then he'd check out the calls still coming in from victims' families at a steady pace and make sure the system he and Anne Kelly had put in place to provide answers and help was working at least reasonably well. But at about 9:30 one of the firefighters who'd been at Tim Haskell's wake last night called and said that Giuliani wouldn't be able to make the funeral tomorrow morning and the Haskell family would like Cross to give the eulogy. Cross had never given a eulogy but said he would be honored to do so—but only if the family *really* wanted him to do it. He didn't want to be intruding on a family's grief. The fireman said the family definitely wanted Cross to speak, and Cross replied that he'd start preparing the eulogy right away.

Cross ordinarily spoke with no prepared text or notes, but this would have to be different. He would actually write it out, word for word. Not so much because he thought that would make it eloquent but because he didn't want to make any mistakes. He didn't want to have even one word misunderstood or subject to misinterpretation. The family had enough grief to endure. Cross had finished writing and rewriting the eulogy and was reading it over when the firefighter called him back at about 11:15 to say, "It's important you put something in the eulogy about his brother Tommy still being alive and how there's hope we'll rescue him."

"You know that no one's alive."

"There's no way the family will get through Timmy's funeral unless they have hope for Tommy."

"I'll do it."

The interview at Channel 12 was live and in studio. It went about ten minutes, with no new ground being broken. Cross gave his assurance that Bush would take whatever action he had to take, that the battle would be fought on many fronts and could go on for many years, and that Congress would stand united with the president. As Cross was being interviewed, the news ribbon along the bottom of the screen said, "Taliban considered extraditing bin Laden to country other than U.S."

Next was a taped interview with WABC for its 6:00 p.m. *Eyewitness News* program. The interview was taped outside Nassau Police Headquarters in Mineola. Cross repeated pretty much verbatim what he'd said on Channel 12. Following the interview, Cross entered headquarters and walked up to the second-floor assembly hall that had been hastily converted into a makeshift processing and information center for families of World Trade Center victims. Long plain tables had been set up around the perimeter of the hall. Behind the tables, at designated locations, sat representatives of various government and charitable entities including the Police Department, the Nassau Crime Victims Center, and the Red Cross. The Red Cross provided money for fuel and mortgage payments. The Crime Victims Center paid for burial costs and counseling expenses. And the police took DNA samples to help identify the remains that were found. Down the middle of the hall was a row of plastic chairs where the family members would wait until it was their turn to go to the appropriate station. Depending on why they were there, the relatives sat in the chairs clutching mortgage statements, oil bills, bankbooks, marriage certificates, or toothbrushes with traces of their relatives' DNA.

Mary Rose worked for Crime Victims. Prior to September 11th her work had related almost entirely to victims of street crimes and domestic violence. Now she was dealing with the worst massacre in American history. Cross looked around and saw his wife seated behind a table on the right side of the hall. She was taking information from a woman seated across the table from her. The woman appeared to be in her mid-thirties. She had long, straight, blonde hair and was wearing no makeup. Her face looked frozen, almost catatonic. Cross stood off to the side until Mary Rose and the blonde woman had completed their business. As the woman left to go to another station, Cross walked over to Mary Rose.

"She looks absolutely shattered," he said in a whisper.

"She's thirty-four. Has four children. Her husband was a bond trader. They haven't found his body," answered Mary Rose in a flat, mechanical monotone.

"What did you do for her?"

"I told her we'll pay for counseling for her and the kids, funeral and burial costs if they find a body, and a memorial service if there is no body," she said, as if she were reciting by rote. "Where are you going now?"

"I've got some TV spots in the city."

"When do you think you'll be home?"

"About eleven or eleven thirty."

"How about you?"

"I should be finished about nine."

"Can you get off in the morning for the funeral?"

"I'll work it out."

"See you tonight. Take care of yourself."

"Yeah. You too."

Walking from the hall, Cross saw Loretta Brennan, the deputy inspector running the operation.

"Good job, Loretta. You got it set up pretty fast."

"It's really great, isn't it?" she answered sardonically. "*One stop shopping* for relatives of murder victims."

The shows in Manhattan were Catherine Crier on *Court TV;* an MSNBC interview at the NBC studio at 30 Rockefeller Center; the *Geraldo Rivera Show;* and then the ten o'clock news on Channel 11. At each stop Cross's message was still identical to what he'd said on Channel 12 and Channel 7. *Bush would get the job done.* And the commentators didn't press him—almost as if they wanted reassurance as much as the public did.

Driving home to Long Island that night, Anne Kelly, who'd been staring out the car window as they were going across the 59th Street Bridge, turned and looked toward Cross and said, "I don't know why, but it didn't really hit me until tonight just how bad this really is."

"What do you mean?"

"When we went to Catherine Crier's show this afternoon and got out of the car on Third Avenue, I was struck by all the photos and missing persons signs on the light posts, the newsstands, the mailboxes, and even the sides of buildings. But walking through Grand Central Station tonight to get to Channel 11 was the worst."

"That was bad."

"It was just so dense. Those pictures and missing persons signs with descriptions and phone numbers were everywhere. Covering every inch of space. And we know that unless there's some miracle, they're all dead."

"I can't imagine anyone being alive. They have to be dead."

"And their poor relatives can't accept this."

"You can't blame them."

"Not only are they dead, but their relatives will probably never even get to know what their last moments were like. It's really sad."

"It certainly is."

Tim Haskell's funeral at St. William the Abbott Church this Wednesday morning was very much the same as Pete Ganci's had been four days before. Crowds lining Jackson Avenue in quiet reverence. The muffled beat of the drums of the FDNY bagpipe band leading the funeral cortege beneath a giant American flag stretched across the avenue. The pained, anguished faces of family members and brother firefighters. And mourners overflowing the church.

The funeral Mass itself was conducted with dignity and honest emotion. Unlike the priest at Sunday's 10:15 mass, today's celebrant—Fr. Steve Camp—made no apologies for America and did not ask the mourners to examine their consciences. Instead he compared Tim Haskell to Christ dying on the cross—a heroic man who had given his life for peace and justice.

After the congregants had received Holy Communion, Father Camp asked Cross to come up to the altar and deliver the eulogy. Standing at the pulpit, Cross adjusted the microphone, took a fleeting look at the Haskell family seated in the first row directly in front of him and began: "We often say on occasions such as this that we have come together to celebrate the life of a person who has died. . . . Today it must be difficult for Tim Haskell's family to see any cause for celebration.

"But it is true that the courage which Tim Haskell demonstrated in living his life and enduring his death has given America much to celebrate.

"Tim Haskell's bravery rallied our nation when we could have stayed down for the count. Because of his courageous example, America knows that it must stand with our commander in chief in rooting out and destroying international terrorism.

"And I must add that because of Tim Haskell's bravery we must have hope for his brother Tom and the other missing victims.

"President Bush has said that we are at war. It is a war we must win in memory of Tim Haskell.

"Now I would ask all of you to give Tim Haskell the send-off he deserves and give him a loud standing ovation."

In less than an instant everyone was on their feet applauding loudly for Tim Haskell. And the applause went on and on and on. And grew louder and louder.

Following the funeral and another in-studio interview with Channel 12 in Woodbury, Cross went to Manhattan to CNN's studio on Eighth Avenue for a *Talk Back Live* appearance with Ed Koch and David Dinkins. The show was scheduled to begin at three o'clock but was delayed by breaking news that U.S. aircraft had just been ordered deployed in prelude to the expected attacks on Afghanistan. Sitting in the green room waiting to go on, Cross and the two ex-mayors discussed the horrible events of the past week.

"All those cops and firemen killed," said Koch, in a particularly bitter tone, "and all those innocent civilians. It's an outrage. A damn outrage."

"I was at Father Judge's funeral," said Dinkins. "That was sad. I was talking to Jimmy Boyle. It's terrible about his son."

"Jimmy Boyle's son was killed?" asked Koch.

"Yeah, Michael, he was a firefighter," said Cross.

"I knew he was a fireman. But I had no idea he was killed," said Koch. "How's Jimmy doing?"

"Jimmy's being Jimmy. He's totally devastated but acting as if life couldn't be better," answered Cross.

"Jimmy will never change," said Dinkins with a sad smile.

"I really think Bush is going to destroy Al Qaeda," said Koch. "I saw him at Ground Zero last Friday. The look on his face told me a lot."

"He's the commander in chief," said Dinkins. "We have to stand with him."

"It was interesting driving in here today," said Cross. "There were no car horns. People just seemed quieter."

"I hear that people are even being *nice* to each other," said Koch, with his trademark grin. "Can you imagine—New Yorkers being nice, being polite!"

The three politicians laughed heartily—probably more so than Koch's humorous remark warranted, but it was a welcome respite from what had become the standard talk of death, funerals, and war. When they got on the show, their segment was less than ten minutes. But it was long enough for them to demonstrate bipartisan solidarity with the president and against bin Laden.

The segment ended, Cross shook hands with Koch and Dinkins and walked from the studio to the elevator. The ex-mayors stayed behind to discuss the prayer session that Rudy had asked them to co-chair this Sunday in Yankee Stadium. Anne Kelly was waiting for Cross at the elevator, her cell phone in her hand.

"While you were on the set, Tom O'Connell called," said Kelly, as they walked into the elevator and Cross pressed the lobby button. "Bush is going to address a joint session tomorrow night."

"What time?"

"Nine o'clock—but Tom thinks you should get down there a lot earlier than that."

"How early?"

"Early enough that you'll probably have to miss Farrell Lynch's memorial service."

"What's the problem? Security?"

"Yeah," answered Kelly, as they stepped from the elevator into the lobby. "If you go to the memorial, the earliest you could get to D.C. would be six o'clock—probably more like seven. And any delay could keep you from getting there at all. Security is supposed to be the tightest they've ever had. Capitol Hill will be an armed camp. Tom said that if there's any threat at all, against Amtrak for instance, they'll just shut down Union Station."

"You're right. I do have to be there for the president," said Cross as they walked along Eighth Avenue toward 34th Street. "The least I can do for Farrell, though, is go to the wake tonight."

"That means you'll still miss the votes in the morning."

"I was going to miss them anyway for the funeral . . ."

"'Memorial service,'" corrected Kelly, with a grim smile.

"Being there for the president is different from being there for a few procedural votes. I'll go to the wake tonight and catch the early train in the morning."

Because Mary Rose was working again tonight at Police Headquarters, Cross drove alone to the M. A. Connell Funeral Home in Huntington Station. Cross was going to the wake as much out of concern for Farrell's family as he was for Farrell's memory. His concern was that there might be a small turnout at the wake. Cross knew that Farrell had been popular, but he didn't know if the community had recovered enough from last week's trauma to be attending wakes, funerals, and memorial services for victims who had not been in the public eye. It was different for cops and firemen. By tradition and there being so many active and retired officers, NYPD and FDNY funerals were always well attended. Civilians did not have such built-in followings.

As he drove north on New York Avenue, however, and got his first look at the funeral home, Cross realized how entirely unwarranted his concern had been. The line of mourners poured out of the funeral home, through the parking lot, and then continued for at least another four blocks. After driving around nearby streets, Cross finally found a parking spot more than a quarter-mile from the funeral home. Walking in the middle of the street toward the funeral home, he saw how slowly the line was moving and realized it would be hours—if at all—before he would even get to the door. Cross also observed how solemn and silent the mourners were. All these people—but no sound louder than a whisper. Just then an Irish-American woman he knew to be a friend of Farrell's parents said hello and introduced Cross to a man she said was over from the Irish parliament. She was going to bring the Irish senator in through a side door and said, "Sean, I suppose we can qualify you as some sort of dignitary, so I'll sneak you in as well."

The room inside was filled tight with people, and it seemed as if no one was leaving. There was no casket, but there were pictures and mementos everywhere. Cross recognized Farrell's widow Eileen in a corner of the room, surrounded by friends. He had met her but didn't know her well and saw no need to bother her. He did, however, talk to Farrell's parents, expressing his sorrow that two of their sons had been murdered, offering to help in any way that he could, and having not the slightest idea what else to say. The parents were shattered but brave, as were Farrell's two surviving brothers and sister.

Terrible grief engulfed the room. In true Irish form, however, emotions were kept under tight rein. Suffering was intense but driven inward. Cross spoke briefly with several other people he recognized. Then he said good bye to Farrell's mother and father and walked out into the night. The line now extended more than five blocks.

13

It had been almost twenty years since Pete Cairney had left Belfast and arrived at Kennedy Airport by way of Dublin. He carried with him false papers, which he used to maneuver his way through Customs and Immigration. Cairney's departure from Belfast had been hastily arranged. It was his only option, since he was barely one step ahead of the British army, and it was closing in fast.

Pete Cairney had joined the IRA in the early 1970s, and by the time he left for New York in the mid-eighties had become one of that guerilla group's senior commanders in the republican stronghold of West Belfast. Cairney was like many Catholic men who'd grown up in Northern Ireland's six counties in the middle of the twentieth century. His neighborhood—Ballymurphy—was a classic ghetto. Terrible housing, virtually no jobs, police brutality. Cairney and his family—mother, father, two brothers, and three sisters—considered themselves thoroughly Irish but lived under British rule, as second or third-class citizens.

When Catholics sought equality in the late 1960s, they utilized peaceful demonstrations modeled on the American civil rights movement. They were met by loyalist mobs who beat them back and then rampaged through Catholic neighborhoods burning down their homes. The police—the Royal Ulster Constabulary—

sided with the mobs. The British army, sent over to protect the Catholic neighborhoods, soon turned its sights on the Catholics. The IRA, which had been largely defunct for almost a decade, emerged from the ashes to defend the Catholic neighborhoods, and before long Northern Ireland was ravaged by war. The fighting in Belfast was particularly fierce, and Ballymurphy was at the center of much of it.

Pete and his two brothers—Liam and Brendan—had been among the first to join the resurgent IRA, and their Ballymurphy unit was particularly effective and lethal. It was urban guerilla warfare, and the battleground was their neighborhood. The IRA men knew the streets and the alleyways, the lights and the shadows, how to move in and how to move out. The fighting encompassed sustained battles and hit-and-run sniper attacks.

Despite his young years, Pete was soon recognized as a leader in the republican movement. He was a skilled gunfighter, showed a lot of guts, and always kept a level head. Just as important, he was lucky—always managing to elude the probes and snares of the British Crown forces. His brothers were not so lucky. Liam was machine-gunned to death by a British foot patrol on Belfast's lower Falls Road in 1973, while Brendan was arrested in 1978 and sentenced to life imprisonment for multiple murders of British soldiers and police officers. As the war continued on its seemingly endless course, Pete's IRA reputation extended beyond Belfast's mean streets; he would often attend planning sessions with IRA men throughout Northern Ireland's six counties.

One leader Cairney met with on a fairly regular basis throughout the early eighties was Rory McAllister from South Tyrone, a rural republican stronghold near the border with the Irish Republic. McAllister's exploits against British troops in Tyrone's rolling fields and tree-lined roads had earned him an almost mythic status among the republican rank and file. During their early meetings, Cairney was struck by McAllister's intensity and sense of purpose. He could sense straight away why McAllister's supporters saw him as such a charismatic leader in their struggle against the British. But as their contact increased, a darker side of McAllister came into focus—a side that saw killing as an end in itself rather than a means to remove the British presence from Ireland.

It was during this time that Gerry Adams and Martin McGuiness were taking their first significant steps toward establishing Sinn Fein as a credible political force for the republican movement. This political initiative generated intense debate among IRA leaders. The Adams-McGuiness supporters saw it as a logical, necessary extension of their struggle to end British rule. It would demonstrate popular support and give legitimacy to their movement. Also, unlike the IRA, which by necessity had to operate in the shadows, Sinn Fein leaders would be able to advocate their cause in the court of public opinion. Opponents of the political route feared that any support given to Sinn Fein would deny the IRA needed weapons and supplies. The republican movement just did not have the resources necessary to fund both a military and a political wing—not when it was up against the full might of the British Empire. Besides, the only message the British would ever understand was the one that came from the end of a gun. There was also the pervasive belief that politics and politicians could never be trusted. Whether it be DeValera and Collins in the 1920s or the quislings in Dublin since then, Ireland's political leaders invariably failed Ireland's people.

Pete saw merit on both sides of the argument but came down alongside Adams and McGuiness. Almost fifteen years of fighting had demonstrated that the British army would never be able to defeat the IRA; it had also demonstrated that the IRA would never defeat the British army. Establishing a strong political force would at least offer hope of a way out of this deadly impasse. What Cairney could not accept was McAllister's reaction—an absolute refusal to discuss the issue other than to exclaim that "Adams and McGuiness are fucking traitors. Fuck politics." After that, Cairney would encounter McAllister on only the rarest occasions, and their conversations would be fleeting and perfunctory.

McAllister increasingly distanced himself from the IRA leadership and confined his activities to the environs of South Tyrone—first carrying out operations without IRA approval, and then formally leaving the IRA altogether to lead a small band of like-minded malcontents. It was during his tenure as leader of this dissident pack that McAllister earned the moniker "Mad Dog" for his arbitrary killing of combatants and civilians alike.

Soon after McAllister left the IRA, Pete was forced to leave Ireland. Though the Brits had known for years of Cairney's IRA exploits, they had never been able to find any evidence to link him to what they were convinced he did. The British were similarly unsuccessful in getting the goods on other top IRA men. Then in the early 1980s they unveiled a new weapon in their legal arsenal—"supergrasses." These were paid informers who would testify against anyone the Brits had targeted and recite from whatever script was prepared for them. Since there were no juries, and the Northern Ireland judges did what they were told to do, the result was a series of show trials where as many as thirty-five or forty defendants would be convicted at a time, on the sole basis of this perjured testimony. When Pete got word that the Brits had turned in an informer who lived just two blocks from him in Ballymurphy, he realized he had to go on the run. IRA operatives in Ireland and New York obtained false papers for him—passport, visa, drivers license, Social Security card; Pete drove to Dublin and took an Aer Lingus flight to New York, where, after maneuvering through the Customs and Immigration maze at Kennedy Airport, he stepped into a waiting car and was driven to a safe apartment in an Irish section of Sunnyside, Queens.

For the first several years in New York Cairney kept a low profile. The Brits had charged him in absentia with a series of conspiracy crimes. Cairney's papers identified him as Eddie Ward, and that was the name he assumed. He got a job with the carpenters union working construction in midtown Manhattan and did some writing for Irish-American newspapers and magazines, under various pseudonyms. He pretty much kept to himself at the construction site each day, not telling his coworkers anything about himself except for the obvious—that he was from Ireland. Most guys in the carpenters' union were Irish born or of Irish descent, and their heritage had conditioned them not to ask anything about a person's background that he didn't volunteer. There were a few people from Belfast living in New York whom Pete would get together with in various pubs around the city. They knew Pete was on the run but made no mention of it, preferring to talk of hurling or the latest Irish elections. Any women he met had no idea who he was or what was in his background, and his relationships with them never lasted more than a few months. Despite the restrictions on his lifestyle, Pete thoroughly enjoyed the experience of living in New York—the museums, the theaters, and the world-class sporting events. And on a less grand scale he became fascinated with the subway system. On his days off from work he would often spend hour after hour riding and transferring from one train to the other, mastering the art of exploring the city's subterranean depths while paying only one fare. The subways lost some of that magical allure after he had to fight off two muggers on the E Train one Saturday night, but he still marveled at the complexity of this elaborate network of tracks, tunnels, and elevated lines.

Life eased quite a bit for Pete when, after the Northern Ireland appeals courts began reversing the convictions of scores of IRA men convicted in the supergrass trials, the British quietly dropped all charges against Pete. This about-face resulted primarily from the international spotlight focused on the supergrass system following a series of scathing reports and exposés from American lawyers and politicians, including Sean Cross. The charges dropped, Pete eased himself from the shadows and began to edge into the mainstream of American life. He took night courses at St. Francis College in Brooklyn, studying English literature and government. His newspaper columns now ran under his real name. He met Nicole Long, an Irish woman from Cork who was making good money with a Manhattan ad agency, and several months later they moved into an apartment that they rented in Woodside. And he began the process of trying to regularize his residency status. After several false starts and with considerable help from Sean Cross's congressional office, Pete's status was legalized, and he got his green card.

Cross had gotten to know Cairney during the time of the supergrass investigations. Sean had been in the forefront of American politicians who exposed the supergrass system—traveling several times to Belfast to observe the trials and then issuing reports condemning the use of these informers. Cairney had briefed Cross extensively not just on the supergrasses but on the entire Northern Ireland judiciary system, which—Cross came to believe—had become a mere extension of British military policy. Pete also put Cross in contact with quite a few republican activists and lawyers in Northern Ireland.

Cross had been introduced to Cairney by John Maloney, an Irish-American labor leader who headed a Teamsters local in Brooklyn. At their first meeting Cairney revealed his true identity and full background to Cross. This didn't concern Cross, since Cairney wasn't the first Irish guy he'd met who was on the run. He was struck, however, not just by Pete's extensive knowledge of all aspects of the Irish issue but by his support of Gerry Adams's long-term attempt to reach a political solution. When Cross and Cairney had first met in the mid-eighties, war was raging throughout the six counties. By 1994 Bill Clinton had given Adams his visa, the IRA had declared its ceasefire, and the peace process was under way. That process was complicated and tortuous, taking unexpected turns and hitting too many dead ends. But it did keep going. And in April 1998 the Good Friday Agreement was signed, giving all the people in Ireland—north and south—their best chance for peace in eight hundred years. Throughout this time Pete worked relentlessly in New York's Irish-American community—particularly among its many hard-core militants—urging them to follow the political path. Pete's IRA exploits were by now well known among New

York's Irish and gave considerable credibility to his call for politics over war.

All the while that Pete was in New York advancing the political route, Rory McAllister was in Ireland striving mightily to derail it. Finally, in the fall of 1997, McAllister merged his group of dissidents with another band of ex-IRA men led by Marty McDevitt, a former member of the IRA's Army Council, to form the small but lethal "Real IRA." It didn't take long for the Real IRA to attain infamy. In August 1998—just four months after the Good Friday Agreement was signed—the Real IRA set off car bombs in the heart of the city center in Omagh, in the middle of a Saturday afternoon, when weekend shopping was at its height. When the explosions ceased, there was carnage everywhere. Bodies blown apart. The smell of burning flesh and the screams of victims. Twenty-nine were dead, and more than two hundred were injured. They were Catholics and Protestants, locals and tourists, young and old. The worst carnage in all the years of the Troubles. Every Irish politician—north and south—denounced this atrocity in the harshest possible language. The world was repulsed by it. But to "Mad Dog" McAllister it was a wondrous victory—a clarion message that he and his type would never allow peace to come to Ireland. This was the type of slaughter he had been building toward for all these years. Finally, however, McAllister's depravity became too much even for the Real IRA. In the spring of 2000, as he walked into the back room of a pub in Dundalk, just across the border in the Irish Republic, for what he had been told would be a meeting of the Real IRA leadership, he was shot dead in a hail of bullets. The Real IRA itself never recovered from the Omagh atrocity and faded steadily into insignificance.

Though Ireland was no longer a front-burner issue, Cross still followed it closely. He stayed in regular contact with Adams and McGuiness, and with his contacts in the Irish and British governments. Pete, however, was his main source for what was going on in New York's Irish community. Despite his support of the peace process and his unyielding opposition to McAllister and the Real IRA, Cairney had managed to stay on speaking terms with even the most unrepentant dissidents. After learning from Frank Hennessy about McAllister's old girlfriend Fiona Larkin and her involvement with Al Qaeda and her meetings in New York with the Muslim terrorist Haddad and with Real IRA supporters, Cross had reached out to Cairney and asked him to find out what he could. They were meeting this afternoon in Rosenfeld's Bagel Shop on Montague Street in Brooklyn, just around the corner from St. Francis College.

"Pete, I appreciate you taking the time to see me," said Cross, as he sat down at the corner table Cairney had secured for them.

"No bother at all Sean," answered Cairney.

"It must be some bother. After all you are working full-time construction plus taking the night classes."

"It sounds worse than it is. I've enough seniority in the union that I don't have to be killing myself on the job anymore, and the literature course I'm taking is just terrific, so it is."

"What's the course?"

"You'll never believe it—'The Contemporary Irish-American Novelist.' It's a gas. Hamill, Breslin, Ryan Travis. All the guys I'm always reading."

"What time's your class?"

"Six o'clock."

"This gives us almost an hour and a half. Plenty of time."

Each ordered a cup of coffee and a toasted raisin bagel with cream cheese.

"What you told me about Fiona Larkin certainly took me by surprise," said Pete.

"Did you know her at all?" asked Cross.

"Not personally. She was still in secondary school when I had to leave the country. But I knew of her later on."

"Sinn Fein thought she was a rising star."

"Until she went off with the Real IRA and started knocking around with that fucking madman McAllister."

"You actually *knew* him," said Cross with a grim smile.

"I did indeed. He was brilliant, so he was. But after a while, he just went off the deep end. When I'd talk to him and he'd be talking about some Brit he killed, his eyes would just light up."

"He wasn't always that way?"

"When I first met him, I thought he was steady. It was almost a year or so later that he started to go—and once he started, he went very quickly."

"Anything in particular put him over?"

"I don't think so. It was probably just the accumulation of it all. People who knew him years ago—long before I did—say he was sound as a bell."

"Were you surprised the Real IRA whacked him?"

"I don't pay much attention to what that type does. It could have been a calculated decision that Rory was doing more harm than good. Or it could just as easily been a group of leaders who were jealous of all the publicity Rory was getting."

"I agree with you they were a bunch of wackos. But how do you explain someone as smart as Fiona Larkin getting involved with them?"

"For the same reason she got involved with the fucking Muslim . . ."

"Abdul Bajal."

"As smart as she is, Fiona sees everything in black and white. When Adams decided to go the political route and accept less than 100 percent, Fiona couldn't handle that. The Brits are evil; you can't compromise with evil. Rory McAllister wanted to kill all the Brits—so he was her man. And I'm sure she felt the same about the Real IRA. All she heard was them saying 'Brits out.'"

"You think it's the same with Bajal?"

"Listen, it's taken me a lifetime to try to figure out the fucking Irish, so I'm not going to pretend that I understand Muslims or know how they act. But from the outside looking in, bin Laden and the others, like this guy Bajal, remind me in many ways of McAllister and McDevitt. They're all absolute fanatics with no thought of compromise and no sense of remorse for anyone who gets killed that isn't one of them. So it would make sense that Fiona would go from Rory to Bajal."

"Have you been able to learn anything about what Fiona was up to when she was over here?"

"I've been very careful what I ask people. I don't want to tip anyone off."

"I appreciate that."

"But I still got more than I thought I would."

"Why?"

"In Real IRA circles in New York, Fiona Larkin is still a celebrity. So even though she was in and out pretty quickly and was very low-key, word still got around."

"What do you have for me?"

"The first thing I can tell you is that she never mentioned a word about being involved with Muslims at all. Anyone she spoke to just assumes she's still with the Real IRA."

"I guess it's safe to say that bin Laden and Abdul Bajal aren't exactly folk heroes in New York's Irish pubs?"

"That's the fucking truth—except maybe for a fringe of a fringe. But we can talk about that later."

"Who'd she meet?"

"Real IRA holdouts. Mickey McDonough in the Bronx and Jimmy Regan in Inwood."

"You still have much contact with these guys?"

"On and off. McDonough's from the Short Strand in Belfast. He was in jail with my brother Brendan. As for Regan, he's actually from the south. Cork. But he was very active over here in the seventies and the eighties. Raised a lot of money and bought a lot of guns for the IRA. Neither of these guys could ever accept a ceasefire or the peace talks and certainly not the Good Friday Agreement. They saw that as just a sellout to the Brits."

"These guys still trust you?"

"They do. They know exactly where I stand. But we go back together so far, they just seem to put the political issues aside and think back to the good old days."

"Are they still active?"

"As a practical matter, not for years. The Real IRA's lucky if it's got more than a handful of members in Ireland. The most guys like Mickey and Jimmy can do is stay in contact with whoever's left in Ireland and be ready in case the war breaks out again."

"But they're not into fund-raising or buying guns?"

"Christ, no. Mickey and Jimmy can dream about how it used to be, but that shit's all in the past. So they just sit and wait for the day the bullets start flying again."

"Are these guys the same type as McAllister?"

"Not really. They're like Rory in the sense they think politics will never work and the only Brit you can trust is a dead Brit. But, believe it or not, guys like Mick and Jimmy don't enjoy killing for the sake of killing. Rory, on the other hand, after a while he killed for the thrill of it."

"Did they know Fiona was coming over?"

"They hadn't a clue. Each of them found a note under their apartment door from Fiona asking them to meet her. Mickey at the Shamrock Arms bar in Riverdale, and Jimmy at the Soldier Boy pub in Inwood."

"Isn't Inwood all Dominicans these days?"

"It's mostly Dominican, but there's still a few Irish holdouts."

"How'd the meetings go?"

"They were both pretty much the same. Very cordial and brief. No longer than a half-hour."

"What did she tell them?"

"That she was sorry for the short notice but the trip had come up very unexpectedly. Things were happening back in Ireland and friends in America might be needed again very soon. She couldn't tell them any details yet, because everything was still in the talking stages—but there could be something very dramatic happening that no Irish group had ever done before."

"I can guess where this is going."

"She told them that even though it's always been strict republican policy—whether it was the IRA or the Real IRA—not to carry out any operation in America, they were considering an attack on a major British installation in the New York area."

"How did Mickey and Jimmy react to this?"

"Obviously, it caught them off guard. But Fiona assured them that no American would be hurt in any way. That this was a British site, separate and by itself."

"Did they accept that?"

"These are guys who are used to following orders, and besides, they assume that no Irish republican would do anything that would threaten Americans."

"Did she tell them what they were supposed to do?"

"Nothing specific—but they think it has to do with explosives. Maybe even car bombs."

"Why do they think that?"

"She told them they would get a few weeks' notice and they'd have to prepare something. But that guys from Ireland would be over to actually carry the operation out."

"Would McDonough or Regan have the capacity to put together explosives or car bombs?"

"Mickey would. He was one of the best we had in Belfast. Jimmy's lucky if he could set off a firecracker, but he could get a lot of the supplies they need."

"How reliable is all this?"

"I think it's pretty reliable. But I do have to tell you that I'm piecing this together from what I got from Mickey and Jim and from some friends of theirs. None of them knows I got as much as I did and—like I said—I'm trying to make sense of it. What I told you is my best information."

"I trust your judgment, but isn't Fiona being reckless dealing in the open like this? And isn't Al Qaeda risking a lot?"

"Having Fiona meet in out-of-the-way Irish bars with has-beens like Mick and Jim isn't really that risky. Especially when the feds and the cops are focusing almost entirely on the Muslims. And Fiona's been off everybody's radar screen for years. If that one FBI informer hadn't spotted her by chance, this would have worked perfectly for them."

"Thank God we caught a fucking break."

"Where do we go with this?"

"That's not for me to decide. I wish I were James Bond, but I'm just a messenger. I'll give what you told me to Frank Hennessy and Lou Bianchi."

"What do you expect them to do?"

"I'd assume they'll put a tight surveillance on McDonough and Regan. It wouldn't make any sense to lock them up now, because Fiona and Bajal would know we were onto them."

"They better watch them *very* carefully, because we're literally playing with dynamite."

"I know. That's why I'm sure they'd want you to keep your ears open and try to find out whatever else you can."

"I'm not a fucking cop," said Pete, displaying, for the first time, traces of reluctance and annoyance. "I said I'd find out what was going on. I didn't say I'd be a detective—or an informer."

"Pete, I can understand where you're coming from. A lot of us wanted to look the other way when it was the IRA against the Brits. Whether that was right or wrong, the fact is—as you just said—'that shit's all in the past.' This is a different time; a different world. And America's the target."

"Christ, Sean. I've known Mickey for more than thirty years and Jimmy for about twenty. Like I also told you, these aren't bad guys. They aren't madmen like Rory McAllister or that fucking bin Laden."

"I'll take your word that they're not. But they're both living in this country, and they both became citizens. And once they decide to do a job for Fiona Larkin in this country—no matter who they think it's against—they've crossed the fucking line. I could understand your loyalty to them if this were fifteen years ago and they were going against the Brits in the North or in England—but not now; not in this country; and, for that matter, not anywhere since the Good Friday Agreement."

"So you're asking me to be a tout, a fucking informer," said Cairney. "I don't have to tell you how that's the lowest form of Irish life."

"I know this isn't easy for you. But, to me, you're an informer when you rat on someone you know is right or when you're just trying to save your own ass. That's not the case here. You think McDonough and Regan are 100 percent fucking wrong, and obviously you get no personal gain out of going against them."

"You're leaving something out—the human element. Sure I know these guys are wrong. But they're friends of mine. They trust me. That's the only reason I've been able to find all this out."

"We're not talking about some hurling match in Gaelic Park or a Mets-Yankees game—or any of the other shit we usually argue about. These are human lives. Innocent Americans working in New York who could be blown apart with car bombs put together by *your friends*."

"I'm not saying you're wrong. I'm saying it's tough to do."

"How would you feel toward some New York Muslim if you found out that he'd known about the World Trade Center or that he knew about the attacks last month? You'd want to kill the guy. If it's wrong for the Muslims to look the other way, it's just as bad for us."

"You think there's any way Mickey or Jimmy would be able to cut a deal?"

"Maybe—but that's for the cops and the feds to decide, not us. If we do anything at all to tip them off, we could fuck up the whole investigation."

"I've become as American as anyone, and I know what's the right thing to do. But emotionally it's still a no-win for me."

"I can understand that."

"I'll do what I can."

"Thanks Pete, I can't tell you how much this means. You've really stepped up."

Cairney looked up at the waiter. It was just past 5:30. "How are we doing for time?" asked Cross.

"We're fine. We've got about a half-hour," answered Cairney.

"Since we have a few minutes, one thing I've been wanting to talk to you about is how disappointed I've been in a lot of the fucking Irish. Not here—but the ones back in Ireland."

"Sean, I know what you're talking about, and I agree with you completely. After all that America did for the Irish—especially with the North—they've really been disgraceful, so they have: first Afghanistan and then Iraq. And it keeps going."

"It really caught me off guard. In the very beginning Ireland was great. Right after September 11th there was a national day of mourning, and thousands of people lined up to sign condolence books at the American embassy in Phoenix Park."

"Yeah, but Jesus, it didn't last long. There were thousands demonstrating against you in Dublin just the very next month."

"That was after we started bombing Afghanistan. I remember the yelling about American imperialism and civilian casualties and war crimes and all that shit."

"And I can tell you that the whole ten years the Russians were invading Afghanistan and slaughtering people by the thousands, there were no demonstrations at all. The Irish didn't say a fucking word."

"To listen to the demonstrators and media types, you'd never know it was America that had been attacked."

"And you'd never know that so many Irish-Americans had been killed."

"Can you explain it?" asked Cross.

"I can try—but that's about all," answered Cairney with a grim smile.

"You know them better than I do—so go ahead."

"If there's one good thing to say, it's that by no means are all the Irish anti-American—though it certainly seems that way, because the ones who are have such access to the media."

"You mean the elite?"

"Yeah. The Dublin 4 crowd—the rich ones who think it's chic and sophisticated to be anti-American. Then there's the same types who make up your antiwar movements—the intellectuals, the media stars, and the students."

"Isn't there something else?"

"What?"

"The worst Irish trait of all—begrudgery."

"Christ, Sean, that goes without saying, so it does. The Irish are the worst fucking begrudgers."

"And there's so much about America to begrudge. We have so much money and so much power, and we've given tens of millions of Irish the opportunity to come here and get better jobs than they could never have gotten at home."

"The sad thing is that there is so much truth to what you're saying. I've seen it so often myself over the years. Some guy would go to America, do well for himself and then at home, instead of being happy for his good fortune, they'd be saying 'And Jesus, I wonder what he had to do to make that kind of money,' and all that kind of stupid talk."

"I understand all that. I've seen it with my own relatives. But I just thought that September 11th was so horrific and so unjust, even the Irish wouldn't let begrudgery get in the way. Not this time."

"Never make the mistake of overestimating us."

"And all this morality and self-righteousness bullshit. It's not as if Ireland has such a stellar record."

"Jesus, you're really worked up on this," said Cairney with a wide grin.

"It's just that I've seen, over the years, how many Irish-Americans did so much for Ireland, without any thought of getting anything out of it for themselves. There were some of those killed in the World Trade Center. And the Irish don't even give us moral support. Maybe we shouldn't have given them the benefit of the doubt in World War II."

"Now you're really hitting a raw nerve—Irish neutrality."

"With hundreds of thousands of Americans getting killed in World War II, it was hard to see why it was 'moral' for Ireland to stay neutral against Hitler."

"The argument was that once the fighting started and us being such a small country, we'd have to rely so much on the Brits that we'd be giving them the keys to take us over again."

"How about when Hitler died and the war was virtually over, DeValera went to the German embassy and signed the condolence book?"

"That was unexplainable and inexcusable."

"Or during the next fifty years when NATO and the United States were protecting Western Europe, the Irish insisted on being 'neutral'? As if there were some moral superiority in being neutral against communists!"

"Let me ask you—with all these negatives, why did you go out on a limb for Ireland for so long?"

"I don't like being psychoanalyzed," Cross answered with a ironic grin.

"Seriously, I'm interested," said Cairney.

"Like anyone else the Irish have their good and their bad," Sean responded after a slight hesitation, "and for the most part they're good people. After all, I'm one of them. And a lot of the anti-American bullshit came from the elite—at least that's what I told myself—and they were the same ones who were turning their backs on the Catholics in the North."

"I remember it was part of your standard speech during those years that the North was a human issue, not an Irish issue."

"Yeah, and I meant it. It also annoyed the shit out of me that you'd have all these micks in the South screaming and demonstrating about human rights abuses, thousands of miles away in

Nicaragua and the Philippines, but not saying a word about what was being done to their own people in the North, less than a hundred miles away."

"Jesus, I can tell you that used to drive us mad in the North."

"I remember when I was in Ireland with Clinton in '98, just a few months after the Good Friday Agreement, and one of my cousins got hold of me. All he wanted to talk about was East Timor."

"The Irish are good for talking about 'something else.' Especially something they know that they can't do anything about."

Cairney looked at his watch. "Maybe someday I'll write a great novel about the Irish psyche—and why it's so fucked up. But if I want to do it, I'd better get my ass over to the literature class. It starts in five minutes."

"Go ahead, Pete. I don't want to get in the way of the next Hamill or Breslin."

"Or James Joyce. By the way, leave the waitress a good tip. We tied up the table long enough."

"I'll leave her ten bucks."

"I always knew you were a big-hearted Yank."

"I'll be talking to you," said Cross, leaving the tip on the table and walking toward the cash register to pay the bill. "And I really do appreciate what you're doing. I know it's not easy."

"Yeah," replied Cairney with a grim smile as he walked out the door and into the warm evening spring air.

Thursday, September 20, 2001

There were still no airplanes flying into Washington. Cross stood on the platform of the Seaford LIRR station. His travel bag in his hand, he looked east and saw the westbound 7:56 to Penn Station approaching. It was right on time.

While Cross did not have much occasion to take the LIRR, he did take it enough and had campaigned at this station enough to know that the platform today was no less crowded than it would have been prior to September 11th. The commuters, never particularly jovial at this time of day, appeared serious but not subdued. Virtually all the commuters were headed to work in Manhattan. Some would be within blocks of Ground Zero. None would be farther away than a few miles. No one looked apprehensive.

As the 7:56 pulled to a stop, Cross glanced through the car windows and saw that the train was crowded. When the doors opened, he was lucky enough to get one of the few remaining empty seats. He placed his travel bag in the overhead rack and sat next to the window. He'd brought with him the full array of New York papers. *Times. Newsday. Post. Daily News.* The lead stories in each paper were about Bush's speech to Congress tonight. Cross would start with the *Times.* Before unfolding its first section, he looked around the train. Several people gave him approving nods.

Headline stories on the attacks and their aftermath still filled the papers. Estimates on the body count were fluctuating. More accounts of heroism were emerging. The coverage of the funerals for those whose bodies had been located was heartbreaking. Today's dominant theme, of course, was speculation on how effectively the president would rally the nation in his speech tonight. As evidenced by the composed commuters on the 7:56, the immediate trauma of the attacks had eased. The country was moving to the next stage of the struggle. And it would be looking to President Bush for direction and leadership in that struggle.

The train stopped at the Jamaica station at 8:23 to accommodate the relatively few passengers who would be transferring to the Brooklyn line. One of the commuters—a middle-aged, well-dressed guy with a gruff demeanor—made eye contact with Cross. Pausing for a moment before stepping out of the car onto the platform, he said in a graveley voice encased in an unyielding New York accent, "Congressman, tell 'W' we're with him all the way. We're going to kick their ass!" Cross smiled approvingly, and the commuter thrust his right thumb into the air.

The train continued its trip to Penn Station and arrived as scheduled on track 13 at 8:51. Cross walked up the two flights of stairs into the main terminal, where throngs of commuters were moving about more quietly than usual but with their customary great energy. Lugging his travel bag, Cross made his way through the crowd to the Amtrak terminal, where he would pick up the ticket he had reserved for the ten o'clock, 2153 express train to Washington. Extra police were deployed throughout the station, and Army National Guard troops were on duty as well. Cross recalled how jarring it had been just nine days ago to see soldiers on the streets of Washington. Now their presence in Penn Station was reassuring. A clear sign that we were on our guard and fighting back.

Cross got his ticket without incident after waiting in line for only a few minutes. He bought a coffee at the donut stand and made his way to the waiting area, where a uniformed Amtrak clerk asked him to show his ticket and ID before allowing him entry. The process was repeated at the top of the staircase to the platform when boarding began at 9:50. When he got on the train, Cross again took a seat by the window. The trip was to take less then three hours. He finished reading the papers, and as the train was pulling into the Newark station put his head back and fell fast asleep. About two hours later, with the train somewhere between Wilmington and Baltimore, Cross was awakened by the vibration of the cell phone in his left shirt pocket. It was Kevin Finnerty telling him that Channel 12 wanted to do a live interview in the next five minutes—a phoner. Cross said okay.

To ensure a clear signal and some privacy, Cross walked to the phone booth at the other end of the car. Fortunately, no one was using the phone. He sat down, closed the glass door, and dialed the number Finnerty had given him. The Channel 12 program director picked up the phone at the other end and said that Carol Silva and Doug Geed were anchoring the noon news show. Geed would be doing the interview, which would start in about thirty seconds and was scheduled to last about six minutes.

Geed: "We're joined this afternoon by Congressman Sean Cross, who is traveling back to Washington by train. Amtrak. How's the trip so far, Congressman?"

Cross: "Everything is going fine. There were a lot more police at Penn Station, and the National Guard is out in force."

Geed: "How are the people reacting? Americans aren't really used to that type of military presence."

Cross: "From everything I could see, they had no problem at all. In fact, I'm sure just about everyone was happy to see them. People realize we're at war. America is a battlefield, and we want to see our soldiers on the battlefield with us."

Geed: "Of course, the main reason all of you are returning to Washington is the president's address to a joint session of Congress tonight. We've been talking about it on the air all morning. How do you expect the president to do? What do you think he will say?"

Cross: "President Bush will do fine. He'll show how the country has regained its equilibrium and how we're fighting back. We know what's happened. We know what we have to do. And we know how to do it."

Geed: "What type of response do you expect Congress to give the president?"

Cross: "He will get overwhelming support. As I've been saying for the past nine days, we're not Republicans or Democrats—we're Americans."

Geed: "Sean, I believe this will be the first time you've been back in Washington since you traveled with the president to Ground Zero last Friday. I know that was only six days ago, but what do you expect to find in Washington when you get there? How much do you think things will have changed?"

Cross: "I suppose in many ways it will be like New York. Both cities were attacked. New York is the financial center of the world, and Washington is the governmental center of the world—so we know that we're both still under the gun. And I'm sure the security level will be unprecedented—especially with the president, the Congress, and all our nation's leaders in one building tonight."

Geed: "Thank you for taking the time to talk with us—and stay safe."

The engineer brought train 2153 to its slow, grinding halt on track 5. It was almost precisely on schedule. Cross stepped from the train, walked along the lengthy platform, and entered into Union Station and its main concourse. No matter how often he was there, Cross always marveled at the station's architectural grandeur. Its ornate gates. Its ninety-six-foot-high, barrel-vaulted, coffered ceilings. Its white granite and classic lines. And its energy and vibrance—more than 130 shops and restaurants, plus Amtrak's headquarters and executive offices. Today there were the passengers and customers walking throughout the station, but there were also patrols of police and National Guard troops. Washington was on wartime footing.

Exiting the station through its main door, Cross saw Adam Paulson waiting for him in his Jeep Cherokee.

"You been here long?" asked Cross, putting his luggage in the back seat and easing himself into the front passenger seat.

"Just about ten minutes, sir. You were right on time," answered the young staff assistant as he pulled the Jeep away. "Should I take you to the office first or your apartment?"

"Unless there's votes coming up, I'll go to the apartment and leave all my stuff there."

"There're no more votes scheduled now."

"How many did I miss this morning?"

"There were several votes. But only one was recorded. The others were all by voice."

"What was the one I missed? Anything important?"

"Nothing important at all. I've got the title right here: 'A bill to amend the District of Columbia Code, to redesignate the Family Division of the Supreme Court of the District of Columbia as the Family Court of . . .'"

"Okay. That's enough. You were right. It wasn't important. What was the count?"

"408-0."

"408. That's a big number for a morning vote, the first day back. We should be at 100 percent for tonight."

"Yes. They're saying just about everyone intends to be here."

"What's the mood on the Hill?"

"Among the younger staffers—and they're the ones I'd be talking to—it's very concerned. Very somber. We've never been through anything like this."

"None of us have."

"But didn't you have the air-raid drills when you were in school? And the Cuban missile crisis?"

"Yeah, we did. But nothing ever happened, and unless it actually happens, most people don't worry about it. At least I didn't, and my friends didn't either. That's human nature."

"The World Trade Center and the Pentagon being attacked was bad enough. But there's a lot of talk from the Capitol Police that the plane that went down in Pennsylvania was headed toward Congress—probably the Capitol Building."

"I guess a lot of parents are concerned."

"They are. They're calling all the time. Some of the staffers have gone home."

"How about you?"

"My family's right nearby in Maryland. It makes it easier for them knowing that I'm not far away."

"How's the security situation?"

"Like an armed camp. Especially on the Hill. Cops and troops are everywhere. Barricades are set up. And there's F-16s and helicopters in the sky all the time."

"I suppose the only upside of this is that we're living in historic times."

Sean Cross arrived in the House chamber at about seven thirty that evening. The president wasn't scheduled to begin his address for another hour and a half, but seventy-five or so members of Congress were already milling about. Under the unwritten rules of protocol, members claimed seats as they arrived. Even though he'd gotten there early, the best seat available for Cross was in the back row on the Republican side, three seats off the center aisle.

Not that the purpose of his early arrival was to get himself a good seat. Any seat on the House floor on such a historic night would be a good seat. Cross wanted to make sure that the extraordinarily high security didn't delay or prevent Danny from getting into the chamber and to his seat in the gallery. Each congressman is allotted one reserved seat in the House gallery for ceremonial events, such as the State of the Union Address and speeches by foreign leaders. The seat location improves with the seniority of the member. The seat allotted to Cross was in the second row of the gallery, directly overlooking the center aisle and just above the rear doorway where the president would make his entrance into the hall. In normal times Mary Rose would use the ticket. Tonight Danny would use it.

When Sean and Danny had walked over to the Capitol Building, the security had been as intense as Cross anticipated. Repeated ID checkpoints between the Cannon Building and the Capitol. All pedestrian traffic narrowed to one sidewalk footpath. Police and military everywhere. Army snipers on rooftops. Police with submachine guns. Antiaircraft missile batteries encircling the Capitol grounds. Bomb-sniffing dogs. Ambulances and emergency vehicles in the parking lot. AWACS aircraft in the sky along with the F-16s and helicopters. Once inside the Capitol Building, Cross was able to go directly to the House chamber. To get to the gallery, however, Danny had to run the altogether necessary gauntlet of metal detectors, body frisks, and more ID checks. It wasn't until about ten past eight that Cross saw Danny making his way down the gallery steps to his second-row seat. They made eye contact and exchanged nods.

The president's arrival was still more than forty-five minutes away. On the night of a State of the Union speech, the chamber would maybe be half-filled by now. Tonight, as Cross looked around the hall, it appeared just about every member was already there. And unlike the squalid posturing that had pervaded the intelligence briefing on this floor just eight days ago, there appeared to be a genuine camaraderie among the members. A shared exhilaration arising from their joining together in this united act of mass defiance.

Dignitaries and guests were introduced to warm applause as they walked down the center aisle to their assigned seats on the House floor. The members of the Senate. The president's cabinet, led by Colin Powell. Supreme Court justices. There were the foreign ambassadors. But the most attention during these preliminaries was centered on a person who was not there—the vice president of the United States. During presidential addresses to Congress it had been custom and tradition for the Speaker of the House and the vice president, in his capacity as presiding officer of the Senate, to sit on the rostrum in the two chairs just above and behind the president, a large American flag draped on the wall behind them. Tonight, however, Dick Cheney was not there. He was still at the undisclosed location to which he'd been evacuated, his absence a vivid reminder that the situation was too perilous for all the leaders of our government to be in one place at one time. Cheney's seat was occupied by the president pro tempore of the Senate, Robert Byrd—the octogenarian West Virginia windbag. This was the first time since Gerald Ford spoke to the Congress in 1974—after Richard Nixon had resigned and there was no vice president—that a vice president was not present in the chamber for a presidential address. Also absent was Dick Armey, the House majority leader and number two in command, who had heeded Hastert's direction to go to his own undisclosed location.

It was several minutes before nine when the door to the west wing of the gallery opened and Laura Bush walked slowly down the steps to her first-row seat. The chamber erupted in loud, sustained applause, and many waved toward the gallery. The First Lady was accompanied by Rudy Giuliani and Governor George Pataki and by New York City's fire, police, and emergency services commissioners—the commanders of New York's ground troops who had performed so heroically in the first great battle of this new and brutal war. Also seated with Mrs. Bush, directly to her right, was the British prime minister, Tony Blair. To Cross this appearance by the British leader was reassuringly reminiscent of the World War II alliance of Franklin Roosevelt and Winston Churchill.

Sean Cross had been impressed by Tony Blair since their first meeting in February 1998. It was in Washington, at the appropriately named Blair House, a mansion on Pennsylvania Avenue just across from the White House that was used by foreign leaders visiting Washington. Blair, only in his mid-forties, had been elected prime minister the previous May, leading his Labour Party to victory after eighteen years of Tory rule. It had been no surprise that Labour swept the elections. Conservative corruption and a sluggish economy had virtually guaranteed a Labour win. What had been surprising was the margin of victory—a 179-seat majority, the largest of any party in more than a century. This overwhelming Labour victory, after so many years in Britain's political wilderness, was largely attributed to Blair's political acumen and leadership skills in forcefully moving Labour from its decades-long infatuation with far-left-wing pacifism to solidly centrist positions of strong national defense and tough law enforcement.

The 1998 visit had been Blair's first to the United States since his landslide win. The official purpose was to lay out the wide range of issues that engaged the Brits and the Yanks, including NATO expansion, Serb aggression, and easing trade barriers. An unofficial purpose was the situation in Northern Ireland. The morning gathering that Cross attended was a breakfast meeting with congressmen and senators, including Ted Kennedy, Chris Dodd, and Pat Moynihan, who'd been involved in the Irish peace process. In his brief, nine-month tenure Blair had already devoted more time and effort to finding a real solution to the Irish issue than had any previous British prime minister. The peace talks were expected very shortly to enter their final stage. Blair wanted his American visit to facilitate and strengthen the process. As the American politicians waited in the living room for Blair to come down for breakfast that morning, no one knew that within two months the peace process would culminate in the historic Good Friday Agreement.

Tony Blair's 1998 visit to Washington had been set against the bizarre backdrop of the Monica Lewinsky scandal, which had so unexpectedly intruded itself into American life just two weeks before and was threatening the very survival of Bill Clinton's presidency. Clinton was reeling. He had to demonstrate he was still capable of functioning as president. He had to be seen as presidential. Blair was the first foreign leader to visit the United States since the Lewinsky soap opera began. This would give Clinton the opportunity to display his nonpareil world stage skills. By standing with him at this perilous moment, Tony Blair was affirming Bill Clinton's position as the tested leader of the free world.

When Blair had made his way down the staircase that morning and entered the room, Cross had been struck by how totally at ease and distinctly nonpatrician he looked. After the introductions were completed and they'd all seated themselves in the dining room for breakfast, Blair led off with a ten-minute update on the peace process, breaking no new ground but demonstrating a full grasp of detail and nuance. During the discussion period that followed, Cross stated that he could not see how the talks could ever succeed if the unionist leader David Trimble continued his refusal to talk with Sinn Fein. Blair gave a cordial but entirely nonspecific answer.

About a half-hour later, the breakfast ended, Cross had walked up to Blair for what he expected to be the usual courtesy handshake. They said it was a pleasure to meet one another, and Cross turned to leave. Blair, however, continued to talk, saying in a low voice, "I heard what you said about David Trimble and Gerry Adams. If you're speaking with Gerry Adams, tell him we're trying to find a way to have Sinn Fein and Trimble engage directly."

"That's encouraging. I'll pass it on," answered Cross.

"It might take a bit of give on both sides, but I agree with you it's important and could be very helpful."

Just an hour later Cross had been at the White House for the official welcoming ceremony. After the Marine Corps band had played "Hail to the Chief," "God Save the Queen," and the "Star-Spangled Banner," and Clinton and Blair had made their remarks, Cross made his way along the receiving line. Clinton and Blair greeted him warmly, with Blair saying, "I meant what I said about Gerry Adams and Trimble."

Blair's visit had been a success on all fronts. His demonstration of solidarity with Clinton gave the beleaguered president a much-needed respite from the Lewinsky morass, facilitated the

Irish peace process, and established the Labour Party's pro-American bona fides.

It was seven months later on the evening of September 4, 1998, in the rear room of a nondescript house in Armagh City, that Cross had next met Blair, and he was similarly impressed. Cross was accompanying Clinton on a trip to Northern Ireland and Ireland. The original purpose of the trip had been to advance the implementation of the Good Friday Agreement. It was also expected to be a bit of a celebratory victory lap for Clinton, who'd done so much to bring about the agreement. All thoughts of celebration were stunningly halted on Saturday, August 15th, however, when the Real IRA set off its car bombs in Omagh, killing twenty-nine and injuring more than two hundred. The victory lap had become a rescue mission.

Clinton and Blair and their wives traveled to Omagh on the afternoon of September 4 to demonstrate their solidarity against terrorism and their determination to go forward, for as long as it might take. That evening they addressed a massive outdoor crowd on the mall in Armagh City and emphasized their commitment to see the process through. Cross and the other congressmen who accompanied Clinton were standing to the side of the stage. Just before the program concluded, a military escort came up to them and led them behind the stage and across the street to a sturdy but unimposing three-story house. Inside, Cross saw Hillary Clinton; the British Secretary of State for Northern Ireland, Mo Mowlam; Clinton's national security advisor, Sandy Berger; various Secret Service agents; and several men he recognized as members of Blair's staff. Cross realized that this was the governmental equivalent of a safe house and that none of the thousands of people who'd be walking by this building as they left the mall this night would know it contained the two most important leaders in the Western world and their entourages.

Mowlam and Hillary were discussing the scene at Omagh. "All that devastation," said the First Lady. "I can't believe anyone would do that." Just then, a door at the rear of the building opened, and Tony Blair stepped in. He and Cross walked toward one another.

"Sean, it's been a marvelous day."

"It certainly has, Prime Minister."

"Do you mind if we speak for a moment?" asked Blair, indicating a vacant area of the room.

"Of course not," answered Cross, following Blair toward the corner.

"This Real IRA has me quite concerned. How much support do they have in America?"

"None. Except for some isolated individuals who have no following themselves."

"That's reassuring, because we can't have another Omagh."

"Prime Minister, let me put it as bluntly as I can. I know most of the people the Real IRA would go to for weapons, and believe me, they're supporting the Good Friday Agreement. They're entirely behind Adams and McGuiness."

"It's very gratifying to see how united we all are on this issue," concluded Blair.

Blair would later go on to stand with the United States in the war against Serbia in the spring of 1999, and Cross would meet him again briefly in Belfast during Clinton's farewell presidential visit to Ireland in December 2000. When Bush took office, it was speculated that Blair might grow distant—that his relationship was a personal one to Clinton, not to the United States. Soon after Bush's inauguration, however, Blair visited him at Camp David, and by virtually all accounts they got along very well. Any lingering doubts about the depth of their relationship had been forever extinguished on September 11th. Blair was among the very first foreign leaders to call the president and pledge his fullest support. He also issued a public statement not only offering President Bush "our solidarity, profound sympathy and our prayers" but reaffirming the lasting alliance between the two nations: "This is not a battle between the United States of America and terrorism, but between the free and democratic world and terrorism. We, therefore, here in Britain stand shoulder to shoulder with our American friends in this hour of tragedy, and we, like them, will not rest until this evil is driven from our world."

At a moment when Tony Blair could have paused or ducked for cover, he stepped forward and made America's war Britain's war as well. Today, Thursday, he had flown to the United States. First, to New York, to witness Ground Zero; then to the White House, to meet with the president in late afternoon. Following their meeting, they spoke to the reporters. Bush spoke first: "It's my honor to welcome my friend, and friend to America, Prime Minister Tony Blair to the White House. I appreciate him coming to America in our time of need. One of the first calls I got was from the prime minister. He was reassuring to me. He showed himself to be a true friend, and I appreciate that. And I look forward to giving a speech tonight. The prime minister has kindly agreed to come and listen to it."

Blair responded, "Thank you, Mr. President. It's my honor to be here, and also to pay tribute to your leadership at this immensely difficult time. I was in New York earlier today, and it's perhaps only when you are actually there that the full enormity and horror of what happened comes home to you.

"And I said then, I would like to repeat, that my father's generation went through the experience of the Second World War, when Britain was under attack, during the days of the Blitz. And there was one nation and one people that, above all, stood side by side with us at the time. And that nation was America, and those people were the American people. And I say to you, we stand side by side with you now, without hesitation.

"This is the struggle that concerns us all, the whole of the democratic and civilized and free world. And we have to do things very clearly: we have to bring to account those responsible, and then we have to set about at every single level, in every way that we can, dismantling the apparatus of terror, and eradicating the evil of mass terrorism in our world. And I know that America, Britain, and all our allies will stand together in that task."

George W. Bush had not yet proven himself to be a Franklin D. Roosevelt, nor Tony Blair a Winston Churchill. But as this great war began, each knew that—like their predecessors six decades ago—they belonged together . . .

It was just nine o'clock. All introductions had been completed. Every seat on the floor and in the gallery was filled. The air throughout the chamber was simultaneously electric and still. All eyes were on the rear doors, which were shut. From his back-row vantage point Cross had a direct view of the doors. As the seconds ticked by as if they were hours, the doors remained shut, and the silent chamber felt even quieter. Then Cross saw the two doors being pulled back and locked in place. First to step through this opened doorway was Bill Livingood, the House sergeant-at-arms. Just behind him was the president, standing in the entranceway, wearing a crisp blue suit, white shirt, and light blue tie. Everyone in the chamber—floor and gallery—rose at once. There was still absolute silence. Livingood stepped forward in the center aisle, stopping at the second row from the back. This was where he would formally announce the president's arrival. The chamber remained silent. The president stepped just inside the entranceway, stopped, and waited. He looked serious but calm. The look of a guy who knew he faced the fight of his life but knew he was ready for that fight. He slowly glanced from one side of the aisle to the other, and then back again, nodding reassuringly toward the members of Congress looking toward him. All of this could not have taken more than several seconds.

"Mr. Speaker," Livingood shouted as loudly as he ever had, "the President of the United States!"

The very instant Livingood concluded his announcement and before the president even took his first step forward, the audience erupted in ear-ringing cheers, roars, and hand-clapping that cascaded through the venerable chamber, crashing off the walls and against the ceiling. It was as if a lid had been lifted from a giant cauldron. Nine days of suppressed rage, fear, hope, and pride were unleashed, filling the chamber with a relentless energy—an energy that fueled the president as he deliberately made his way down the aisle, shaking the hands thrust toward him from both sides of the aisle. As he stepped onto the Speaker's rostrum, positioned himself behind the podium, and looked out toward the crowd, the decibel level soared even higher into the stratosphere. The ovation went on for a seemingly endless time. When the clamor began to subside, the Speaker gaveled for order and then made the required reintroduction of the president, and the ovation began all over again. Finally the applause, cheering, and roaring ended. The chamber again fell silent. The president began.

Cross saw right away that Bush was on his game. The voice was clear and strong. The delivery direct and confident. The presence commanding. The attacks of nine days ago had been brutal and the days since then perilous, but Bush was making it clear that now he was controlling events. That it was America that would set the agenda—and that agenda was to destroy bin Laden, Al Qaeda, and international terrorism. Cross's evaluation of the Bush performance was shared by the other congressmen and senators, who interrupted the speech thirty-two times with thunderous applause.

Bush set the tone at the very outset: "In the normal course of events, presidents come to this chamber to report on the state of the Union. Tonight, no such report is needed. It has already been delivered by the American people. . . . It is strong.

"Tonight we are a country awakened to danger and called to defend freedom. Our grief has turned to anger, and anger to resolution. Whether we bring our enemies to justice, or justice to our enemies, justice will be done."

The president went on to thank the countries throughout the world who were pledging their support, stressing the help from the British. "America has no truer friend than Great Britain. Once again, we are joined together in a great cause—

and I am so honored the British prime minister has crossed an ocean to show his unity of purpose with America. Thank you for coming, friend."

Friend. If Cross knew anything about George Bush it was that he wasn't a touchy-feely, hearts and flowers, psychobabble type of guy. He didn't let people get very close to him. So if he said *friend,* he meant it. It wasn't a throwaway line or the superficial bonhomie that characterizes so many political "friendships." George Bush had just given his friend, Tony Blair, his highest compliment . . .

Bush left no doubt who was responsible for the attacks—and who would be held responsible. All evidence "points to a collection of loosely affiliated terrorist organizations known as Al Qaeda . . . Al Qaeda is to terror what the mafia is to crime. . . . The group and its leader—a person named Osama bin Laden— are linked to many other organizations in different countries."

So Al Qaeda and bin Laden would be brought to justice, or justice would be brought to them. But so too would others suffer our wrath. Al Qaeda was based in Afghanistan, with the full acquiescence and support of the Taliban regime. Bush demanded that the Taliban turn over all Al Qaeda leaders and shut down all training camps. As important as the demands was the ultimatum: "These demands are not open to negotiation or discussion. The Taliban must act, and act immediately. They will hand over the terrorists, or they will share in their fate."

Nor would our sights be limited to Afghanistan: "Our enemy is a radical network of terrorists, and every government that supports them. Our war on terror begins with Al Qaeda, but it does not end there. It will not end until every terrorist group of global reach has been found, stopped and defeated.

"Every nation in every region, now has a decision to make. Either you are with us, or you are with the terrorists. From this day forward, any nation that continues to harbor or support terrorism will be regarded by the United States as a hostile regime."

The speech was a call to arms. It was also a reality check. This would not be a quick or easy war. Nor a war suited to the demands and expectations of cable TV's twenty-four-hour news cycle: "America should not expect one battle, but a lengthy campaign, unlike any other we have ever seen. It may include dramatic strikes, visible on TV, and covert operations, not even in the news."

It would also be a war where we would not be immune to domestic attacks. To coordinate the defensive effort, Bush would establish the Office of Homeland Security. It would be directed by Pennsylvania governor Tom Ridge. Ridge was a Vietnam War hero. Cross had served with him in the House. He was tough and sturdy. A solid choice.

The president also made a call for tolerance. A call that at the time Cross thought to be particularly appropriate and beneficent: "The terrorists practice a fringe form of Islamic extremism that has been rejected by Muslim scholars and the vast majority of Muslim clerics—a fringe movement that perverts the peaceful teachings of Islam. . . . No one should be singled out for unfair treatment or unkind words because of their ethnic background or religious faith."

Bush concluded by pledging that America's future would not be one of fear. "I know there are struggles ahead, and dangers to face. But this country will define our times, not be defined by them. Great damage has been done to us. We have suffered great losses. And in our grief and anger we have found our mission and our moment. . . .

"It is my hope that in the months and years ahead, life will return almost to normal. Even grief recedes with time and grace. But our resolve must not pass. Each of us will remember what happened that day, and to whom it happened. We'll remember the moment the news came—where we were and what we were doing."

Bush then took a police shield from his pocket and displayed it to the nation and the world. "This is my reminder of lives that ended, and a task that must not end." It was the shield of George Howard. He had been a constituent of Cross. It had been given to the president by Arlene Howard, George's mother. She was also Cross's constituent. He knew her well from her active involvement in veterans' groups . . .

"I will not forget this wound to our country or those who inflicted it. I will not yield; I will not retreat; I will not relent in waging this struggle for freedom and security for the American people.

"The course of this conflict is not known, yet its outcome is certain."

A cacophony of shouts, roars, and applause enveloped the president as he slowly worked his way back through the well-wishers and up the center aisle. As Bush was passing the final row, Cross shook his hand, saying, "Great job, Mr. President," which was what just about everyone else had said to him.

Cross stood in the hallway outside the chamber, until Danny came down from the gallery. Then, saying little, they walked downstairs and out the door into the night. The sky was dark and still protected by F-16s.

It was early evening as Sean Cross navigated his car through the tree-lined roads of Cove's Neck, a very upscale community on Long Island's north shore. Recognizing two large brick columns coming up on his left, he turned his car from the road, between the columns, and along the long, unpaved driveway leading to the luxurious twelve-room home of Dr. Abdul Ahmed.

"These guys really know how to live," said Tom Barfield, who was seated in the front passenger seat.

"Yeah, but Ahmed's earned it," answered Cross. "He's got a terrific reputation, one of the top heart surgeons in the country."

"I'm not denying he's a good doctor, and I certainly don't begrudge him his money. I just wish he'd remember that the only reason he's made that kind of money is because he's living in America."

"Maybe he is starting to remember. That's supposed to be the reason he invited us up here tonight."

"We'll see."

Several weeks had gone by since Cross and Ahmed had met in the doctor's Northern Boulevard office, and Cross had heard nothing. Then Ahmed telephoned Cross and asked him if he could come by his Cove's Neck home this evening. Cross said yes.

Ahmed said he might have some information that might be help-ful. Cross asked if he could bring Tom Barfield. After a moment's hesitation, Ahmed had said yes.

Cross moved his car slowly toward the two-story Victorian style structure. Ultra-bright security lights came on, illuminating the grounds around the house. Cross parked the car in a pebble-filled area adjacent to the front porch. As Cross and Barfield walked from the car and up the porch steps, Ahmed was waiting at the door to greet them.

"Congressman, it is indeed my honor to welcome you to my home," said Ahmed, extending his right hand toward Cross.

"It's my pleasure, Dr. Ahmed," answered Cross as they shook hands. "I think you know Tom Barfield."

"Certainly I know Mr. Barfield. I met him at several of your fund-raising events. And, of course, everyone knows of his dis-tinguished reputation as a security expert," replied Ahmed, shak-ing Barfield's hand and leading both guests into his expansive and elaborately furnished living room. Cross and Barfield sat down on the long damask-covered sofa, and Ahmed asked if he could get them a drink. Knowing that Ahmed was a strict, observant Muslim and that alcohol would be out of the question, Cross asked for apple juice. Barfield requested orange juice. Ahmed returned from the kitchen less than a minute later, gave Cross and Barfield their drinks, and sat down in one of the two high-backed, wooden chairs located in the center of the room, less than eight feet from the couch, which he faced directly.

"I gave considerable thought to what we discussed at our last meeting," said Ahmed, "particularly the issues you were raising about the level of cooperation from my community. To be very honest with you, that conversation was distinctly painful for me."

"As you know, Doctor Ahmed, it was never my intention to cause you pain," answered Cross, "but I do believe that friends owe each other the truth. Especially in such perilous times."

"I understand that. I do indeed. I must also say that, as I thought it over and over again in the following weeks, I came to understand—or at least partially understand—why you might conclude that Muslims are not doing all that we should be doing in cooperating with law enforcement agencies."

Cross leaned slightly forward as Ahmed was speaking; Barfield leaned back, more observer than participant.

"Did you have the opportunity to discuss this at all with any of the leaders in your community, in your mosque?" asked Cross.

"Yes. I did. And some of those conversations did not go so well. Certainly not at first."

"You don't have to give me any names. But what type of people did you speak with?"

"A fairly good cross section. Doctors, of course. But also shop owners, accountants, and cab drivers."

"Did you talk to the imam?"

"No. I did not believe that would be appropriate on so sensitive a topic."

"Well, where do we stand?" asked Cross, signaling that it was time to cease the formalities.

"I have very reluctantly concluded that there is indeed some merit to your contention. I think there may well have been some incidents going on around us. Incidents that should have given us a signal but, for whatever reason, we chose to ignore."

"Anything in particular?"

"Yes. But first, if you will indulge me, I would like to speak generally. There is someone I will introduce to you later who can speak more to the specifics."

"Certainly," answered Cross, who until that moment had no clue that anyone else would be joining their meeting. To his side he could sense Barfield sitting more upright.

"As with your Bible, there are sections of the Koran that taken in isolation could be interpreted as justifying violence against non-Muslims and by extension against the West. When I was growing up in Islamabad, that was not the type of Islam I was taught. We certainly weren't particularly open-minded about other religions, but . . ."

"Don't worry about that," interjected Cross. "I grew up Irish-Catholic, and we weren't open-minded at all."

"See, we do have a lot in common," replied Ahmed with a broad smile.

"I'm sorry I interrupted you."

"Not at all. We weren't open-minded or ecumenical, but neither did we attempt to hurt or injure anyone. There was never a feeling that our religion would justify us attacking someone from another religion. Also, there was always a strong feeling of affection toward the United States."

"How was it when you came over here to live?"

"I think it was basically the same. At least in the beginning. But, as I look back on it, there were changes that began about twenty years ago. They were very subtle at first but increased steadily."

"What type of changes?"

"Toward fundamentalism. In our religion we call it Wahhabism. A very literal reading of the Koran."

"How did the changes come about?"

"As I said, it was subtle. But during the eighties and nineties, there was a large influx of immigration from Muslim countries. A good number of immigrants had fought as mujahedeen against the Russians in Afghanistan. They were almost all fundamentalists, and they became very active in the mosques."

"And the imams?"

"The imams who immigrated here were also much more fundamentalist than what I'd been used to, and they began to take over in more and more mosques."

"But you said it was subtle?"

"It was. As I'm describing it to you now, it sounds very black and white, very clear-cut. But when it was happening, it didn't appear that way at all. For instance, while I certainly try to live up to the tenets of my religion, I've never been particularly active in the operations of the mosque. So when the new, younger immigrants showed so much energy and enthusiasm, those of us who'd been here for a while were happy to step aside and let others do the work."

"But wasn't the fundamentalism an obvious change?"

"Again, not as obvious as you might think. As I listened to it, it seemed more an expression of Muslim pride than hatred against others. And while it was different from my own experience, I realized that the younger immigrants coming over in large numbers and having the experience of fighting a Muslim war against the Soviets would prefer imams who were more dogmatic and forceful than what we were used to. Also, with so much drugs and teenage pregnancy, some of us felt that maybe it wouldn't be so bad to restore traditional values—if you don't mind me using that term."

"There was no anti-Americanism?"

"Nothing at first. And what criticism I'd hear was nothing different from what you'd expect to hear in a democratic society."

"Like?"

"Like the fact that Pakistan was America's staunch ally but that America sided with India even though India voted against America in the United Nations. Like the fact that when there was genocide against Muslims in Bosnia, the United States and the Europeans waited years before they did anything about it. And, of course, that in the Middle East, the United States always took Israel's position over the Palestinians."

"You don't see that as anti-American?"

"No. I thought it was fair comment. After all, on Pakistan and Bosnia, you, yourself, agreed with us, and, as with your own issue, Northern Ireland, I recall you saying that the State Department invariably took the British side."

"I see your point, but only to an extent. I did think American policy was wrong on Pakistan and on Bosnia, but I didn't think it was because our government was anti-Muslim. And as strongly as I felt about Ireland, I didn't think the United States was anti-Irish or anti-Catholic."

"And I didn't consider what I was hearing in the mosque to be anti-American. I knew what this country had done for me, and I never would have conceived of being anti-American. What I was missing was that the newer immigrants *were* anti-American and that what they were hearing from the imams was fortifying that prejudice, that . . ." Ahmed hesitated for a moment—" . . . that hatred."

"Was there anything besides the imams and the mosques?"

"Yes. And again this is more obvious to me in hindsight than when it was occurring. When we would have gatherings, the Muslim Political Alliance for instance . . ."

"I spoke there once. I think you were the one who invited me."

"I remember that well. And I recall how well received you were—particularly your message that we should become more politically involved."

"But apparently something was going on at the convention that shouldn't have been going on."

"That is my belief. When I first started attending gatherings of this type, the people were very dignified, very respectable."

"What happened?"

"I don't mean this to sound as if I'm class conscious, but more and more in recent years, these meetings started attracting a much harder element. They would almost always be unshaven. None wore a tie. And they would stay together in small groups. An air of conspiracy about them. They seemed very confident and also very angry."

"Do you know where they were from?"

"Most came from Saudi Arabia, and quite a few had fought with the mujahedeen."

"Do you ever talk with them? Or have any dealings with them?"

"Nothing except to say hello. But in their own way, they gave me the clear impression that I was not in their circle."

"You definitely have drawn us a general picture. I suppose we could disagree over whether you should have taken more notice than you did. But I have no reason to doubt your word.

What do you have as far as specific information on what's been happening lately?"

"The actual information is from one of the young men active in our Muslim Political Alliance."

"He's the guy who's here tonight?"

"Yes. He has been waiting in the den. With your permission I shall ask him to join us."

"By all means."

Ahmed left the room and walked from the living room through the dining room to the rear of the house. Moments later he returned with a Middle-Eastern-looking man, about six feet tall, with a wiry build. Wearing jeans and a blue Yankee sweatshirt, he appeared to be in his late twenties. He also appeared somewhat uncomfortable and ill at ease.

"Congressman Cross, this is Omar Aziz, one of our finest young men."

"Very good to meet you, Omar. This is Tom Barfield, a friend of mine, who gives me a lot of advice on security issues."

"It is my pleasure to meet each of you gentlemen," said Aziz, as he shook hands with Cross and Barfield, before sitting down in the chair next to Ahmed.

"With your permission," said Ahmed, "I will tell you what I know of Omar, as a means of introduction, and then ask him to tell you the information that he and I believe might be of help to you."

"Sure," said Cross, as both he and Barfield leaned slightly forward.

"Omar is from Saudi Arabia. He originally came to this country eight years ago to study at New York University. After several years, however, he left school and has worked in a number of jobs, including managing a gas station near here in Wantagh, and being a foreman in a trucking company."

"So far, there's nothing particularly unusual," said Cross.

"We're coming to that," answered Ahmed. "For the past four years Omar shared an apartment in Astoria with another young

Saudi, Ali Said. Mr. Said is also active in the Muslim Political Alliance, and his uncle is a member of our mosque, but in all honesty, I do not know Mr. Said that well. Certainly not nearly as well as I know Omar."

"Pardon me for interrupting," said Barfield in an almost Columbo-like manner, "but just to make sure I can keep track of who's who, could you tell me who Mr. Said's uncle is?"

"That would be Khalid Mustafa."

"And he is a member of your mosque?" asked Barfield, in an extremely casual, uninterested tone.

"Oh yes. He lives in New Hyde Park. Very respected indeed."

"I'm sure," said Cross, remembering that Mustafa was the name given him by Barfield and Lou Bianchi as an explosives expert, but not wanting to tip his hand. "I'm sorry we keep interrupting you with these side issues."

"No problem," answered Ahmed. "I myself will conclude in just a moment. What I was starting to say was that in the past several weeks Omar came across some very troubling information. So troubling that he came to me to discuss it, and after listening to him, that is when I called you and asked you to come to this meeting. Now I will let Omar tell what he knows."

"Before Omar even begins, I want to thank him for being willing to help us out like this," said Cross, moving slightly to look directly at Omar. "I know this can't be easy for you. But this could be very helpful to us and to all Americans."

"I appreciate your kind words, Congressman Cross," said Omar, in broken but very understandable English. "I do hope that I can be of assistance to you. You were very correct, however, when you said this is very difficult for me. For while I think I have come upon some things that might well be significant, I am also aware that often there are coincidences for which innocent people are made to suffer. There is also the added fact that if my suspicions are true about the information I have, then a person for whom I have had a deep friendship could be in great trouble."

"I understand your concerns," said Cross. "But I do believe you have made the correct decision in coming forward."

"Let me begin," said Omar, his voice growing stronger. "The eight years I have been in this country have been very beneficial to me. I have nothing but good things to say about the United States. I wish I had been able to stay in the university longer, but that was my own fault. My grades fell behind, and then I couldn't afford the cost of making up courses and staying in school that much longer. So I started working full-time, sometimes having second and third jobs, and I've always managed to do well."

"How did you meet Mr. Said?" asked Cross.

"A little over five years ago I started working for a trucking company in Brooklyn. Ali was one of the first guys I'd met. We were both looking for an apartment. He found a good-sized place in Astoria, within walking distance of the el, and we decided to share it."

"What do you know about his background?" asked Cross.

"We're just about the same age—I'm twenty-nine, he's thirty. We're both from Saudi Arabia, though I didn't know him before I met him over here."

"Was he politically active at all?" asked Barfield.

"He's always had strong political and religious views—and the two ran very much together. I've always considered myself to be an observant Muslim—even what you might well call a fundamentalist—but nowhere near as observant as Ali. He also had very intense feelings about American foreign policy being controlled by the Jews—especially in regard to Palestine."

"Would you say he was anti-Semitic?" asked Cross.

"Not really. He was anti-Israel, because he believed that Jews were on Palestinian land. But it had nothing to do with the Jewish religion or Jewish people."

"What other foreign policy issues?" asked Barfield.

"He was almost obsessed with American troops being on Arab soil—such as in Saudi Arabia. To him this was a desecration of holy land. In that way he was very much like bin Laden."

"Did he speak much about bin Laden?" asked Cross.

"He was generally favorable toward bin Laden, saying that Muslims needed someone to give them a sense of pride, of dignity—and someone who had the courage to speak out against the decadence of modern society."

"Did he talk this way even after September 11th?" asked Barfield.

"I'm afraid he did—though not as directly. But—and this is something that as a Muslim I am not particularly proud of—there were many American Muslims who did not think the case against bin Laden was as black-and-white as other Americans thought it to be."

"How did Ali and those Muslims feel?" asked Cross, who cast a quick glance toward Ahmed.

"They believed that while what bin Laden did was wrong, in many ways it showed the world that Muslims could no longer be ignored, that we were a real force. Just think about it—you had the most powerful nation in the world brought to a halt and the most famous city in the world in flames because of a few unarmed Muslims."

"I don't think it's fair to say that most American Muslims shared that feeling," interjected Dr. Ahmed.

"With all respect," answered Omar, "I think it is fair to say that too many Muslims either felt that way or didn't care enough to speak up. And I'm including myself in that category."

"Was Said involved with any groups or organizations that supported bin Laden?" asked Cross.

"Nothing that I was aware of. To be very honest with you, all the time Ali was talking about bin Laden and religious fundamentalism, I just thought it was what Americans call 'barroom talk.' I never thought he'd act on it."

"'Barroom talk' is pretty good for guys who don't drink," said Barfield with an ironic smile.

"Seriously, I never thought Ali had any connection to a group like Al Qaeda . . ."

"Until two weeks ago," said Ahmed.

"Yes, until two weeks ago," answered Omar. "But, as I look back on it, probably several months ago as well."

"First things first," said Barfield. "What happened two weeks ago?"

"It was on a Tuesday night. I'd told Ali I would be getting together with some guys from work and probably wouldn't be home until about midnight. Instead, things pretty much fell through, and I showed up at the apartment at about eight-thirty or so."

"He wasn't expecting you?" asked Cross.

"No. And that shouldn't be such a big thing. After all, we have our own lives, and we come and go. But this night when I came in, he was taking a shower—so he didn't hear me. I saw papers spread out all over the kitchen table. I just casually looked at them and was confused at first."

"How so?" asked Barfield.

"There were what looked like blueprints or plans and then professional-type photos—some eleven by fourteen, most eight by ten—from all different angles. Ground level and from overhead."

"Photos of what?" asked Cross.

"The New York docks."

"And the plans?" asked Barfield.

"I assume the docks as well. But I didn't know for sure."

"Are you sure it was the docks?" asked Cross.

"I have no doubt the pictures were of the docks," answered Omar. "The blueprints I'm pretty sure about—but not as definite as the photos."

"How long were you looking at them?"

"I guess about two or three minutes. But it didn't mean much to me. I didn't think there was anything wrong with it."

"So what made you suspicious?" inquired Barfield.

"Ali's reaction. He went mad. I'd never seen him act this way before."

"What do you mean?" asked Cross.

"He'd just come out of the shower, had put on a robe and was rubbing his face with a towel—when he saw me in the kitchen. He started screaming: 'What are you doing here? How dare you look at these pictures! Who do you think you are?' His face was beet red, and I thought the veins in his neck were going to burst."

"You said he ordinarily didn't have a bad temper?" queried Barfield.

"From my experience he had no temper at all. He was always very calm, even when he was talking about politics or religion."

"What happened next?" asked Cross.

"He started gathering all the photos and drawings together. Scooping them up off the table. Then he took them to his room and slammed the door shut."

"What did you do during all this?"

"When he was doing all the yelling, I tried a few times to tell him that I'd meant nothing by it. The pictures were out in full display, and I was just being curious. We'd never had any secrets with one another. But I really couldn't get a word in."

"How long did he stay in the room?" asked Barfield.

"About ten minutes or so. When he came out, he was dressed and had all the photos and drawings in a large folder. He must have had other papers in the folder—because it seemed bulkier than just the photos and the drawings. He told me, 'What you did was wrong,' and he went out the door."

"Have you seen him since?"

"Just once. He stayed out all night. He came back the next morning and started packing his clothes. He said 'After what happened last night there's no way I can stay here.'"

"Did he say where he was going?" asked Cross.

"To live with his uncle in New Hyde Park."

"Khalid Mustafa?" asked Barfield.

"Yes. He works in a furniture store in Brooklyn. On Atlantic Avenue."

Cross and Barfield remained stoic, making sure not to show any reaction.

What are you doing with the apartment?" asked Cross.

"There's only sixty days left on the lease, so I told the landlord I wouldn't be renewing it. And Ali—to give him credit—sent me a check for his share for the final two months."

"Omar, I can understand you being upset over Said's outburst and his strange behavior," said Cross. "And I can see why you might be suspicious. But was that really enough for you to come to me and tell me all about it? Because, let's face it, the implications of what you're suggesting are absolutely terrifying."

"I understand that, but fortunately—or unfortunately—there were other incidents that caused me to have these grave suspicions and convinced me I had to speak to someone."

"What can you tell us about these incidents?" asked Barfield.

"They actually go back several months, and at the time I paid absolutely no attention to them. But after what happened that night, I forced myself to do a lot of thinking. I particularly thought back to the days before the attacks on the office building in Westbury and the Armory in Brooklyn and the train tunnels. And I realized there had been very suspicious behavior."

"What specifics can you give us?" inquired Cross.

"About two or three weeks before the attacks, Ali got a call from his uncle, Khalid Mustafa, to meet him at the Empire Plaza towers—the two buildings that were attacked."

"Did he tell you this?"

"Yes. Apparently his uncle had left him a message to meet him there the next day. Ali knows nothing about Nassau County, so he asked me what the closest LIRR stop was, and I told him Westbury."

"Did he tell you what they were going there for?"

"Only when I asked him—which I did only to make small talk. He said the Muslim Political Alliance was thinking of opening a Long Island chapter office in Empire Plaza."

"That was untrue. Entirely untrue," said Dr. Ahmed. "I am involved in the Alliance, and I can tell you there was never ever the slightest decision of starting a Long Island chapter, never mind opening an office. There would be no purpose in opening such an office—or any justification for paying the cost it would involve."

"I'm active in the Alliance as well," said Omar, "though at a much lower level. And I'd heard nothing about a separate Long Island chapter, and since then I've asked friends who are in the Alliance, and they all say they never heard anything about it."

"Do you remember what time he was supposed to be there?"

"He said as close to 10:30 as possible. And it's about a five-minute walk from the station. So we checked ticket information, and he took a train arriving in Westbury at 10:24."

"That means they would have arrived at the office complex just about an hour prior to the time of day the attacks were ultimately carried out a few weeks later," said Barfield. "It's standard procedure for these guys to check the target out and do a dry run."

"There's just one thing I can't accept about this scenario," said Dr. Ahmed. "It is beyond my belief that Khalid Mustafa could be involved in any type of illegal activity. He has always been a perfect gentleman. Never associates with any unruly element. And is very much respected."

Cross did not want Ahmed to know that Inspector Bianchi had told him of Mustafa's connections to Ali Shibh, the dirty-bomb scientist. Nor did he want him to know that Barfield had been suspicious of Mustafa all along.

"How would you account for Mr. Mustafa scoping out Empire Plaza, if he was entirely innocent?" Cross asked Dr. Ahmed.

"No one saw Khalid at Empire Plaza," answered Ahmed. "No one knows that Khalid ever even spoke to Ali Said about going to Empire Plaza. All we know is that Ali told that to Omar. If Ali could lie about everything else, he could certainly lie about that."

"You could be right," said Cross, eager to take the spotlight off Mustafa. "I think our focus should be on Ali Said."

"Is there anything else you can tell us about Mr. Said?" asked Barfield, who knew exactly what Cross was up to.

"There is," answered Omar, "but again it's the type of thing that I took little notice of at the time. Beginning about four or five months ago, he began spending quite a bit of time with Sheik Hassan . . ."

"He's from Yemen," said Dr. Ahmed.

"Yes, he is from Yemen and a very strong Al Qaeda sympathizer," said Omar. "Probably more importantly, even though he has never—as far as I know—held a job for the entire year he's been in the country, he's always had plenty of cash."

"He would be an example of the unsavory element that I was mentioning," said Dr. Ahmed.

"What kind of contact would Ali have with Hassan?" asked Barfield.

"Like I said, Hassan has been in the United States for just about a year," said Omar. "For the first seven or eight months I never knew of any contact between them. But starting last fall, probably in November or December, Hassan started calling the apartment on a regular basis. It seemed like at least once a day—occasionally two or three times. They would also get together once or twice a week that I knew of."

"Did Ali give you any idea about what his dealings were with Hassan?" asked Cross.

"He says they were raising money for an Islamic Academy they wanted to establish in Brooklyn. It would be for grades one to six and would have separate wings for boys and girls."

"Again, I must say that I did not hear any discussion in our community about the creation of such an academy," said Dr. Ahmed.

"Do you remember anything about the telephone conversations?" asked Barfield.

"I certainly wasn't eavesdropping or paying very much attention," said Omar. "But my recollection is that they were brief. Ali never said much more than yes or no, and he often left the apartment five or ten minutes after the conversations were ended."

"How did Hassan react to last month's attacks?" asked Barfield.

"I have no idea. He hasn't called the apartment since the day before the attacks. And afterward I never heard Ali mention Hassan's name or anything about the academy."

"Have you had any contact with Ali since he left the apartment?" asked Cross.

"I haven't spoken with him at all. The only contact was the rent check he mailed me."

"Don't you work for the same furniture factory?" asked Barfield.

"We did, but he quit about six months ago," answered Omar. "Since then he told me he was driving a cab."

"Omar, as I said earlier, I really want to thank you for coming forward," said Cross. "I'm not the professional. I'm going to pass on what you've told us to the appropriate law enforcement people. So I'm not in any position to evaluate this information. But it certainly appears to me to be very disturbing, but also very helpful."

"I hope so," said Omar.

"I'm sure you've thought of this yourself," said Cross, "but I think you have reason to be concerned for your own safety. If Ali Said was involved in any way in last month's attacks or in any attack that is being planned for the future, then we are dealing with some very dangerous people."

"I don't want to be an alarmist," said Barfield, "but we could be talking about life and death."

"I have thought about it," answered Omar. "I've actually thought about it quite a bit."

"I've told him that he is free to stay here in my home," said Ahmed, "until some other arrangement can be made. But, in all fairness, I do not want to put my family at sustained risk. I was thinking, Congressman Cross, that you might be of assistance."

"That was why I asked," said Cross. "When I talk to the FBI and the NYPD, which I'll do almost immediately, I'll urge them to provide Omar with protection. In the meantime, I think it would be best for Omar to stay with Dr. Ahmed—I hope for a short period of time. In no event, though, should you go back to your apartment."

"Thank you, Congressman," said Omar.

It appeared that Omar had more to say but was having difficulty saying it. After several long seconds, Dr. Ahmed spoke.

"Congressman, there is one other matter we should discuss, which I must admit is somewhat awkward."

"Why don't you tell me what it is, and we'll decide what can be done," answered Cross.

"It concerns Omar's status," said Ahmed.

"His immigration status?"

"I'm afraid so."

"Give me the details," said Cross, looking toward Omar. Omar hesitated for a moment, then began.

"When I first came here to attend NYU, I had a student visa. Obviously, when I left school, the visa expired. I just stayed here, kept a low profile, and nobody bothered me. Even with all the crackdowns after September 11th, INS never came after me."

"That's fairly common, isn't it?" asked Barfield.

"Actually, it is," answered Omar. "Despite the talk of dragnets and door-to-door searches for illegals, many of us—maybe most of us—have not been caught. My concern now is that by coming forward and trying to assist the government, I will be deported."

"And if he is deported," said Dr. Ahmed, "he will be sent to Saudi Arabia, which would put him at great risk."

"I guess this goes under the heading of no good deed going unpunished," said Cross with a rueful smile. "But assuming the information you've given me is accurate, I'll do whatever I can to help you out."

"Could you give us some idea what steps you might be taking?" asked Ahmed.

"I told you I'll be talking with my contacts in the FBI and the NYPD as soon as possible to tell them what Omar's given me," answered Cross. "At the same time I'll tell them about his visa problem and ask them to make sure Immigration leaves him alone."

"Do you think that will work?" asked Ahmed.

"There are never any guarantees when you deal with the feds," answered Cross. "But I'm pretty sure I'll be able to keep them off your back for a while."

Cross maneuvered his car to the end of the long driveway, stopped for a moment, and then turned right onto the main road.

"Jesus Christ, with all their money you think these people could afford streetlights up here," grumbled Barfield.

"Maybe they just want to make it difficult for people like you to show up uninvited," answered Cross. "Or maybe darkness adds mystery and ambience."

"Darkness or not, this trip will have been worth it if just half the shit that guy told us turns out to be true."

"You're right. Ahmed seems to have delivered a lot more than I expected."

"The real shocker was them giving us Mustafa's name without us having to say a word."

"That certainly fits in with what you and Lou Bianchi were trying to piece together."

"We might actually be making some progress."

Cross then contacted Bianchi and Hennessy from the car phone, briefly telling them what he and Barfield had learned from Omar. Bianchi and Hennessy agreed to meet face to face tomorrow so the NYPD and the FBI could coordinate this information with whatever other evidence and leads they had. Bianchi also said he would assign a security detail to Omar within the hour, and Hennessy said he'd make sure the feds stayed away from Omar for now.

Barfield looked in the rear-view mirror and then back over his right shoulder.

"Sean, I don't want to sound paranoid, but there's been a car following us for the past few miles."

"Actually he's been following us from the moment we left Ahmed's house, and he followed us all the way up there as well," answered Cross with a laugh. "It's Brian Sullivan."

"The Nassau detective?"

"Yeah. He's still giving me security—but we didn't want to intimidate Ahmed. So Sully drove behind us and then stayed close to the house in case anything shitty came down. It was the same when I met with Pete Cairney—Sully just blended in, and nobody knew he was there for me."

"You're a lot smarter then you look."

"If I were that smart, I wouldn't need police protection."

"Good point."

"What did you think of what Omar told us?"

"Obviously we'll have to check it all out. But if I had to bet, I'd say it's probably on target."

"It shocked the shit out of me when Mustafa's name came up. You'd told me from the start that the FBI was looking at him, and then Bianchi told me his name came up in Hamburg. But I'd never mentioned his name to Ahmed or any of those guys."

"That's why I think Omar is probably being straight with us."

"Of course, Omar could still have his own agenda here. For all we know, he could have been involved with Ali Said, and they had a falling out. He's probably also petrified of being deported. So he comes to us and tells us what we want to hear."

"This guy could have the worst motives in the world, but how would he have known what we wanted to hear? How would he have known we were onto Mustafa? We never had to bring up his name. And as far as the visa, he's probably taking more of a chance by coming to us than if he just continued to lie low—especially if he's giving us phony information."

"You're right. You know, we might actually be starting to connect the dots!"

"Let's hope we're able to connect them all before it's too late," said Barfield.

October 2001

Life in Washington and New York was returning to a level of normality far greater and far more rapidly than Sean Cross would have dared to imagine during those first devastating days after September 11.

Planes resumed flying into Washington again—first to Dulles Airport in Fairfax County, Virginia, about twenty-five miles from downtown Washington, and then, on October 4th, to Reagan National Airport just across the Potomac from Washington, D.C., itself.

Congress was meeting again in regular session. Voting on the House floor. Holding committee hearings. Meeting foreign leaders such as the emir of Qatar, who assured Cross and other congressmen on October 4th that his Arab state would stand with the United States against Al Qaeda.

New York was continuing to fight back. Pataki and Giuliani met with Washington lawmakers to lay out their proposals to rebuild lower Manhattan. Larry Silverstein, who had signed a ninety-nine-year lease to operate the World Trade Center just before September 11th, met with New York congressmen to assure them he intended to rebuild all the structures on the World Trade Center site. Labor leaders, especially from the unions representing the hotels and restaurant employees, described how jobs in their industries had been decimated and how much they needed short-term help. Major league baseball had been suspended during the week after September 11th, but the Mets and Yankees had come back to play before capacity crowds in Shea Stadium and Yankee Stadium. The Mets, after almost a full season of lackluster play, made a last-minute surge but fell just short. The Yankees, however, won their division and league championships and would be playing Arizona in the World Series.

But all this, of course, was peripheral to the central issue of when the war against Afghanistan would begin. When would the president unleash America's military might against the terrorist forces that had caused so many innocent civilians to suffer so much? Bush made it clear that he would not move until our military was positioned to strike effectively. When the attack came, it would be very meaningful and very lethal. The president also wanted to enlist as much international support as possible—not so much because America needed the military assistance of other countries but because Bush wanted bin Laden and the regimes who supported him to realize how outnumbered they were. It would also debunk the inevitable charge that the United States was an international Lone Ranger attempting to impose itself on the world. But while Bush wanted maximum military and diplomatic support, he also knew, and made it clear, that he wouldn't wait forever. This was not a time for anguishing or waiting for the perfect moment. As September 11th demonstrated, this is a very imperfect world.

In the immediate aftermath of September 11th, the media had demonstrated much of the same patriotic fervor and sense of unity that gripped most Americans. Dan Rather went on the David Letterman show and broke into tears attempting to describe his pride in America and his admiration for the rescue workers. Television reporters and anchors took to wearing American flag lapel pins. And much of the almost knee-jerk antigovernment cynicism that pervaded the psyche of so many American reporters since the days of Vietnam and Watergate actually receded. At least for a while. Then ABC instructed its reporters and anchors not to wear the lapel pins. Cablevision on Long Island issued a similar decree against on-air patriotic displays, though some reporters quietly rebelled by wearing discreet combinations of red, white, and blue apparel. Reuters actually decreed that the word "terrorist" should not be used, while CNN said the murderers of September 11th should be described as "alleged hijackers" rather than "terrorists."

From his dealings with the president, however, Cross was convinced that George W. Bush paid no attention to reporters and generally did not care what the media thought—except as he could use them to advance his policies. Unlike Lyndon Johnson, who kept three televisions in his bedroom so he could see and hear what the network anchors were saying about his Vietnam policy, Bush would decide what he thought had to be done, and he would do it.

Bush decided that the war would begin on Sunday, October 7th. Cross and Mary Rose were at the Sands, an ocean-front catering hall in Atlantic Beach on Nassau County's south shore, attending a baby-naming brunch for the grandson of Larry and Helen Elovich, two of their close friends. Larry was one of Long Island's most successful lawyers. He was also a top Democratic operative, who nonetheless gave Cross strong political and financial support. Larry was tough and hard to impress, Helen much more open and trusting. Together they were a great blend. When Cross and Mary Rose arrived that morning, just after 11:30, hundreds of guests were already there. It was a Jewish ceremony, of course, but many Christians were present, including the Eloviches' good friend Al D'Amato. And the ceremony would have a strain of ecumenism. A rabbi would perform the actual ceremony naming young Matthew Jake, but at Larry's request, Cross's son-in-law John Sweeney would deliver an Irish blessing. *Leave it to Larry to cover all bases,* thought Cross.

Driving to the Sands that morning, Cross listened to the radio reports that the war might well begin today. There were hints and indications but nothing definite. And that was all he knew when he arrived at the Sands and Larry asked him, "Any word on the war? There's a lot on the radio." "No," answered Cross, "but Tom O'Connell is monitoring it in my D.C. office. He'll let me know as soon as he hears anything." "The sooner we get them, the better it is for everyone," said Larry.

When the guests took their seats in the banquet room shortly after twelve noon, Sean, Mary Rose, John, and Kara sat at a table in the rear of the room, so there wouldn't be any disturbance in the event O'Connell telephoned Cross during the ceremony. The ceremony itself was moving and uplifting as the rabbi said prayers and invoked blessings upon this baby boy who was embarking on life in such a changed and dangerous world. John Sweeney then concluded the ceremony with an invocation that the Jewish guests must have thought came from a Catholic book of prayers for occasions just such as this, but that Cross knew to be a Sweeney composite of Irish Catholic mysticism and barroom philosophy. But it sounded good and struck the appropriate chord of life and hope.

As John was returning to the table, Cross felt his phone vibrating in his shirt pocket. It was Tom O'Connell. The time was just after twelve thirty. "There was a television report that the war is on," said O'Connell. "I called a friend in the Pentagon, and he confirmed it. The president will speak to the country in about half an hour." Cross closed the phone and quietly told the news to Mary Rose, Kara, and John. They said nothing but nodded quietly. Trying to be unobtrusive, Cross slowly got up from the table and walked along the side of room toward the front, where Larry was standing while his daughter spoke from the microphone about what a joyful gathering this was.

"Do you have any news?" asked Larry, with a look of expectation and apprehension.

"Yeah. The war's just started. The president will be announcing it very soon."

Larry was silent for a moment.

"Should we announce it to the people?" asked Larry.

"That's up to you."

"I think we should. Do you want to do it?"

"No. I really think you should. These are your guests. It's not a political event."

When his daughter concluded her remarks, Larry walked toward the microphone.

"May I have your attention for just a moment?" asked Larry, his voice betraying an uncharacteristic tremor.

Sensing the seriousness of his tone, the room quickly fell silent.

"Congressman Cross has just told me that the war has begun."

A low but pronounced gasp went through the room.

"The president will be making an official announcement very shortly. I . . . "

Larry was unable to continue. He stepped to the side as the rabbi came forward to recite a prayer for the country. The moment he concluded, the crowd spontaneously began singing "God Bless America."

Food had been prepared for a lavish feast. Cross had been looking forward to it. But with the war under way, he wanted to be home to make and receive phone calls. He also wanted to hear the president's speech. Sean and Mary Rose said good-bye to Larry and Helen and to Al D'Amato. Kara and John decided they would stay for a while.

Cross was driving eastbound through Long Beach along Lido Boulevard. The radio was tuned to News 88. The president began his speech. He was speaking from the Treaty Room in the White House. His voice firm, he appeared in control from the outset.

—"Good afternoon. On my orders, the United States military has begun striking against Al Qaeda terrorist training camps and military installations of the Taliban regime in Afghanistan."

—"We are joined in this operation by our staunch friend, Great Britain. Other close friends—including Canada, Australia, Germany and France—have pledged forces as the operation unfolds. More than forty countries . . . have guaranteed air transport or landing rights. . . . We are supported by the collective will of the world."

—"More than two weeks ago, I gave Taliban leaders a series of clear and specific demands. . . . None of those demands were met. And now the Taliban will pay a price."

—"The United States of America is a friend to the Afghan people, and we are the friends of almost a billion worldwide who practice the Islamic faith. The United States of America is an enemy of the barbaric criminals who profane a great religion by committing murder in its name."

The president pointed out that this "military action" was only another part of the overall war against terrorism that already included "diplomacy, intelligence, the freezing of financial assets of known terrorists by law enforcement agencies in thirty-eight countries." He then concluded: "The battle is now joined on many fronts. We will not waver; we will not tire; and we will not fail. Peace and freedom will prevail. Thank you. May God continue to bless America."

Just as Americans were focusing their gaze on the war in Afghanistan, troubling reports of anthrax were emanating from Florida. On October 5th, a sixty-two-year-old photographer, who worked in the same building where the *National Enquirer*, the *Star*, and other scandal sheets had their offices, died in a Boca Raton hospital. The cause of death was anthrax—the first recorded anthrax death in this country since 1976. First reports speculated that the reporter had contracted anthrax after being exposed to polluted water on a recent fishing trip. By the next week, however, it became apparent the anthrax was coming not from polluted water but a bioterrorist. Two other employees—a man on Monday, a woman on Wednesday—who worked in the same building as the photographer were diagnosed with anthrax. Unlike the photographer, they were fortunate enough to survive. But this was only a temporary respite from the anthrax siege. At a dramatic news conference in Manhattan on October 12th, Rudy Giuliani announced that anthrax had been found in NBC's Rockefeller Plaza offices; one of Tom Brokaw's staffers had been stricken. The anthrax had been contained in a letter to Brokaw that the staffer had opened in her third floor office on September 19th. Because anthrax spreads rapidly once it is released, NBC announced it would provide testing for its employees. Anne Kelly, remembering that she and Cross had been at NBC's third-floor studios for an MSNBC interview on the evening of the 18th, told Cross, "We lucked out on this one. Just a day later and we'd have been in the middle of this."

But they weren't as lucky as they thought. Cross was in his district office on Monday, October 15th, watching the news of the latest anthrax attack. An anthrax-filled envelope had been delivered to the Washington, D.C. office of Senate majority leader Tom Daschle, where it had been inadvertently opened by a young staff assistant. Hundreds of Senate employees were to be tested for anthrax and given Cipro—an extremely powerful antibiotic—as a precaution.

"This anthrax situation keeps getting worse," said Cross to Anne Kelly.

"Worse than you think. Read this e-mail you just got," answered Kelly, handing the computer-illiterate Cross the e-mail she'd just printed out for him. It was from MSNBC's booking office:

"As you are aware by now, a confirmed case of cutaneous anthrax has been discovered in an NBC *Nightly News* employee at 30 Rockefeller Plaza in New York. The anthrax is linked to a letter that arrived on the 3rd floor of the building on September 18th. We have absolutely no reason to believe that the exposure will be widespread and every reason to believe that only those coming in direct contact with the particular letter may have been exposed. However, we here at MSNBC feel it necessary to let all of our guests know that there is help and information available. For any guests that joined us for interviews on the 3rd floor of 30 Rockefeller Plaza between September 18th and October 12th, here are the resources available to you."

"The New York Health Department and the FBI will be at 30 Rockefeller Plaza today until 8:00 p.m. They will be available for counseling if you have any fears or questions and they will also be conducting testing if you have reason to believe you may have been exposed in some way. . . . Please call if you will be using these services today so that we can alert security at 30 Rockefeller Plaza and make travel arrangements if necessary."

"I guess God is punishing us for presuming too much," said Kelly with an ironic grin.

"I think NBC is just being extra cautious," answered Cross. "We were down at the other end of the hall that night and the letter wasn't even opened until the next day."

"You're probably right. The only worry could be if the letter had been opened when we were there. But I should probably be extra cautious and call my doctor," said Kelly who was almost four months pregnant.

"And I'll call the congressional doctors. They'll probably tell me to forget it."

Kelly's doctor told her to be tested right away, and she made arrangements with the Nassau County Medical Center to get a test the next day. But since she was pregnant, she couldn't be given Cipro.

The congressional doctor Cross reached told him to come to the medical office as soon as he arrived in Washington the next day. Cross would be tested and put on Cipro as a precaution.

"This is turning out to be more than I expected," Cross said to Kelly. "But I still think they're just taking every precaution."

"You're probably right. But we might as well play it safe."

"Assuming the worst, since you can't take Cipro, what do they give you if there is a problem?"

"I'll jump off that bridge when I come to it. But I can always sue you for bringing me in there that night!"

The congressional doctors—collectively known as the Office of the Attending Physician—are located on the first floor of the Capitol, just off the main lobby leading from the House to the Senate. The office is staffed by four navy doctors. Today, October 16th, one of those doctors was inserting a long cotton swab like a Q-tip into each of Cross's nostrils.

"We should have the results in two or three days," said the doctor. "I don't expect anything, but here's a ten-day supply of Cipro. Take two each day."

"Thanks Doc. How are the Senate staffers doing? It sounds pretty serious," asked Cross.

"It is serious. I wouldn't be surprised if at least thirty or so tested positive. But the Cipro should stop it in time. So be sure to take yours."

The next morning at nine o'clock, the House Republicans were holding their weekly conference meeting in HC-5, a stark, cavernous room in the bowels of the Capitol Building. Denny Hastert was almost always present at the start of these conferences, but this morning he was still at the White House meeting with the president and the other legislative leaders—Dick Gephardt, Trent Lott and Tom Daschle. When Hastert arrived at HC-5 about 9:20, Cross thought he looked unusually somber. When the Speaker got to the microphone, he spoke in a particularly deliberate tone.

—The meeting at the White House ran late because they were discussing the anthrax attack on Daschle's office.

—The situation is far more serious than we thought.

—The anthrax was weapons grade and very lethal.

—It could have spread through the office buildings, possibly in the ventilating ducts.

—More letters could have been delivered that we are not aware of.

—The police and the medical people want the House and Senate office buildings shut down as soon as possible so they can conduct a complete investigation.

—Anyone remaining in the buildings could contaminate the crime scene.

—All the leaders—Hastert and Gephardt; Daschle and Lott—have agreed to recess this afternoon.

—Alternative offices will be found as soon as possible so we can come back into session, ideally by next week.

Cross had no doubt that Hastert was making the right call. It wasn't even close. The police and the doctors had no idea how far the anthrax had spread or if it had all been found. Clearly the offices had to be evacuated, and with no alternative office space available yet, it made no sense for congressmen to be hanging around Washington when they could be working in their district offices. The Senate and House leaders were in agreement—which meant there wouldn't be any grandstanding. Anthrax was too serious for that—and it would be the height of irresponsibility to showboat. But that's exactly what the Senate did.

Just as the House was concluding its business at the agreed time that afternoon, word came across the Capitol that the Senate might not be recessing. That Daschle and Lott were saying they'd never agreed to recess in the first place. *What bullshit this is,* thought Cross. *They're sandbagging Denny and Gephardt.* Cross realized right away what was up. The anthrax was feared to be in the House and Senate office buildings—not the Capitol building. House members had offices only in the main office buildings—Cannon, Longworth, and Rayburn. Generally unbeknownst to the public, however, about seventy-five of the one hundred senators had secret hideaway locales entirely separate from their official offices. These hideaways, located surreptitiously throughout the depths and bowels of the Capitol, could be used for whatever the senators might want—whether it be drinking, entertaining, sleeping—even work.

So, by reneging on the agreement, the senators could hang out in their hideaways, portraying themselves as heroes manning the ramparts while the House members abandoned their posts. Hastert and Gephardt, realizing the issue was too important for cheap headlines, kept their end of the agreement and recessed the House. It was the right thing to do. Besides, Cross was certain the media would see through the Senate's tawdry stunt.

He was wrong. The next morning, blaring headlines in papers throughout the country hailed the heroic Senate and blasted the duty-shirking House. Television and radio newscasters parroted the newspapers' line. Senators took to the floor to hail themselves for this their "finest hour." Particularly self-congratulatory were Bob Torricelli of New Jersey, who had just barely escaped indictment in a sordid corruption scheme, and Robert Byrd of West Virginia, now in his ninth decade but never tiring of posing as a statesman rather than the Klansman he had once been. Finally, when the senators could think of no more self-congratulations to bestow upon themselves, they also recessed for the week. Though it was never noted by the media, the only item the senators voted on that day was legislation the House had completed the day before.

Cross went on CNN's weekend show with Kate Snow that Saturday to belittle the senators as "self-important windbags" who had put their own phony image-making before the national interest. The media weren't listening. They were too busy buying the senators' act. But then Washington, D.C. postal workers who'd handled the Daschle letter died from their anthrax exposure. *Surely,* Cross thought, *this will show everyone how serious this is.* But again Cross would be disappointed. This time the story line was that black postal workers had been allowed to die because they weren't given the same access to anthrax testing as congressmen and their staffs. Ordinarily an argument like this would embarrass even the likes of the *National Enquirer,* but now it was the lead story on all the network and cable news shows.

On Wednesday morning, October 24th, Cross was seated in Fox's Washington studios waiting to be interviewed from New

York for the morning news show *Fox and Friends*. The topic was to be military strategy in Afghanistan. The questioners would be the show's hosts—a sophomoric, thirty-something trio, two males, one female—who had never met an issue they couldn't trivialize. As soon as the interview began, they said they'd get to military strategy later. First they wanted to discuss why Congress let postal employees die. Cross asked if the interviewers realized just how stupid they sounded and proceeded to point out that:

—All the medical experts had previously said anthrax was only a danger after it was released into the air, not when it was in a sealed enclosure like an envelope; this was the advice Congress had followed.

—The congressional staffers received the same testing as the NBC employees.

—No New York City postal employee was tested when anthrax was delivered to the NBC studios.

—It was disgraceful and dumb even to suggest that members of Congress, or any American for that matter, would knowingly allow anyone to die from anthrax.

Believing it their privilege to accuse congressmen of being accessories to murder, the sophomoric trio reacted furiously at Cross's audacity in defending himself and the Congress. They said they were outraged by his attacks; he replied that he was appalled at their ignorance—and the interview continued at this high level for the next several minutes before the trio finally turned to military strategy for the last thirty seconds. The interview concluded, Cross removed his ear piece, unclipped the microphone from his tie and walked from the room, pleased he had exposed the trio for being the low intellects they were and certain he would never be invited back on the show.

In speech after speech following September 11th, the president had emphasized and reemphasized that we were not at war with Islam; that Muslims were not our enemy; that our effort had to be against the terrorists who had hijacked the Muslim religion.

Cross had shared the president's sense of magnanimity. At least for a while. He soon noticed, though, that there was very little Muslim reciprocity for Bush's extraordinary gestures of good will. No flying of American flags in Muslim neighborhoods or rallies of support for the United States. And there was a pronounced anti-American sentiment emerging, as well.

For instance, Sheik Muhammed al-Gameli'a, a prominent Manhattan imam, speaking in Egypt on October 4th, urged other Muslims not to help America any in a war against Afghanistan because it was "a betrayal of Allah and his Prophet." Then on Sunday, October 14th, there was a large interfaith solidarity gathering at the North Shore Islamic Center. The theme was brotherhood and—more explicitly—a clear demonstration by religious leaders that Muslims were an integral part of American life and should in no way be blamed for the atrocities of September 11th. The Catholic bishop spoke. As did rabbis, ministers, and priests. Each echoed the president's theme that Islam was a religion of peace hijacked by agents of evil. Then there were the two final speakers—Dr. Masri, who was the coordinator of the event, and the imam. They had their own theme. It was the United States that was wrong. Bombing innocent Afghan women and children. Oppressing Palestinians. Starving Iraqis. They made no condemnation of Al Qaeda. No mention of bin Laden. It was becoming more and more clear to Cross that brotherhood, love, and solidarity were going one way—toward the Muslims—with very little being returned.

Cross's son-in-law, John Sweeney, worked in an office building just several blocks north of where the World Trade Center had been. His twenty-eighth-floor office had provided him an unimpeded view of the September 11th attacks—seeing the explosion coming from the North Tower and watching the plane flying directly toward, into and through the South Tower. He'd evacuated the building, made it home safely, and then returned to work the following week. John considered himself lucky to be alive and, being Irish, tried not to dwell on any emotional impact the attacks might have on him. But he did find himself wanting to see the actual Ground Zero site. Though he worked nearby, the area around the site was entirely cordoned off to the general public. John spoke to Sean, who said that he also wanted to visit Ground Zero—not as a voyeur or sightseer but as a congressman who had not been there since September 14th. Cross called Rudy's office, and an inspection tour was set for Sunday afternoon, October 21st, which was the day after the attending physician told Cross the anthrax test had come back and he was fine. Anne Kelly got the same result.

Cross, Mary Rose, John, and Kara drove to the Chelsea Piers on Manhattan's West Side, which had been set up as the Ground Zero command post. They were met by a mayor's aide and a deputy sheriff, who drove them in a sheriff's vehicle down the West Side to the site. It was a beautiful fall day. The sun bright. The sky clear. The air with just a hint of fall chill. Yet the presence of death was still there—and would probably always be there. And the flames were still burning. But firefighters, cops, and construction workers were working around the clock, as they had been day after day, for forty days. Rubble was being removed, and the site now resembled more a construction project than a war zone. Clearly progress was being made—far more than Cross would have thought possible when he had been there on September 14th. And the remains of victims were being recovered—including three this afternoon. As Deputy Inspector John Codiglia, NYPD's commanding officer at Ground Zero, slowly guided Cross and his family around the site, Cross was struck by how focused the rescue workers were—how they could maintain such a level of intensity after almost six unremitting weeks. Cross also walked over to two office buildings in which he'd worked in 1970 and 1971—30 Vesey Street at the northeast tip of Ground Zero and 100 Church Street, the building where Giuliani had been trapped on September 11th, about two blocks directly north of the site. Both structures had windows blown out, suffered structural damage, and were now surrounded by scaffolding. For three decades these buildings had literally been in the shadow of the Twin Towers. Now 30 Vesey and 100 Church were bloodied but still standing, and the towers had been reduced to dust and rubble.

Afterwards, Cross, Mary Rose, John, and Kara were in Pete's Tavern on East 18th Street, sitting at a rear table eating burgers and drinking pints of beer. This landmark watering hole, the oldest bar in Manhattan, had been a hangout for O. Henry, who had written *The Gift of the Maji* there.

"That was very worthwhile. I'm glad we did it," said John. "I hate to use psychobabble, but I felt a definite sense of closure."

"I don't know how the cops and firemen go there every day," said Kara. "It must wear them down."

"Psychologically and physically," interjected Mary Rose.

"I hear it has had a real impact on some of them," said Sean. "Some cops have had their guns taken away, and quite a few firemen have been ordered to go on medical leave and get counseling. But I can't believe they've gotten so much done. From what I saw when I was there that first week, I wouldn't have thought it was possible," said Sean.

"It was very moving when they found those bodies," said John.

"Human nature is really funny," said Kara. "Would you ever have believed there would be such a sense—of joy almost—in finding the remains of murder victims?"

"Maybe I'm too patriotic, but I just think Americans are able to adapt very quickly and do what has to be done," said Mary Rose.

"Especially New Yorkers," said Sean.

The bombs were no sooner dropping in Afghanistan than the American media began doubting the effectiveness of the war. It was almost as if this generation of American reporters, conditioned to viewing all foreign crises through the liberal's prism of Vietnam, accepted as gospel that the United States could not win a war and was indifferent to the killing of innocent civilians. Added to this seemingly congenital bias against the use of the American military was the feeling of many reporters that they had to make up for what they thought was the free ride they'd given the president in the aftermath of September 11th.

The network correspondents would breathlessly report "Taliban charges" of civilian deaths—and then, after detailing the atrocities told to them by the Taliban, issue the perfunctory disclaimer "but there's no way to verify any of it." Almost as if the Taliban were a credible source—otherwise, why report the charge?

When the media didn't want to rely solely on the unverified accounts of America's enemy, they would turn to Al-Jazeera, the Arab television network, which so willingly allowed itself to be used as bin Laden's mouthpiece. So, on October 23rd, ABC television would report that "footage from Al Jazeera today shows body bags lined up in a hospital hallway in Kandahar" and then show the Afghani doctor at the hospital saying, "My sympathies are with the Afghans."

It wasn't bad enough, of course, that Americans were randomly killing innocent Afghans. We also weren't winning the war—or at least that's how the media saw it.

On October 29th, ABC's White House correspondent said he thought "the bad guys are winning." *At least he thinks the Taliban are the bad guys,* thought Cross.

Nor were the print media any more supportive. The *Boston Globe*, for instance, reported sources among the coalition forces suggesting that "the Bush administration had underestimated the resilience of the country's hard-line regime."

The ultimate pronouncement, of course, was issued by the venerable *New York Times* and its almost equally venerable correspondent R. W. "Johnny" Apple. On October 31st the *Times* ran Apple's analysis of the war on page one, headlining it "Another Vietnam?"

"Could Afghanistan become another Vietnam? Is the United States facing another stalemate on the other side of the world?

"Despite the insistence of President Bush and members of his cabinet that all is well, the war in Afghanistan has gone less smoothly than many had hoped."

But if George W. Bush knew or cared about what the *Times* and Johnny Apple thought about his war policy, he certainly didn't show it when he met with Cross and several other northeastern Republicans in the cabinet room of the White House that afternoon.

The focus of the meeting was to be the Airline Security Act, introduced to revamp and upgrade security procedures and personnel at the nation's airports. There was bipartisan consensus that the qualifications and training of the airport baggage inspectors had to be increased and standardized. Democrats favored making all baggage inspectors federal employees. Bush supported federalizing most inspectors but allowing airports to use a limited number of private employees so long as they were federally trained and certified. Cross leaned toward Bush's proposal as being more effective than a "one size fits all" approach. But he was holding back his support, because Dick Armey and other House Republican leaders were selling the Republican plan as a way to impede the growth of federal unions. Cross thought it wrong to exploit September 11th as an anti-union lever. The others at the table also had reservations, and that was why they had been called to this meeting.

The president entered the cabinet room through the side door leading from the Oval Office. He appeared in good spirits and, after shaking hands with everyone, took his traditional seat at the center of the table, the window to the Rose Garden at his back. Cross was seated three seats to the president's right. The president made his case and then opened up the meeting for questions. Cross was the third questioner recognized by the president.

"Mr. President, before I ask my question, I just want you to know that you have strong support in New York for what you're doing in Afghanistan. I've gone to a lot of wakes and funerals for cops and firefighters, and all the people I talk to you are with you. And many of them are Democrats."

"Thank you," said the president in an almost whispered tone.

"Mr. President, I support this bill on its merits, but I have real problems with leaders in our party saying we should vote for it because it's anti-union. That's the wrong message to send. This should be about national security and nothing else."

"I fully agree with you, and I've told them that. And I will make it very clear. I'll get that message across."

"Thank you, Mr. President. That's all I was looking for."

When the meeting broke up, Cross shook hands with the president, who said, "I heard what you said about those firefighters and police officers. You're doing God's work by going to those wakes and funerals. Those people mean so much to me."

"They're certainly with you."

"You know I'm flying to New York to throw out the first pitch at Yankee Stadium tonight," said Bush, speaking of the third game of the World Series between the Yankees and the Arizona Diamondbacks. "I'll be wearing an FDNY jacket."

"The crowd will go crazy when they see that."

"I've been practicing the last few days. I want to make sure I get the ball over the plate."

"Are you ready?"

"I think so. I've been throwing with the vest on. When I was getting ready to throw out the first pitch on opening day in Baltimore back in April, I forgot I'd have to wear the vest. So when I threw the pitch from the mound, I bounced it in front of home plate. I hated that."

"Well, better luck tonight."

"Don't worry. I'll get it over."

Cross and Danny were sitting in the living room of their Washington apartment that evening looking at the television as the World Series pregame show was concluding. The announcers discussed the unprecedented security that was in place for the president's appearance that night. The extraordinary NYPD presence. Police sharpshooters on the roofs of neighborhood buildings. The metal detectors at all entrances to the Stadium. F-16s in the sky.

Then the players were introduced onto the field. The Yankees lining up along the first base line, the Diamondbacks along the third base line. The players standing at attention as the Irish tenor Ronan Tynan sang the national anthem.

The start of the game was minutes away. All the players were now off the field except for the Yankee starters, who were at their positions. Then the baritone voice of legendary Yankee public address announcer Bob Sheppard was heard intoning that the first pitch for tonight's game would be thrown out by "the President of the United States, George W. Bush." As the president walked onto the field toward the pitcher's mound wearing the FDNY jacket, the crowd rose as one to give him a roaring and sustained ovation. When Bush got to the mound, he looked toward the crowd to acknowledge their continuing applause. Then he put his right foot on the pitcher's rubber and looked toward Yankee catcher Jorge Posada, who was positioned behind home plate.

"Christ, I hope he gets it over," said Cross.

Bush began his windup, lifting his left foot forward. Raising his right arm, he positioned his left foot on the mound and brought his right arm around, pushing hard off his left leg for extra velocity. For the briefest moment, as the ball left the president's hand, the crowd hushed with anticipation—then erupted louder than ever.

The pitch was over the plate. In Posada's glove. A perfect strike.

"It even hooked a bit at the end," said Danny. "It looked like a slider."

The president strode off the field wearing his FDNY jacket and a proud smile.

The next morning Cross called Jack Kilbride, an old friend and an NYPD detective who'd been on duty at Yankee Stadium the night before.

"Jack, talk about high tension, you guys mustn't have been able to let up for a minute last night. What a security nightmare!"

"I don't think I've even seen that much pressure. But I'll tell you, it was worth it. The president was protected, and, just as important, he threw a strike—a perfect fucking strike!"

"He was practicing at the White House for the last few days to get ready."

"He also warmed up under the stands last night."

"I'm not surprised. He was really serious about it."

"Let me tell you something that may surprise you."

"Go ahead."

"You're pretty smart, right? After all, you are a congressman."

"I hope I'm smarter than you, anyway."

"Okay, wise guy. Did you notice anything different about the umpires last night?"

"What do you mean?"

"Do you know how to count?"

"I can count votes."

"Well, if you'd counted the umpires, you'd have noticed there was an extra one on the field when the president was there."

"Who was he?"

"A Secret Service agent with an Uzi under his jacket. What do you think of that?'

"I hate to keep saying this—but our lives will never be the same."

"That's the fucking truth!"

Sipping his Dewars and water, Sean Cross glanced up at the clock behind the long mahogany bar. It was just a few minutes past noon. He was at the Tribeca Grill, the renowned restaurant owned by Robert DeNiro, at Franklin and Greenwich Streets in lower Manhattan, just blocks north of where the World Trade Center had been. From his vantage point at the corner of the bar, he had a clear view of the front door. He was waiting for Bernadette Hanlon, an old friend from Belfast. When she'd called him last evening and said she was just in from Ireland and had to meet with him about something important, he had immediately said yes.

Cross had first met Bernadette Hanlon more than two decades ago, when he was in Belfast to observe the notorious supergrass trials being conducted by the British against accused IRA members. These trials, based on paid informers and perjured testimony, had convinced Irish republicans like Pete Cairney that it was time to leave Northern Ireland. Bernadette's husband, Dermot, had not been so fortunate. He was arrested in a dragnet sweep, charged with multiple murders, and convicted solely on the uncorroborated testimony of an alcoholic psychopath whose testimony was riddled with obvious lies and flagrant inconsistencies. But the informer had said what he was told to say, and that was enough for the pro-British unionist judge to convict Dermot and sentence him to life imprisonment, plus a few hundred years. Cross knew that Dermot was no saint or angel. He was a known IRA man. But he wasn't guilty of, or even remotely connected to, the crimes for which he was convicted.

At the time of Dermot's arrest, Bernadette was a young Catholic wife and mother of three children living in a run-down Catholic ghetto. Her brother had been in the IRA until several years before, when one of his own bombs detonated prematurely and blew his body into small pieces. Bernadette, however, had no interest in politics or any involvement with the IRA or Sinn Fein. Her way of coping with the Troubles that surrounded her had been to ignore the reality of her husband being in the IRA and to focus her life on her children and the few hard streets around her small home in West Belfast.

But Dermot's arrest and the murder of a young neighborhood girl by British soldiers changed all that. Bernadette became radicalized and transformed. She organized families of other supergrass defendants, led street demonstrations, appeared on television and radio, and conducted a speaking tour of the United States. At the end of the day, the Northern Ireland Appeals Court threw out the convictions of Dermot and all the other supergrass defendants—effectively forcing the British to scrap the supergrass system altogether.

There was also—as she would later confide to Cross—yet another side to Bernadette. A lethal side, which led her to carry out the IRA-ordered assassination of a local Catholic politician who'd been informing for the British. In a perfectly planned execution, Bernadette came up behind him on an empty street and blew his skull apart with a .38-caliber pistol before escaping in a waiting getaway car.

Cross had stayed in touch with Bernadette over the years. After Dermot was released, she remained an active force in the community—campaigning for Sinn Fein, working with released prisoners and their families, and trying to establish cross-community ties with Protestant women. After the Good Friday Agreement was signed, she formed and headed a community redevelopment association that brought investment and jobs to West Belfast. She was successful at what she did, and part of her success owed to the frequent visits she made to Washington and New York, attending trade and investment conferences and meeting with corporate leaders. Still, Cross had not been expecting Bernadette's call last night, since, as far as he knew, she wasn't due over here for at least another month. But if she said it was important, he knew it was, and that was why he was here today . . .

It was only a few minutes later that Bernadette walked smartly through the doorway, wearing a stylish blue business suit and white blouse. Bernadette was in her fifties now but as striking as ever—shoulder-length auburn hair, silklike skin, and a magnificent body. As Cross walked from the bar to greet her, she stepped forward with a wide smile. Cross hugged her and kissed her on the cheek.

"It's great to see you," said Cross. "Did you have any trouble finding it?"

"No bother at all," answered Bernadette. "I got off the subway at Chambers Street, and it was just a few minutes' walk, so it was."

"You sound like a veteran New Yorker. I remember when you were afraid to even look up at the buildings because they'd make you dizzy."

"Ah, Sean, we've all come a long way," said Bernadette laughingly.

"I've got a table reserved near the back. Do you want to have a drink first at the bar?"

"No. The table will be grand."

The manager, Martin Shapiro, led them to their table and told them a waiter would be by with menus and to take their orders.

"This is a beautiful restaurant," said Bernadette, sipping some ice water. "I love the exposed brick walls."

"Yeah. It gives the impression that the place is a landmark. But it's only been open for about fifteen years."

"I'm very sorry I've given you such short notice for this meeting. But it was just yesterday that it all came together, and I decided I had to come over."

"Just yesterday! Christ, the plane ticket must have cost a fortune."

"Don't worry yourself about it. I was able to bill it to a government account—industrial development work. And I'm covering myself. I'm meeting later today with some of the mayor's people at City Hall on possible joint projects. That's one thing I've learned from dealing with politicians—how to get a free trip."

"City Hall's just a few blocks from here."

"I know exactly where it is. Remember, I'm an experienced world traveler."

"Of course. But, more important, what was it that 'all came together?'"

"I'm afraid it has to do with someone you might have some interest in—Fiona Larkin."

"What makes you think I'm interested in Fiona Larkin?"

"Sean, you might be a good enough liar to get the eegits over here to vote for you all the time—but you're not clever enough to put it over on me."

"I know it can be difficult for you Belfast women to keep a cool head, but try not to get too carried away. Of course I know Fiona Larkin. I met her more than ten years ago. I've met a lot of people from Ireland—some good, some bad. She's been good and bad. So if you have information about Fiona that might be important to me, I'll certainly be interested."

"Thank you so much for the clarification," said Bernadette with an ironic smile.

"I always try my best," answered Cross with an equally ironic smile.

They'd each achieved what they had to. Bernadette letting Cross know that she thought he'd been tipped off about Fiona. Cross neither confirming nor denying. They might be good friends—but they still had to go through this conspiratorial dance.

"Since I'm the one who asked for the meeting," said Bernadette, "I'll tell you what I know, and you can do with it what you like. You're the best judge of that."

"Thanks. And I do appreciate your interest."

"Sean, I'm a bit older than Fiona—to be perfectly honest, it's more than a bit—and I've known her since she was a wee girl. She was always very smart and very determined—so I was delighted when she became so active with Sinn Fein."

"She was probably only in her early or mid-twenties when I first met her, and she really seemed to be on the fast track."

"Fiona was exactly the type that the republican movement needed. Young, articulate, and a woman."

"I was really surprised when she split from Adams and McGuiness."

"You've probably heard this before—but all the time you saw her during the nineties, when Gerry and Martin were pushing the peace process, she never thought they were for real. She thought they were just stringing the Brits along."

"The irony is that the hard-core Brits thought the same thing. They always said the IRA ceasefire and the peace process were all part of some evil master plan Gerry had concocted."

"I remember her actually being startled when she realized Gerry truly wanted an agreement. Even before the Good Friday Agreement was signed, she officially resigned from Sinn Fein and joined what they called the Thirty-two County Sovereignty Committee."

"But that was just a front for McDevitt, McAllister, and the Real IRA."

"Aye. It was nothing but a front. And then she began living with Rory McAllister."

"The 'Mad Dog.'"

"That he was indeed. A complete header he turned out to be. No wonder his own people killed him."

"That seems to happen quite a bit with these splinter groups."

"Aye. It does."

Bernadette and Cross were treading water, stalling for time. Cross was content to wait. He was not going to volunteer anything he knew about Fiona and Abdul Bajal. After a silent interval that probably seemed to be of greater duration than it actually was, Bernadette resumed.

"I don't know whether you've heard this or not but, after Rory was killed, Fiona became involved with a Muslim living in Dublin."

"Actually we hear so many rumors, it's hard to decide what to believe."

"This is more than a rumor. She was with a guy called Abdul Bajal. He's one of bin Laden's people and was supposed to be the leader of an actual Al Qaeda cell in Dublin."

"I've heard about Bajal."

"Apparently the Gardai had him under surveillance, but he snuck out of Ireland just before September 11th, and Fiona went with him."

"Any idea where they went?" asked Cross, attempting to feign a lack of knowledge but realizing he was probably not doing a very good job.

"The word that got back to Belfast was that they went to Indonesia."

"That's a real hotbed of Islamic militants."

"Apparently it is."

The waiter came by to take their orders. Caesar salad for Bernadette. Steak sandwich for Cross. Sparkling water for each.

"You said 'the word got back to Belfast.' Is there somebody who stays in touch with Fiona?"

"Aye. Indirectly."

"I'm listening."

"Rory McAllister's first cousin, Irene Turner, lives in Twinbrook," said Bernadette, referring to the republican stronghold on the outskirts of West Belfast. "She's very involved in the community, coordinating a drug rehab program. I'm with her several times a month at different community-type meetings."

"And she's kept in touch with Fiona?"

"Apparently so—but I didn't know any of this until the last two days."

"And that's why you're here."

"Aye."

"She must have really gotten your attention to get you to come over so quickly."

"Aye. I had to tell you straight away, and I don't trust the phones."

"I don't blame you."

"Two nights ago there was a meeting at the Europa about teenage drug awareness," said Bernadette.

The Europa Hotel was located on Great Victoria Street in the heart of Belfast. During the times of the Troubles it was known to be the most bombed-out hotel in Europe. But that was then. Now it was an integral part of the new and resurgent Belfast.

"Years ago who'd have thought you'd be able to have community meetings in the Europa at night without fears of being shot?"

"Oh, aye. Things certainly have changed for the better."

"And Fiona Larkin would rather be in fucking Indonesia!"

"That's what Irene wanted to talk to me about. When Fiona and Rory were knocking about, Fiona and Irene became friendly."

"Was Irene into the Real IRA?"

"Not at all. In fact she was entirely nonpolitical. But she'd always got on well with Rory since they were wee children and stayed friendly with him through it all."

"How did she manage that?"

"I suppose she just ignored his dark side. That's not terribly unusual when you grew up the way we did. With so many people around you being shot and killed, you realize early on that no one's perfect. With someone like Rory though, you can end up ignoring too much."

"So Irene stayed friendly with Bernadette after Rory was killed?"

"Aye. They would get together for lunch or dinner every few weeks or so."

"From the way you describe Irene, it doesn't seem as if she'd have much in common with Fiona."

"Irene says they never discussed politics at all. Just ordinary things that women would talk about—friends, clothes, holidays—or vacations, as you Yanks call them—and also Irene's work against drugs. It's almost as if Irene filled a void in Fiona's world."

"Did she have any dealings with Bajal?"

"Apparently she'd met him a few times."

"What did she think of him?"

"She says they got on well enough. He was very quiet and reserved. Never said a word about politics or Islam."

"Was Irene surprised when they took off from Ireland?"

"Not really—and it wasn't because she suspected anything about terrorism or Al Qaeda. It's just that there was a strong anti-immigrant feeling in Ireland at the time, and Bajal was very active in the Muslim community—so she thought the pressure might be too much."

"Irene knew nothing about bin Laden or Al Qaeda?"

"Nothing. She said neither Fiona nor Bajal ever said a word about any type of Islamic terrorism. Of course, after September 11th she started to have her doubts. And the police questioned her . . .'"

"The police?"

"Aye, the Gardai Special Branch had been keeping a surveillance on Bajal, and Irene's name had come up and the Northern Ireland Police let them question her in Belfast."

"What did the cops say?"

"They told her about Bajal's involvement with bin Laden and Al Qaeda, and asked what she was doing with them."

"How did Irene react to that?"

"It jolted her, so it did. Fiona was her good friend, and now she learns Fiona and her Muslim lover are connected to the mass murderers of September 11th. Irene told the Gardai, of course, that she knew nothing about any of this."

"Did they believe her?"

"Apparently so. They haven't come back to her since."

"What did they say about Fiona?"

"They told Irene there was no evidence Fiona had done anything illegal with Al Qaeda. But being involved with Bajal and before that with Rory and the Real IRA certainly raised very serious suspicions."

"I guess they would," said Cross. "When did Irene hear from Fiona?"

"Actually, she never has heard from Fiona directly. But messages have gotten to her from Fiona."

"That's intriguing."

"I suppose it is. About six months ago after Fiona and Bajal left, one of Rory's old mates contacted Irene."

"From the Real IRA?"

"Aye."

"Is he still with them?"

"I don't think anyone is. But—and this does sound like intrigue—he's one of those types who runs in terrorist circles."

"You mean beyond Ireland?"

"Aye. He met with a number of terrorist groups when he was trying to buy weapons for the Real IRA, and he's kept his ties with them. I know he goes back and forth to the mainland quite often."

"What's his name?"

"Padraig Foley."

"Do the Gardai and the Northern Ireland Police know about him?"

"They do indeed, and I'm sure they've informed the police in other countries about him, but he's a clever one, so he is. Hard to pin anything on him."

"Did Irene know him before this?"

"Maybe enough to say hello. Nothing more than that. Then he came alongside her one night in a church hall in West Belfast after a community meeting and said he had 'a message from Fiona.'"

"Anything special?"

"The fact that there was any contact at all from Fiona was special enough. But that was when Irene learned Fiona was in Indonesia and that Fiona wanted Irene to know that all was going well."

"What about Bajal?"

"Foley didn't mention him that time, but Irene assumed he was with Fiona. Why the hell else would she stay in Indonesia?"

"And this contact continued?"

"Aye. Every three or four months Foley would tell Irene that things were the same with Fiona."

"Was anyone else getting these messages?"

"Somehow the word got out to the street about the two of them being in Indonesia. Irene doesn't know if that was from Padraig or from the police. But it was known—certainly in republican circles."

"The contact with Foley shows a terror connection, I guess, but these were pretty bland messages."

"Not all of them were bland. Remember the terrible bombing in Bali in October of 2002?"

"That was brutal."

"Everyone pretty much concluded straight away that Al Qaeda was behind it."

"They were."

"But just about a month afterwards—in November or early December—Padraig told Irene that Al Qaeda had nothing to do with it. That the group Jemaah Islamiah was responsible."

"They were tied directly to Al Qaeda. Al Qaeda funded that whole operation."

"Of course they did. But Foley was pushing the Al Qaeda line at that time that they were separate groups."

"What did Irene say?"

"To be honest, she wasn't that interested in the difference between Al Qaeda and Jemaah Islamiah. She just wanted to know who told this to Padraig."

"And?"

"He told her this came from Bajal."

"Did she ask Foley why he was telling her this?"

"Padraig said it was important for people to know that Al Qaeda was being unjustly accused. That this was propaganda being put out by the Americans and the Brits."

"Even the most gullible anti-American wouldn't believe that. But it does show that Foley probably did have some kind of contact with Bajal."

"Aye. There's no way Padraig would have known anything like this on his own."

"Did Irene consider taking any of this to the police—either in the North or the South?"

"No. Padraig was telling her this because she was Fiona's friend and Fiona wanted her to know that she was doing fine. There were no crime being discussed or any of that carry on."

"But if the cops could have questioned Foley, that could have gotten them closer to Bajal or at least the operatives in Europe that Foley was talking to."

"Sean, I understand what you're saying, but that's just a step too far. That would have put Padraig at great risk and also violated Irene's friendship with Fiona."

"The old informer stigma?"

"Aye. It's in our tradition that the informer is the lowest form of life. And then living through the supergrass trials reinforced that for us. Besides, it's still difficult for us to trust the police after all they did to us over the years."

"Wasn't the purpose of the Good Friday Agreement to end all that?"

"It was indeed—but we're just not there yet."

"But you are here today."

"Aye. Because what Irene heard from Padraig the other day was—as you Yanks say—a wake-up call. She realized she had to do something."

"What did she hear?"

"Padraig actually told her two things that Irene saw right away as being very troubling. The first was that people in Rotterdam said they'd be seeing Bajal soon. The second was that Fiona had been to New York."

"New York? Does Foley have connections over here as well?"

"Some holdovers from the Real IRA. One of them met with her and couldn't keep his mouth shut. He had to tell Padraig."

"Did Foley give Irene the guy's name?"

"No," said Bernadette, with a look indicating that she thought Cross already knew the name.

"Irene told you this right away?"

"The very next morning."

"Why you?"

"She realized she had to tell someone. After the attacks here last month, she didn't want blood on her hands. This was more than just finding out where Fiona was living or how she was doing. It sounds like it could be another attack. At the same time she still wanted some distance between herself and the police. She knew that I had contacts with Americans, so she told me everything. And here I am."

Each had finished eating. The waiter brought Bernadette a cappuccino and Cross a coffee.

"Bernadette, we've known each other too well, for too long, for me to play games with you. There are things I know that I can't tell you."

"I understand that."

"But I can tell you that this information you've given could be very helpful. I also want you to know that it was great of you to get it to me as quickly as you did."

"So you can use it?"

"Yes. There are people I'm dealing with who will be very interested. I'll give it to them, and they can fit it in with whatever other leads they've gotten. And if an attack is being planned, hopefully this will help us head it off."

"My concern, of course, is that Padraig might be using us by intentionally giving out false information, to throw everyone off."

"That will be up to the experts to decide. But, to be honest with you, I doubt this is disinformation. For one thing, Foley had been giving Irene information for several years now, and she never told anyone—including you. Then he would have to assume that if she were going to give the Rotterdam story to anyone, it wouldn't create problems for him."

"What do you mean?"

"Suppose, instead of going to you, Irene went to the Northern Ireland Police or the Gardai. Foley would be lifted right away, and God knows how long they'd keep him locked up. Or worse yet, put him back on the street and let the word out that he'd told them more about Al Qaeda than he was supposed to."

"Are you suggesting the police would use dirty tricks? Didn't you just finish telling me how we should trust them?" asked Bernadette with a knowing grin.

"There's an exception to every rule."

"So you think this was just a case of Padraig wanting Irene to know that he was on the inside?"

"I'd say so. As clever as he is, everyone's got an ego."

Cross did not tell Bernadette that what Foley said about Fiona coming to New York was entirely true and accurate. That it was not disinformation. Cross didn't want to disclose anything more than he absolutely had to, and Bernadette chose not to pursue the issue.

"Those attacks last month must have been terribly troubling to the people in New York," said Bernadette. "The pictures and the news reports we got were just horrible."

"It was bad. But since September 11th everything seems manageable. Almost as if it's our patriotic duty not to let it get us down."

"It's remarkable how much New York has come back from September 11th. Not just the spirit but the actual work that's being done. I see all the construction that's going on at the World Trade Center site."

"The destruction at the Twin Towers was more than anything I ever could have imagined. I got there about three days after the attacks and couldn't believe what I was seeing. And this whole area up here had to be evacuated. It was all covered with dust and ash like a nuclear attack. This restaurant was closed down for two weeks after the towers were attacked."

"Don't the people ever get worn down having to live under all this pressure?"

"Of course they do. Not everyone's a hero all the time. And I suppose there's always some who are never heroic. But as a people, no—the city has never let down. From the first minute that the first tower was attacked and right through all the death and rubble there was never even a hint of surrender."

"I realize there's so much that you can't tell me, but are you surprised by what appears to be this link with the Real IRA and Al Qaeda?"

"Actually, I think it's more of a fluke. Someone like Fiona is attracted to fanatics, and after Rory was killed, the first fanatic she ran across was Bajal. And, as for guys like Padraig Foley, there's always fringe characters in every country. But what has bothered me is the attitude of a lot of the Irish since September 11th."

"You mean the demonstrations against your policy in Afghanistan and Iraq?"

"I mean the whole anti-American attitude among so many Irish people."

"The government hasn't been so bad."

"No. Bertie Ahern in particular seems to have done the best that he could. But why should he have to fight so hard just to let our military flights refuel at Shannon? It's not as if we're asking Irish troops to do anything."

"Sean, you don't have to talk to me about this. I know full well that—no matter all the picketing and demonstrating and television interviews we did at home in the eighties—my own husband would still be in jail if it hadn't been for the people in America, and there never would have been peace in the North if it weren't for your government."

"Listen, I'm not trying to make a big thing out of this, but it is disappointing—especially compared to how supportive the Brits have been."

"Fair play to him. Tony Blair was never afraid to stand up."

"He was the best—straight through from September 11th."

"He was also good on Ireland. He took some real chances."

"When are you going back?"

"Tonight. The meeting at City Hall shouldn't last more than an hour. And a car will take me directly to JFK."

"You really are the twenty-four-hour wonder-woman."

"I felt I had to make this trip. I just hope what I gave you will be of some help. We have to be together on this."

"Thanks. And I'm sure it will be helpful."

November–December 2001

As America entered the first days of November it became increasingly apparent that the anthrax attacks that had killed five and sent paralyzing fear through millions more had run their course, ending almost as quickly and silently as they had begun. The FBI had tentatively concluded that the attacks had been of domestic origin and had no link to Al Qaeda.

If the anthrax attacks were receding, however, increasing numbers of Democrats were intensifying their political attacks on the president. Frustrated by Bush's continuing high poll numbers and realizing it was too early—even for them—to attack him on the war, Democrats sought to undermine his credibility by charging that he had already turned his back on New York. That the president who had so willingly pledged on September 13th to provide twenty billion dollars to New York was reneging. As New York Democrats said in one of their more statesmanlike pronouncements this first week in November, "Bush is with bin Laden instead of New York." Clearly they were not concerned about rhetorical overkill or shameful excess.

The basis for these Democratic fusillades was the vacuous premise that since New York hadn't received the full twenty billion yet, it was never going to get it. These attacks caught Cross unawares. As far as he knew, the administration was giving the city the money as it needed it. Thinking that maybe he had missed something along the way, Cross called Gene Turner, a deputy mayor, who told him "the Democrats are full of shit. We can't spend the money we already have. We've gotten every nickel we've asked for and more. These guys are fucking shameless."

Cross went on offense, blasting the Democrats' attacks as "unconscionable" and accusing them of intentionally undermining the commander in chief in time of war. The Democrats were undeterred, however, and charged that if a tornado had hit a trailer park in Texas the president would have come up with the money already. Fortunately, the American people and the people of New York showed good sense and chose to ignore these transparently partisan attacks.

What New York was not ignoring was the seemingly endless line of memorial services and funerals for the victims of the World Trade Center. It was not unusual to have as many as ten in a day. Some families waited for a body part to be found—a finger, a tooth, a trace of spinal fluid—before holding a funeral. Others would decide they could wait no longer and schedule a memorial service. Either way it was wrenching and heartbreaking.

The families of Michael Boyle and David Arce decided it served no purpose to wait any longer. They would have a joint memorial service for their sons, and it would be in St. Patrick's Cathedral on Monday, November 5th, at 9:30 in the morning. A few days before the service Jimmy Boyle asked Cross if he would give one of the eulogies.

"Jimmy, I'd be honored, but you've told me you already have Giuliani, Von Essen, and Pataki giving eulogies. Didn't the archdiocese set a limit of three eulogies by politicians?"

"Actually, Hugh Carey is going to speak for Pataki."

"Jimmy, that doesn't change a thing. He's still a politician."

"As always, you're being difficult, and you're refusing to show any imagination. Can you get a letter from the president for Michael and David?"

"I can get a letter."

"Great. Cardinal Egan is celebrating the Mass, but I'll tell the monsignor who's putting it all together that the president has given you a letter he wants you to read. And then once you're up on the pulpit, just go ahead and say whatever you want to say. What's the cardinal going to do, throw you off the pulpit?"

"Jimmy, your mind is in its own universe."

The morning of November 5th was clear and bright with barely the slightest hint of chill in the air. A classic fall day. St. Patrick's Cathedral stood proudly on Fifth Avenue. Its majestic Gothic structure spanning the entire east side of the block from 50th Street to 51st; its spires rising 330 feet toward the heavens.

Cross was standing on the westerly side of the avenue facing toward the front steps of the cathedral. He was in the line of "dignitaries"—as the FDNY ceremonial officer insisted on calling them. Hugh Carey was on his left; Ed Koch on his right. For as far as Cross could see, Fifth Avenue was closed to traffic in both directions. It was, however, bursting with more firefighters than he had ever seen.

It was about a quarter past nine when they were told the procession would be coming down from 53rd Street and was expected to begin in about ten minutes. As the "dignitaries" waited and spoke in hushed tones, their conversations were the usual disconnect of heartfelt sorrow and political rumor.

Carey—"Jimmy's the best. What a heart of gold."

Koch—"He's a great guy to deal with. When I was the mayor and he was the head of the union, he was tough but always straight."

Cross—"Jimmy was actually right across the street when the North Tower came down on Michael and David."

Koch—"What can be worse than losing a child?"

Carey—"What's wrong with these wacky New York Democrats? Attacking the president after what he's done for the city."

Cross—"That's your party, Governor."

Carey—"That's not my type of Democrat."

Koch—"I think Bush has been terrific. I thank God every night that he's the president."

Cross—"How about the mayor's race? Can Bloomberg win tomorrow?"

Koch—"Bloomberg *will* win. Too many people know Mark Green," answered Koch, referring to the Democratic opponent of Michael Bloomberg.

Just then two police cars—with lights flashing but sirens silent—traveling west on 51st Street, entered Fifth Avenue and stopped in the middle of the street.

"There's the mayor," said Koch, looking toward Giuliani, who was getting out of the back seat of the second car.

Cross was struck by Koch's enduring reverence for the office of mayor. Though he'd endorsed Giuliani, Koch had bitter political and personal differences with him—going so far as to write the book *Giuliani Is a Nasty Man*. But today Giuliani was here to represent the city, honoring two fallen heroes, and so to Ed Koch he was "the mayor."

"He must be exhausted," said Cross to Koch. "I never thought he'd make it."

Giuliani had been in Arizona last night for the seventh game of the World Series and had watched the Yankees' quest for another championship come to a shattering end when the Diamondbacks pushed across two runs in the bottom of the ninth inning. The game had ended at just about midnight New York time. Rudy had to have been flying all night and come directly from the airport.

Giuliani walked over and shook hands with the "dignitaries" and took his position to Governor Carey's left.

"Tough game last night," said Cross in a hushed tone as he leaned across Carey. "I thought the Yankees had it locked up."

"Especially with Rivera pitching," answered Giuliani.

"How did the Yankees take it?"

"I was down in the locker room after the game. They took it well. Joe Torre is a class guy. He set the standard."

At the first beat of muffled drums, coming from several blocks away, all conversations ended, and everyone stood in absolute silence. Virtually at attention. Their heads turned slightly to the left to catch the first glimpses of the FDNY band and of the Boyle and Arce families slowly making their way down the avenue.

Cross got his first clear view of the families when they were about halfway between 52nd and 51st Streets. Jimmy was in the center of the street with his wife Barbara, David's mother Marge, and the sons and daughters from both families. They extended across the avenue, with many relatives and friends walking in procession behind them.

The procession crossed 51st Street and stopped in front of the cathedral. Now that they were no more than twenty or so feet away, Cross saw how their faces were wracked and torn with pain and grief.

Since there were no bodies to bury and no coffins to carry, firemen carried two boxes of dirt from the World Trade Center and the helmets of Michael and David up the steps and into the cathedral.

St. Patrick's Cathedral seats more than 2,200. Today every seat was taken, each inch of standing room filled. The crowd overflowed onto Fifth Avenue.

Cardinal Egan was the celebrant. Family members gave individual readings. The Boyle and Arce members were sitting in the front rows on the right side of the cathedral as you faced the altar. The "dignitaries" were in the front rows on the left side.

The principal eulogies were delivered by John Mills for the Boyle family and David Arce's brother Peter for the Arces. Just recovered from a long illness, Mills walked on a cane and slowly made his way to the pulpit positioned on the altar about thirty feet directly in front of the families. Mills was a former fireman and an extremely respected attorney. He and Jimmy had been close friends for more than thirty years. His words were moving and poignant, describing Michael's heroism and how everyone knew he'd been destined to follow Jimmy as union president. Peter Arce was equally effective, using humor and warmth to describe how caring his brother was. The guy they called "Buddha" because he was so quiet. The guy who anonymously delivered gifts to needy children every Christmas.

Then there was Giuliani, who showed no signs of jet lag as he described how much Michael and Buddha had meant to New York and how they would always be remembered. And Tom Von Essen, who brought the mourners to their feet in a roaring ovation as he described Jimmy as the "greatest leader the union ever had." Hugh Carey was superb. Though he was in his eighties, Carey's voice bellowed off the walls and ceiling of the cathedral as he spoke of the new spirit of patriotism that had spread across America since September 11th.

As the former governor concluded his remarks to loud applause, the monsignor said, "We will now hear from Congressman Cross, who will read a letter from the president." Cross was sitting in the second row on the left, two seats from the aisle. He climbed past Ed Koch and walked to the pulpit. He took the president's letter from his pocket—as well as the eulogy he'd prepared. Just as he was to begin, he looked at Jimmy sitting in the front row. Two guys from Sunnyside. Together today in this improbable moment in this celebrated cathedral. Cross hesitated for a moment, looked around the cathedral, and then focused his eyes back on Jimmy. "We've come a long way from St. Teresa's, Jimmy," said Cross. Jimmy smiled. *Thank God*, thought Cross.

Cross began by expressing his condolences to the two families and explained how Mike and David had volunteered in his campaigns. He then pointed out that "just last year Mike ran a fund-raiser for me in Rockaway and—as I always remind Jimmy—it was more successful than all the events Jimmy had run for me over the previous twenty years!"

"On September 11th Michael Boyle and David Arce died as they had lived, with a sense of duty and courage that inspired our people and rallied our nation at our moment of greatest need." The monsignor was sitting off to the left. Sensing his growing impatience, Cross told the mourners that President Bush had asked him to read a letter. Cross began reading the letter, and the monsignor sat back. He was relaxed. The letter thanked the families for what their sons had done for their country and said that Michael and David would always be in the prayers of the president and the First Lady.

Cross concluded the letter. He intended to finish the eulogy, but he saw from the corner of his eye that the monsignor was getting ready to get up from his chair. Cardinal Egan was seated on the other side of the altar to Cross's right. Cross had no idea what the cardinal might be doing. All Cross knew was that Jimmy would never let up on him if he let the monsignor keep him from completing the eulogy. Cross looked quickly at the monsignor and gestured his left hand toward him—behind the pulpit and out of sight of the mourners—signaling that he had more to say and was going to say it. The monsignor hesitated for the briefest moment, and Cross immediately began:

"Let me conclude by saying that I was not surprised when Jimmy Boyle told me on September 12th that Michael was missing. Because I knew that if there was one person who would rush to the World Trade Center, it would be Michael Boyle—whether he was on duty or whether he had signed out from the firehouse. That was the way he was raised. That was how he lived. That was how he died.

"Michael Boyle and David Arce were firefighters, and they were soldiers in the first great war of the twenty-first century. And it is because of their courage that America will win this war."

Cross looked at Jimmy, who gave him a smile. Cross did not look at the monsignor.

This was Cross's week for memorial services and eulogies. Like the Boyles and the Arces, the family of Tommy Haskell also decided that they should go ahead with a memorial service rather than continue to wait until his remains might be found. Tommy Haskell's brother Tim had also been killed at the World Trade Center. His body had been recovered right away, and his funeral had been held on September 18th.

Now it was Saturday afternoon, November 10th, and Cross and Mary Rose were arriving at St. William's Church in Seaford when they were greeted by Fr. Steve Camp in the parking area between the rectory and the church. He told them there'd be a half-hour delay, because the band was running late, and also that the mayor had been able to change his schedule at the last minute and would be coming. Father Camp invited them into the rectory for coffee and buns. Cross and Mary Rose gladly accepted and a few minutes later were joined by Giuliani and his girlfriend, Judy Nathan.

Rudy appeared almost to welcome the news of the half-hour delay. It would give him the unexpected opportunity to actually sit and relax. *I'm sure this hasn't happened too often since September 11th*, thought Cross. Sipping a cup of coffee, Giuliani leaned back in his chair, expressing random thoughts:

—How classy Torre and the Yankees had been after such a heartbreaking loss.

—How delighted he'd been to make it back in time for the Boyle and Arce service.

—How great it was for the city that Bloomberg had been elected.

—What exceptional leadership Bush was demonstrating.

—What spirit the people of New York had shown.

—How heartbreaking it must be for a mother like Maureen Haskell to have had two sons killed at the same time.

It *was* heartbreaking. The service for Tommy was almost identical to the one for Tim less than two months before. The same church. Same celebrant. Same family members and friends. Same grief and sorrow. Just a different son.

Cross referred to this overwhelming tragedy in his eulogy: "The expression 'brother firefighter' has a special meaning here today, because Tom's brother Tim was also killed in the World Trade Center. This is more than any one family should ever have to bear. And it should make all of us realize how lucky we are to have people like this in our community. Most of us in Seaford see ourselves as ordinary people doing the best we can. But September 11th made us realize what an *extraordinary* family the Haskells are and how fortunate we are to be able to say that they grew up in our community, attended our schools, went to our church, and achieved greatness."

A lot of neighborhoods around New York were hit hard by the World Trade Center attack. But none was hit harder than Rockaway. A peninsula on the northwest end of Queens—between the Atlantic Ocean and Jamaica Bay—Rockaway was a blue-collar town, home to more than five hundred firemen and many young guys in the financial services business. Almost a hundred of them were killed on September 11th.

As a kid—and through his college years—Cross spent many a summer day at Rockaway. With its miles of beachfront and multitude of gin mills, it was know as the "Irish Riviera." Later, in 1986, he was grand marshal of Rockaway's St. Patrick's Day parade. The parade breakfast was held at the Harbor Light Restaurant on 130th Street. The Harbor Light was also where Michael Boyle had run a firefighters' fund-raiser for Cross in October 2000. The Harbor Light was owned by Bernie Heeran, a retired firefighter. His son Charlie had worked for Cantor Fitzgerald. In the World Trade Center. On the 104th floor. He was killed on September 11th.

When Cross woke up in his Seaford home on Monday, November 12th, he was looking forward to the day. It was Veterans Day, and the weather was bright and clear. At noon he was going down to the local Knights of Columbus Hall to present special service medals to Korean War veterans. Now he was sitting in the living room reading the newspaper. It was just before 9:30. He heard Mary Rose call from the den, "I can't believe this.

There's a plane down in Rockaway." Cross ran to the den to look at the television. On the screen was a long-distance view of Rockaway, but all that could be seen were swelling mounds of smoke that filled the sky. All the channels—local, national, and cable news—were covering the crash. Many facts came quickly.

—The downed plane was American Airlines Flight 587, an Airbus A300, en route from New York to Santo Domingo in the Dominican Republic.

—The flight had taken off at 9:14 a.m. and crashed just five miles away in Rockaway at 9:17.

—President Bush, who was at a National Security Council meeting, was informed of the crash at 9:25.

—All air space over New York was shut down and all New York bridges, tunnels, and airports had been ordered closed.

—Rudy had declared a Level One alert, and forty-four fire trucks and two hundred firefighters had been dispatched to the scene.

—The center of the crash appeared to be near 131st Street.

Tom O'Connell called from Washington to say he would find out what he could from the Pentagon and the FAA. He also said that Kevin Finnerty's family lived just about ten blocks from the crash site and that Kevin still hadn't been able to get through to them by phone. From what Cross could see on television, the smoke was extending a lot farther than ten blocks. Cross told O'Connell to let him know as soon as he got any more details from his contacts, and especially about Kevin's family.

At about 9:45 Cross received a phone call from Mary Murphy from Channel 11 News. She was calling from home. Cross had gotten to know Mary well over the years and considered her the best street reporter in the business. Neither had much information to give the other, but she asked him if he'd call Channel 11 and do a phone interview at 10:00. Cross said he had nothing to add to the story, but Mary said the station wanted someone who could describe what the government would be doing. Cross, of course, agreed.

Cross called the station several minutes before ten. He stood in the den, holding the cordless phone, looking at the television. As soon as the interview began, he muted the sound on the television. The screen showed ever more billowing smoke, with Cross's name across the bottom. The interview ran about five minutes. Cross's main point—which he repeated in several variations—was that while it was wrong to jump to conclusions, because of September 11th the government had to assume this was a terrorist attack and work its way back. That's why the air space had to be shut down and why the tunnels, bridges, and airports had to be closed. The public could be sure that the federal government was fully mobilized and cooperating completely with the city, the state, and the Port Authority. *None of this is particularly profound*, thought Cross, *but it's the answer we have to give since September 11th.*

An hour later Cross was in Channel 12's Woodbury studios repeating pretty much what he'd said on Channel 11. Some positive news was coming in, however. The FAA said there was no evidence of terrorism. The bridges and tunnels were reopened. Kevin Finnerty called Cross just seconds before he went on the air to tell him he'd contacted his parents and they were fine. They'd been jarred by the tremendous explosion, and their street was filled with smoke—but, for them at least, there was no harm done.

Within a few more hours the numbers were in—260 passengers and crew were killed on the plane and five Rockaway residents killed on the ground. Yet the almost universal reaction was relief. It could have been so much worse. It could have been a terrorist attack instead of a structural malfunction. The plane could have plowed through streets of houses and killed many hundreds more people instead of crashing straight down and destroying "only" six homes. It could have destroyed the Harbor Light instead of plummeting to the ground just across the street.

Just as Seven World Trade Center received barely any mention when it collapsed on the afternoon of September 11th, today there was the second-worst aviation disaster in American history, thought Cross, *and we think we caught a break!*

Meanwhile the American war effort in Afghanistan was moving forward. Air power in the sky; 2,500 troops, hundreds of CIA operatives, and Northern Alliance and Pashtun allies on the ground. The effort was going forward, but you would never know it from many elements of the American media. Robert Novak said there was a "mood of foreboding" about the war, which was a "a long way from being won." The *New York Times* pronounced that the United States "is not losing the first round against the Taliban; it has already lost it." Evening news reporters described how the war would drag on inconclusively through the long winter months, causing mass starvation of Afghans. Clearly the United States had underestimated the strength of the Taliban. Now we understood why the British and the Soviets had been so unsuccessful in Afghanistan over the centuries.

But suddenly the war was just about over. On November 9th Northern Alliance troops advanced into the Taliban stronghold of Mazari-i-Sharif, and on November 13th they liberated Kandahar, now controlling more than half the country. By December the Taliban had been deposed, and Al Qaeda was in full retreat—its forces either dead, captured, or fleeing the country. No one knew where bin Laden was—or whether he was even alive—but he had lost his base of operations, and his terror apparatus had been severely disrupted. Afghans reacted joyously to their liberation. Dancing in the streets. Men shaving their beards. Women shedding their burkas. And on December 5th Hamid Karzai—who was pro-West and anti-Taliban—was selected as president following a conference of the various Afghan factions.

Cross and Mary Rose were at the White House in the first week in December for the annual Christmas Party. As they went through the receiving line, Cross shook the president's hand and commended him on the successful war effort. Bush thanked Cross and urged him "to keep working with those police and firefighters the way you've been doing." That Friday there was another firefighter's memorial service in Cross's district. Firefighter Brian McAleese was being buried at St. Christopher's Church in Baldwin. As usual for these funerals and memorials, Cross and Anne Kelly arrived about an hour early—mainly to avoid traffic delays, but also in case there were any last-minute changes or complications. The temperature was unseasonably mild. Cross was speaking with some firefighters when he saw Hugh Carey walking robustly along Merrick Road. He was accompanied by Tom Regan, a retired firefighter and longtime Carey aide.

Hugh Carey was a legend in New York politics. World War II combat veteran. Seven-term congressman from Brooklyn, two-term governor. Carey was in his eighties, and the past few years had been rough for him. A severe neck operation had immobilized him for a while and left him slightly stooped. The death of his son Paul from cancer earlier in the year had been a wrenching loss, and friends worried if all this had just been too much for the old warhorse. Curiously, the agony of September 11th had revitalized Carey. It was as if he had been given one more mission. Though he was a lifelong Democrat, Carey represented the Republican governor George Pataki at any number of funerals and memorial services. Whenever Cross had seen him, Carey had been brilliant. Extolling the courage of the victim who'd been killed and commenting so movingly on the new spirit and patriotism that had arisen from the ashes of September 11th.

"Governor, how are you? I'm seeing you at too many of these," said Cross, as they shook hands.

"One is too many, but it seems as if they will never end," answered Carey, almost crushing Cross's hand in an iron grip.

Carey paused for a moment, looking first at his watch and then scanning the buildings near the church.

"We have at least forty minutes," said Carey. "Let's go to the rectory."

"The rectory?"

"Yeah. That's the first thing a politician should do if he's early for a funeral. Go to the rectory. They'll always fix you a cup of coffee or tea and give you something to eat."

"You're the boss."

Carey, Cross, Anne Kelly, and Tom Regan walked around the corner to the rectory. Carey knocked on the door and started to introduce himself to the Irish housekeeper who stood in the doorway. He'd hardly gotten a few words out when the housekeeper, speaking in a pronounced Irish brogue, almost fell over herself inviting him in. She told Carey what an honor it was to meet him and how delighted the monsignor would be. She then said hello to Cross, who introduced her to Kelly and Regan.

"Governor, let me fix you something," she said. "Follow me to the kitchen."

As the housekeeper led them to the kitchen, Carey turned toward Cross with a wry smile and a big wink.

The monsignor *was* delighted to have the former governor as his guest and was very cordial to Cross as well. As they sat around the table sipping tea and eating toast, the focus was on Carey, who regaled them for the first several minutes with tales of Brooklyn, Albany, and Washington, and of Irish bars everywhere. But then the conversation took a serious turn.

"I've been around a long time, and I thought I'd seen it all, but what happened at the World Trade Center was worse than anything I could have imagined," said Carey.

"That was absolute evil," said the monsignor.

"These funerals and memorial services just tear you apart," said Carey who, besides Paul, had lost two boys in a car accident years ago. "To see these young widows and their children go through all this agony is just dreadful."

"Every death is tragic, but to keep seeing those towers burning on television means this tragedy will never go away," said the monsignor.

"Governor, you really seem to have been affected by the patriotism and the spirit since September 11th," said Cross.

"Sean, I have never seen anything like it—even after Pearl Harbor. It's so deep, so intense—so much determination. All the flags—they're an important symbol. But it goes beyond that. I have never been so proud to be an American."

"It's too bad all the politicians don't get that message," said Cross.

"I just can't believe some of the people in my own party," answered Carey. "I was mentioning this to you at Michael Boyle's service last month. We're at war. The president is doing a magnificent job. He is really demonstrating amazing leadership. He's doing everything he can to rebuild the city, and all these Democrats do is take cheap shots at him. They're lucky he doesn't tell the whole city to go to hell—sorry, monsignor."

"That's quite all right, Governor."

During the days and weeks following September 11th, the victims' families had been ridden with anguish and sorrow. Many were despondent and in almost trancelike states as they scheduled funerals or decided whether or not to have a memorial service and tried to explain the inexplicable to their kids. Spouses of firemen and cops know all too well that these are dangerous jobs and that each day could be the last. But they also know fatalities are rare and that the odds are with them. If tragedy does strike, as overwhelming as the grief would be, the whole world would not be watching, and the circumstances of the death would not be shown over and over and forever on television. However, the spouses and families of the civilian victims—primarily from the financial services sector—never had any reason to expect, anticipate, or plan for such a horrible end. Now in November and December, though the sorrow remained for all these families, the shock and trauma of September 11th began to ebb, and hard reality was setting in. The reality of how to go forward and where to go. As they confronted this reality, they realized how much the shock and trauma had actually served them as an emotional shield during the previous months.

Congress had anticipated some of this during the first days after September 11th when, as part of overall legislation designed to make the airline industry solvent, it set up the Victims Compensation Fund. The basic purpose of the fund was that, in return for families agreeing not to sue the airlines, they would be compensated what the victims would have earned during their lifetime, minus whatever life insurance polices there might be. At the time Cross thought this was a win-win solution. It protected the airlines from the threat of lawsuits that would have made it impossible for them to get financing, and the families would get reasonable compensation and be spared the delay and added trauma of prolonged litigation. Whatever the ultimate cost to the government might be, the price would be small relative to the dimensions of the tragedy. Cross soon realized, however, that he should have remembered nothing in life could ever be that neat and clear-cut.

Cross's office was dealing with the survivors of more than a hundred victims—uniformed and civilian. Not surprisingly, Jimmy Boyle was his main contact among the families of firemen and cops. Cross's link to the financial services families turned out to be Ashling Lane, whose husband Liam had worked with Tom Barfield. Cross had known Liam and knew his parents even better. They had supported him for many years when he was involved in the Irish peace process. He had met Ashling but didn't know her well. Cross had gone to Liam's wake and spoken with his parents and brothers. He saw Ashling that night, but she was surrounded by a sea of friends and relatives, and he decided there was no need to bother her. When Ashling had called him in early October, it was not because she had any particular concern or dilemma; it was mainly to make the connection and have the security of knowing there was someone in the government she could reach out to should a problem develop. Cross told her that Liam had been a good friend and that she should feel free to call at any time. During the next several weeks Cross and Ashling had spoken a number of times. He also spoke with several of her friends—widows whose husbands had also been killed in the World Trade Center—who'd called him at Ashling's suggestion. Most of these conversations would be informational—dealing with such coldly mechanical but necessary issues as obtaining death certificates or contacting the medical examiner. Other times it would involve tracking down and dispelling rumors, such as the erroneous report that the city was calling off the search for remains.

As November turned into December, however, the concerns of the uniformed and the financial services families turned increasingly toward the Victims Compensation Fund. Not because they wanted to become rich but because they wanted to know what their financial position would be and what they'd have for their kids. Progress with the fund proved to be a lot slower than Cross had anticipated when it was set up back in September. So far the only decision that had been made was to appoint Kenneth Feinberg as the "special master" of the fund. Feinberg was a bipartisan choice—a former Ted Kennedy staffer appointed by the Republican attorney general, John Ashcroft. His first responsibility—and really the main part of his job—was to set up the payment schedules, or "guidelines," as Feinberg preferred to call them. Cross didn't expect this to be a particularly difficult or lengthy process. It was the type of thing that was done every day in courtrooms throughout the country. Working with actuarial charts and income projections was not exactly rocket science. But as the process lingered into mid-December with no results, concern grew that Feinberg might be using the "guidelines" as a pretext to rewrite the law.

The families, of course, each had their own reasons for concern—the most basic being finding out how much money they'd have to go forward. Cross had the luxury of being able to consider a big-picture concern—whether Feinberg's maneuvering would cause a division between the families of the rescue workers and the financial services people. Cross had seen some of this already. Not often. But he had heard some of the complaints. Not from any of the widows he was working with. But he knew it was out there. The widow of the bond trader who was "sick and tired of hearing about the firemen being such heroes. Didn't my husband count for anything? He's just been forgotten." Or the fireman's widow lamenting that her husband "had to die trying to save all these rich people. Now that he's dead everyone's calling him a hero. But the firemen never got a good contract. That's why he had to work two jobs." Cross thought any split along these lines was unfortunate and unnecessary. The firemen and cops *were* heroes. Anyone who without hesitation runs into a towering inferno has to be a hero. And almost all the financial services guys he knew came from the same backgrounds as the cops and firemen. Blue collar. From the neighborhood. Good athletes. Many went to Catholic schools. As for their courage— no one would ever know what they had done on September 11th, but many had been exceptionally heroic when the World Trade Center was attacked back in 1993. To Cross the bottom line was that there was no reason for a split, and the government should be doing what it could to prevent one from developing. The families didn't need to be divided. And certainly the country didn't need it.

Cross's first meeting with Feinberg came on Monday, December 17th, in an auditorium-like room in the lower level of the building where Feinberg had his New York office—780 Third Avenue, between 48th and 49th Streets. Hillary Clinton was also there. As were about a hundred relatives of financial services victims. The stated purpose of the meeting was "informational." To give the families an idea where Feinberg was going and how he was getting there. *The real purpose,* Cross thought, *is to give these people faith that the fund would be fairly administered. And that means Feinberg would have to convince the families that they should trust him.*

"What do you think?" asked Anne Kelly as they were driving back from Manhattan to Massapequa Park. "Did Feinberg convince them?"

"Actually, I like the guy. I like his style. Brash. Aggressive. Very smart," answered Cross. "But I don't know if it worked with those women. I'm a politician. I've been a lawyer. I know what it's like to make deals or go overboard to make a point. That's all part of the game. But I don't know if Feinberg realizes that these women are just coming out of shock. They're not geared for games or one-upmanship."

"When do you expect him to put the guidelines out?"

"From what he told me, I'd say in the next two or three days."

"What do you think he'll do?"

"I don't know. I'm just afraid he might be too cute and create divisions that we don't need."

"Between the families?"

"Yeah. And also between the families and the general public. If the families object to what he offers, the public could see them as money grubbers."

"What did you think of the families?"

"That was rough. Before today I'd met about ten of them individually and spoken to some of the others on the phone. But it was really unsettling seeing them together like that. They all had the look of people waiting outside an emergency room . . ."

"Or a funeral parlor."

"Maybe it's worse when they all see each other. Every face must bring back a flood of memories."

"How was Hillary?"

"She was fine. We're on the same side on this. She's definitely putting time into it—and I don't think there's much political mileage in it. And she knows that."

Cross's dealings with the families also made him realize how vulnerable they were to unintended consequences. American troops searching an abandoned Al Qaeda headquarters in

Afghanistan in December came across a video of bin Laden meeting with Muslim clerics some time after September 11th. The video had not yet been shown to the public, but its contents were being reported in the media. Bin Laden was discussing the attacks in great detail and clearly taking credit for them. Regaling in the collapse of the Twin Towers. To the administration this video was a smoking gun. It would remove any trace of doubt of bin Laden's guilt and responsibility. The Pentagon was doing its final analysis and completing its translation. Then the tape would be made public. It would be a significant victory for the United States in the court of world opinion. But the morning the tape was to be released, Cross received a telephone call from Ashling Lane giving him another side of the story. A side he hadn't thought of. That Ashling's kids and other victims' kids would have to see and listen to the man who killed their father. Hear him bragging about it. And it would be like the burning towers, shown over and over again. She asked whether anything could be done. Cross knew the tape had to be shown. America's national interest demanded it. But could the impact on the families be at least somehow ameliorated? Cross gave it his best shot. Contacting the White House, he spoke with Karl Rove, who was Bush's political guru, and Mary Matalin, who was Dick Cheney's top aide. Both said they had not thought about this problem but realized it had to be addressed. The result was a statement by the Pentagon, which accompanied the release of the video, expressing regret at the pain that it would cause the families. This, of course, did not address the underlying issue of the trauma that would be inflicted upon the kids, but it seemed to work. Ashling appreciated it, and so did the other widows. It demonstrated to them that their government was listening. And that it did care. Cross also noted that the day the tape was released the imam at the North Shore Islamic Center acknowledged for the first time that bin Laden might well have been involved in the September 11th attacks! *That was nice of the imam,* thought Cross.

In the weeks after September 11th Cross concluded that it was not enough for everyone to know and talk about the heroism of the rescue workers who died on September 11th. It was essential for the sake of history that Congress officially commemorate that heroism. He introduced the True American Heroes Act, which would award posthumously the Congressional Gold Medal—Congress's highest civilian award—to all the police, firefighters, and other rescue workers who had died in the line of duty on September 11th. The legislation would also honor those who brought down Flight 93 over Pennsylvania. The bill came to the House floor on December 18. Speaking as the manager for the bill, Cross said:

"In going into those burning towers, the firefighters and police faced almost certain death. Mr. Speaker, our country has responded very dramatically to the tragedy of September 11th. One of the reasons why is the example that was set that day, when the eyes of the nation and the eyes of the world saw these people running in to save lives, saw them meeting their death. They saw that nobody wavered in the face of those fires and those falling buildings."

After others had spoken in favor of the bill, Cross reclaimed the floor to ask for a vote. Before doing so, however, he looked away from the Speaker's rostrum toward the camera that was located in the gallery and said, "And to my friend Jimmy Boyle, who's watching this on television, I told you we'd get this done, and today we're doing it." The vote was called, and the bill passed by an overwhelming margin.

Cross had little time to savor the victory, however. Two days later Ken Feinberg issued his "guidelines," and they were what Cross had feared. Feinberg had gone beyond the statute in some instances and interpreted it far too strictly in others. The result was that, as written, his guidelines would shut out or severely limit financial recovery to the groups affected the most—the uniformed services and the financial people.

—Spouses of cops and firemen who were killed would get *nothing* from the federal fund. Not one cent. Feinberg's reasoning was that the NYPD and FDNY continue to pay full salaries to survivors when their spouses are killed in the line of duty, offsetting the obligation of the federal government.

—Survivors of financial services victims who were earning in the top 2 percent of the country would not get their spouses' projected income but an amount determined by Feinberg on a case-by-case basis. Since most of the bond traders were in this top bracket, this ruling put their spouses at Feinberg's mercy.

The cops and firemen were the very symbols of September 11th, thought Cross. *Certainly Congress didn't intend for them to get nothing. The financial services people were targeted by bin Laden precisely because they were so successful and were symbols of the American economy.*

As soon as he saw the guidelines, Cross contacted Jimmy and Ashling. He told them that not very much could be done over the next few weeks because of Christmas and New Year's, but assured them he would work with the families after the first of the year to get the guidelines at least modified. He also wished them well over the holidays, what he feared would have to be a very rough time for them.

Cross knew that the fight against the guidelines would be tough. Legally a special master is given a lot of leverage, even if it might appear that he's acting against the will of Congress. More importantly, Ken Feinberg had won over the editorial writers, and the New York papers uniformly endorsed the guidelines. This would put the families even more on the defensive. While he'd told Jimmy and Ashling the fight wouldn't start until after New Year's, Cross thought he should at least fire a few warning shots now, stake out some territory. So, on the weekend before Christmas, he told the papers the guidelines were "unjust" and "discriminatory" and then on Sunday afternoon appeared on Fox News to say that those who suffered the most from September 11th would now be penalized the most under the guidelines—unless those guidelines were changed.

On the same Sunday that he appeared on Fox, Cross and Democratic congresswoman Carolyn Maloney held a news conference to publicize the gold-medal legislation, which had passed the House that previous Tuesday. They held the conference at the Engine 22/Ladder 13 Fire House on East 85th Street in Manhattan. This house had lost nine firemen on September 11th. Kara and John accompanied Cross to the firehouse. When they arrived, they were met by firemen—who were gracious and friendly but obviously preoccupied. There was a longtime veteran who'd been off from work on September 11th and seemed unable to shake the guilt that he'd survived when nine died. There was another veteran—who appeared to be strong enough to carry a fire engine on his back—emotionally telling Cross how much it meant that Congress had cared enough to pass this bill. *Are you kidding?* Cross thought. *You guys run into two burning skyscrapers that were attacked. Three hundred forty-three of you get killed. And you think we're great because we passed legislation thanking you for it!* Cross shook hands with each guy in the firehouse and thanked them for what they'd done. They couldn't have been more genuine. And though somber, none appeared depressed or unable to go forward. The news conference itself went well with virtually every New York station covering it.

"They're really tough guys," said John, as Sean drove the car from the firehouse toward the 59th Street Bridge.

"Yeah, but they're also pretty sensitive," suggested Kara. "They've got a lot hanging over them. I don't know how they'll ever get over it."

"I just hope they're able to get some satisfaction from realizing how indebted the country is to them," said Cross.

Christmas seemed more solemn this year. Cross, Mary Rose, Danny, Kara, and John went to Midnight Mass at St. Patrick's

Cathedral. Following the mass, Cross spoke briefly with Rudy and Tom Von Essen and wished them a Merry Christmas and a Happy New Year.

New Year's Eve, though, was spent at home. Sean and Mary Rose watching television. Looking at the Time Square throng, which spread for blocks and blocks. Viewing the great ball come down at the stroke of midnight.

Though its memory would remain forever, 2001 was finally behind everyone. Cross knew it was now time to face the new year, which had already begun.

Driving the black car west along Queens Boulevard in the Sunnyside section of Queens, Detective Brian Sullivan turned left toward 47th Avenue, and then made a right. He drove several more blocks until he spotted the two-story brick factory building they were looking for. It was on the street off to the left. He turned onto that street and pulled the car in front of the factory. Sean Cross and Tom Barfield got out of the car into the clear spring air. Several blocks ahead of him Cross could see the spire of St. Raphael's Church reaching into the sky toward the bright midday sun.

"I'll wait out here," said Sullivan. "You guys will have enough protection inside."

"Thanks Sully," answered Cross. "We'll probably be a few hours. So don't worry if you want to disappear for a while. Just keep your cell phone on."

"If I go anywhere," said Sullivan, "it'll just be to the Boulevard to grab a sandwich in a diner."

Cross and Barfield looked up and down the street at the rows of light-industrial buildings and the trucks driving to and from them. The building they wanted was second from the corner. They walked toward the gray, steel, windowless door and pressed the button on the wall next to it. Within seconds they heard a buzzing sound, and the door opened. They walked into an entirely plain and austere waiting area. Lime-green walls. Linoleum floor. Four government-issue plastic chairs that looked like retreads from the motor vehicle bureau. A uniformed NYPD sergeant, probably in his mid-thirties, was waiting for them. "Congressman Cross, I'm Sergeant Ragone. Inspector Bianchi and Mr. Hennessy are waiting for you in the central command room." Cross and Barfield followed Ragone as he walked toward the door that led from this waiting area.

Walking through the door, it was as if they'd entered another country—even another century. The room was massive and without windows. But it was brightly lit. Workstations were situated throughout the room. There must have been a hundred people, all busy. Though most were not in uniform, they had the look of cops and FBI agents. Almost all were wearing pistols. Most were male, but there were a good number of women. The maps and screens on the walls and the equipment throughout the room reminded Cross of what the Strategic Air Command communications center must be like. He had no knowledge of computers or technology, but he knew this was state-of-the-art telecommunications and computer equipment. More than state-of-the-art—almost futuristic. He could also tell that the people working here took their jobs seriously. This wouldn't be a place for Cross to be doing any political glad-handing or looking for a photo-op.

Sergeant Ragone said nothing as he led Cross and Barfield through this cavernous room toward a staircase in the rear of the room. They walked up the stairs and down a short hallway to another gray, steel, windowless door. Ragone pressed a code that caused the door to unlock. Inside the door was a good-sized windowless conference room, with a long, rectangular oak table in the center. Lou Bianchi and Frank Hennessy got up from the table to greet Cross and Barfield. Sergeant Ragone left the room, closing the door behind him.

"How do you like our holiday retreat?" asked Bianchi.

"I don't know if any of that stuff that we saw downstairs works or not," answered Cross. "But it sure as hell is impressive."

"You could never tell anything at all from the outside," said Barfield. "These few blocks around here are about as *unimpressive* an area as you could find."

"Tell me about it," said Cross. "I grew up less than a mile from here, and these blocks were always dark and depressing."

"Maybe that explains your personality," quipped Barfield.

"We are pretty much incognito here," said Bianchi. "Most of the guys are in plain clothes, and we use unmarked cars. But it's not top secret or anything. We just don't publicize it or tell anyone about it."

"Same with the FBI," interjected Hennessy. "We have about twenty of our people here. It's obviously a top priority, but we don't put press releases out on it."

"Is this an NYPD or FBI operation?" asked Barfield.

"This actual building is run by the NYPD. It's the base of operations for our Counterterrorism Bureau," answered Bianchi. "The FBI agents are here as a support force for the NYPD."

"Just like the NYPD has guys working at our Manhattan office," said Hennessy.

"How's the cooperation level?" asked Barfield.

"We're doing okay," answered Bianchi. "It'll probably never be perfect. But it's a helluva lot better than it was before September 11th."

"I guess the information never stops coming in," said Cross. "Now that you've got guys all over the world."

"Stationing the NYPD overseas was one of the most effective things Ray Kelly's done," said Bianchi, referring to the city's stellar police commissioner. "It gives us access to raw data we never could have gotten otherwise. We also have direct, instantaneous contact with just about every intelligence agency in the world—at least the ones that are on our side."

"The trick is to interpret that data," said Hennessy. "Most of what we get, we end up throwing out. And we almost never get a smoking gun. The most we can hope for at any one time is a piece of the puzzle."

"How's the puzzle coming along?" asked Cross, as he and Barfield sat down directly across the table from Bianchi and Hennessy.

"To be honest with you," answered Bianchi, "it looks as if we've got quite a few pieces."

"That sounds good," said Cross

"Good and bad," replied Bianchi. "The bad part is that if there's that many pieces, they're probably very close to pulling off the attack."

"Any idea of a time frame?" asked Barfield.

Bianchi and Hennessy looked toward one another. For a long moment they were silent. Then Hennessy spoke.

"We think we're talking about the next week or ten days. The pieces are fitting together."

"And it's not a pretty picture," interjected Bianchi. "They're planning to really come at us."

"How does it look?" asked Barfield. "Can you head it off?"

"That's why we're here today," answered Bianchi. "We want to lay the whole damn thing out."

"You guys are smarter than I am," said Cross. "So it would really help me if—before we do anything—we do this by the numbers and start from the beginning."

"Sort of a who's who," said Barfield.

"That's actually what I'd planned on doing," said Bianchi. "We've got all the charts and computer files, and still I find myself getting mixed up."

"That's what happens when you mix Irish and Arabs," said Barfield with a smile.

"Thank God there's no Italians," said Hennessy.

"I was wondering how long it would take you fucking micks to start with the Italian jokes," said Bianchi. "All I know is that with all the names and places we have—there's not one Italian name or one Italian city."

"I hate to admit it, but for once your people are in the clear," said Cross. "But it is time to get serious, so why don't you start laying it out for us?"

"Thanks Sean," said Bianchi, "it is serious. Very serious. First, I'll give you a rundown on what we all know. Then each of us can add any new evidence that we have. But don't worry about jumping in along the way—especially if you've got a question."

"Fair enough," said Barfield.

"I'll start with the Irish side," said Bianchi.

Opening a file folder resting in front of him, Bianchi described what they had on the Irish connection.

—Fiona Larkin from the Real IRA and Abdul Bajal from Al Qaeda had been living in Dublin. Just prior to September 11th they left Ireland and made their way to Indonesia, where they were still living.

—Last month Fiona traveled secretly to New York and met separately with Ramzi Haddad, a henchman for Mohammed Hawasi; and two Real IRA supporters—Mickey McDonough, a car-bomb expert, and Jimmy Regan, an old-time gunrunner.

—Pete Cairney, a former IRA man living legally in New York, told Cross that Larkin had instructed McDonough and Regan to be ready for a possible operation in New York. Cairney said he would try to get any further details that he could.

—Late last week Bernadette Hanlon, an old friend of Cross from Belfast, traveled to New York to tell Cross she'd heard that Fiona had been to New York and that Bajal would soon be in Rotterdam.

Closing the first file folder and opening a second, Bianchi turned to the Muslims.

—Mohammed Hawasi is an antiques dealer in Brooklyn and runs the Islamic Medical Service Foundation. Both operations are money-laundering fronts for Al Qaeda.

—Khalid Mustafa came to the United States in the early '90s. He is an explosives expert living in New Hyde Park. The German police—the Bundeskriminalamt—told Bianchi they believe Mustafa and Ali Shibh, another explosives expert known as the "scientist" and operating in Hamburg, could be involved in planning an Al Qaeda nuclear or dirty-bomb attack.

—Ali Said is a twenty-nine-year-old nephew of Mustafa. He lived in an apartment in Astoria, Queens, with Omar Aziz.

—Omar Aziz is a thirty-year-old Muslim who shared an apartment with Ali Said. Omar told Cross and Barfield that Said had reacted angrily and moved out of their apartment when Omar came across photos and plans that Said had of the New York City docks. Omar also disclosed that Said and Mustafa had visited the Empire Plaza office complex the week before the recent truck-bomb attack, at the same time of day as the attack occurred, and that Said associated with another young Muslim, Sheik Hassan, who had large amounts of cash that he claimed was for an Islamic academy that was nonexistent.

"Everybody on board?" asked Bianchi, as he concluded the presentation.

Hennessy, Cross, and Barfield nodded in agreement.

"Let me just add," said Hennessy, "that Immigration won't be bothering Omar about his visa problem."

"I'm glad they've done something right," said Barfield. "Will this be permanent, or is it just temporary?"

"It's temporary for now," answered Hennessy. "But if his story checks out, we should be able to protect him for good."

"How does the story look so far?" asked Cross.

"So far everything he told us is fitting in," answered Bianchi. "And like I told you after you met him at Dr. Ahmed's, the NYPD is giving Omar around-the-clock protection. We've got him in a safe apartment with bodyguards."

"How much of what Omar told you have you been able to track down?" asked Barfield.

"Probably the main thing is that Ali *is* Hawasi's nephew. And despite what Dr. Ahmed might believe, Hawasi *is* a bad guy. A very bad guy."

"We also checked out that Ali did spend a lot of time with Sheik Hassan, the guy from Yemen who always carried around a lot of money," said Hennessy.

"Even though he never had a job," injected Barfield.

"That's the guy," said Bianchi. "He was tied very tight to Ali Abdullah, the imam from that radical mosque in Brooklyn who is personally close to bin Laden."

"Tom, isn't Abdullah one of the guys you told me about at the beginning?" asked Cross.

"Yeah. He reminds me of that blind sheik who orchestrated the '93 attack on the World Trade Center," answered Barfield.

"There's something else we think we learned about Sheik Hassan," said Bianchi. "We don't think he'll be bothering us again."

"What's up?" asked Cross.

"We're pretty certain he was killed in the explosion at Empire Plaza," said Hennessy.

Cross and Barfield said nothing.

"We have someone in the Brooklyn mosque who started picking this up about a week after the attacks," said Bianchi. "There was talk of 'martyrdom' and 'a warrior in our midst.' And Sheik Hassan hasn't been seen since the attacks—and he was always at the mosque before that."

"You have an informer in the mosque?" asked Bianchi.

"He's actually more than an informer," answered Bianchi. "He's working for us. He's a Saudi who came over here in the mid-nineties and became active in the Muslim business community."

"What kind of business?" asked Cross.

"Talk about fitting the stereotype," answered Hennessy. "He's a rug merchant."

"How did you find out about him?"

"He was working with the local precinct on community issues and after 9/11 quickly let it be known that he wasn't pleased with how the radicals were taking over the mosques," said Bianchi.

"Did he belong to Abdullah's mosque?" asked Barfield.

"No. He attended occasionally but was not a member," answered Bianchi. "Almost two years ago, he reached out to the lieutenant at the precinct and said he wanted to do something. That he was disgusted with the fundamentalists. The lieutenant sent him over to us, and we worked with him—telling him it was important that he get active in the mosque and find out whatever he could for us. It's so seldom we get any cooperation from the Muslim community."

"Are you sure you can trust him?" asked Cross

"About as sure as we can be. You never can be certain. All you can do is go with your best judgment, and we think he's with us," said Bianchi.

"Have you had any problems with the civil liberties crowd?" asked Barfield. "This is a house of worship."

"Obviously they don't know about this guy," answered Bianchi, "but the whole issue of house of worship surveillance is a difficult one. On one hand you have the constitutional right to freedom of religion; on the other you have the reality that so many of the terrorist plots are actually planned in the mosques. We've been in and out of federal court the past few years on the overall issue, but so far we've done okay."

"You feel you're on solid ground?" asked Cross.

"I really do. The lawyer we have is the best on constitutional issues," answered Bianchi. "Professor Bonenberger from Notre Dame. I went to law school with the guy. He was always the smartest in the class—and now he's running rings around the ACLU."

"How effective has your guy been in getting information?" asked Cross.

"First he had to work his way in, and that took a while," answered Bianchi, "and he still isn't close to the imam or the power structure. But he was helpful as far as letting us know what the mood of the community was and when activists from overseas would show up at the mosque."

"When did he tell you about Sheik Hassan?" asked Barfield.

"Pretty much around the same time as Omar mentioned him to you," answered Hennessy.

"That either corroborates what Omar said or it could mean they're acting in collusion to throw us off," said Barfield.

"There's always the possibility in the intelligence business," said Bianchi, "but our analysis is that Omar and the rug merchant have no dealings with each other—and probably have never met one another."

"Was there any DNA evidence on Sheik Hassan at Empire Plaza?" asked Barfield.

"Nothing. The explosion and the fire just vaporized whoever the drivers were," answered Hennessy. "But we're still pretty confident that Sheik Hassan was a driver."

"And that's an ominous sign," said Bianchi. "This means they're willing to use one of their top talents on a suicide mission."

"Like Mohammed Atta on September 11th," said Hennessy. "It shows they're serious."

"Any idea where Ali Said is?" asked Cross.

"We spotted him on Atlantic Avenue three days ago," said Bianchi, "and we've put a tail on him."

"What's he up to?" asked Barfield.

"For one thing, he's not working," said Hennessy.

"Didn't he tell Omar he was driving a cab?" asked Cross.

"If he was, he's not any more," answered Bianchi.

"We've only had him under surveillance for three days," said Hennessy, "and there's been nothing incriminating. But he has stopped in to see his uncle Mustafa at the furniture store in Brooklyn a few times, and then yesterday—and this is ominous—we followed him to the Brooklyn docks."

"What did he do?" asked Cross.

"Nothing. Just walked around and looked—like he was a tourist."

"Obviously, that fits in with what Omar said about the pictures and plans for the docks," said Bianchi.

"It also means that we're getting closer to show time," said Hennessy. "This type of activity—contact between the principals, checking out the site—usually means the countdown has begun.

Remember Omar told us that Ali and Mustafa visited Empire Plaza the week before the attack."

"Sean, that's why that tip you got about Rotterdam from your friend Bernadette could be so helpful to us and so frustrating," said Bianchi. "Helpful because it could direct us to the ship that has the dirty bomb; frustrating because it could be a false lead and also because Rotterdam is so damn big."

Cross knew about Rotterdam from his work on the International Relations Committee. It is a port city of almost six hundred thousand, in the Netherlands. It was founded in the fourteenth century and by the sixteenth century its access to the North Sea made it a major European port of trade. Rotterdam continued to flourish and expand its port facilities into the twentieth century. Then it was devastated by the Nazis during World War II. Extensive aerial bombardment with blockbusters and firebombs left the city in ruins. But after the war Rotterdam steadily rebuilt, and today it is the largest port in the world, with more than three hundred million metric tons passing through it every year . . .

"I assume that means you've started looking in Rotterdam," said Cross.

"As soon as you told us what you heard, we contacted the Dutch police and their intelligence units," said Bianchi. "Plus the feds have people working for them who are supposed to preinspect the ships coming over here. We also got in touch with the Brits and the Germans."

"No luck so far?" asked Barfield.

"We're not even certain exactly what we're looking for. We're assuming the tip is real and that Bajal is planning something in Rotterdam. And we're assuming that it involves some type of bomb or explosive device on a ship that's leaving there and coming here. But there's hundreds of ships, and some of these freighters carry more than seven hundred containers. And we don't have the technology to detect every radioactive device that could be hidden away in these containers. Besides, we're not just talking about a single harbor in Rotterdam. There's a whole range of harbor complexes in and around the city. And all of this assumes that Bajal is in Rotterdam as part of a plan to attack the United States. Instead he could be there to attack Rotterdam. At least five major oil companies have refineries there, and more than twenty chemical companies have processing plants in the city, with extensive piping systems transferring chemicals from plant to plant."

"In other words," interjected Hennessy, "Rotterdam has many rich targets besides the ships coming in and out of its ports."

"Which means," said Barfield, "that we could end up preventing an attack in Rotterdam but miss the attack against the United States."

"The more I do this shit," said Bianchi, "the more I realize there's endless possibilities. The bottom line is that we don't have the luxury of tracking down every possibility. We're running out of time. So while we'll keep our eyes open for everything, we've got to focus on what looks like the most likely shot—and that's Bajal in Rotterdam."

"Lou's right," said Hennessy. "We hope we're right and pray that we're not wrong. But we can't fucking agonize and get caught up in the process. We've got to go straight ahead."

"And you have to remember that with all our effort, and even if we are right," said Bianchi, "it's still going to be tough to get Bajal and head off the attack."

"Let's switch to the micks," said Hennessy. "Sean, how did you do with Pete Cairney?"

"I met him last night after he got off construction," said Cross. "We had dinner at P. J. Clarke's."

"At least it was appropriate that you went to a donkey joint," said Bianchi.

"What would you want us to do—go to some mafia hangout on Mulberry Street?" answered Cross.

"Spare us the ethnic shit," said Hennessy.

"After I met with him over a week ago," continued Cross, "Pete touched base with McDonough and Regan. He's pretty sure he didn't tip his hand. He said McDonough told him nothing—absolutely nothing—which Pete thinks means something."

"How so?" asked Bianchi.

"After Fiona first came over, McDonough had no problem talking with Pete and with some other guys in the Bronx that Pete knows," answered Cross. "But now he's totally clammed up and has virtually gone underground—Pete thinks this means that McDonough has gotten his orders. He's in war mode."

"How about Regan?" asked Hennessy.

"Regan's being helpful," answered Cross, "and Pete thinks Regan knows what he's doing. That he wants to be helpful—even though he's not actually putting it that way."

"What's he giving to Pete?" asked Bianchi.

"The first thing is that he hasn't heard anything back from Fiona but he's sure that McDonough has," said Cross. "A few days ago McDonough met Regan and told him he should be ready if something comes up soon. Regan assumes that McDonough was delivering a message for Fiona. Since that day Regan hasn't heard a word from McDonough. He did hear two days ago, though, that someone saw McDonough up in Pearl River," referring to an Irish-American enclave in Rockland County, north of the city.

"Let me try out this scenario," said Hennessy.

The three nodded their okay for him to go ahead.

"Fiona met with Haddad, who's an agent for Hawasi. Hawasi has access to cash from that phony foundation that he runs. McDonough is a car-bomb expert. Haddad can give him the cash he needs to assemble whatever car bomb or truck bomb Bajal wants."

"Carrying this scenario out, what kind of bomb do you think it would be?" asked Barfield.

"I would say it'd be one or two car bombs. Working on a truck might attract too much attention. But whether it's car bombs or truck bombs—I'm almost certain it's going to be a dirty bomb."

"How bad would that be?" asked Barfield.

"It wouldn't be a fucking picnic," said Bianchi. "That's for sure. But to be honest with you, the impact would be more psychological than deadly."

"We simulated a car-bomb attack in lower Manhattan with conventional explosives and ten pounds of highly enriched uranium," said Hennessy. "It would cause absolute havoc, spreading radioactive dust over Chinatown and Tribeca and would reach Brooklyn. But we doubt it would kill more than twenty people."

"So you don't think the car bomb would be the main part of the attack?" asked Barfield.

"Listen, twenty people or forty people getting killed and radioactive dust being spread all over lower Manhattan is bad, no matter how you look at it," said Bianchi. "But if they're going to all this effort, they must be planning to kill a lot more than that."

"We're pretty certain that by far the central part of this attack will be from a massive bomb—probably a dirty bomb—hidden on a large freighter," said Hennessy. "And it will probably go off either at the docks or near a bridge. And based on what Omar told us about the pictures and the plans that he saw, we're leaning toward the docks."

"Do you think the Irish are tied in with the attacks on the docks?" asked Cross.

"Certainly not McDonough or Regan," answered Hennessy. "We think Fiona's only job over here involved the car bombs. The same with Haddad and Hawasi. They're supplying cash for that part of the operation. I'm sure Fiona knows from Bajal what's happening with the ship, but she's not involved in any of the details."

"It looks like the ship part of it is being run completely by the Muslims. Mustafa and his nephew are certainly involved—as I'm sure they were with last month's attack, especially the one at Empire Plaza. But the money for the New York end of the freighter attack is coming from Abdullah, the imam in Brooklyn. He raises a fortune in the Brooklyn mosques, and he's definitely connected to the crowd that runs Al Qaeda."

"If your scenario is the right one, and it certainly seems to be the most plausible," said Cross, "doesn't all this come down to finding the ship? We know about the players over here—Mustafa,

Ali Said, and the imam Al Abdullah for the ship; Hawasi, Haddad, and McDonough for the car bombs. And we know that Bajal and Fiona are coordinating this from Indonesia or Rotterdam, or wherever the hell they are."

"By the way," interjected Barfield. "I know there's been no sign of Bajal or Larkin in Rotterdam, but how about Indonesia? Didn't you have them under surveillance?"

"We did," answered Hennessy, "but last week we lost them. It was a tough surveillance from the start, because the country is so damn big and in many ways impenetrable for Westerners. We did get a good level of cooperation from the Indonesian police and the military. But they still have a lot of corruption. Anyway, whatever the reason, they disappeared—which could mean nothing, or it could mean they're on their way to Rotterdam."

"In the meantime, what do you do with the guys in New York?" asked Cross.

"We have to watch them as closely as we possibly can," said Bianchi, "without letting them know that we're onto them. The main thing we have to worry about right now with these guys is the car bomb. We can't let that go off. So we have to find out where McDonough is in Pearl River and watch him like a fucking hawk. As for the others, I think they've pretty much finished what they have to do. Grabbing them now wouldn't serve any real purpose and would only let Bajal know that we're onto him."

"But couldn't that scare him into calling the operation off?" asked Barfield.

"That's the toughest call of all, and we've been in touch with Homeland Security on the final decision," answered Hennessy, "but we think—again—that this is so far along, Bajal would keep it going. He knows we're looking for the needle in the haystack."

"And in some ways it would be an even greater victory for them if they hit us even when we knew they were coming," said Bianchi.

"So, as of now, Homeland Security won't be raising the alert level?" asked Barfield.

"I don't think so," answered Hennessy.

"We all better hope to God that McDonough's car bomb doesn't go off prematurely in Pearl River," said Bianchi. "That would be a helluva thing—since basically we're going to let him build it."

"Tom and I are taking up a lot of your time," said Cross, "and that's one thing you don't have a lot of. But can you tell me where you think you might catch a break?"

"Two things," answered Bianchi. "The first, of course, would be to spot Bajal in Rotterdam; the second would be to intercept a message to any of their guys over here. We're following them; we got their phones tapped; and we're monitoring their e-mail."

"Let's hope for some luck," said Barfield.

"We need a lot of it," answered Hennessy. "And soon!"

Detective Sullivan drove the Crown Victoria away from the factory toward Greenpoint Avenue, where he made a left, angling his way through the streets of Woodside until he made a right onto 48th Street, which led him to the Long Island Expressway.

"It's always good to change the route," said Sullivan.

"After what we heard inside, we're going to have to do a lot more than change our route over the next week," said Cross.

"Bad stuff?" asked Sullivan.

"Nothing really new," answered Barfield. "We just didn't realize how quickly it was coming to a head."

"Tom, I've asked you this before, but is Frank Hennessy doing any work for you, or is he spending all his time with the FBI?" asked Cross.

"Well, I'm still paying him, but today is the first time I've seen him since we had dinner that night at Bobby Van's," answered Barfield. "I know he's got an arrangement with the FBI—so I guess you'd say he's on some sort of detached service. But I don't really care. If he can help stop this attack, we all benefit. And if he doesn't, then it won't really matter very much who the hell he's working for. That will be the least of our troubles."

January 2002–August 2002

As the new year began, New York was enjoying one of its mildest winters in years. It was a welcome calm amidst the storm clouds of war and the harsh reality of the search for body parts that continued unabated in lower Manhattan.

The first official event that Cross attended in the new year was the swearing-in of Ray Kelly as NYPD commissioner. Cross had first met Kelly when he was appointed commissioner in the last year of David Dinkins's administration. By all accounts he'd done a good job, but understandably enough, when Giuliani took over he wanted his own man. Ray moved to Washington and into the Clinton administration, where he served first in the Treasury Department and then headed up Customs, where he was responsible for some major drug interdictions. When Clinton left office, Kelly went into the private sector and made big bucks as a security consultant on Wall Street. He and his wife lived in an apartment in Battery Park, directly behind the World Trade Center. Fortunately they'd been away on September 11th, but their apartment had been badly damaged.

Kelly became fixated with the war against terrorism. So when Mike Bloomberg was elected mayor, Ray gave up his high-paying private-sector post and returned to the police commissioner's job.

It was the job he'd always wanted the most and the job for which he was uniquely suited. Marine Corps. Vietnam. Street cop. Law degree. Harvard degree. Up through the ranks. Tough as nails. Cross and Kelly didn't know each other at the time—Kelly was a few years ahead of him—but they had gone to the same grammar school, St. Teresa's in Woodside. And Kelly never lost his neighborhood style. He ran in the highest circles but was still a neighborhood guy.

Cross was pleased that Kelly had invited him to today's ceremony at Gracie Mansion. For as far into the future as anyone could see, New York would be the terrorists' prime target. It was reassuring that Ray would be the top guy leading the fight against them. He knew the city and the NYPD inside and out. And he knew how the federal government worked and didn't work.

As he was driving over the Triborough Bridge toward FDR Drive and Gracie Mansion, admiring the unobstructed view of the Manhattan skyline and lost somewhere in his thoughts, Cross was quickly brought back to reality by the sharp ring of his car phone, mounted on the floor beneath the radio. It was Betty McLarnan. Her husband Eddie had been on the 105th floor of the North Tower. Neither his body nor any part of it had been found.

"Sean, I didn't want to be bothering you over Christmas, but these guidelines from Feinberg have been driving me mad. It really tears me apart. Ashling told me you thought we might be able to do something."

"There's no guarantee we'll be able to get him to change, but we can give it our best shot. Put the pressure on. But to have any chance, you and as many of the other widows as possible have to be willing to go public. And be ready to take some heat from the media."

"That's going to be difficult. I think I can force myself to do it, but so many of these women have barely been able to get their lives back together—and their children's lives."

"I'm not saying it's easy. And I'm not saying I'd be able to do it if I were in your position. But it won't have any chance of working unless a lot of you get out front."

"Ashling told me about the demonstration for this Sunday."

"Yeah, outside Feinberg's office on Third Avenue."

"What kind of turnout are you talking about?"

"To make an impact we've got to have at least fifty or sixty family members. And it should be financial people along with the cops and firefighters. You have to show that you're not going to be divided."

"I just hate for Eddie's memory and all the other guys who died that we have to do this. It trivializes their lives. It looks like we're fighting for blood money. I just wish to God Feinberg hadn't put us in this position."

"I have no doubt it's the right thing for you to do. But it can't be easy. Not after all you've gone through."

"It's as if the Congress said that we're entitled to this compensation and Feinberg is saying 'Eddie wasn't worth as much as Congress thought he was.' What are our chances?"

"I honestly don't know. We've never had anything like this before. But I do know that unless you do something soon, you have no chance."

"I'll be on the phone all day, trying to get as many widows as I can."

"Jimmy Boyle told me he's doing the same with the firefighters' families."

"I'll call you tonight and tell you how many I think I'll have. I'll also try to work on a statement for a widow from the financial sector to read. I don't think we should have a million people speaking."

"I agree with you. Three or four should be the most we have. Also—and I hate to sound callous—but you can't have people up there who are going to be crying or seem like they're looking for sympathy. The country is past that. It's a new year. There's still sorrow—but now it's deep rather than emotional. The approach has to be reasonable and dignified."

"Even though we're still torn apart and shattered . . ."

"Yeah."

"I'll talk to you tonight."

Ray Kelly's swearing-in went well. The room was overflowing with friends, well-wishers, and political heavyweights. The media coverage was extensive. When the ceremony ended, Cross had a chance to shake hands with Kelly and wish him well. "You've got a tough fight ahead of you," said Cross. "That's why I came back," he answered.

Leaving Gracie Mansion, Cross spotted Mario Biaggi—another of those New York political legends from the Hugh Carey era. Mario—now in his eighties—had been a much-decorated hero cop and had gone on to serve twenty years in Congress before being convicted in a kickback scheme. Biaggi, though, was one of those guys who remained popular with the people no matter what the jury said. Cross had first met him in the 1970s when—as an Italian-American—he was the most outspoken voice on the Irish issue. To this day—criminal conviction or not—Mario Biaggi still received the loudest and most sustained applause at any Irish-American gathering.

"Sean, it must be tough down in Washington these days," said Biaggi. "The war in Afghanistan, the threat of another attack here in New York. You're earning your money these days."

"I wouldn't go that far," answered Cross, with a smile. "But it is tough—not for us personally but for the country. Everything seems so different."

"I think of all the things we used to debate and fight about when I was there—and remember, I was in Washington during the sixties and during Watergate and the Iranian hostage crisis. But nothing like this. I'm sure you've heard this a million times since September 11th, but I never thought I'd live to see our city attacked."

"We just have to make sure it doesn't happen again."

The white-haired Biaggi nodded his head in quiet agreement, shook Cross's hand, and slowly walked away.

It was overcast and gray, and there was a slight chill in the air this Sunday morning as Cross, Mary Rose, and Anne Kelly walked into O'Neill's Restaurant on Third Avenue between 45th and 46th Streets. It was just after nine o'clock. Hemmed in by buildings on either side, O'Neill's could well have been a rural Irish pub transplanted to midtown Manhattan. The exterior was a bright blue with the American and Irish flags extending over the entranceway. Inside, the walls were lined in dark wood; the waiters, waitresses, and bartenders spoke with pronounced Irish accents; and the Irish whiskey, beer, and stout flowed freely. And the food—Irish staples of meat, potatoes, and green vegetables— was distinctly Celtic. Most days and evenings the crowds were wall to wall. But not Sunday mornings. That was one time O'Neill's was closed. Except for today. The owner, Kieran Staunton, offered to open up to accommodate Cross and the relatives who were coordinating the news conference they would be holding at ten o'clock outside Ken Feinberg's offices just a few blocks up the avenue, between 48th and 49th Streets.

Staunton was standing inside the front door. The bar was still darkened and the chairs upturned on the tables from the night before. Kieran shook hands with Cross and directed Cross, Mary Rose, and Anne upstairs.

"There's a few arrived already," said Staunton, with a slight Mayo brogue. "The tables are all set, and breakfast will be ready in a few minutes. As the others get here, I'll send them on up to you."

"Thanks, Kieran. I really appreciate this."

"It's no bother at all. It's the least I can do. Mother of God, it could have been one of my family that was down there on September 11th."

Cross had known Staunton since the mid-eighties and had worked with him over the years on the Irish peace process. Staunton had opened O'Neill's in the mid-nineties, and it had been a success from the start. Kieran was a guy who could be counted on to do the right thing. So when Cross called Staunton late yesterday afternoon and asked if he would open up this morning, he was pleased and appreciative that Staunton said yes—but not surprised.

Betty McLarnan was upstairs, seated at a table next to the window overlooking Third Avenue. Widows of two firefighters and one cop were sitting with her at the table. The waitress had already served them tea.

"Sean, I think this is going to work out well today. It looks like we'll have a good turnout, and Angela and I are on the same page," said Betty, referring to Angela Scarpetti, sitting directly across from her, whose husband Mike had been a cop killed in the South Tower.

"We realize we're in this together," said Angela. "We're not looking to get rich, and we want to get this behind us as soon as possible—but we owe it to our kids and to our husbands to get what Congress intended us to get."

"It's too bad you have to go through this—after everything else that's happened to you—but you really have no choice," said Cross.

As they were talking, eight more relatives—including Ashling Lane and Jimmy Boyle—came up the stairs.

"I just passed Feinberg's building," said Ashling. "About twenty or so relatives are already there."

"Sorry I'm late," said Jimmy, "But I was on the phone with Kerry Kinirons at the *News,* and she says there should be a big media turnout."

The new arrivals sat at tables grouped together near the window. The waitresses took orders and served massive Irish breakfasts of ham, bacon, sausage, eggs, potatoes, and soda bread. Just before 9:30, Congressman Felix Grucci from Long Island and Carolyn Maloney, the congresswoman from the East Side, made their way up the stairs.

"Leave it to the Irish guy to make us walk up a flight of stairs to get our breakfast," said Grucci.

"Stop complaining. It's probably the most exercise you'll get all day," answered Cross.

After a few minutes, Cross, Grucci, and Maloney spoke briefly—thanking everyone for their cooperation and laying out the format for the news conference. Very short introductory remarks by the members of Congress, then statements by the relatives—Betty McLarnan and Ashling Lane for the financial services victims; Jimmy Boyle and Angela Scarpetti for the firefighters and cops. Jimmy then got up from his table to say a few words.

"This is a wonderful moment. It really is. I lost my son Michael on September 11th, and you lost your husbands. For us to be able to join together like this—to be united, to speak out for the memory of our loved ones—means so much, and I'm just proud to be with you."

Jimmy's remarks struck just the right tone and balance. Everyone applauded warmly. Jimmy walked back and sat down at the table in the chair next to Cross.

"Great job, Jimmy. You said it beautifully," whispered Cross.

"This is a great breakfast they've served us," answered Jimmy. "I'm sure you're not paying for it."

Several minutes before ten, the assemblage got up from their tables and walked down the stairs and out onto Third Avenue. Staunton was just outside the doorway.

"Should we settle up now?" asked Cross.

"Jesus, no, this one's on me," answered Staunton. "And why don't you come back afterwards for some brunch. They'll need it after the news conference."

"You're the best."

The group turned right and followed Cross and Boyle for the two-and-a-half-block walk up Third Avenue. As they crossed 46th Street, Cross—who prided himself on his knowledge of useless trivia—looked easterly and pointed toward Spark's Steakhouse, where John Gotti had gunned down Paul Castellano in the winter of 1985. Cross had said it just to say something. At most he expected a perfunctory response. Instead the widows started asking him detailed questions.

—Did Gotti actually pull the trigger?

No. He sat in a parked car and watched . . .

—Was anyone shot in the restaurant?

No. Just Castellano and his bodyguard, out in the street . . .

—Is that what made Gotti the top guy?

Yeah . . .

The conversation lasted almost until they got to 47th Street, where they crossed Third Avenue for the last block and half of their walk. Cross doubted that any of these women had any interest in Spark's Steakhouse, John Gotti, Paul Castellano, or the mob. It was just nervous talk to take their minds off the upcoming news conference and the reasons for the news conference.

They were still more than a block away, but Cross could tell that the crowd in front of 780 Third Avenue had to exceed one hundred. Just as importantly, news trucks from every New York station lined the west side of Third Avenue from 48th to 49th Streets. As they crossed 48th Street, Cross was greeted by Kevin Finnerty, who'd flown up from Washington that morning to handle the press.

"This is a home run," said Finnerty. "They're all here. Television. Radio. And the relatives are terrific. Very calm and dignified. This should send Feinberg a message."

Finnerty led the relatives toward the battery of microphones that had been set up on the sidewalk in front of the large office building. Waiting for them was Vito Fosella, the Staten Island congressman, who'd arrived just a few minutes before.

"Vito, it's too bad you couldn't have walked up with us," said Cross. "We just saw where one of your most famous constituents was killed."

"Who's that?"

"Paul Castellano."

"You dumb Irish guys never let up. At least he died on his way to a good meal—not that garbage you serve in those Irish joints."

The news conference couldn't have gone better. The relatives were very moving and articulate. Every evening news show in New York was to carry this as a lead story. The next day's papers gave it up-front coverage, and Cross was invited to make the talk-show rounds, including Bill O'Reilly on Fox, Jeff Greenfield on CNN, and Imus on MSNBC. And Finnerty was right. Feinberg did get the message. He appeared on Greenfield's show to rebut Cross and started showing up on various news and talk shows. *Good*, thought Cross, *we're drawing him out.*

Over the next few weeks Cross set up meetings with Feinberg for the families of firefighters and the financial services survivors. At the firefighters' meeting Jimmy Boyle made the argument that since firemen took lower salaries to get higher pensions, those pensions shouldn't now be used to penalize the survivors of the firemen. The financial services widows reemphasized the point that their husbands had been killed by bin Laden precisely because they were so successful, and it would be wrong for their own government to penalize them again for the same reason. As always, Cross found Feinberg friendly and engaging. He also seemed less inclined to make academic arguments or rhetorical points. All the meetings seemed to go well—or as well as could be expected under the circumstances. One meeting with Betty McLarnan and Ashling Lane was exceptionally cordial. At its conclusion the two women shook hands warmly with Feinberg. As Cross opened the door, though, he saw a minister and a police officer in the waiting area. They looked past Cross toward Betty, and she broke into tears. She knew why they were here. They told her the medical examiner had just identified her husband Eddie's remains. Cross later learned it was a piece of thigh bone. Seeing Betty in tears with her pastor, Cross knew there was nothing constructive for him to do. So he mumbled something inaudible to Betty, said good-bye to Ashling, and left.

Feinberg ended up issuing revised guidelines. They weren't perfect, but they were an improvement. Survivors of firefighters and cops would be penalized only a portion of the pensions, and financial services people would have more doubts resolved in their favor. There was still too much left to chance, but the gap was narrowing, and Cross took some solace in that. More importantly, so did many of the survivors.

Most effort and attention still focused on Al Qaeda and other potential terrorist threats. In his State of the Union address on January 29th President Bush pointed to the military success in Afghanistan. He brought the senators and congressmen to their feet when he introduced Hamid Karzai, Afghanistan's new president and the symbol of victory over the Taliban. Karzai met the following day with the International Relations Committee and was effusive in his gratitude to the United States. He also made it clear, however, that Al Qaeda was a vicious and resilient foe that had to be kept on the run and not allowed to regroup.

While there was at least surface agreement that Bush was on the right track regarding Al Qaeda, the Taliban, and Afghanistan, he generated real controversy in his address by labeling Iraq, Iran, and North Korea an "axis of evil." Some Democrats and columnists saw this as rhetorical excess and charged that Bush was attempting to extend American influence and power too far and too fast. Cross joined the debate, defending Bush's position on various talk shows—arguing that a dangerous world required direct talk and an end to endless process. In many ways the axis-of-evil debate was a metaphor for the debate between the very different foreign policies and world approaches of Bill Clinton and George W. Bush.

This was a debate that Cross would make no attempt to avoid, though it would have its awkward moments. He supported Bush's initiatives—indeed, thought them absolutely vital—but he had been and continued to be friendly with Clinton. Cross had been elected to Congress the same year that Clinton entered the White House. It hadn't been long before they began working together on the Irish peace process—Clinton making the big plays like giving a visa to Gerry Adams and actually inviting him to the White

House over the most vehement British opposition; Cross using his longtime connections with Adams and the republican movement to establish contacts and pass along messages that would be inappropriate for a president or White House official to engage in directly. Cross had numerous meetings and conversations with Clinton throughout the maze of intricacies and complexities that was the Irish peace process and traveled to Ireland and Northern Ireland with him three times. The bottom line was that after centuries of bitter fighting and brutal killings, the 1998 Good Friday Agreement gave the Irish people a genuine opportunity for peace, and it couldn't have been done without Bill Clinton.

While Cross had opposed Clinton on virtually every economic and social issue and was critical of such foreign policy ventures as Somalia and Haiti, he was one of the few Republicans who had supported Clinton's use of military force in Bosnia and Kosovo. Indeed, he believed the Bosnia deployment prevented Al Qaeda from gaining a European base of operations. Most significantly, though, Cross broke with his party not only to oppose Clinton's impeachment but to argue his case in repeated television appearances and on the floor of the House. During all this time and through all their dealings, Cross found Clinton to be a straight guy.

Cross saw Clinton's true skill in conciliation. He could listen endlessly to rival parties, make some sense of what they were saying, find common ground, and build upon that. That's why he was able to sort out the Irish miasma, after scores of Irish leaders and British prime ministers had failed over the centuries. Clinton also had the ability to appreciate and understand every aspect and angle of key foreign policy issues. And all the possible resolutions to those crises. But Cross saw that Clinton had difficulty accepting that certain major issues did not lend themselves to conciliation. That some crises could only be resolved by deadly and sustained force. And that was where Clinton seemed to fall short. So it was that in the summer of 1998, when bin Laden destroyed American embassies in Kenya and Tanzania, killing hundreds, Clinton responded by firing cruise missiles at an abandoned Al Qaeda training camp in Afghanistan and at a factory in Sudan, which may or may not have been producing chemical weapons. That was it! When Saddam Hussein ejected the weapons inspectors from Iraq later that year, Clinton said Iraq was a grave menace to the world and that "regime change" was essential. His response, though, was limited to *four days* of bombing against Iraq. And when Al Qaeda attacked the USS *Cole* in Yemen in October 2000, killing American sailors, Clinton did nothing. Nothing! No wonder bin Laden was emboldened to plot and plan even greater and more spectacular atrocities.

As for North Korea, another component of Bush's "axis of evil," Clinton had negotiated an agreement with the North Koreans in 1994 giving them billions of dollars of aid in return for their scrapping their nuclear weapons program. When Clinton left office, the North Koreans were still getting their aid, but it was becoming increasingly evident that they had resumed their development of nuclear weapons.

Cross realized full well how difficult the presidency was and how easy it was to Monday-morning-quarterback and second-guess. Still, though, he felt that the attacks of September 11th had stemmed in significant part from the belief of bin Laden and others that the United States no longer had the guts to go all-out for the long haul. That too much of our foreign policy would be defined by process rather than action.

None of this affected Cross's friendship with Clinton. Just this week Cross had asked the former president—and Clinton had readily agreed—to endorse a book Cross had written. Indeed, Clinton had invited Cross and Mary Rose to a party he was having at his office in Harlem on Sunday evening to watch the Super Bowl, between the St. Louis Rams and New England Patriots.

It was a few minutes past six o'clock that evening. Cross had just driven over the Triborough Bridge. He went across 125th Street and found a parking place between Fifth and Lenox Avenues, less than a hundred feet from the federal building where

Clinton had his top floor office—55 West 125th Street. Cross and Mary Rose were standing in the lobby waiting for the elevator when the former president and Hillary arrived. They all greeted one another warmly.

"I'm really delighted that you were able to make it," said Clinton. "This should be a fun night."

"It certainly should, Mr. President," answered Cross. "Thanks for inviting us."

Another couple arrived. Cross didn't get their names, but they were friends of Clinton and had some sort of Hollywood connection.

"I just want you to know," said Clinton, talking to his friend and pointing toward Cross, "that this man—even though he's a Republican—stood up on the House floor and defended me during impeachment. Not only defended me, he threw it right back at the Republicans."

Cross smiled and said to Hillary Clinton, "That seems like a lifetime ago." She smiled back.

The party was a classic Clinton event. Celebrities, intelligentsia, and plenty of food and drink. The offices were magnificent, extending room after room from east to west. Clinton's personal office had large windows—running the whole length of the wall—facing south. Providing an unobstructed view not just of Harlem but extending down over Central Park. Two walls were lined with floor-to-ceiling bookshelves—with books occupying every inch of space. Clinton led Cross and Mary Rose to the shelves behind his desk, where he animatedly detailed his method and formula for categorizing and assembling his books. It was a sort of Bill Clinton version of the Dewey Decimal System. Basically, they were broken down by presidential administration—so that all books relating to historical events that occurred while a particular president was in office, even if that president had no relation to those events, would be placed in the area reserved for that administration. After Clinton excused himself to greet some arriving guests, a female staff assistant who'd been standing nearby said, "He takes that so seriously. He personally placed every book in the shelves. God help us if anyone moves one of them. He notices right away."

The kickoff would be in a few minutes. Five large-screen televisions were located throughout the offices. Most of the guests had arrived. Sidney Poitier and Alec Baldwin were among the entertainment celebrities. Israeli defense minister Shimon Peres topped the diplomatic elite, while former secretary of state Madeleine Albright and United Nations ambassador Dick Holbrooke represented the Clinton foreign policy team. And there was Christiana Amanpour from CNN.

It soon became evident that the party—not the game—was the principal event of the evening. And Bill Clinton was the star of the party. There had to be over a hundred people there, but it seemed as if most of them were always wherever Clinton happened to be as he ambled from room to room. Again Cross was struck by the depth and expanse of Clinton's knowledge. Discussing policy options for North Korea with Albright and Holbrooke. Exploring Middle East possibilities with Peres. And films with Poitier.

Though not many at 55 West 125th Street—including Cross—were watching very closely, the game turned out to be one of the most exciting Super Bowls ever, as New England upset the Rams on a sudden-death field goal.

Cross and Mary Rose were in their car driving back across 125th Street.

"Before you have a chance to think it over and analyze it," asked Mary Rose, "give me your impression of Clinton tonight."

Cross paused for a moment, then answered. "He's got just as much charm. I can tell that it must kill him to wake up every morning knowing that there's so much going on around the world and he can't do anything about it. That he can't just pick up the phone and call Blair or Chirac or Mubarak. He's as smart as ever—maybe even smarter."

"Do you think he'd do a better job than Bush?"

"Not in these times. Bush won't get caught up in process. As he says, he won't use a two-million-dollar weapon to attack a four-dollar tent. We need a guy who knows when it's time to stop talking and start shooting."

"And keep shooting."

An array of foreign leaders made their way to Washington over the next several months. Cross was particularly encouraged by the level of support from the heads of Muslim governments. President Musharraf of Pakistan. President Mubarak of Egypt. And King Abdullah and Queen Renia of Jordan. All were with us against Al Qaeda. Providing invaluable intelligence data. Routing out Al Qaeda cells in their countries. This solid support from Muslim leaders who were literally in the line of fire was a welcome contrast to the ambivalence of such European leaders as Ireland's former president Mary Robinson, who announced she was "very concerned" that the United States might be violating the human rights of Al Qaeda prisoners being held at Guantanamo. The basis for this great concern was pictures she'd seen of the prisoners being walked through the camp blindfolded. The fact that it was the United States government that had released the photos and that the prisoners were being led to their cells where their blindfolds were immediately removed seemed unimportant to Robinson. Cross's retort about Robinson was, "It's great to be a critic when you're three thousand miles away and it's American soldiers who are risking their lives."

In February the Democrats resumed their attacks on Bush for not delivering on his promise for twenty billion dollars in emergency aid. The charges were just as baseless as they'd been back in the fall, but this time the White House people had no one to blame but themselves. Pressed by the Democrats as to when the money would be paid, the budget director, Mitch Daniels, gave all sorts of conflicting doubletalk. First, he said, New York would probably end up getting more than twenty billion. Then he said that the estimated $5 billion that would be going to New York residents from the Victims Compensation Fund could be considered part of New York's aid package. Finally he said that the New York Democrats asking the questions were "money grubbers."

Reading the transcript of Daniels' remarks that afternoon, Cross realized that nothing Daniels said technically contradicted Bush's twenty-billion-dollar pledge but that he'd created a public relations nightmare and gift-wrapped an issue for the Democrats. The next day's headlines confirmed Cross's worst fears. Bush was reneging. The White House was double-counting. Victims compensation money was being diverted to cover up the betrayal.

Cross decided to attack on two fronts. On one front he assailed the media and the Democrats for distorting what Daniels had said. *The weaker your case, the louder you yell,* he thought. On the other he told Tom O'Connell to call his contacts at the White House and tell them they'd fucked up royally. "Those fucking morons must have their heads permanently on mountain time," said Cross. "Do they always have to be so fucking cute when they're talking about New York? Bush is giving New York the money, and that should be the whole fucking story. Instead those morons continually box us in for no good reason. And this is the last time I'm defending them."

Over the next few days Daniels did some backtracking and clarifying, and the furor receded. And then the president quelled it once and for all. He invited the entire New York congressional delegation to the White House. He detailed how much money would be spent, how it would be spent, and when it would be spent. The total came to *$21.4* billion. Bush then invited them to join him in the Rose Garden, where he would make the formal announcement to the press corps. Once in the Rose Garden, the same Democrats who had been assailing Bush over the past few months fought and jockeyed for position to be seen on camera with him. When Bush concluded, Hillary Clinton came to the microphone to thank him and got off the best line of the day: "Mr. President, I knew you promised us twenty billion dollars. But I never knew you promised us a Rose Garden as well."

For the previous nine years that Cross had been in Congress, the events of the week leading up to St. Patrick's Day were hectic. They were often filled with the drama of high-level negotiations and bargaining, as the various players in the peace process attempted to use the good offices of the American government to advance positions or resolve differences. This year though, there would be little of that. There were still problems in implementing the Good Friday Agreement. Real problems. But they didn't seem insoluble. Certainly nothing compared to September 11th.

The week began on March 9th, with another service for another firefighter killed on September 11th. George Cain of Massapequa. Like too many other funerals and services, this was also held at St. William's in Seaford. The only difference between this and the long line of funerals that had begun the previous September was that Mike Bloomberg was now the mayor delivering the eulogy.

On Monday night, March 11th, Cross traveled to Hoboken, New Jersey, for an outdoor telecast of *Hardball* with Chris Matthews. Hoboken was directly across the Hudson River from Ground Zero, and that evening at nightfall two large beams of light would be projected from the site into the heavens to commemorate the six-month anniversary of the destruction of the two towers. Looking from the set with Matthews toward lower Manhattan, Cross found the giant beams both majestic and haunting.

The next night was the annual extravaganza at the Irish ambassador's residence in the luxurious northwest section of Washington. As always, the crowd flowed through the residence and out into the massive grounds behind the house. The Irish prime minister, Bertie Ahern, was there. As were many Washington luminaries. And there was more than enough food and booze. Still, the mood was somber. The embassy had been good enough to invite many guys from the FDNY, and their uniformed presence was a grim reminder of just how many Irish-Americans had died that terrible September day. Appreciating the solemnity of the moment, Ahern walked from firefighter to firefighter shaking hands and wishing the men well.

The next morning President Bush hosted a reception at the White House, and again the New York firefighters were the guests of honor. Jimmy Boyle had taken the train down that morning, and Cross brought him to the White House. Within minutes, Jimmy was shaking hands with everyone in sight—from Colin Powell to Karl Rove.

Cross went directly from the White House to the Capitol, where Denny Hastert was hosting the annual St. Patrick's Day Speaker's Luncheon for Bertie Ahern and Bush. Cross and Gerry Adams were assigned to table two, which was right next to the table for the president, the prime minister, and the Speaker. As they sat here today, the president of the United States less than ten feet away, Cross remarked to Adams that it hadn't been until just eight years before that the Sinn Fein leader had even been allowed to set foot on American soil. They also discussed the Unionists' attempt to thwart the peace process and Adams's basic belief that the process would work. Adams also reaffirmed what he had said so many times before—the Real IRA had no real support and was virtually defunct. When they gave their brief speeches, Ahern thanked Bush for his continued involvement in Ireland and praised the spirit of the American people; Bush pledged that America would always work for peace in Ireland. Following the lunch, Cross and Adams stood at the bottom of the Capitol steps. Before saying good-bye, Adams noted with some emotion how strongly the county seemed to have come back from September 11th.

The nation's return to normalcy continued apace during the spring months. "Normalcy," of course, meant that instead of focusing almost exclusively on the tragedy and consequences of September 11th, our political, cultural, and social discourse could shift to such other terrible occurrences as the upsurge in suicide bombings in Israel, the child-abuse sex scandal in the Catholic Church, and the corruption and downfall of such corporate giants as Enron, Global Crossing, and Tyco. The war in Afghanistan continued—but it seemed more of a police-work, clean-up operation. Americans knew there was always the threat of another attack at home, but bin Laden hadn't been heard from since the fall before, and Al Qaeda operatives were being apprehended all over the world.

September 11th was never entirely distant, however. For one thing, there were still funerals and memorial services to be held and attended. Remains of Michael Boyle and David Arce had been identified—for Michael it was a piece of spinal tissue inside an FDNY uniform—and their families decided to go ahead with a joint funeral at their home parish of St. Brigid's on Post Avenue in Westbury. Cross visited with the families during the days leading up to the April 19 funeral; it was almost a reenactment of the anguish that had preceded the November 5 service at St. Patrick's. Jimmy's grief was compounded even more when the investigators told him that based on where Michael's uniform had been found, he must have been at the *exit* of the North Tower when the building came down upon him. Just several more seconds—or at most a minute—and he would have lived.

The passage of time from September 11th did, however, embolden Democrats and sensationalist elements of the media to take more cheap shots at Bush. The cheapest came in mid-May, when a story, leaked by some disgruntled intelligence officer, said that Bush had been warned about September 11th and had chosen to do nothing. *He Knew!* blared the banner headline in the *New York Post*. "What did he know?" asked Hillary Clinton on the Senate floor. "What did he know and when did he know it?" asked Dick Gephardt and Tom Daschle, evoking the spectre of Watergate.

If true, of course, the president would have been guilty of an outrage comparable to treason. The story broke the afternoon of May 16th. That evening Cross flew to Manhattan to attend the fortieth anniversary of the New York State Conservative Party at the New York Hilton. He even missed several votes to make sure he was there on time. Dick Cheney was the principal speaker, and Cross wanted to demonstrate solidarity. The vice president strongly defended Bush and emphasized that the administration would cooperate with any legitimate investigation—but wouldn't allow American intelligence procedures to be torn apart by publicity-seeking witch hunters. Following the dinner, Cross went directly to the MSNBC studios at 30 Rockefeller Plaza, where he defended the president on the Alan Keyes show—saying it was disgraceful even to raise an issue of this magnitude until at least some facts were known.

The next morning the facts did begin to emerge. And they showed nothing. Indeed, if anything, they affirmed Bush's judgment. The previous August, a CIA official—not the director— had presented Bush a report showing that Al Qaeda was increasing its capability and expanding its scope. American targets were particularly vulnerable. It listed potential targets as bridges, tunnels, large buildings, and national monuments. It spoke of various means of attack, such as car bombs. Also mentioned in the report was a 1998 British warning that a plane might be hijacked and its passengers held hostage to force the release of Al Qaeda prisoners. There were no details of threats any different from what had been known during the Clinton years. What was new was the conclusion that the Clinton policies hadn't worked. After receiving the CIA report, Bush had ordered the National Security Council to formulate an action plan against Al Qaeda. That report would call for, among other things, military action against the training camps in Afghanistan. It was ready to be submitted to the president on September 10th. Cross made the media rounds that evening and over the weekend defending Bush. But the president really didn't need that much defending. The American people just weren't buying that any president would knowingly allow September 11th to happen. The polls reflected that, and the Democrats retreated, insisting they had never questioned the president's conduct or blamed him for anything. All they'd ever wanted were more facts.

Memorial Day, May 30th, marked the official end of the recovery effort at Ground Zero. All that could be found, had been found. The work had been completed far more quickly than anyone had projected. Relatives and public officials were invited to the solemn ceremony that would mark the close of this chapter. Cross decided not to attend. He did not want to be a voyeur of other people's grief. Cross and Mary Rose, however, did go to the site on their own the Sunday before—May 26th—to see what had been done. They were escorted around by Lt. John Ryan—a Seaford neighbor—who played a key role with the Port Authority Police Special Operations Unit. Cross was amazed at the extent of the "clean-up"—a terribly insensitive but accurate description of the work. Looking down into the vast pit where there had been tons and tons of debris and searing flames, one saw nothing but almost perfectly manicured grounds. And subway tracks. That was what struck Cross the most. Undamaged, still-intact subway tracks, which had somehow survived all the destruction above and around them, deep below ground level along the eastern perimeter of the pit—a stark reminder of what had been.

The summer months were pleasant and tranquil. In June the president hosted the congressional barbeque at the White House—the barbeque that had been scheduled for the previous September 11th. Virtually all of official Washington was walking casually around the White House south lawn, listening to country music, eating the plentiful food, and not evincing any concern for their security. They were all there—Dick Cheney, no longer at his undisclosed location; Colin Powell and Condoleezza Rice, the foreign policy team; and Denny Hastert, the next in line to the presidency, after the vice president. Also there was Tom Ridge, the director of Homeland Security. And, of course, the president and First Lady, enjoying one of those rare Washington nights when people were actually being friendly to one another.

This was also a congressional reapportionment year. That event occurring every ten years when the state legislatures are mandated to redraw the lines of congressional districts to reflect population shifts. Fortunately for Cross, the lines of his new district, which now extended out into Suffolk County, were favorable to a Republican. He looked forward to a successful campaign and spent considerable time visiting the communities in the new part of his district.

The Mets were a major disappointment, playing below-.500 ball, but the Yankees were surging toward another division championship and a hundred-win season. And the Jets and Giants were both viewed as legitimate NFL playoff contenders. Yeah, life was more and more normal.

But not completely. Sometime in mid-August people began to accept that the first anniversary of September 11th was coming upon them. They began to think back not just to the horror of that day but the sorrow and dread that had suffused them in its aftermath. Now they were becoming increasingly apprehensive—not so much fearing another attack but concerned that the memory of that sorrow and dread might enshroud their lives yet again.

21

It was late Thursday morning, and Sean was sitting behind his desk in his district office in Massapequa Park when he got the phone call from Lou Bianchi.

"This could be the day," said Bianchi. "About an hour ago the Dutch police spotted Bajal and the scientist going into a warehouse in Rotterdam. It's near the docks."

"What's the situation now?"

"We're monitoring it in real time. The warehouse is surrounded by SWAT teams. We see it on our screens, and we're in direct contact with an NYPD guy who's on the ground with the SWAT team."

"What do you think?"

"It's going to be tough. There's others in the warehouse with them, and they have some heavy artillery."

"How about Fiona?"

"We assume she's in there with them."

"What about over here?"

"We have all our people—NYPD and FBI—in place and ready to grab everyone. We're especially watching McDonough, with his fucking car bombs. But we're holding back until we have a better idea of what's going to happen in Rotterdam."

"Do you want me in there?"

"That's why I called."

"Sully's here. I'll be leaving in two minutes."

"How long will it take you?"

"The traffic shouldn't be bad at this time. If it is, Sully can throw on the lights and siren. So about a half hour to forty minutes."

"See you then. I'll call Tom Barfield and ask him to come in."

"I'll be on the cell phone if anything happens in the meantime."

Traffic was light. Sullivan had the car at sixty-five most of the way. It was five minutes before noon when he got off the LIE at the 48th Street exit and worked the car through the streets toward St. Raphael's, before making a right across Greenpoint Avenue and parking in front of the second industrial building from the corner. Sully and Cross got out of the car and walked toward the gray steel door. They were met by Sergeant Ragone, who said he'd take them directly to Lou Bianchi and Frank Hennessy in the central command room on the second floor. As Ragone hurried them across the vast room on the first floor, Cross saw that the cops and agents were talking into their phones and working their computers with an almost ferocious intensity.

Sergeant Ragone opened the door to the central command room. Bianchi and Hennessy were standing in the center of the room holding phones to their ears while looking at two large screens recessed in the dark oakwood walls. There were another fifteen or so NYPD and FBI around the room. Cross didn't know any of them. But this wasn't the time for introductions. Everyone had a look of deep concern. Cross could see from the screens that a brutal gun battle was under way.

"Doesn't look so good, Sean," said Bianchi.

"The SWAT team got in place and kept calling in more reinforcements to totally surround the place," added Hennessy. "They were also trying to get the architectural plans for that warehouse and the buildings around it to see if they could make an entry. They didn't fire any shots but were strengthening their position."

"Then about five minutes ago, the shit hit the fan," said Bianchi. "Bajal's guys started firing. And they've got some heavy stuff. M-60s. Grenade launchers. AK-47s."

Just then Tom Barfield walked into the room. Saying nothing, he stood next to Bianchi and Cross and looked up at the screens. Then they saw the explosion.

"Make all arrests and execute all search warrants immediately," shouted Bianchi into his phone. "Immediately!"

The pictures on each of the screens said it all. There had been one massive explosion and then another. The Rotterdam warehouse and all the buildings around it were engulfed in roaring flames and billowing black smoke.

"Son of a bitch!" shouted Bianchi. "They're dead, and we don't know what they've sent our way. All we can do now is get the bastards that are over here and hope for a break."

Within minutes NYPD and FBI agents were moving throughout Brooklyn, Queens, Nassau, and Rockland. And they moved effectively.

—Mickey McDonough was nabbed in a closed-down car wash in Pearl River. The bomb squad was carefully dismantling the two car bombs he had finished assembling.

—Ali Abdullah, the radical imam, was arrested in his Brooklyn apartment, and papers and records were seized from his mosque.

—Mohammed Hawasi was arrested in his office at the Islamic Medical Service Foundation in Brooklyn. The foundation's records and the records in his antiques shop on Atlantic Avenue were seized.

—Ramzi Haddad, Hawasi's henchman, was arrested in a Court Street restaurant.

—Khalid Mustafa was arrested as he left his two-story home in New Hyde Park. Boxes of documents in his attic and a computer in his basement were seized.

—Ali Said had still not been apprehended, but many of the records and documents seized in Mustafa's home appeared to be his.

At about 4:30 that afternoon Cross was sipping coffee from a styrofoam cup and eating a buttered roll. He was sitting at a side table with Barfield and Sullivan. Bianchi and Hennessy were constantly going in and out of the central command room. Cross stayed out of their way.

"It's that fucking freighter," said Barfield. "It could already be on its way. Or it could still be in Rotterdam ready to leave tomorrow, or the next day, or next week. We just don't know."

"Or it could be at another port altogether," said Cross.

"Listen, my job today is to just hang back with you guys," said Sullivan. "But I've been a cop a long time. And one thing I've learned is that it's almost never as bad as you think it is. The worst thing you can do is give up."

"I guess that's the old saying—it's darkest just before the dawn," said Barfield.

"From the look on Bianchi's face the past few hours, I'd say it's pretty fucking dark," said Cross.

It was shortly after 6:00 p.m. Two cops had brought in platters of roast beef and ham and cheese sandwiches and put them down on the large conference table in the center of the room. Cross and Barfield walked over to the conference table and sat down. Cross grabbed a roast beef sandwich, Barfield a ham and cheese. Sullivan stayed back at the smaller table alone in his thoughts for the moment, his cop's mind at work.

The door opened and Bianchi entered again. He had several sheets of paper in his hand. He appeared a bit more relaxed than he'd been for the past few hours. Or maybe he was just exhausted. In any event, Cross said nothing to him. Bianchi walked to the far end of the room where Hennessy was talking on the telephone. Bianchi showed him the papers, and Hennessy put down the receiver. They spoke for about a minute. Hennessy picked the phone back up and pressed just one button on the keypad. This call was speed dial.

Bianchi approached Cross and Barfield, allowing himself the barest hint of a smile. Sullivan, his police instincts working overtime, got up from the small side table and walked toward the conference table, stopping to the side of Cross and Barfield.

"I don't want to speak too soon," said Bianchi, "but we may have caught the break we were looking for."

"What can you tell us?" asked Cross.

"Mustafa's home in New Hyde Park. We got a shitload of papers there, and the guys downstairs have been going through the computer that we picked up. It looks like that kid Ali Said was the brains behind the whole operation over here—not the uncle."

Bianchi paused for a moment but Cross, Barfield, and Sullivan said nothing.

"From the computer and from two bills of lading we found, it looks as if Ali made a deal with St. Vincent—the small island nation in the Caribbean—where they'd let him use their flag on a ship for a price . . ."

"Is that those 'flags of convenience?'" asked Barfield.

"You got that right," answered Bianchi. "Anyway, we got the ship's description. It's a big mother. A five-hundred-foot freighter. And Ali's records seem to say that it's due to leave Rotterdam tomorrow."

"Are you sure it's in Rotterdam?" asked Cross.

"That's what Frank's checking right now."

Bianchi reached down and grabbed half a roast beef sandwich.

"This is the first thing I've eaten all day," said Bianchi, with a reluctant smile.

All eyes were on Hennessy. But then he put down the receiver and no one had to ask him anything to know how the call had gone. His smile was from ear to ear.

It was shortly after midnight when Lou Bianchi called Sean Cross at home and gave him the final word.

"It's over, Sean. We made it. The Dutch SWAT teams and our guys just got finished. They found two containers and deactivated them. They tell me there were enough explosives and radioactive material to blow apart half of lower Manhattan and downtown Brooklyn."

"Thank God you stopped it," said Cross.

"I can't believe we got so lucky."

"It was more than luck. You guys broke your asses."

"Thanks. But believe me there was a lot of luck."

"Let's just hope, then, that we stay lucky."

September 2002

Cross and Mary Rose walked south along Broadway. As they reached the narrow, cavernous confines of Wall Street, they turned left. They were heading toward Federal Hall, on the corner of Wall and Broad, where on this day—September 6, 2002—the U.S. Congress would be meeting here in joint session for the first time since the adjournment of the second session of the First Congress on August 12, 1790.

Federal Hall was where both houses of Congress first met after the Constitution was ratified, and it was where George Washington took his oath of office as our first president. But all that was more than two centuries ago. In the remaining 212 years Federal Hall had served as a city hall, then as the customs house and, since 1920, as the Federal Reserve Bank. It was long ago designated a National Historical Site and National Memorial.

Today's special meeting reflected the efforts of the New York congressional delegation, the mayor and the governor to have the Congress officially commemorate what New York had achieved over the past twelve months. As the House and Senate resolution stated, this special meeting would be held "in remembrance of the victims and heroes of September 11, 2001 and in recognition of the courage and spirit of the city of New York."

The NYPD had blocked off all the streets near Federal Hall. Cops were seemingly everywhere. On foot. In squad cars. On motorcycle. In vans. And, of course, the sharpshooters on the rooftops. Yet the mood on the street this bright, clear morning could not have been more upbeat—almost festive. As if it were a victory party. And that's what it was—a victory over fear.

Less than one year ago, just blocks from here, the Twin Towers had been destroyed. This very area of Wall and Broad had been filled and covered with clouds of smoke and ash. But today New York was back. Hundreds of members of Congress from all over the country had come to join in the commemoration. Vice President Cheney would preside over it.

The meeting itself went off without a hitch. The congressmen, senators, and spouses took their seats within the chamber. Speaker Hastert called the session to order, and the chaplain gave the invocation. The Pledge of Allegiance was recited, and the soloist, LaChanze, sang the national anthem. Hastert and Cheney spoke briefly and appropriately, as did selected House and Senate leaders. Then the Stuyvesant High School choir sang "God Bless America," and the congressmen and senators filed from the hall and down the front steps past the statue of George Washington. They were led by a color guard composed of the NYPD, the FDNY, Port Authority cops, court officers, and the U.S. Capitol Police. It was a proud and exhilarating moment.

But nothing could extinguish the reality that this pride and exhilaration had its origin in the death and carnage of September 11th. And the commemoration of that was just days away. Cross was struck by how differently various victims' families were reacting to this first-year anniversary. Some would stay at home with their loved ones. Others would take their children to the beach so they could walk along the sand, look out at the ocean, and think back. And there were those who would attend and take part in the actual commemoration ceremonies at Ground Zero.

Cross watched the September 11th ceremonies on television from his district office. He saw relatives—including Jimmy

Boyle—walk down into the pit amidst a swirling wind and read aloud the names of victims. Later that afternoon he watched President Bush—who first went to the Pentagon and then to the field in Pennsylvania—arrive at Ground Zero and meet and speak with each of the many family members who had waited for him.

That evening the Seaford community held a special service to commemorate ten of its neighbors who had been killed on September 11th. The service was held at St. William's, where so many of the funerals had been held over the past year. Members of the community arrived early, and more than a half-hour before the scheduled beginning time of eight o'clock, the crowd was overflowing onto the street. Jackson Avenue, leading to St. William's, was lined for several blocks as a procession of family members and local officials marched from the local firehouse to the church. The procession was led by the combined bagpipe bands of the neighboring Wantagh Fire Department and a British marching unit that had come over especially for the occasion.

As the processional line filed into the church, the organist played "America the Beautiful." All of the front rows on both sides of the center aisle were reserved for family members. Wives. Children. Parents. Brothers and sisters. Cross sat with the other local officials in the front row of seats off to the side of the altar. Fr. Steve Camp spoke, as did Rabbi Robert Applestone and Lutheran minister Ronald Klose. American flags that had been flown over the Capitol were presented to each of the families. Cross was the principal speaker. After a year of eulogies, Cross had difficulty thinking of saying anything different—a point he pretty much acknowledged when he began:

"Certain events in human history are so unique and so transcendent that they truly do speak for themselves. No words are necessary to describe these events, and no words *can* describe them.

"Certainly the events that we are commemorating here at St. William's this evening speak for themselves with an eloquence exceeding any words we could ever hope to compose."

He then went on to describe the heroism of those who had died and the "grace and determination" of their survivors. Cross concluded by saying the "undying obligation to the memory of those who died is to defeat and destroy those who carried out this atrocity."

The service concluded with stirring renditions of "My Country 'Tis of Thee" and the "Battle Hymn of the Republic," and then everyone was invited to the basement of the church, where a reception was to be held.

The reception was subdued but not sorrowful. Just about all the family members were there, as were hundreds of people from the community. No one was laughing, of course, but neither were there any tears. The deep sorrow that affected everyone who had lived through the events of September 11th would always be there—certainly and more intensely for the families of the murdered. But we had made it through the ever-changing and unprecedented challenges of the past year. And we were stronger for it. Much stronger. So as Cross said goodnight to these people he had worked with and come to know over the past year and then walked up the stairs and out into the night air, he knew that he was far more at peace than he had been this very day exactly one year before.

23

P.J. Clarke's is a true New York City landmark. Built in the 1890s and located on the corner of 55th Street and Third Avenue, this tough, brick watering hole is the ultimate gin mill—dark wood walls, crowded tables, and standing-room-only bar, plenty of drink, and inexpensive food. It was chosen as the setting for the booze film classic *The Lost Weekend;* its clientele includes neighborhood regulars, interested tourists, and a variety of political, athletic, and show business celebrities.

Lou Bianchi had called earlier today to reserve a back table for four at eight o'clock this evening. When Cross and Barfield entered the restaurant, they were greeted by Pat Moore, their favorite waitress and aspiring young blonde actress.

"Big week for you guys," she said.

"I just hope it keeps going that way," answered Cross.

"Your friends got here a few minutes ago. Let me take you back there."

Bianchi and Hennessy were drinking pints of beer. Cross and Barfield ordered the same.

"Lou, I've been thinking and rethinking everything over the last few days," said Cross. "And I still can't believe the job you did. This could have been a disaster."

"Don't forget to give Frank and the FBI credit," answered Bianchi. "They were great."

"It shows what we can do when we work together and forget the turf battles," said Hennessy.

"We also owe a lot to Dr. Ahmed and Pete Cairney," said Barfield. "They really came forward and delivered the goods on their own kind."

"That had to be tough for Ahmed," said Bianchi. "The Muslims are still a very insular community."

"Maybe this will show them that their real loyalties should be to America," interjected Hennessy.

"Pete Cairney has no trouble being loyal to America," said Cross, "but this one was tough for him, because that dumb mick McDonough had been in jail with his brother in Belfast. So they go back quite a few years."

"Thank God Cairney found out what he did about the car bombs," said Bianchi.

"The guy who was really a great help was that Muslim guy Omar," said Barfield. "Without him we'd never have known about Ali Said."

"Like I was telling Sean last week," said Bianchi, "it turns out that Ali was coordinating the whole operation—the freighter and the car bombs."

"He was also behind the attacks in April," said Hennessy. "He's one of Al Qaeda's top guys."

"What are your chances of nabbing him?" asked Cross.

"We think they're pretty good," answered Bianchi. "Our intel is that he's probably holed up in Brooklyn or Jersey City, and we're tightening the noose."

"Speaking of leads," said Hennessy, "we wouldn't have known anything about Rotterdam, Sean, if your friend Bernadette hadn't tipped us off about Bajal."

"That was some explosion," said Barfield. "It reminded me of Waco and the Branch Davidians."

"It wasn't just the artillery that was being fired," said Bianchi. "The warehouse was filled with explosives and chemicals."

"Any idea how many were in there?" asked Cross.

"Once it went up, there was nothing left," answered Hennessy, "so there was no way to count bodies. But we know Bajal and 'the scientist' were in there, and based on the amount of firepower, we figure there must have been at least eight or nine gunmen."

"How about Fiona?" asked Cross.

"We assume she was in there," answered Bianchi.

"Fortunately, the Dutch were able to evacuate all the surrounding buildings," said Hennessy, "so there were no civilians killed."

"If you hadn't been able to locate the freighter before it left, how long would it have taken to get here?" asked Barfield.

"Six or seven days," answered Bianchi, "But they had that stuff so well hidden. I don't know if we would have known enough to intercept it and find anything if we hadn't come across Ali's records leading us to that ship."

Cross's cell phone went off. He recognized the overseas caller ID and said hello. He excused himself from the table and stepped out the side exit onto 55th Street so that he could speak freely.

"Bernadette, how are you doing? We were just talking about how much help you were."

"Sean. I'm sorry to bother you like this, but I rang you at home and Mary Rose said it was okay for me to call you on the cell phone."

"Of course it is. But it must be after one o'clock in the morning over there."

"It is—but it was very important that I speak to you."

It was about three minutes later that Cross came back into the restaurant and sat back down at the rear table.

"Who was that?" asked Barfield, with a smile. "Your bookie?"

"No, it was Bernadette Hanlon," answered Cross.

"I hope you told her how much we appreciate the information she gave us," said Bianchi.

"I did," said Cross with some hesitation.

"And?" asked Hennessy.

"She gave me some more information."

"What information?" asked Bianchi.

"Her source told her that Fiona Larkin is in Yemen."

"Yemen?" asked Barfield.

"Yeah," answered Cross.

"What's she doing there?"

"She's with Ali Said," answered Cross.

Barfield motioned to the waitress who was standing nearby and ordered another round of beers.